SHADOWS MOVE AMONG THEM

T0149122

ALSO BY EDGAR MITTELHOLZER

Creole Chips
Corentyne Thunder
A Morning at the Office
Children of Kaywana
The Weather in Middenshot
The Life and Death of Sylvia
The Adding Machine
The Harrowing of Hubertus
My Bones and My Flute
Of Trees and the Sea
A Tale of Three Places
With a Carib Eye (nf)
Kaywana Blood
The Weather Family
A Tinkling in the Twilight
The Mad MacMullochs (as H. Austin Woodsley)
Eltonsbrody
Latticed Echoes
The Piling of Clouds
Thunder Returning
The Wounded and the Worried
A Swarthy Boy (nf)
Uncle Paul
The Aloneness of Mrs Chatham
The Jilkington Drama

SHADOWS MOVE AMONG THEM

EDGAR MITTELHOLZER

INTRODUCTION BY RUPERT ROOPNARAINE

P E E P A L   T R E E

First published in Great Britain in 1951
by Peter Nevill Limited
This new edition published in 2010
Peepal Tree Press Ltd
17 King's Avenue
Leeds LS6 1QS
England

ISBN13: 978 1 84523 091 3

The quotation on p. 329 from Edward Thomas's *The Glory*
(published by Faber & Faber Ltd.) is reproduced by kind
permission of Mrs H. Thomas.

Supported by
ARTS COUNCIL
ENGLAND

RUPERT ROOPNARAINE

INTRODUCTION

Religion, Sex and Utopia in *Shadows Move Among Them*

While it may be too early to speak of a Mittelholzer revival, there are encouraging signs of a reawakening of not only academic but wider general interest in the work of this prodigious pioneer of the Guyanese and Caribbean novel. Between his *Corentyne Thunder* of 1941 and *The Jilkington Drama* of 1965, Mittelholzer made, in the words of Arthur Seymour, "a long and tireless assault upon the publishing world of London."[1] The spurt of overdue critical attention that followed Seymour's inaugural Mittelholzer Memorial lecture of 1967 subsided after the 1970s, though by then important assessments had been made by Frank Birbalsingh, Michael Gilkes and Patrick Guckian,[2] among others. Judging from the attentive critical work newly resumed by Juanita Cox, as can be seen in her introduction to the Peepal Tree Press reissue of *Corentyne Thunder*, we are hopefully nearing the end of the neglect of the last quarter of a century, during which, at some point, all his novels fell out of print, some never reprinted since their first publication. Unsurprisingly, this absence has been accompanied by a deafening critical silence.

In a letter of the 1950s to Seymour, responding to the latter's comments on *A Morning at the Office,* Mittelholzer wrote:

> "Yes, Arthur, you'll come to learn that sex and religion are my 'themes' as a writer. I hold very strong views on these two subjects and in everything I write, you will note that I shall touch on them. In some works I shall emphasize them heavily, in others I shall introduce them as a background accompani-

ment; but they will always be there. In my latest *Shadows move among them*, religion is the main theme. I'm simply itching to hear what you think of it."[3]

Given Seymour's prominence in the Georgetown Protestant establishment, there is a hint of mischief in that "itching" for his opinion on what he did come to see as "Edgar's major assault against orthodox religion."

Religion in *Shadows*

Shadows Move Among Them is the first of a pair of novels written in the early 1950s that have tended to be classified as novels of ideas. The other is *The Mad MacMullochs*, written in 1953 but not published until 1959 under a pseudonym, H. Austin Woodsley.[4] In the latter the scene shifts from the slow, black water and myth-laden jungle up the Berbice River in Guyana where "Berkelhoost teems with passionate, cruel spirits" and "the whole neighbour-hood bristles with the residual effluvia of past violence" (p.94; page references are to this edition) to the undulating hills and coast of sunny Barbados. In both novels, just as significant as the plot action, is the documentation of the day-to-day happenings, opera-tions and discussions within these Utopian communes dedicated to ways of thinking and acting that are held up by their fictive protagonists as bright banners of liberation against the grey rot of Western civilization. In *Shadows* Mittelholzer mounts a satirical assault on orthodox Christianity, an assault that does not restrict itself to the practice of the religion, but slyly challenges elements of its doctrinal and philosophical foundations. In *The Mad MacMullochs,* the sexual life replaces religion as the major theme.[5]

Mittelholzer's authorial voice almost certainly coincides with his characters' critiques of the anti-life soullessness of the "civi-lized" world beyond the confines of the commune, but how far he wanted his readers to think that the Reverend Harmston and his utopians in *Shadows Move Among Them* had found a genuine alternative is very much less clear. Readers will have to decide for themselves *where* Mittelholzer might be in a narrative that is characterized by some rewarding instabilities and contradictions. In any event, the reader is urged not to make retrogressive assump-

6

tions about where authorial sympathies might lie on the basis either of later novels, or critical commonplaces about Mittelholzer's attraction to "right wing" or "authoritarian" ideas. In *Shadows*, at least, there is a strongly libertarian spirit and a lively dramatization of contrary ideas, but above all a willingness on Mittelholzer's part to follow where his imagination led him. This is to a narrative that is by turns gothic, light-hearted, satirical (and not always in expected directions), darkly comic and sometimes chillingly serious.

As is not uncommon in a novel dealing with ideas, the primary function of some characters, sometimes very volubly, is to act as mouthpieces articulating some aspect of the novel's debate. In Chapter IX of *Shadows*, Garvey, the older Harmston boy, notably lacking the rich fancy and fertile imagination of his younger siblings, Olivia and Berton, plays just that role when he interrupts the visitor, Gregory, as he is sitting by the landing place watching the jungle reflected in the water "with leaf detailed clarity". Increasingly bemused by what Berkelhoost seems to offer, Gregory (who has come to see his aunt and uncle (the Reverend and Mrs Harston) following the presumed suicide of his wife and his own breakdown) takes comfort in the fact that the forest: "…seemed very safe in its inarticulation. No matter how long he watched it it would never talk back at him or advise him how to keep sane" (p.250). Not so the teenage Garvey, who brims over in youthful confidence with advice and instruction. To Gregory's admission that he finds the way of life at Berkelhoost absurd, no doubt brooding over the punishment inflicted on Mabel, the Harmston's eldest child, for failing, at his urging, to report Sigmund's fatal fourth offence, Garvey launches into him:

> "As absurd as we find your way. You are a good example of the misery and emptiness of your pseudo-civilization. Look at you! Rudderless, unhappy, cynical. And look at us… We're full of life and fire… we're happy and I mean when I say happy that we're not burdened with a sense of world-guilt as you are." (p.251)

He berates Gregory and his like for taking life so seriously that they leave no time for enjoying it. They spend too much time inflating their egos and trying to convince themselves how superior they are to the baboons and the chimpanzees: "We don't suffer from such egotism, you see; we take life with a big pinch of salt, because we know it has no purpose beyond today; that's why we can throw ourselves into it with such heartiness and extract all its richness" (p.252).

Gregory is ready to accept the accusation about himself, and there are certainly aspects of what he sees and hears at Berkelhoost that he finds plausibly attractive, not least Garvey's assault on the doctrine of the resurrection (which is made with ebullient Mittelholzerian humour), attacking the conceit that man has been fashioned in the image of a God that he has created out of his own superstitions, including ideas of a soul and an afterlife. It is this fundamental conceit, according to Garvey, that drives people like Gregory to invent things like morality and piety to keep them "pepped up and to prepare… for the Afterlife." Such doctrines so trap the believer that he has to deny himself most of the things that could give him fun. Not so at Berkelhoost where myths and conventions are created day by day and discarded just as easily:

> "But you – you have to be content with the stale gods your forefathers forced down your throats. We get life at first-hand; you get it at second or third… No really civilized man can be religious or patriotic. There's nothing that limits your range of thought – and your enjoyment of life, as a result – more than religion and patriotism…" (p.253)

Later, his aunt, Mrs. Harmston, tells Gregory of her own conversion, of how she has come to understand that "one's morals are only the results of an attitude – an attitude that we ourselves, through ignorance or superstition, build up." She argues for a morality that derives from the dictates of the individual conscience and makes Gregory understand what a curiosity he is to the rest of them, how much of a savage he seems:

> "What passes for civilization in the world you've come from seems, in our eyes, just laughable barbarism – at least, it would be laughable if it weren't so pathetic – and tragic. Millions and millions of people all being bamboozled by sentimental moralists and pious charlatans." (p.284)

It is in the phrase "pious charlatans" where we might suspect that

Mittelholzer's satire is double-edged, with respect to the commune's unassailable leader, the Reverend Harmston, particularly when the darkness beneath Berkelhoost's sunnily comic surface shows through. We might note, too, that it is the dictates of individual conscience that Gregory and eventually Mabel follow in the case of the condemned Sigmund, whilst the members of the commune follow the rules (no doubt introduced by Harmston).

But how seriously are we intended to take the commune as a alternative to the values of the outside world? Mittelholzer allows his characters to be entertainingly slippery about just what Berkelhoost stands for. When the hyper-imaginative Berton is taunted by Garvey – "a case of too much myth hath made thee mad, young fellow" – he hotly accuses his elder brother of making fun of their religion. Garvey retorts that its core tenet is that they are free to make fun of it. Reverend Harmston, called upon to adjudicate, reminds them of the importance of never allowing themselves to "become slaves to rigid doctrine". Religion must be kept "elastic" if it is to be enjoyed.[6] They must be able to make fun even of the most sacred precepts: "Religion without a sense of humour to dilute it can only result in being an awful bore" (p.196).

That is an undoubted truth regarding the church in the commune. As Harmston explains to Gregory (somewhat dismayed that there is to be no ceremony to mark his proposed marriage to Mabel): "We encourage fantasy, but fantasy doesn't necessarily call for superstitious belief. Superstition results from ignorance – and ritualistic forms." According to Harmston, it was ritual that obfuscated the "honest, down-to-earth myth-scheme" with which Christianity started out: "It is as much an example of mumbo-jumbo as the practices of the African witch-doctors." (p.254). All of which, in Harmston's view, explains why official religion has become "such an impotent factor" in world affairs.

Not so the church at Berkelhoost that, far from being an impotent factor, is at the structural and ideological centre of the novel. In its opening pages, we enter the church and the gothic imagination of Olivia, with bats squeaking and fluttering among the rafters and down into her mind. (She fantasizes their "little timid teeth that sank without pain, almost with pleasure into her throat" (p.33).) In the closing pages, we are back in the church

9

with the bats and an Olivia whose precocity, clairvoyance, and yearnings we have come to know. The church is our point of entry into Berkelhoost and our point of departure from it. It is though its windows that we and Olivia watch Gregory disembark from the corial and take his first step onto Berkelhoost soil.

It is in the church, where Gregory sits next to Mabel, to whose charms he has begun to awaken, that he is treated to Reverend Harmston's serio-comic lampoon of the Apostles' Creed. To the accompaniment of Olivia's wheezily stagey harmonium, he cajoles, instructs and entertains his flock. In unison they intone the Berkelhoost creed: "I believe… in what I can sense, and I believe in the reality beyond the shadows, the shadows that move among us. Verily, I believe in God the Father of all Myth, himself the most wonderful Myth, and in Jesus Christ, born of Joseph and Mary, in natural union. Jesus, among men, the King of Dreamers, creator of many beautiful parables …" They chant their belief in "a life of cultured simplicity,… in fairies and phantoms, in hard work, frank love and wholesome play, always spiced with make-believe." They are enjoined to "revel in the day but hope for nothing beyond this life, for in this life is the Kingdom of Heaven. And after death only shadows, nothing but shadows, shadows." (p.160) Gregory is caught up in the enthusiasm of the congregation and impressed by the "spirit of intense sincerity":

> "For an instant it shattered his neutrality… he could sense the elation and almost quivering spirit of freedom that flickered through the congregation. He felt a buoyancy within, and for no reason wanted to laugh and dance." (p.160)

His indoctrination continues at the hands of Robert of Art Squad, Mabel's old lover, who tells Gregory that attendance at church is completely voluntary, that those who go do so because they enjoy the service. If they are not in the mood, they stay away and are not considered sinners: "we have no Hell to be afraid of." At Berkelhoost, Robert tells him, their religion doesn't make them "miserable with fear and remorse". And while they all believe in God, they don't "shiver in awe at the thought of him." They regard him as "a good jumbie-friend". And why should anyone be afraid of a mythical friend?

10

Is *Shadows* the "major assault against orthodox religion" that the churchman A.J. Seymour claimed for it? Mittelholzer might well have been amused that sections of the contemporary church have developed liturgies, though not of course the theology, that resemble the gaiety and spontaneity of the Berkelhoost Sundays. But even within the Brethren's exuberant rationalism Mittelholzer plants a contrary element. The church ridicules the idea that the spirit survives physical death. Olivia, though, "gifted with ghost sight", can see the ghosts of church-haunting Dicky and of the lascivious, man-loving Luise, the sister of Mevrouw Adriana Schoonlust, whose bones lie in the cellar of the old Dutch ruins.

Serio-comic teasing might more accurately describe Mittelholzer's approach to religion in this novel, which can be seen to be in the satirical tradition of such early 19th century radicals as Joseph Hone or Richard Carlile.[7] The reader will decide whether Mittelholzer presents Harmston's church as a serious alternative to orthodox Christianity, or – in parts – a playfully inverted mirror image of the civilized world that Harmston despises, and of which, of course, he is a product. His chat with Gregory spells out the church's moral relativity, that "the keynote of our happiness here is evasion" (p.217). And Harmston's Berkleyan idealism ("we ourselves, unwittingly, have created reality…") and his assertion of the "close affinity between actuality and dream" (p.218), become in practice rather less than a search for epistemological truth and more of a justification for a universe where Harmston plays a role scarcely less authoritarian than Prospero's on his island – an intertextual reference discussed below. The blurring between dream and reality is, of course, also used as an excuse for Mr Buckmaster's (or rather his oversexed "doppleganger's") sexual exploitation of the local Amerindian women. If the critique of the civilised world is that it evades the truth about itself, lives in a state of false consciousness, can Harmston claim any better for his counter-world? It is not surprising that Gregory reaches a point where he wants to yell at his aunt: "Keep your philosophy! I'm sick of philosophy! I'm sick of you and sick of mankind!" (p.286) Mittelholzer also has Gregory mock this dream/reality evasiveness when he excuses himself from having eavesdropped a Harmston family conference: "All in a dream, so I'm entirely without blame" (p.143).

11

Whilst the apologist Garvey sees the Brethren harmonising opposites – "We're positive in our approach to living, even though our philosophy has much in it that is negative" (p.251) – a careful reading suggests that Mittelholzer wants us to see the unresolvable contradictions. Garvey claims "we don't have to nail ourselves down to any philosophy or flat conventions" when in reality the household is intensely rule bound. He claims that "we have our rules and can break them and not be horrified" (p.255), but this is just not true (except in the case of letting off Mabel, and certainly not for Logan and Sigmund.) Garvey's boast that Berkelhoost equals "Evasion. Hedging. Make believe" (p.256) is double-edged.

Sex in *Shadows*

Sex, Mittelholzer's other grand theme, is relegated to the background in *Shadows* in comparison to *The Mad MacMullochs*. Take the issue of nudity. Gregory's introduction to the easy way with nudity at Berkelhoost occurs on the occasion of his first bath when he is interrupted first by Berton, then by Olivia. Gregory "shielded himself with the towel", prompting Olivia to observe that his attitude is "atavabistic." (p.63). It is in this comic and understated way that nudity is introduced in *Shadows*. We are far from the serious business of the MacMulloch plantation where nudity is a banner of defiance and a celebration of the unperverted life.[8]

The subject is not broached again until Gregory's brooding introspection by the side of the river is interrupted by Mabel who has come from bathing naked in the creek, and he "smelt the creek-water smell of her, refreshing and wholesome." He would love to join them, he tells her, but confesses that he "hasn't yet taken to nudism", which Mabel asserts is: "Wholesome and sensible and civilized. ... We think you barbarous in many ways. Your views on sex and religion and clothes – they're what one would expect of savages." When Gregory queries why they mostly go about clothed, Mabel's answer is practical. It is for the benefit of the authorities. Berkelhoost would be shut down and Harmston denounced as "immoral and no fit person to be a protector over the Indians here." (In *The Mad MacMullochs* there are elaborate security arrangements and protocols designed to protect the nudist plantation from just such an eventuality.)

It is at the point when Gregory seems to have finally broken free of his torment and opened himself to love for Mabel that he is newly destabilized to learn, in conversation with her mother, that Mabel has had lovers since she was sixteen. Mrs. Harmston assures him that it would be perfectly fine for him to "associate" with Mabel, since it would be the natural thing to do as they are in love. She tells him that she would have been upset had Mabel gone into his room on his first night at Berkelhoost: "That would have been shameful wantonness, and we frown very much on that sort of thing… but so long as she's in love with you and you respond – well, that's quite all right." (Or, in one of Olivia's more creative malapropisms, to engage in sex without love is "probitchscrewity".) Mrs Harmston affirms that "natural urges must of necessity be normal and healthy or they wouldn't be natural, so why should we stifle them and turn ourselves into warped, unwholesome personalities?" She challenges Gregory to say if he has witnessed any "orgies of licentiousness" at Berkelhoost. She claims that the people in the commune aren't "obsessed by sex. They treat it as an ordinary everyday function, and enjoy it when it's time to indulge in it. They make jokes about it as they make jokes about eating and swimming and going to church."

However, the pastoral innocence of Mabel's love life is not quite the last word on the matter. "…in Berkelhoost, the Flesh is powerful, and the Devil lurks in the shadow of every twig" (p.142). This is a matter of "local influences" and history. During their tour of the Dutch ruins, Olivia tells Gregory of the history of the Schoonlust family, the original owners of Berkelhoost, who were murdered in the 1763 slave revolt. She tells of the 17 year old Luise who enjoyed being raped and became Cuffy's mistress and secretary: "She's blind and deaf to women in the real world; that's because she died wanting men so badly."

We are also led to wonder what is "natural" when we meet the Harmston's servant Ellen, who is nothing but the erotic instinct in its rawest state, with her frequent invitations for "lil' quick-quick sweetness" and the "graphic circular motion" she regularly makes with a finger. Far from inviting, in Gregory's first sight of Ellen he is confronted by the "nipples of her sharply jutting breasts" protruding through her dirty dress. To Gregory, "it was as if two bristling eyes were hidden behind the cloth evilly focused upon him" (p.68). At this stage, Gregory sees eyes watching him every-where: the "mass vigilance of his fancy". Ellen is sexually aroused by the beating and chaining of Logan, lusts after Berton, who is no more than a child, and misses no opportunity to cling on to him. Later, Garvey's preaching on the absurdity of the "civilized" world's sexual taboos is comically undermined by his complaint about catching fleas off Ellen after a sordid little episode of master/servant bedding. The lascivious Ellen, no doubt inhabited by Luise, is at the far end of carnality; at the opposite end is the guilt-ridden, cramped sexuality of Gregory.

In his tortured sexuality and its comic possibilities, Gregory is a familiar Mittelholzer type.[9] He tells his aunt when she enquires about him and Mabel that he hasn't had sex for three months. He has earlier admitted to Olivia that the flesh was one of his worst weaknesses, that he slept with another woman the night after his wedding and has been promiscuous from his adolescence. In Olivia's brilliant malapropism, Gregory has suffered from "de-mentia peacocks", a self-preening madness. To Olivia's question whether he had come to realize that it didn't pay, he admits: "Yes. Lust is clinker. It glows entrancingly when it is hot. It fascinates you. Then it cools and reveals itself as clinker" (p.121). His boat ride with Mabel is classic, playful Mittelholzer. Gregory catches:

> "a whiff of the perfume on her person, and desire scooped a hollow in his stomach. He scowled in self-contempt, remem-bering Ellen's obscene gesture and seeing himself on a par with her. With an excruciating desperation he wished he could burn all physical urge out of his body. Christ! Why must he want not to feel desire for a woman and still have to!" (p.288)

Gregory's recovery at Berkelhoost eventually leads to relief from the burden of guilt over his failed relationship with his dead wife Brenda. He concludes that they were both suffering from "the filthy sickness of ultra-civilized people (p. 206)." However, in *Shadows*, Gregory's restoration has little to do with the preach-ing to which he is subjected, but is about the rediscovery of his feelings in a sensuous natural environment – and redemption through Mabel's love. If in *MacMullochs*, the case for trouble-free sex is made explicitly at the level of ideas,[10] *Shadows* suggests that the relationship between sex and love is altogether more complicated than the Harmston ideologues pretend.

Nature in Shadows

If there is a gap between what Garvey claims as the ecological virtues of the Berkelhoost community in not exaggerating "the importance of *homo sapiens* on the earth", and its leader's actual behaviour, nature is entirely truthful. As Gregory observes, "Trees are different... Trees don't reach to the sky for power" (p.191). And it is during the play-acting of the Easter Sunday service in church that the violent storm erupts, occasioning Gregory's epiphany and the onset of his resurrection:

> "Gregory watched the column of water. Bits of dry leaves, the dung of birds, pollen dust, dead insects, all must be mixed together in the turgidity of this water – the accumulation of a week of dry, blazing days... It could be the dross of my own spirit I'm watching being washed away..." (p.265)

Under the tutelage of Olivia and the spell of Mabel, he has been opened up to the world outside himself, to the movement of leaf and the whispering of wind. The fury of the storm outside is the fury of the turmoil within.

> "He opened his eyes and saw the sky ripped across by a network of fire, and the air shook with a bang. Rain came down with new force, new vengeance, the grass about his feet hissed as though alive with unseen snakes. Suddenly he saw point in things. He felt a sense of direction. He identified himself with the weather, and saw the rain as possessed of a tremendous immediate purpose: a passionate perseverance that was almost human. The lightning too: its swift vivid spite. And the ramming impact of the thunder. Yes, he thought, I can see shape here. It gives me shape." (p.266)

Whilst the Harmstons would undoubtedly want to claim responsibility for Gregory's recovery through their rational efforts at re-education, the narrative suggests a cause located in the natural – and altogether more haphazard. Previously, Gregory has found it strange that storms always seemed to threaten Berkelhoost, but not break: "It is almost as though we were outside their notice: in a sector of contempt." When the climactic storm comes, it takes everyone by surprise. And it should be noted that in Mittelholzer's portrayal, nature (which is rich with an animacy that looks forward to novels such as Wilson Harris's *Heartland*) is by no means wholly beneficent. Whilst Berkelhoost is located in a natural world of "a vibrant, replete livingness (p.140)", with "Crystalline rivers of living spirit in leaves and branches (p.191)", it is also a place of "savagely vigorous verdure (p.38)", with plants "sullen with their burden of sap (p.50)", where the images of a poisoned old-world "civilization" is mirrored by images of poisoned berries in the bush.

Utopia in *Shadows*

> "I readily admit that there is much in the Utopian commonwealth that I wish rather than expect to see realized in the cities of our world."
>
> — Sir Thomas More, *Utopia*

Seymour has identified "at least three attempts Edgar made, half in seriousness, half in fun, to create a Utopia in his books… They are in *Shadows Move Among Them, The Mad MacMullochs* and *A Tinkling in the Twilight* …"[11] And indeed, both Berkelhoost and the MacMulloch plantation are utopian communities in the classic sense. Italo Calvino, discussing Fourier, describes them: "They [utopias] come to us as mechanisms that function perfectly in every cogwheel, self-sufficient, self-regulating, and self-reproducing, innocent of any teething troubles at the start and of an end that is always possible." However, the brief sections of *Tinkling in the Twilight* where the narrator/protagonist Brian Liddard – experiencing the "gap in [his] vision: the shift in Space along the curve of Time" – is hurtled into the Coterie State of 2039, then 2046, belong more accurately to the literature of anti-utopia, journeys into the infernal regions of the future, more in the manner of Huxley's *Brave New World* and Orwell's *Nineteen Eighty-*

Four than Fourier's Society of Harmony: "the vision of a hellish future where the best that can be seen is a condemnation."[12]

Writing in *Bim* in 1961, Geoffrey Wagner claimed that "every element of the Fascist state in embryo is represented at Berkelhoost",[13] while Michael Gilkes, in the fifth of the Mittelholzer Memorial Lectures in 1975, *Racial Identity and Individual Consciousness in the Caribbean Novel,* also found that "beneath all the liberalism and naturalness, the idyllic atmosphere of freedom and creative expression lies a disturbingly perverse element of cruelty and sadism."[14]

Both Wagner's and Gilkes's remarks seem to imply that the fascist elements in Berkelhoost represent in some part Mittelholzer's ideological tendencies, or at least his unconscious fantasies. This seems a retrogressive reading from some of the later fiction onto *Shadows*, particularly of patterns that become more explicit in the treatment of utopian elements in *MacMullochs* and in *Tinkling in the Twilight*: the education of children, eugenics and population control, and in particular discipline, crime and punishment. In short, the rationalist project. However, whatever the direction his later fiction and public pronouncements might have taken, *Shadows* can be read convincingly as showing Mittelholzer's position as altogether more libertarian and aware of the contradictions and dark underside of the Harmston project. It is to this underside that the publishers' note no doubt alludes in making the observation that "such an utopia cannot be taken at face value, and it is impossible to read the novel, first published in 1951, without seeing in it elements of prophecy: of the descent into sexual abuse, mass murder and suicide of the People's Temple commune at Jonestown in Guyana in 1978."

Education

From the earliest designs of the pioneer utopians, Charles Fourier and Robert Owen, the education of the child was at the very centre of their engineered communities, the *phalanstère* and the New Lanark Institute for the Formation of Character. The most exhaustive treatment of life in Fourier's Harmony is reserved for the educational system. Fourier had no time for motherly virtues and fathers were to be kept far away if they were not to cause actual damage to the child. What in Fourier is more than a little chilling in its systematic rigidity is a rather more flexible and benign affair in *Shadows* and *MacMullochs,* though the organization of the children at Berkelhoost into the Labour Squad, School Squad, Music Squad, Book Squad, and Art Squad seems to owe something to Fourier's Little Hordes and Little Bands, the former made up of those children who enjoy playing with muck and so are made responsible for collecting garbage, the latter composed of gentler children who tend flowers. The children at Berkelhoost are streamed into the various squads depending on their performance at the half-yearly intelligence test for six to ten year olds. Children in the Labour Squad who show signs of "bookishness" can be moved into the School Squad. The Book Squad will spend the summer vacation reading *Macbeth.* The Music Squad will have the privilege of occupying the first four rows at the concert where Mr. Buckmaster will bring his radiogram and play, among other uplifting delights, Beethoven's Seventh Symphony. The Berkelhoost curriculum consists of a heavy dose of high European culture, or a parody of it. It is the civilizing mission at work with a vengeance among the unspoiled "children of the forest" in the dense jungle up the Berbice River. The children learn to identify pieces of music and the names of their composers. There is a nice scene where a child at such a musical session reads from her exercise book: "The Moonlight Sonata, Beethoven. The 1812 overture, Tchaycowsky. The minute waltz, Chopin. The ride of the Valeries, Wagner…" (p.114). We find the Harmston children in the dining room, absorbed in their daily hour of improvement: "Olivia with Darwin's *A Naturalist's Voyage,* Berton with Gray's *Anatomy,* and Garvey deep in Byron's *Childe Harold…*"(p.184). After his talk on personal hygiene, followed by his lecture on the Restoration, Harmston passes on his credo: "I take pride in these children. I want them to grow up into men and women with rich minds. And I want them to lead full but quiet, natural lives in this their jungle home. My aim is to teach them to be civilized without cynicism" (p.112).

The evidence for the positive effects of the Harmston regime on his own children is far from convincing. Olivia, for instance, becomes enmeshed in self-harming and harbouring jealously murderous thoughts towards Mabel over Gregory. If there is a real heroine in the novel, it is Mabel, and her courage in standing up to her family and Berkelhoost in refusing to give evidence against Sigmund, particularly since we also see how indoctrinated she has been by Harmston.

Population Control
From the pulpit of the church at Berkelhoost, Reverend Harmston makes the announcement that a fresh shipment of contraceptives is expected by the next steamer from New Amsterdam, and he informs the communards that finances at Berkelhoost are healthy enough to allow for a new clearance scheme and the building of several more *benabs* in the residential area:

> "As a result, I'm glad to tell you that at least ten couples will be given permission to have babies. Their names will be announced shortly. We'll probably have a get-together ... and discuss how these couples should be selected – that is, whether you prefer to draw lots or whether you prefer to let those who are first on the waiting-list have the preference..." (p.263).

It is a light treatment of a theme, "half in seriousness, half in fun" in Seymour's phrase, that will take on a more sinister aspect when we come to the Eugenics Department on the MacMulloch plantation, charged with keeping the population "free of human vermin".

It is in the treatment of the issues of crime and punishment that the dark side, the "disturbingly perverse element of cruelty and sadism" (Gilkes), makes itself felt.

Crime and Punishment
Apart from Mabel, whose punishment for failing to report Sigmund's fourth offence involves a more subtle form of shaming, the Harmston children as well as Ellen come in for their share of slaps, clouts and whippings. Significantly, they are all punished not for the original infraction, but for the more serious offence of disobedience to Harmston. Properly brought up to respect authority, they all accept that they are guilty of disrespect and deserve to be punished. "I shouldn't have done it a second time", says Berton. For failing to turn up at the concert – having gone

19

hunting for *labba* instead, and been stung by a *marabunta* – Garvey gets a sarcastic comment from Harmston instead of the praise and sympathy he feels he deserves. He flies into a temper and tells Harmston to kiss his arse: "Naturally, he landed me a clout, and that got me madder and I let loose some more lurid language at him." This is followed by a "walloping with the balata whip and that brought me to my senses." While he is being beaten, Garvey, in a rare moment of nonconformism, calls his father a tyrant, "no better than a dirty Mussolini." For a moment Harmston interrupts the beating to say "We'll discuss that later" – then resumes the beating until he thinks Garvey has had enough. Later he tells Garvey that he has "touched on his tender spot", that he "couldn't stand being looked upon as a tyrant" (p.256).

The punishments of Olivia lead to murkier territory. Abusing Ellen as a "dog-bitch girl and a stink-puss girl" she is so harshly slapped by her father that it leaves "the imprint of his hand on her cheek. She trembled but not a tear came. Her eyes were marbles of hate" (p.88). But unlike her siblings, who shrug off the cuffs and slaps, Olivia responds to violent punishment in ways that lead into what Gilkes calls "erotic or sado-masochistic titillation." On another occasion of defiance, Olivia is again slapped across the face. This time she leaves the room in triumph, "her face afire but a smile on her lips", thinking that she's "suffering in body as well as in spirit." She goes and asks her enemy Ellen to slap her hard and kick her – which she does – and pisses on her as well:

> "Ellen, a dim, grey, trembling phantom of hate, kicked her in the chest, in the face; the darkness whirled with her female musk, and in the sound of her panting gurgles was malice, long pent-up, foetid and turgid. Olivia lay quiescent and took the punishment. Shivers of elation ran through her, and she thought, even as stars spattered the gloom behind her shut eyes: I now know how Logan feels when Daddy beats him. This is joy." (p.201)

Is this a genuine exploration of Olivia's gothic taste in martyrdom, an observation about the connections between regular physical punishment and the stimulation of sado-masochistic sexuality (was this something that Mittelholzer, who was much beaten as a child, knew about?) or merely Mittelholzer teasing, titillating and

trying to offend the Georgetown bourgeoisie? Such playful am-
bivalence of fictive intent is harder to see in the portrayal of
Harmston's treatment of Logan which, along with the fate of repeat
offenders like Sigmund, takes *Shadows* to its darkest place. On top
of his propensity for beating his own children (with a frequency
that rather points to his hypocrisy in denying any pleasure in the
act) Harmston appears locked in a sado-masochistic double-act
with Logan that involves frequent whippings and chainings up.

We see clearly what Logan's role is in the narrative when he is
discovered manacled and chained and groaning by the workshed, the "place of penal shadows", with the children gathered
round, chanting lines from *The Tempest*:

> "'Ban, 'Ban, Ca-Caliban!
> Has a new master: get a new man!
> 'Ban, 'Ban –" (p.106)

Olivia who with the other children has been recently memorizing
passages from *The Tempest,* "could not help thinking that he did
look a little bit like Caliban". She reflects that the "deep compassion" she sometimes felt for him was because "he could be so half-
animal in his looks." Nor is this the only point at which the shadow
of *The Tempest* falls onto Mittelholzer's text. Written in the same
year as O. Mannoni's influential *Prospero and Caliban*[15] and a full
decade before George Lamming's celebrated chapter in *The Pleasures of Exile,*[16] "A Monster, a Child, a Slave", Mittelholzer was
drawing on the variations on obedience and authority that are at
the centre of Shakespeare's play. Harmston's Prospero whips the
loyal beast of burden Logan/Caliban into submission. Obedient
Olivia/Ariel ("a regular little sprite" who goes "off at a dart") is
Harmston's intelligence agent, flitting here there and everywhere,
spying, eavesdropping and reporting back. There is even an echo
of Ferdinand and Miranda in the wooing and betrothal of Gregory
and Mabel, even if Mabel's parents, unlike Prospero, and to
Gregory's chagrin, have little use for pre-marital chastity.

In the inhuman treatment of Logan, the Caliban figure, punishment becomes systematic and indistinguishable from torture.
The novel is barely under way when Logan receives a whipping
for disobeying the order to take Gregory's baggage up into the

house before he moves the provisions that have come in on the steamer from New Amsterdam. His howls of pain reach Olivia: "Long, mournful and telling of pain. Poor fellow, she thought, he must have done something again. I've got to go and beg for him" (p.57). Harmston uses a balata whip with knotted cords, while Logan cringes and howls. After the whipping, Logan's "high cheekbones [were] shiny with tears but his wide, thick-lipped mouth curved in a smile." Harmston assures Olivia that he "enjoys being flogged." But for Logan there is something worse than being flogged. About once every three months, according to Harmston, he is manacled and chained for indulging in "really disgusting behaviour" – in reality something absurdly trivial. When the squeamish Gregory, who is still learning the ways of Berkelhoost, discovers Logan howling and beating his forehead against the corrugated iron wall, Harmston tells him: "One of the jobs I don't like doing, my boy… but I have to do it. Part of my programme of discipline. He'd get completely out of hand if I didn't punish him… hardly a week goes by that I don't have to give him a flogging. He's an intractable, perverse fellow…" (p.93). Later, he amends his initial description of Logan from "distinctly abnormal" to "sub-normal." At various points of the narrative, it is Logan's monstrous animality that is forced on our attention. His laughter is "a sound that wavered through the air, half-human, half-beast in timbre" (p.234), "a raucous quark of mirth". And after some inventive and musical playing of the church bell that "sounded mad and idiotic and grave in turn; joyous and whispering and bizarre", Logan is described as galloping "round and round the belfry… He turned somersaults and let out hoarse quarks (p.339)." Caliban, too, did famously sing, though for Logan there is no jubilation of imagined freedom, or ultimate seeking of wisdom or grace.[17]

Aside from his crimes of disobedience, Logan's small acts of rebellion consist of attempting to entangle Mabel and Gregory in a frame-up and later of pelting the house with sawari nuts. For the rest he is a thoroughly domesticated servant, showing no sign of what Auden called Caliban's "passion of resentment". But notwithstanding the docility of the victims, *Shadows* holds up the civilising mission of the imperialist penetration of the New World to not so gentle ridicule. What Harmston is repressing in Logan is "Lil nancy-story fun", and we are never allowed to forget that Berkelhoost is created on the ruins of the old Dutch plantation that perished at the hands of the slaves in 1763 and exists in the jurisdiction of the colonial power. It is no accident that Logan, in a predominantly Amerindian/European settlement, is half African.

In the case of Sigmund, we move from slaps and clouts and whips and chains to the death penalty. The Berkelhoost code decrees that after three serious offences, the offender, in the words of Cedric of the Music Squad as he whistles the Habanera from *Carmen*, "must be considered an outcast who, because of his fourth major criminal offence, has to be regarded as incurable and thus worthy of death" (p.320). [18] The congregation gather and the vote is taken: Sigmund is to die. Gregory, who had earlier persuaded Mabel not to report Sigmund's uninvited entry into the Harmston's house, finds this fascistic: "this is what thousands of poor devils are fighting against in Spain." Mabel, torn between her love for Gregory and her loyalty to the code, is puzzled by Gregory's response: "Why should you consider it Fascistic to get rid of a man who has proved himself a hopeless crime-addict? Don't you think four times enough? And he *knew* what the penalty would be if he was caught a fourth time... Surely you don't expect us to wait until he commits a murder before taking steps to get rid of him!" (p.325). Of course, nothing that Sigmund is claimed to have done in the novel actually amounts to a "major criminal offence" or suggests any propensity for violence, as Gregory discovers when he apprehends him with pathetic ease.

When Gregory tries to persuade her not to give evidence, she argues that Sigmund would be worse off for being pardoned and that he would begin to turn violent: "Look what happens in America... If the American authorities were sensible they'd wipe them out before they get to the homicidal stage and turn gun-men. It seems so absurd to let criminals shoot up and hack people to death when they could have been stopped by being put out of the way before they got to the point where their frustrations and hatred of society compelled them to take to violence..." (p.326). Whilst this is a "logic" evidently found persuasive by some of the world's more brutally fascist police forces in dealing with street children, it is surely not one that Mittelholzer wants the reader to see as other than cruelly absurd. In the end Mabel yields to Gregory's pressure and withholds her evidence. Sigmund is spared. That is, until the bushmaster or, as we are free to imagine, some less feral force restores the Harmston order of things.

Rationalist project vs. "local influences"

The utopia of Berkelhoost is a rationalist project with an ancestry that reaches back through Owen and Fourier to William Godwin and Thomas More. As we have seen, Mittelholzer cleaves close to this rationalist tradition of perfectability in the creation of his Guyanese and Barbadian communes, but in a reiteration of the collision between the rationalist/utilitarian project and the insurgent romantic assertion of individual feeling and emotion, as exemplified in Mary Shelley's *Frankenstein* (or even in Godwin's own fiction), the Berkelhoost project is forever at risk of being undermined by the "local influences". This conflict is a source of imaginative tension in the novel.

Harmston explains Ellen's abnormal behaviour by the "unusually powerful effect" the local influences have on her. Unlike Olivia and Berton, who are the most receptive to the influences, Mabel, according to Olivia, "doesn't really respect the local influences." Like her mother, she is not troubled by shadows. Nor is Harmston, though he is all too aware of the influences and their power to disrupt. He even goes so far as to invent an occasion when he was "caught napping" by the influences and sleepwalked to a "pretty Buck girl" who gives birth to Osbert nine months later. We learn later (though we might wonder whether this is another fiction) from Garvey that Harmston created this fiction to demystify himself to the Indians and his wife, who regarded him as "a hero who could do no wrong". He even manages to convince his outraged wife that guilty though he has been of a breach of discipline, he is not really to be blamed: "The local influences had taken him unawares; he was as much vulnerable to the local influences as anyone else." As the architect of the rationalist project, he, of course, claims to be properly aware of the threat of the subversive power of these influences.

What goes hand in hand with "local influences" is the other

phrase that describes something regrettable in the Berkelhoost universe: "the human element". In the rhetoric of Harmston and his acolytes, the "human element" is what is responsible for Sigmund's wife's tears when she agrees that he deserves to die. When Mabel refuses to testify against Sigmund (defying "the Secret Code before all the people", as Olivia accuses) this, too, is seen as a weakness born of "the human element". It is in the clash between the utilitarian project and the mysterious ways in which "pity and love" enter the human heart that the moral centre of the novel is to be found. Mabel, still at this stage arguing the necessity of Sigmund's fate, speaks in Benthamite tones: "It's practical and sensible and necessary to our happiness to do them" (p.212), whilst Gregory, one suspects, speaks for Mittelholzer when he replies: "Compassion. It is the enemy of every human endeavour, yet we must cherish it, for without it we cease to be human" (p.225). And, as if wanting to give the reader a clue about where he is in the novel, Mittelholzer has Gregory declare the ultimate Mittelholzer credo: "All life is conflict; nothing was meant to be at rest or peace" (p.194).

Olivia

A J Seymour is at his most fulsome in talking about Olivia whom he sees as "the conscience of the story", a role she hints at when she describes herself as "a stupid, romantic dolt who had allowed her reason to succumb to things mythical" (p.47), and he puts his finger on what is at the imaginative heart of the novel when he describes Olivia as:

> "the most attractive character to my mind to have come out of Caribbean fiction in English, and reading the novel again, I fall even more in love with her from the opening chapter to the last when she begins to grow up; such passionate imagination hoping and desiring to grow up to become passionate flesh, such insight, such sympathy, so conscious of the shadows that move among us and so at home among them."[19]

She is Ariadne leading Gregory out of the maze of his torment. I differ with Seymour though when he finds Roxanne, the youngest of the MacMulloch sisters, an "image of a developing Olivia".

It is true that they share certain qualities, like rebelliousness, impishness, self-dramatization. ("I am a protaxonist in a tragedy"). What Roxanne shows no sign of is the rich imaginative life that makes Olivia glow in the dark. Then there are no subversive local influences in sunny Barbados, no myth-laden jungle where the "whole neighbourhood bristles with the residual effluvia of past violence." "Gifted with ghost-sight" and on familiar terms with the shadows, Olivia is an enchantress of concealment and revelation. In a book with its share of cardboard figures, caricatures and stereotypes, Olivia is a full presence, our eyes and ears, engaged and engaging. Capable of dark imaginings, like slicing off Mabel's breasts, her final morbid, melodramatic hoax on Gregory is cruel and spiteful. Her full effect on Gregory is still to come, which is to say that he is yet to fall under her spell, "her lasso of love". For the span of the novel he remains torn between sensing in Olivia "security and peace – or infinite catastrophe" (p.137), but there is a premonition of her potential effect when, early in their relationship, he "of a sudden grew keenly aware of Olivia's absence" and "in his fancy he saw her as a milky shadow upon a veil of evening dusk." This "quaint flitting child" is far and away Mittelholzer's most appealing creation.

> "Perhaps I might mention," he writes further in that letter to Seymour with which we began, "that I am prepared to be judged on *Shadows*...it is a novel that I like ... I wrote it to please myself entirely, without a thought to publishers or public." [20]

Not yet a revival perhaps, but let the reawakening continue.

Mahaica,
East Coast Demerara

Endnotes

1. Quoted in A.J. Seymour, *Edgar Mittelholzer: the man and his work*, Georgetown, The Edgar Mittelholzer Memorial Lectures, 1st Series. Georgetown: National History and Arts Council, 1968, p. 14.
2. See for instance Frank Birbalsingh, "Edgar Mittelholzer: Moralist

or Pornographer?" *Journal of Commonwealth Literature 7*, (July 1969), pp. 88-103; Michael Gilkes, "Edgar Mittelholzer", in *West Indian Literature*, ed. Bruce King, 1979, pp. 95-110; and Patrick Guckian, "The Balance of Colour: A Re-Assessment of the Work of Edgar Mittelholzer", *Jamaica Journal 4* (March 1970), pp. 38-45.

3. Seymour, ibid., p. 14.

4. Mittelholzer explained the anonymity in a letter to A.J. Seymour: "The object of this letter is to ask you to keep a secret. Not long after receiving this letter you'll be getting a book entitled THE MAD MACMULLOCHS, by an author called H. Austin Woodsley. I told the publishers to send you a copy. This is an occasion when I'm not sending out any presentation copies as I usually do. But I do want you to read the book, hence the review copy. You'll probably wonder why this book appears under a pen-name. Well the story is as follows: I wrote this book in Barbados in 1953, but Secker & W. (regular publishers) turned it down, saying that they thought it might damage my reputation, that the critics might give me a raspberry. I reluctantly had to put it aside, because I was 4,000 miles away from London and couldn't do much about it. But meanwhile a friend of mine (English girl) in Barbados read the script and liked it very much, and a year ago I met her in London here in a night-club, and she asked me why didn't I unearth the script and try to get it published because she liked it next to SHADOWS. I took her advice, read it and thought I ought to publish it. So I gave the script to Peter Owen (whom I know personally and who was once a director of the now defunct Peter Nevill, the firm that brought out SHADOWS and CHILDREN of K. Peter now has his own firm). Peter snapped it up at once, and it appears under his imprint next Friday. 24th. but I had to use a pen-name, because it would have been embarrassing for Secker & W. if I'd published it under my own name when they are already my regular publishers. The literary world would naturally think I must have fallen out with them or something like that, which, of course, isn't the case. Again, I thought it would be good fun to see how the critics would react to the work of a "new" novelist. Think, Arthur, if one of them should say: Mittelholzer had better watch his step. Mr Woodsley seems on the way to over-shadowing him." That is why I want to keep it a dead secret. I don't want it to leak out for quite a while that I'm the author of this book." [Grateful thanks to Juanita Cox for supplying this material from her research notes.]

5. In *The Mad MacMullochs* (1959), the plantation is where the uninhibited natural life is celebrated in defiance of the repressive practices of the society beyond its gates. The thesis is set out by Mr. Lambert, manager of the Income Tax Evasion Department, as he

declares to the assembled communards: "the men outside the boundaries of this plantation with their sewer-like minds will see obscenity in every gesture relating to the sexual act – even in the circumstance of a nude human body. Even into that passive circumstance men have injected the toxin of their dirt – the crass, cramped pretentious fools outside this plantation who deem themselves enlightened and civilized…" (*The Mad MacMullochs*. London: Peter Owen Ltd., 1959. p. 227-228).

6. The concept of elasticity is deepened and more fully developed in *The Mad MacMullochs* where the rebellious and wilful Roxanne, under the permitted age to marry, sidesteps the prohibition by producing her "EE & E" card granted by the Department of Errors, Exceptions and Elasticity (p. 233).

7. See for instance "The Bullet Te Deum with the Canticle of the Stone" (1817) and "The Litany" from *The Second Trial: the King Against William Hone* (1817), in *Regency Radical: Selected Writings of William Hone*, Ed. David Kent and D.R. Ewen, Detroit, Wayne State University Press, 2003, pp. 38-41 & 106-112.

8. See for instance, Evaline and Albert, and Elsie and Albert in *MacMullochs*. As Mr. Robert MacMulloch propounds to a nervous Albert, going nude prevents them from "indulging in morbid and unwholesome imaginings about what lies hidden behind panties and brassieres and jock-straps…we take human nudity for granted – and we experience no guilt when a pair of breasts or two promising testicles strike us as particularly tempting." (p.136) In *The Mad MacMullochs* all inhibitions have disappeared and sexual intercourse between consenting adults is considered as natural as breathing. On the plantation, there is no requirement for emotional engagement, although the young MacMulloch women are expected to be virgins until their marriage. The fondling of a breast is an expression of courtesy and appreciation and coupling *al fresco* turns no heads.

9. What in Gregory and Albert is mildly neurotic, assumes, in the case of Brian Liddard, in *A Tinkling in the Twilight* (London: Secker & Warburg, 1959), an altogether darker dimension. Five years after the end of his marriage to Elizabeth, "womanless years of solitude and Yoga peace", he revisits the last time they lay together: "And for an instant an ache of anxiety attacked me. … Then the ache faded – the anxiety sifted away like sand from the upper to the lower chamber of an hour-glass. In my fancy I saw an hour-glass. In the lower chamber lay settled the dross of my natural urges. In the upper the air was free and clean. I began to smile to myself, thinking: that upper chamber must always remain free and clear; never again must I reverse the glass; never again must I let the dross

of the flesh filter back into the clear, clean freedom of my spirit" (p.39). In that dynamic from desire to revulsion, and the retreat into the safety of abstinence, the sexual pathology Gregory escapes from finds its most developed expression in Brian Liddard who tells us that his "life of sexless bliss took time and trouble to shape [...]Much crawling through the heated labyrinths of libido had to be achieved. Many nightmares of nymphic horror had to be endured and enjoyed..."(p. 62).

10. In his rebuke to Albert, put out at the sight of Mervyn fondling Euphony's breasts, Ronald declares: "...because you were brought up to feel that every gesture and act connected with sex is indelicate and indecorous – if not outright salacious... we've been brought up to feel that copulation – as natural a function as eating – is a filthy business. It's men, Alby, men and women themselves who have stuffed the filth into sex." (*The Mad MacMullochs,* p.113).

11. Seymour, op. cit., p. 43.

12. Italo Calvino, *The Uses of Literature.* New York: Harcourt Brace Johanovich, 1987.

13. Geofffrey Wagner, "Edgar Mittelholzer: Symptoms and Shadows", *Bim* 9, (July-Dec 1961), pp. 29-34.

14. Gilkes, *Racial Identity and Individual Consciousness in the Caribbean Novel,* The Edgar Mittelholzer Memorial Lectures, 5th Series. Georgetown: Ministry of Information & Culture, 1975., p.27.

15. O. Mannoni, *Prospero and Caliban: The psychology of colonization*, New York, Praeger, 1956.

16. George Lamming, *The Pleasures of Exile.* London: Michael Joseph, 1960, pp. 95-117.

17. "No more dams I'll make for fish/ Nor fetch in firing,/At requiring.../ Freedom, high day, high day freedom, freedom, high-day freedom!" (*The Tempest*, 2:2:175ff.)

18. Mittelholzer develops this theme more stridently in *Tinkling in the Twilight.* Brian Liddard has one of what he calls "the tanglings with the tendrils of Time... the shift in Space along the curve of Time" (p.104). He is catapulted from 1958 into the Coterie State of 2039. There are no prisons in the Coterie State. "When anyone is found guilty of a non-violent crime he is given a slip. For the first offence, a pink slip. For the second, a red slip. For the third, a black slip. There's no fourth slip. At the fourth offence he qualifies as HV. Human Vermin. He's regarded as a potentially violent criminal – and pop he goes. Morphine or cyanide (p. 212)."

19. Seymour, op. cit., p.14.

20. Seymour, op. cit,. p. 14.

PART ONE

I

Up in the darkness of the rafters, every now and then, the bats wriggled and squeaked, and Olivia, who lay on her back in the Buckmasters' pew, saw them, in her fancy, squinting at her with a sleepy slyness. In her fancy, too, they grinned and nodded at each other, plotting midnight murders. Sour berries and insects that saw in the dark would be their victims. But night had not yet come, and now in the twilit church it was she they had chosen.

She waited, not caring, for she wanted to die so that her father could weep and say: "My fault. All my fault." If he had let her have her way she would have taken the harmonium, which was a portable one, out of the church and set it up by the landing place so that when the *corial*★ with her cousin, Gregory, came alongside the logs that served as landing-stage she could have played *See the conquering hero comes.* That was how she had planned to welcome Gregory to Berkelhoost.

"Men who fight in wars are heroes."

"Um. I suppose they are," said her father, the Reverend Mr. Gerald Harmston. "But I don't think your cousin would want such a welcome. And it would be wise not to remind him about the Spanish War. I have an idea he's coming here to forget such things."

"And no loud shouting and horseplay," said Mrs. Harmston. "His nerves are bad."

Very well then. Let her die.

A solemn signal passed between the bats, and down they came whirring and whirling: frayed funereal scarves that fanned her face and settled like soft soot on her chest. Scarves into soot, and out of the soot little timid teeth that sank without pain, almost with pleasure, into her throat.

"Delight for me. Delight for them."

And now her blood rose in mist above the pew; in a minute the

★ Pronounced kree-all.

33

whole church would be filled with a sunset glow... In the jungle, far away, a bird began to sing. It was a sad song, but it soothed her, for the magic-swan was singing it. Her swan-song...

"Olivia!"

That was her mother calling from the house. The mist subsided, and the swan lay clubbed by reality. The bats were only bats in the rafters.

She watched the sunshine on the pulpit. Late afternoon sunshine, it came in through the missing pane of one of the two western windows. Filtered by the fronds of the *cookerit* palm that stood near the rickety belfry, it put a dappled pattern on the varnished woodwork of the pulpit. In some way it pacified her to watch it. It seemed to remind her of a pleasant happening of long ago – a long ago five or six years ago. Sitting on the church steps with Berton and some of the Buck children eating *cookerits* during a big *cookerit* season. Or the excitement and anticipation of the evening before a trip to New Amsterdam. Or hunting for rare ferns or flowers on a Saturday morning... A patch of speckled sunshine on the brown pulpit. It wove an ache inside her and lifted her spirit into a place of leafy breeze... The pattern shifted slightly. A wind must have shaken the fronds. She listened and heard the wind – like a ghost of rain passing through the jungle... Now it was gone, abruptly and mysteriously, as it always came and went.

It was very peaceful in the church. She liked the gloom and the silence and the shut windows with their dark-green panes. And the squeaking of the bats, and the furry, hollow thumps they made as they wriggled. She preferred being in the church on a weekday. On Sunday all the windows were open and the pews and the pulpit and the altar-table looked white with daylight – ordinary. And people came in and shifted their feet along the floor and stamped about and coughed and sang hymns out of tune.

She sat up and cocked her head and hugged her knees, her dark-brown pigtail tickling her long bare legs. She heard the distant mooing of the steamer's siren, and her heart beat faster. Even if Gregory had not been expected it would have been like this; the weekly steamer always gave her an excited feeling.

She could hear voices and rustlings at the landing-place.

Thuds and splashings. Logan must be getting ready to take the *corial* and the skiff out into the stream to meet the steamer. The urge to go outside and join the others moved strong in her – so strong that her head went dizzy-empty as though it had turned into a cavern with pink twilight.

"Olivia! Where are you? The steamer is coming!"

That was Berton calling her now.

She hugged her knees tighter, and giggled, feeling cosy and full of secrets. It was good to know that you were being called and searched for and nobody knew where you were. You were safe from them in a pew in a shut-up church watching a solitary patch of sunshine.

Yet a wisp of regret moved up through her. She could almost see it. Slowly, magically it moved, like smoke. Or like the Genie escaping out of the Green Bottle… She hated not answering when Berton called. He and she were close chums. Though fourteen, he never tried to make her feel she was his inferior because she was two years younger. Not like Garvey who, at fifteen, felt he was a grown-up person. Garvey was stiff and snappish with her, and full of sneering airs.

When she saw Berton later in the evening she must explain why she could not answer… "Daddy was vexed with me because I wasn't at the landing-place to meet Gregory, eh? I'm glad. I wanted to spite him for not letting me play the harmonium."

She turned on to her stomach and leant over and peered under the seat. When her eyes had got accustomed to the dark she made out a milk-white web at the back, in the corner near the aisle where the back-support of the pew joined up with the side-support. In this web lived a blue-black hairy bush-spider. No one but she knew that it lived here.

She smiled with relief and whispered: "My friend. Still alive, eh? I'm so glad. But they will find you before long. Death cometh any day."

"Ollie! Where are you hiding? The steamer is nearly here!"

His voice came from farther off. He must be heading along the track toward the Dutch ruins. She could see him, red-haired and freckled; long-legged and thin like her; with the scar shaped like an L on his right knee. His grey-green eyes must be wide and anxious. He was forever fearing that one day she would lose herself so that nobody – not even she herself – could find her... "You're such a funny girl, one never knows what mightn't happen to you. The Genie might lure you away – or a *kanaima*..."

If only she could have sent her spirit out of the church after him so that it could have followed him along the track and caught up with him and said: "Don't be anxious about me. I'm safe in the church. Tell them you can't find me. I'm not dead yet, Berton dear."

She felt tears coming. Tears for the spider, and tears for Berton who loved her. She raised her head and settled herself on her back again.

The patch of sunshine was moving off the pulpit. It would soon be on the lectern with the big black Bible.

"Olivia!... Ollie!" Much further off. He must be getting near to the fallen palm where the track branched...

"*Into the valley of death,*" she whispered, shutting her eyes, "*rode the six hundred.*"

She could hear the voices of the others at the landing-place – and also a swish and gurgle of water which told her that Logan was pushing off in the *corial*. In the darkness of her closed eyes she saw the skiff following in tow. The smooth, black water parted and started a fan of ripples that ringed out toward the end of the world. She could hear the distant, muffled, churning commotion of the steamer's screws. The steamer must be coming round the bend in the river, wonderful and dirty-grey, charged with all the mysteries of the coast a hundred miles away... It would be good to watch it approach. She could see Logan stacking the skiff with the boxes of provisions from New Amsterdam. In a few minutes he would be doing that. And he would put in Gregory's trunks and suitcases, too. She tried to speculate how many pieces there would be and what colour the trunk would be... Five pieces, say? And perhaps the trunk was the colour of the harmonium – pale brown. What could it contain besides clothes? Two revolvers and a box of ammunition? The statue of a naked woman in bronze? An *Encyclopedia Britannica*? A little bottle of sand from the Sudan? A stereoscope and pictures of the Himalayas?

Her body quivered in a fever of fancies.

"I wonder," she murmured, "what new shadows he's bringing with him."

She sat up, eager to rush out and join the others. But she shook her head slowly. "I swore I'd spite Daddy by staying here, and I've got to carry through my plan. The Genie would think me weak if I didn't."

"Ollie!"

Berton was coming back. She heard his footsteps. After a while, he went past the church toward the landing-place.

"Daddy, I can't find her anywhere," she heard him say. "I've searched in all our regular hiding places – and I can't find her."

"Don't trouble any more, my boy. Come. Here's the steamer." A kindly voice. He was a good father... Strong. A hero-giant...

She struggled with herself, and after a while, lay on her back again and murmured: "I've held out like Verdun, and I've triumphed over my weakness. I stay here and spite him."

She moved her head and saw that the sunshine was on the lectern. Memory-rich. "You make me think of a black lizard, sunshine," she whispered. "It has no tail, and it wriggles very fast on the sand. You make me think of the Ibi Creek, too, when the sun is hot at midday and *mora* blossoms are floating past, and you can hear distant thunder."

II

Since half past seven that morning the steamer had begun its journey up the Berbice. For the first three hours it had laboured with a slight ploughing motion through the choppy water of the lower reaches and then had settled down to an easy gliding, for by this time the water had ceased to be choppy and had taken on a pond-like smoothness, had ceased, too, to be amber and muddy in look and become black and evil. As the stream narrowed and the jungle reared silently higher and higher and denser on either bank the blacker and more evil a smile the water appeared to brew. The shadowed spaces made by the low-hanging foliage momently seemed to gather a deeper gloom and to glower with the sullen menace of many watching eyes: eyes concealed amid poison-berries and slow-drifting blossoms. The trade wind, which had made the heat in the little town at the mouth of the river so bearable as not to be heeded, no more could be felt; gradually it had withdrawn as though sensing in this savagely vigorous verdure spirits alien to its cool, ocean-free careering. And as it had fallen back the heat, poised and silky, entwined itself with stifling power around the steamer.

The steamer, small and rather dirty in appearance, was a two-decker, the top deck first-class and the lower deck second. Cattle and dogs, crates and baskets of vegetables and groceries, lumber, bags of cement, stacks of machine parts and forks and shovels travelled with not-well-off human beings on the lower deck.

First-class passengers, on any trip, seldom number more than half-a-dozen. On this trip there were five. A cattle-rancher with a dark-red, leathery face who was on the first leg of his long journey to the Rupununi Savannah. An olive-skinned, drawling-voiced shopkeeper and his darker-complexioned, silent-smiling wife. A very tall, soft-voiced, diffident Church of England priest. And Gregory Hawke who was on his way to the mission-house at Berkelhoost.

First-class passengers have the use of wicker chairs and the tiny dining-saloon. And lunch is provided if it was ordered at the commencement of the journey: a lunch of chicken or beef, with rice (boiled in loose grains as it is always done in British Guiana and the West Indies) and vegetables – fried plantain and sweet potatoes and perhaps a piece of baked breadfruit. The war may have changed things somewhat, but in July, 1937, when Gregory travelled up the river, this was the kind of meal that was served.

On this particular trip it was curried chicken with a coconut flavour – and rice, fried plantain and yams. It was unfamiliar food, but Gregory ate all of it and enjoyed it, though his fellow passengers could only guess at his enjoyment, for during the meal he said nothing to them nor they to him. Since half past seven, when the steamer left the wharf in New Amsterdam, he had shown them very plainly that he wanted to keep to himself. They had made attempts to be friendly, but he had rebuffed them – not rudely but with polite firmness. Even the cattle-rancher, the least shy and most persistent, had had to give up trying after five attempts within two hours.

Throughout the meal he could sense their disapproval of him, was conscious of the furtive glances they cast in his direction. It bothered him; he found himself wanting to fidget. For he was sensitive to the atmosphere of other people. But he could do nothing about it; he had no desire to talk or to be talked to by strangers. If these people, he thought, knew what was the matter with him they would be sympathetic instead of disapproving. He could tell that they were simple, honest people. Unspoilt by the pampering amenities of big cities. Touched, but not irrevocably poisoned, by civilization. He felt friendly toward them, but must not show it. To do so would be to augment the confusion in him.

They would have to go on seeing him as they must see him – an aloof Englishman; a man from the north with a superior, self-sufficient air. He could not let them have an inkling of the tears that were stored in him, nor of the harsh laughter that fought for escape behind his tight lips. He must conceal from them the violent trembling that only his clenched hands kept in check. They would be sorry for him if they could know of the shadows that made a dancing screen between him and them.

He could not even read a book. He had to recline in a wicker chair and stare at the unvarying versions of jungle that stretch after stretch of the river brought into view, his hands clasped lightly in his lap. If he clasped them too hard it might attract notice, and that he could not stand. Notice could easily engender pity. He could not bear that. There was a space in him waiting to be filled with someone's pity and love, but if he found that someone who was willing to fill it he would have to turn away from him or her with a shudder and a silent whimper. Often when he watched the jungle watch back at him with malicious glitterings in the scorching sun he would think: I have to do something about this. But I can't decide what.

In such moments his pasty face would twitch, though if anyone had been looking at him they would have thought he was smiling at something pleasant he was remembering. In these moments he saw himself outside his body, viewing his body. With sly wonder he would observe the slimmish man of thirty-one, square-shouldered but with sunken chest, pale blue eyes, fair hair, dry and limply brushed back as though breathed upon by a hot wind, and long tapering fingers fashioned specially, it seemed, for frequent clenching and unclenching. Oh, my God, he would cry in careful silence, and stop watching himself. Then perhaps glance aside quickly at the others to make sure they had not heard the cry.

Once or twice, not often, the heat would help him to doze. The heat and the throbbing of the engines. The subdued tumultuous swash of the water as the bows perpetually parted it. A light doze: a momentary drifting away from the intensity of the immediate present, so that in the red gloom curtained off by his shut lids he could sway with the throbbing of the engines and watch without strain the endless waves swelling off from the bows and undulating toward the darkness under the overhanging foliage. Before lunch, he had stood many times at the rail and tried to follow with his eyes clump after clump of foam until it broke up into separate bubbles and became lost in the boiling turmoil that receded toward the vessel's stern. Now in his doze he would build up a picture of these foam-clumps, and the sight of them rushing past would not seem futile and monotonous, nor would they seem symbols of the years gone by; he would see them in his doze as dream-snow, and he was standing at the door of his home in Middenshot on a January evening, a boy of eight excited because the mild winter had, at last, suddenly turned cold and snow was coming down… Only he was still aware of the black water, and the snow became froth on a mug of brown ale, and he was not a boy but a young man of twenty-two in the Ram and Cross and there was a motorcycle waiting for him outside to take him to Staines or Guildford, for it was a Sunday morning in May, and the sun was shining, and the rhododendrons were in full bloom everywhere you looked…

It was good to doze. But the awakening came with a start and the trembling sound in his head, and he was back with reality. Alert. Waiting. His lips pursed and his jaws clamped together in an effort to control himself. The fear was ever with him that the trembling sound in his head would grow into a stammering roar. Innumerable times he had pictured himself breaking up into so many pitiable bits, and the anxiety that closed in around him would seem like the neutral walls of a terrifying limbo. In such instants he cringed outside himself and whimpered in spirit-silence, sorry for his plight and in need of companionship – and the pity and love of his fellow-men.

When, as happened sometimes, the jungle would part to reveal a small cultivated clearing with an isolated hut roofed with palm leaves the tension of anxiety would ease somewhat; he would sit forward with interest, and feel a slow warmth moving inside him, for the palm-leaf roof would stamp itself on his fancy and become changed into a haystack seen from the train or glimpsed in a flash as he hurtled along the highway on his motorcycle… At some of these lonely homesteads the steamer would stop – stop in mid-stream – and a boat would come out to be loaded with crates or boxes of provisions: a canoe precarious in the water yet handled with such skill and confidence by its dark-skinned occupant that though the water came within an inch or two of its gunwale disaster never overtook it…

He would watch wide-eyed, a set smile on his face, and when the steamer moved on again, would feel less lost. Hope would drift like thistledown before his eyes.

For several minutes after he would experience a liquid throbbing in his chest, and he would tell himself with an inward laugh that a clear brook was running over smooth pebbles, and the pebbles were he. This was relief, and when he stood aside from his body he saw a face pale but calm, and limbs relaxed as though infinitesimal panthers were streaking over the surface of the golden-haired skin.

It was during one of these spells of relief that a voice said to him: "The next stop is Berkelhoost." The cattle-rancher's voice.

Gregory did not move. Nor reply. He wanted to – with urgency – but he was unable to; it was part of his illness: his body did not always work in harmony with his will. In terror, he could envisage the breath in him as strands of thread shimmering through his lungs. Pink lungs – sea-sponges in sea-deep twilight. And the shimmer of blue threads… At length, as though his body had answered a delayed telephone-call from his brain, he shook himself and sat forward in the chair.

The cattle-rancher was on the point of moving off, a shortish, solid man in clean khaki-drill shirt and shorts, his red face kindly but with a slighted expression. Gregory almost gasped at him: "Please! Just a moment." He rose stumblingly. Smiling. "Please. The next stop you say is Berkelhoost?"

The cattle-rancher turned and nodded. "Yes," he said, with uncertainty, with some stiffness.

Gregory's hands were cold and damp. He had to exert all his will not to clench them, not to bring them together and clasp them tight.

"Thanks," he said, still smiling. Rigidly. He stood aside and viewed himself. A ghost in wax, smiling. A ghost caught in a photograph.

The cattle-rancher was looking at him curiously. Soon there would be pity in his grey-blue eyes.

"Thanks a lot," said Gregory. In a murmur. He held out his hand. "It's very good of you. I hadn't realized we were so near. What's the time?"

The cattle-rancher glanced at his wristwatch and said: "Ten past five." His manner less stiff – still curious. Almost sympathetic. Had he noticed anything odd? He said something about baggage. Gregory, he said, had better go down and see after his baggage. "I take it the Berkelhoost people are sending out a *corial* to collect you and your things?"

"Yes. They probably will – if it's the custom."

He nodded, keeping himself very still, then said: "You must forgive me. I wanted to be friendly, but – I couldn't."

The cattle-rancher only stared at him. With wonder. On the verge of a smile. Embarrassed.

"I'm sorry I had to keep to myself," said Gregory – in a whisper. And moved toward the companionway, aware of the other man's eyes on him. If only, he thought, I could rid myself of all these eyes... The jungle, he could feel, teemed with them. Palm-berry eyes and blossom-eyes. Each leaf held its ominous orb; each twig its bead of brilliance. And in the chirruping shade of Berkelhoost how many more awaited him? Frogs' eyes filled with emerald fires. Lizard-eyes that mirrored a multitude of haunted rooms. And orchid-specks to lure one's soul to demon-land...

In this dream of vague fears he found himself on the lower deck, and moved aft to the spot where his baggage was piled: a trunk, a large expanding suitcase and two small suitcases. The dusky passengers stared at him, joining the mass-vigilance of his fancy; a silence came upon them as he passed, then the drawl of their creole voices continued behind him. A dog sniffed at his ankles: a brown mongrel with a black muzzle. A smell of food assailed him: boiled rice and perhaps fried salt fish. He stood for several minutes gazing at his baggage. The trunk bore labels in a variety of colours, some of them torn or scratched. In a hotel in Madrid he had stared like this at his trunk. Waiting for conveyance to take him to Barcelona. Raoul had told him not to be upset. His good friend Raoul Bijou... "There comes a day, my friend, when one must leave. On such a day it is better to smile with courage and remember only the good intentions with which one set out. You have helped us as much as you could. Don't weep because you have to leave us. Time has no heart, and Fate is more heartless..." A voice speaking in French in an hotel in Madrid.

"You de gentleman for Berkelhoost, sir?"

"Yes. This is my baggage. I understand we're nearly there so I've come down to see about it."

"Ah'll help you get it down to de boats, sir," said the man. He was a member of the crew, dark-faced, in a greenish shirt and washed-out blue dungarees. The third finger of his left hand was missing. He smelt of sweat and engine-grease; the smell of hard work and stability. A smell honest and real. It stamped upon fantasy – and defeat. Silenced the drums of death. It stood by Gregory and reassured him throughout the whole business of disembarkation.

The man in the *corial* reminded him a little of Miguel Sanchez who had driven the car to Barcelona. He said his name was Logan.

"You Mister Gregory, sah?"

The *corial* rocked on the black water and seemed on the point of being flooded. A half-inch more... But it always avoided catastrophe. It fascinated Gregory. One suitcase went into it – then another. The trunk and the expanding suitcase Logan and the seaman lowered into the skiff, together with the two boxes of provisions addressed to "Rev. Harmston, Berkelhoost Mission, Rio Berbice."

"Come down, sah. Step right down. Don't have no fear."

Logan grinned up with unsound teeth; they were bluish around the decayed cavities.

"I'm not afraid," Gregory told him. "Only interested."

He clambered over the side of the steamer and into the *corial* with a sureness and agility that called forth comment from one or two of the passengers. Seating himself in the frail craft, he was in no way awkward. His will worked in harmony with his body now because he was interested – stimulated by the freshness of the experience. There was a buzzing relief within him. He remembered something before the craft moved off. From his wallet he took a note – a British Guiana one-dollar note – and held it up to the seaman who leant outward and took it with a "T'ank you, sir!" and a smile. Gregory had a whiff of his smell of sweat and engine-grease.

Logan pushed off, grinning and nodding to the seaman as though in congratulation. Then he brought his paddles into play, and the *corial,* with the skiff in tow, began to glide toward the landing-place where the Reverend Mr. Harmston and his family waited to welcome Gregory.

III

The patch of sunshine had moved from the lectern. It was on the lower part of the coloured picture of Jesus with a lamb. Beneath this picture stood the harmonium, pale brown and locked up, with the leather handle on top. It had a look as though it might have been a small trunk, thought Olivia. Gregory's trunk. A whirlpool of bitterness swirled inside her.

"On Sunday," she muttered, "I play hymns for them, but because I want to play something for myself today to welcome Gregory I'm forbidden to do it. I wish I could vanish and turn into an ugly ghost to haunt them."

She watched the harmonium and saw herself unlocking it, throwing back the lid, lifting up the central section and letting down the pedals that pumped air into it. She sat before it at the landing-place, and the sunshine was on her back – not hot noon sunshine but cool, wine-coloured and mixed with long tree-branch shadows. She rested her fingers on the keys ready to play… But it was not real. It was a might-have-been happening. The sunshine was on the wall. On the picture of Jesus, Jesus without a halo. Jesus the man.

She got off the pew and went into the tiny vestry. It was a room eight feet by six, with a cupboard and an iron canister. In the cupboard her father kept his vestments, a letter-wood stick, packets of candles and two Dietz paraffin lanterns. In the canister he kept books and magazines with ghost-stories, and imitation holly sprigs for decorating the church at Christmas time.

She sat on the canister and put her fingers in her ears to keep out the sounds from the landing-place. She shut her eyes tight. She could smell the musty wood-ants smell that pervaded the little room, and a swift picture moved in her head of her father and Logan squirming under the church looking for wood-ants' nests. A pleasant, exciting picture – but bittered over by the plight of the present. She opened her eyes and let her gaze rest on the cupboard. Near the bottom of the door she could make out a pencil drawing of an ugly face – the face of a jumbie as imagined by Berton. He had done it one Sunday when sent into the vestry as a punishment for misbehaving during communion service; he had dropped a chicken's foot down Dorothea Buckmaster's back.

What wouldn't she give to get up from this canister and rush outside!

She rose and returned into the main body of the church. She crept on tiptoe to a northern window and applied her eye to one of the many flaked spots in the green paint on the glass panes. She could see the others at the landing-place: her father, tall, muscular, in white drill shorts and open-necked shirt, her mother, plumpish, in a green flowered dress, Mabel, tall and slim, in a pink dress, Berton in his navy-blue serge pants with the patch in the seat, and Garvey in his new long trousers of yellow drill; he said he was going to wear a red tie, but she could not tell if he had because his back was to her... Beyond them she could see the *corial* and the skiff approaching. Logan and Gregory were in the *corial*. And in the skiff she saw the big trunk – not pale brown like the harmonium, as she had thought it might have been, but dark blue, with labels on it – and two whitish wooden boxes: the provisions from New Amsterdam that arrived every week, sent by S. Wreford & Co.

Gregory looked so thin and pale. But he had to be, of course, because he was ill with his nerves. The war in Spain had smashed up his nerves. She could feel something going out of her to him. A lasso of love. This was not how she had expected she would have felt toward him; in her fancy she had seen him as a strong, handsome man with black hair and wearing perhaps a matador's hat (bought in Spain) and two revolver-holsters at his waist. He might even be carrying a Lee-Enfield rifle. She had expected to feel admiration for him as he stepped ashore. She would have played *See the conquering hero comes,* and he would have stood at attention and smiled, and when she had finished playing the tune he would have bowed in her direction and called: "That's the lass! That's the lass!"

Now she could see the silliness of her dreamings. This pale, thin man, fair-haired and staring straight before him as though seeing something that made him anxious called forth her love and pity. Her father, she realized now, had been wise in forbidding her to play the harmonium to welcome him.

A feeling of depression attacked her. She saw herself as a hopelessly poor judge of people and situations. She was a stupid, romantic dolt who had allowed her reason to succumb to things mythical. Myth was good, of course. At Berkelhoost, myth was the basis…

She had to break off in her thoughts to murmur: "What a pity I can't wait to spy at him as he lands. I've got to go back into the vestry."

For Dicky had come. And the church was getting dark. Out of the corner of her eye she could see Dicky. He was seated in the last pew. He must have entered by the west door. She was not afraid, but uneasy. He always made her uneasy. She glanced aside quickly, and was sure. He was there. He was kneeling, his head bent as though in prayer. How unfortunate that he should have come at this particular moment!

She left the window and went back into the vestry, disturbed now by the bats squeaking and thumping up in the rafters; in a few minutes they would begin to fly around and escape into the open through the jalousies at the front part of the church, above the altar-table. For night was almost here. The sun was gone from the picture of Jesus and the lamb. A chill struck through the twilight gathering in the small building. Just before entering the vestry, she turned and looked toward the western end, and saw that he had not moved. He looked grey and dim, but his black, smooth Buck hair seemed to gleam with a light of its own. In life he had been a good man, Dicky. He had come to church every Sunday, with his wife and daughter, and had always brought eggs and fruit and vegetables for her father from his little farm a mile down-river. When he had died of dysentery in January last she had known that he would come back and haunt the church. One Sunday morning, toward the end of February, when she was in church – after morning service; she sometimes remained after service to practise tunes on the harmonium – she had turned and seen him at the back of the church, in the last pew, the pew he had sat in when he was alive. And as now, she had not been afraid –

only uneasy. She had got up from the harmonium and gone into the vestry. And a few minutes later when she returned into the church he had gone. Intuitively she had known that he would not go unless she went into the vestry.

Twice since then she had seen him. The last time it was a Saturday about two in the afternoon when she and Mabel were sweeping the church and putting flowers in the vases on the altar-table. Mabel had not seen him. She had tried her out by saying: "Is that a flower you left in the font, Mabel?" And Mabel had glanced toward the font – which was just beyond the last pew – and had said: "A flower? No, it's the duster." And had gone on arranging the flowers on the altar-table as unconcerned as before. Mabel, Olivia had known then, was not gifted with ghost-sight.

In the vestry, she sat on the canister and listened to the sounds at the landing-place, her feelings uncertain as though she were in a fine mist that she might discover at any instant to be a chilly rain, or, with delight, to be a puff of sweet woodsmoke. Pity and love, remorse, uneasiness, anticipation of things pleasant and unpleasant to come, a dusk-shape moving within and around her, mingled with wood-ants smell and the splash of paddles in the river, the bumpings of baggage and the voices of her parents and brothers and sister.

A musty breeze whirled about her head. One of the bats had flown into the vestry and out again into the church.

She rose. Hugged herself. Felt undecided, then passed through the open door, paused just beyond the threshold and looked round and round at the now rapidly darkening pews and pulpit and lectern; the Bible on the lectern had taken on the look of a dead black bird. A bird-mummy.

Two bats kept flitting, jagged and tilting, from windows to jalousies and down again, and the dampish coolness of night seemed to move with them through the descending rafter-gloom.

"Genie, I can see myself on this same spot." Her whisper went like a sigh funnelled through the sixty-foot length of the church. "I'll stand here one evening and look around at the six-o'clock darkness, and it'll be me looking, only not me to touch. I wonder if you're still there in that pew, Dicky, but you're so clear now I can't see you."

She shivered. It was as though she could feel another musty breeze. Brushing her cheek. This one not musty with bat but with age; it wanted to shrivel something in her; it made her wonder, with panic, if it was she who had just whispered. She moved back into the vestry and sat on the canister, and, elbows on her lap, chin in her hands, listened to the sounds outside but not caring about them; beyond disappointment.

She watched the floor grow black with night.

IV

Gregory saw that they were all smiling. Except the younger of the two boys – the thin, long-legged one in navy blue shorts; he had a scar shaped like an L on his right knee, and his eyes were wide open but with a faraway look as though the feelings and thoughts that mattered to him were not in him but had left him and alighted, like a lonely bird, on a sand-reef; he might have been listening to the sea.

Behind the group, the jungle towered in dark-green gloom against the crimson glow of the setting sun. The wooden church painted a blue that had faded and the two-storeyed house, wooden, too, but unpainted, grey with weather, had the air of being one with the vegetation: tree-thought, tree-spirit taken solid shape.

Plants with tapering red-veined leaves, stunted grass and feathery ferns grew along the water's edge, sullen with their burden of sap, sly with an abundance of hidden insects, and lusciously engulfing both ends of the two roughly-hewn logs embedded along the bank and against which the black water secretly lapped.

Gregory kept his gaze on the logs, on the plants, fascinated by the way they silently rebuffed the sinister water. He was still gazing at them as he stepped out of the rocking *corial,* and it might have been by sheer accident that he glanced up to acknowledge the Reverend Mr. Harmston's quiet, friendly greeting.

"Had a good trip, young man?"

"No. Not at all. The heat on the steamer was unbearable."

"Yes, it can be very hot on the steamer. Never mind. You'll feel better after a wash-up. We'll get a tub ready for you. This is Joan, my wife – your aunt."

Gregory smiled and held out his hand, but Mrs. Harmston ignored it and leant forward and kissed his cheek. She had cool lips, and he felt suddenly comforted and safe and more self-confident. His smile became less waxen and his manner more relaxed as he was introduced to Mabel.

Almost as tall as her father, Mabel put out her hand with shy hesitation, but her grip was firm, and her greenish-grey eyes, though diffident at the moment, held depths of character. She murmured that she was glad to meet him, a humming purr in her voice that he liked; it made him think of bees among apple-blossoms, and it made her seem sweet and sincere behind her shyness. A tall girl of nineteen with brown hair piled up on her head. He could see her walking between the holly hedges of Middenshot, pink spots in her cheeks from the tingling cold of early spring.

"And this is Garvey," said Mrs. Harmston, who had taken charge of the introductions. "He's named after your father."

Garvey smelt of new cloth. It must be his yellow drill suit; it had the look as though it had come from the tailor an hour ago and Garvey had put it on straight away new and unlaundered. He wore a red tie which contrasted strangely with his pale grey eyes. Gregory thought at once of a cat wearing a red bow. But Garvey had nothing feline about him; if anything, he seemed clumsy and heavy-limbed. He gave the faintest of smiles – and the faintest of winks – as he held out his hand and said: "How do you do?" His hand was warm and dry – not damp – as though he had had it in his trousers pocket for a long time. Gregory liked his hair: it was a dark red merging into mahogany brown. There was in his manner a vague irony, but, somehow, it suited him, Gregory thought; he did not seem precocious.

When it came to the younger boy's turn, Gregory felt some of the tension spreading through him again. He had the illusion that he was confronted with another but unfamiliar version of himself: a nervous herb of a boy not so much watched by baleful eyes as listening and being listened to. Gregory glanced quickly at his aunt and asked: "Did you say Bettie? I didn't quite –"

"Berton," smiled Mrs. Harmston, pinkening a trifle. She laughed and said: "It's spelt B-E-R, though – not B-U-R. We had a good friend of that name in New Amsterdam, and he asked us to name Berton after him."

"Yes, Tommy Berton," said Mr. Harmston. "He's dead. Too much whisky."

Berton had not yet smiled, and the expression on his face was the same faraway one that Gregory had observed from the *corial.*

He uttered a whispering sound as he took Gregory's hand: an echo of distant surf.

"Have you lost your tongue, Berton?" said his mother.

He looked at her sharply, pale, and said: "Mother, I couldn't find her anywhere at all. I searched everywhere – everywhere she hides." The words came out of him in a pelting rush, as though they had been poised within a tight bud and the bud had just burst. He made futile gestures with his hands, and his breath seemed to become wisps of steam about to dissolve out of him in a soft ghastly farewell.

"Everywhere," he breathed. "Everywhere I searched." And turned away tearfully, hissing. His head trembled.

"He means Ollie," Mabel murmured.

Mrs. Harmston laughed. "Olivia will turn up, don't trouble yourself, my boy. She's annoyed with Daddy." She turned to Gregory and explained about the harmonium, and Gregory found it such an unusual explanation that he became relaxed again. He smiled and said: "How strange of her to want to welcome me in such a fashion! Shall we search for her?"

"I'd help you search," said Berton, his eyes eager on Gregory. "Nobody likes to search for her when she's lost herself. Only I. They don't care about her. They don't care what happens to her!"

"They don't?" said Gregory.

"No," said Berton. "Olivia is a special kind of girl. She seems queer, but she's good. But all of them laugh at her. She ought to be protected, but only I protect her."

"From what?"

"The shadows that move among us. Look! See that! Mabel is laughing at me with her chimpanzee laugh! I could kill!" He clenched his hands and trembled. "I could stab everybody when – when – stop laughing, Mabel!"

"I'm smiling, not laughing," said Mabel.

"He's a very highly strung boy," said Mrs. Harmston. "You mustn't take him seriously. Berton, please don't make a display of yourself so soon." But she said it not too scoldingly; her manner was half-playful. Fond. Her plumpish but well shaped body on the verge of laughter-tremors. "He's just a silly little goat, Gregory." She gurgled – like a girl.

"Yes, he can be a regular idiot at times," said Mr. Harmston. "I told you not to bother about Olivia, Berton my boy, didn't I?" He put out his hand, a strong hand gnarled and red as from much hard work, and stroked the boy's head.

"Don't pat his head, Daddy," Garvey growled. "It's only going to make him behave worse."

"Shut up, gargoyle, before I wee-wee on your new trousers." Berton turned to Gregory. "I didn't mean to make a scene," he said quietly, "but I had to speak. I have to wake them up sometimes – for Olivia's sake."

His mother pulled him to her and gave him a hug. "Silly boy. But you're well meaning. He loves his younger sister and feels he must defend her. Well, it's getting late. We mustn't stand here talking when Gregory has to have his wash-up and get settled in."

"I'd better run ahead and get the tub filled, Mother," said Mabel.

"Yes, dear, do. And look in the pantry for a new cake of Lifebuoy."

Mabel went off at a half-run, giraffe-gauche but not unattractive.

"Logan," said Mr. Harmston, "bring up Mr. Gregory's baggage right away. You can leave the provisions until later."

"Yes, sah," Logan replied cheerfully. "Coming wid it right off."

Berton said: "He won't obey. You know he won't. He'll bring the boxes with the provisions up to the kitchen first."

Logan laughed loudly, with a raw bravado, his olive face going purple-olive. He did a caper.

Mr. Harmston gave him an amused glance and wagged a forefinger. "Now, Logan, now! See and bring the baggage up before you do anything else. Understand?"

"Ah will try, sah," said Logan, hollow-voiced with laughter. "Dis is a wicked lil' boy. Satan mek you, lil' boy!" He made a grimace at Berton, and Berton showed him his middle finger phallus-like.

"None of that, please, Berton!" frowned Mr. Harmston.

Berton did it again, and his father gave him a clout on the back of his neck, all the weight of his huge, muscular frame seeming to go behind the blow. Berton staggered forward and whimpered, and Gregory gasped: "Oh, but please! That was a hard blow!"

"Premeditated obscenity," murmured the reverend gentleman, "is against our aesthetic codes. Berton knows that."

"Of course I do," said Berton. He looked at Gregory, fingering the back of his neck. "I shouldn't have done it a second time, but Logan is a most annoying humbug. I can't stand humbugs."

Mr. Harmston uttered a deep laugh and ruffled Berton's hair playfully. They moved off in the direction of the house, and left Logan in quarking bellows of laughter. Mrs. Harmston was laughing, too. She made a comment about Logan that Gregory did not catch, her voice indulgent. The flowered dress she wore blended well with the greens of the jungle and the wild plants along the bank. She herself blended; she could have been a succulent fruit dropped from the sultry-looking fronds of the *cookerit* and *awara* palms that stood between the house and the church.

Insects had begun their night-time wheezing. Gregory listened to them, and envisaged them as hidden demons emitting a twinkle of rays tinted pink and green that pricked through his ears with unceasing eagerness, wishing never to peter out but ever to make a seething in his head, week in week out. He felt a panic coming on, but succeeded in keeping it off. The bat helped. He saw it flutter like a silent spatter of mud from out of one of the jalousied windows high up on the front part of the church. It went wavering toward the river, and he glanced back to follow its flight. It vanished. Vanished above Logan who was unloading the skiff and still laughing, though in abated quarks. His old grey flannel trousers, patched and oil-stained, and white duck shirt with mildew marks, looked like camouflage symbols in alliance with the now dust-buff dark... Dump, went the first box of provisions on the logs. Dump, went the second. Logan hoisted one box on to a shoulder, hoisted the other box on to the other shoulder, and set out after them. And as though he knew Gregory had observed his actions he gave out a sound – half-laugh, half-squeak.

"I hate bats," said Mrs. Harmston.

"I like them," said Berton. "Except those that suck your blood and dance among the languid shadows."

Gregory saw Mrs. Harmston shudder. "There's no chance of them sucking our blood, Berton dear. We sleep under nets, don't we?"

"What's a stupid mosquito-net," sniffed Berton, "to a really earnest, blood-hungry bat!"

"Oh, stop that foolish joke," drawled Garvey.

"Not to please you! They come into the house through the eaves, Gregory," said Berton. "Our houses in the tropics here have open eaves for ventilation. And sometimes they come in through the kitchen door. Big, crouching black ones with sharp teeth."

"Don't let him frighten you, Gregory," laughed Mrs. Harmston.

"I'm not at all frightened," said Gregory. "I'm entertained."

Berton uttered rollicking, hiccupping laughs.

They ascended the short flight of wooden steps to the gallery. The front door gave directly into the gallery; there was no portico. Mrs. Harmston said that she wondered how Mabel was getting on, and Mr. Harmston in a quiet voice asked Gregory to be excused. "I have a little matter to attend to," he said, smiling. "Aunt Joan will show you about the house."

He went out again, and Berton gave Gregory a significant look and whispered: "Disciplinary measures. We must have discipline."

V

Midnight, thought Olivia, has come to the vestry.

The one wooden window, hinged at the top so that it could be pushed out by a stick and kept in place when the lower end of the stick was fitted into a groove on the sill, was shut. No light could enter the vestry; that was why now, at six o'clock when the dusk was only brown outside, it was midnight in the vestry.

"I'm miserable," Olivia murmured. She still sat on the canister. "A wretched being. I'm the protaxonist in a tragedy."

Her hands were pressed to her face, so that it was double midnight behind her eyelids. Who, she asked the Genie in the Green Bottle, could have made me like this? Spiteful and determined like this?

She began to murmur to herself again. "They've met him," she told the darkness, "and now they're taking him up to his room – the room Berton and Garvey used to have. Berton and Garvey are going to sleep in the sitting-room, They've put up a kind of screen-wall and made part of the sitting-room into a bedroom, and Garvey and Berton will have to sleep in camp-cots in there. Our cousin from Middenshot, Surrey, England, is now in our midst. He went to the war in Spain, then his nerves got bad and he returned to England. Then he went to Barbados to get better. But he got worse, so he wrote and asked Mother if he could come and stay with us. 'For a short while or for always. Until my spirit is healed.' I read the letter, Genie, and saw it for myself. I wonder what he meant by that. He could have got wounds in the war, but can war wound your spirit, too? I'll have to investigate that thoroughly. I wish I didn't feel so miserable and loocop-brugious in here. Anyway, I've got to sit on this canister until they find me. I wonder if Gregory will come and look for me when I get lost, as Berton does. Perhaps he'll fall in love with me and do that, and then I could tell him my Secrets and show him the Scar of the Hissing *Kanaima*. As a reward."

She felt sorry for herself, and then was sorry and angry that she felt like this. She stamped on the floor, and snapped her teeth together like a dog trying to catch flies that would not be caught.

She held her breath and kept herself stiff so that she would not cry, and she was like this when the howl reached her. Long, mournful and telling of pain. Poor fellow, she thought, he must have done something again. I've got to go and beg for him. This changes everything now. I've got to forget my spite and go to the rescue.

She got up and went out, taking care to close the door after her and push the slat of wood under it so as to keep it shut tight, for this door that gave into the vestry from outside did not have a lock; not even a hook or bolt. Where the lock should have been there was a hole about a half-inch in diameter, as though long ago somebody had wanted to put a lock but had changed their mind. Years ago she and Berton used to look through this hole, at six o'clock, to see the jumbies dance in the vestry, and they would chortle and say: "Isn't it nice to be outside here safe from the jumbies in there?"

She went dashing across the clearing toward the kitchen. Up the kitchen stairs – seven treaders, shaky and humming when you ran up them.

He was using the whip with the knotted cords, and Logan cringed over the two boxes, and by the sink Ellen stood grinning her cruel Buck smile in the yellow lamplight. Ellen liked to see him flogged, for she did not like him; she would be glad to see him dead.

"Please, Daddy, I beg for him. Don't beat him any more."

Her father desisted at once, and Logan stopped howling but groaned and tapped his head against the white-pine wood of one of the boxes. One day the skin would split and his skull would look white like the wood. She went up to him and stroked his black curly hair and told him not to mind. "Never mind, poor Logan. But you must obey. Why don't you like to obey when Daddy tells you anything?"

Logan stopped groaning but did not raise his head.

"See that he goes down at once to the boats and brings up the baggage, Olivia. He disobeyed me and brought up the provisions first."

"Yes, Daddy, I'll see he does,"

He smiled and patted her head. "Where have you been hiding?"

She did not answer. She took the whip from him and began to wrap the three knotted thongs around the shiny wooden handle. "How many lashes did you give him, Daddy?"

"Seven."

"The mysterious number."

He chuckled. "The mystical number, you mean. Logan, you may go."

Logan groaned. He crouched by the box, his head bowed as if in prayer. His hands gripping his thighs.

"I'll give you some liniment before you go to bed. Get up and go down and bring up the baggage."

"Yes, sah," the man mumbled, and rose and went out, his high cheekbones shiny with tears but his wide, thick-lipped mouth curved in a smile.

Mr. Harmston looked after him and shook his head. "That's the great trouble, my girl. He enjoys being flogged."

"I know. But I don't like you to beat him. I feel the lashes."

"You don't beat 'e hard enough, parson," said Ellen, hate on her face. And Olivia looked at her and clenched her hands. "You say that again and I'll cuff you, Ellen."

Mr. Harmston took her arm and urged her toward the pantry. "Come inside and meet your cousin. Ellen, learn not to bate. Hate eats up the soul." He gave her a stare and added: "Like acid."

Ellen turned away with a sour look.

"One day she's going to poison Logan and me, Daddy. She's going to put Buck poison in our soup. But I'll come back and haunt her. Haunt you until you die! You hear me, Ellen! Try to poison me and see!"

Her father's grip on her arm tightened. In the dining-room she cocked her head. "Is that rain falling? I didn't see any clouds."

"It's Mabel filling the tub for Gregory."

"Why? Can't he use the shower like the rest of us?"

"He's from England. They don't use shower-baths in England."

"Oh, yes, I forgot. You told us that once."

Through the sound of water murmuring on metal she made

out her mother's tread on the stairs that led to the upper storey. And the tread of another.

"Mother is going upstairs with him," she said.

"Go after them."

"It's dark enough for the lamps, Daddy."

"Yes, I'm going to light them. You run up quickly and meet your cousin."

She went into the sitting-room and paused at the foot of the stairs, then suddenly ran up them three at a time. As she got to the top she saw her mother and Gregory stop outside the door of the southwestern room. Their faces looked yellowish in the weak light of the wall-lamp.

"Who lit the lamp, Mother?"

"Olivia, dear. Come and meet Gregory."

"Is this Olivia?"

"Yes, I am," said Olivia. She went up to him smiling. "They told me you were nervous, but I didn't believe them. I read it in your letter, too, but I still didn't believe it. Did Mother tell you how I wanted to welcome you with the harmonium?"

When he had first glimpsed her at the top of the stairs the lamplight had struck full on her face, but now she was with her back to the lamp, and her face had drawn some of the dusk of the evening. But her eyes shone through this dusk, and the light of them fanned through and beyond him as though it were some fiery pollen. It seemed to permeate the astral fabric enclosing the present and set mirrors flashing backward to infinity. All the years blasted one by one and that he had thought forever gone returned in swift reflections. Scented phantasmagoria. Spring in the village lanes. Summer on the fell and the little girls frolicking. And the cedar grove: tier upon tier overhead of dark-green drowsy shade.

"Your mother told me," he replied.

Mrs. Harmston laughed amiably.

"They told you how queer and precocious I am?" asked Olivia.

"Berton did mention that you're queer."

"Berton would. He's my close friend."

He held out his hand, eager to touch her and confirm her fleshly presence. But she seemed not to notice.

"I'm waiting to shake your hand," he smiled.

59

She looked at his hand now – with a critical air – then smiled at her mother. Her mother smiled back and said: "Well, what's wrong? Aren't you going to take your cousin's hand?"

"Where's Mabel?"

"She's in the bathroom preparing the tub for Gregory."

Olivia still ignored Gregory's hand. She took a pace nearer to him and tilting up her face, whispered: "I love and pity you."

Mrs. Harmston shook and gurgled. "Run along, child. Enough of your prankishness. Gregory my boy, come in and let me show you your room. Olivia, is Logan bringing up the baggage?"

"Yes. Daddy told him to and he's gone down for it. Did you hear him howling? Daddy gave him seven lashes with the cord whip."

"Yes, I thought it must be that."

"Was it he I heard howling?" said Gregory.

"Yes. Gerald doesn't stand any disobedience from him," nodded his aunt. "Logan can be very stubborn and whimsical sometimes. We had him since he was eleven. He was an orphan and we adopted him as a servant and sort of companion for the children."

"He's half Indian, a quarter negro and a quarter Portuguese," said Olivia. "His mother was the Buck."

"You call the Indians Bucks, eh?"

"Yes. Logan is twenty-three. How old are you?"

"Don't be rude, Ollie."

"Thirty-one," Gregory answered.

Olivia accompanied them into the room which contained an old-fashioned double bed with mahogany posts and a tester. Through the mosquito-net shone a lamp. It rested on the dressing-table that stood between the two windows. The mosquito-net looked like petrified spittle, and Gregory saw himself already enclosed within it. Unsafe and on the watch for the watchers. A mosquito-net could keep out mosquitoes only. For the first time since leaving the steamer fear crept in little crumpled feet along his limbs.

"You can see the river through your windows," said Olivia. "Mother, where is Berton?"

"I think he went off to search for you again. Where were you hiding, by the way?"

"And where's Garvey? Did he wear the red tie as he said he would?"

"Yes, he wore it, but there's an iron-mould spot on it. Gregory, what do you think of the room? Feel you'll be comfortable in here?"

"I think so."

The water had stopped. Footsteps tapped on the floor in the corridor, and Mabel appeared at the door.

"The tub is ready."

"Did you get the new cake of Lifebuoy, Mabel?"

"Yes, Mother. I've put it in the soap-dish in the bath room."

"I heard a bump," said Olivia.

"What?" Gregory glanced at her sharply.

"Many things go bump in this house, Gregory," Olivia told him. "At this time of the evening especially when the shadows are piling up."

"It must be Logan coming up with the baggage," said Mrs. Harmston.

Mabel glanced out into the corridor and said yes, it was Logan. Tall and shy. She must be very aware that people might consider her awkward and uncomely because of her height, thought Gregory. He asked her: "Was it you who lit the lamp in here?"

"Yes," she smiled, blushing. "It was getting so dark."

"Thank you."

"Oh, it was a pleasure," she said softly.

Logan appeared at the door with one of the two small suitcases and the large expanding one. He had a sad and chastened air, and asked: "Where you want me to put dem, Mr. Gregory, sah?" And showed his bad teeth briefly and in humility.

"Over there, please, Near the washstand will do."

"That's our best washstand. Do you like the marble top?"

"Olivia, Olivia! Now, don't overdo it, dear."

When Logan had brought up all his baggage, Gregory was left to himself in the room. Olivia, the last to leave, told him at the door: "Be careful with the tub. It goes bong! And then plang!"

Before he could ask her what she meant she had gone. A few minutes later, he went to the bathroom. The door, he found, after he had entered, had no means of being secured, so he just shut it.

A lamp burned on a shelf, and under the shelf, in the shadow, a black shadow moved. He kept very still and stared at it, and saw that it was a hairy spider. It seemed very sluggish, and stopped moving after a while, as though deciding that his entrance did not portend danger, after all. He could feel it watching him. He shuddered, and turning his gaze from it, looked about the small room.

The walls, like the walls downstairs and in his room, were of bare, unpainted boards. The rose for the shower overhung a concrete-floored sink, and in this sink rested a round iron tub about three feet in diameter and nine or ten inches in depth. It was two-thirds filled with water. On a low shelf under a single-paned window – a window like a prison-cell ventilator except that it had no bars – rested a blue enamel-ware soap-dish containing a new red cake of Lifebuoy soap. A small stool with soap and water-marks, but quite dry, stood outside the rampart-like edge of the sink, and on this he laid his towel and dressing-gown, keeping a sly eye on the spider as he did so.

When he stepped into the tub, at the first pressure of his foot the tub went bong!, the water shivering with ripples that glittered in the lamplight as they ringed out toward the rim and hillocked inward back upon his ankle. Chills ran up and down his body, for the water was cold. He smiled and relaxed, and put in the other foot, and the bottom of the tub underwent another distortion that resulted in a plang!

When he was soaping himself, the door opened and Berton looked in.

"Do you play chess?"

"What! But – look here, I'm in my bath!"

"I know. I heard you were."

"But don't you knock before you enter rooms?"

"No. We never mind seeing each other naked. Do you play chess?"

The first shock of the boy's appearance passed, Gregory relaxed and smiled. "Yes, I play," he said, "but not very well. Only passably."

"Good enough. You're going to be popular with us. We all play. I'll go and tell Ollie. She wanted to know." He went, shutting the door.

Gregory was drying himself when the door opened again. "How wide is the world? How broad is the bush?"

Gregory gasped and shielded his body with the towel.

"Are you ashamed for people to see you naked?" Olivia smiled. He swallowed.

"Mother said you might be, but I thought not. It looks as if she was right. Your attitude toward things is atavabistic."

Gregory wanted to swallow again but could not.

"That was a password. How wide is the world and so on. Berton and I have passwords. We've just made up our minds to share one or two with you. We've just had a conference over you in our Cavern."

"I see. Thanks." He felt his limbs losing their tension. He smiled but still held the towel before him.

"Dinner will be ready at half-past seven. We generally have it at seven, but as you were expected Mother said we'd better have it half-an-hour later to give you time to get washed up and so on."

"Yes, she's very thoughtful."

"Mabel, too. Mabel and Mother think of everything. You want to get married?"

"Not particularly – no. Why?"

"Then look out for Mabel. She might try to bag you. She only looks quiet like that but she's hot. She talks to herself in her sleep, and not too long ago she was crazy about one of our Buck chaps on the Reservation. He's a painter named Robert."

"Do you associate intimately with the Indians?"

"Of course we do. Aren't they human beings like us? But talking about Mabel, she'd make you a good wife. She's nice. We all like her. Of course you could wait for me to grow a little more if you preferred. Oh, look! A spider under the shelf. Have you seen it?"

"Yes."

"And you're not afraid of it?"

"I am, but I thought if I left it alone it wouldn't crawl around."

"I'm glad you didn't kill it." He saw that tears had come into her eyes. "When you go to your room I'll catch it and take it outside."

"How will you catch it?"

"Berton and I have invented a trap. It doesn't harm them. I'll show you one day. Not tomorrow, but one day – if you don't betray me." She brushed the tears away, but her eyes still looked bright with emotion. "If you don't betray me," she repeated, smiling, her hands clenched. "I can be a tigress to people who betray me," she whispered. She laughed and said: "But I believe you're good," and went, shutting the door.

VI

Gregory had thought Mr. Harmston would have said grace. When in his room dressing he had envisaged them all standing round the dining-table, heads bowed, while the reverend gentleman, in a dramatic rumble, pronounced a blessing on the food they were about to eat. But it turned out otherwise. Mrs. Harmston showed Gregory where he was to sit – between Olivia and Garvey – and they all took their seats and waited for Mrs. Harmston to pass the soup which she ladled out of a large tureen bearing an elaborate pattern of grape leaves and clusters of grapes. Gregory did not like these grapes. The more he let his gaze linger on them the more they took on the appearance of orbs: the symbol of his illness. They eyed him. With evil intent. And tension pushed upward like a telegraph pole through his head.

Some measure of relief came when Mr. Harmston, who sat with his wife at one end of the table – it was a large table capable of seating twelve people with ease – smiled at him and said: "We never say grace, my boy. I don't believe in overdoing religion."

Gregory smiled.

"Daddy is a practical parson," Olivia murmured, and held up her forefinger. And Berton, who sat directly opposite to her, held up his, too.

Mabel, alone at the end of the table, opposite her parents, frowned from Olivia to Berton, and Olivia whispered to Gregory: "That was a secret sign Berton and I gave to each other. It means we both agree with what Daddy said, but Mabel always mistakes it for a bad joke. She thinks Berton and I mean it for the wee-wee sign."

Gregory smiled again, so relieved now that the grapes did not bother him at all. He gave all his attention to his soup. It was thick pea-soup with submerged chunks of vegetables that gradually rose like islands as the surrounding sea went down. Neither by sight nor taste could he make out what these vegetables were, and it was not until long afterwards that he learnt that the slimy grey-blue ones were eddoes and the stringy white ones cassavas. He ate them without question and enjoyed them.

On his left, Olivia, too, was relieved. She had feared that he would not like the soup. In her fancy she had seen him grimacing and trying to make a polite pretence of eating food that was too un-English for his taste. Clammy fingertips of anxiety had tapped upon her heart, and she had had a picture of him, long and orchid-white, stretched out in death on the bed in his room; he had died of starvation, poor fellow. Toll the bell. Toll the bell and hear it echoing in the jungle. Our poor nervous cousin from abroad is dead!… A tear had run down her cheek, and it still glinted there like a diamond magically melted. Berton noticed it – and her father – and then her mother; but they made no comment, for they were accustomed to her swift tears.

While he ate Gregory looked about him at the bare walls of board, and found them hostile. The pictures that decorated them, however, seemed friendly; they were like shutters against any hidden holes the walls might possess. One picture showed a smiling Victorian-looking girl standing by a stile, flowers in her broad hat, and phantom trees in the background. He smiled within, and thought: "She's a grandmother now in Middenshot. She wears a shabby black coat over a faded purple dress as she sets out for Carp's Bun Shop in the High Street. Ten to ten on a grey, misty morning in February, and she has to stand in the short queue on the cobbled pavement and wait until ten, for Carp doesn't open till ten… Another, the one over the mahogany sideboard – it was a sepia monotone lithograph – showed an animated battle-scene; it seemed to be something from the Crimean War… Another depicted a bowl overflowing with fruit – grapes, apples, pears, plums. Overflowing on to a huge fish of many tints.

A boat was going past on the river. He could hear the soft swash of oars or paddies in the water. The insect-chorus had risen to such a pitch that it created silence in massed shrill waves.

In the rays of the gas-lamp that hung from a nail on a ceiling beam, the room and all of them sitting at table had a look of having been flashed upon by lightning and left with the whitewash of its death.

66

So Raoul and his company had looked that morning in March when the yellow plane dived out of the mountain mists. Caught unawares in a large field, they had stopped and stared upwards, too utterly dismayed even to drop flat. Twice the plane roared over them. Then it veered off and sank into the valley that lay beyond the road that wound round the northern and eastern boundaries of the field. It disappeared, but they could still hear its engine. It came back almost at once and tore snarlingly over them for the third time, flying so low now they could make out the pilot's face. He could have strafed them out of existence, but, instead – and none of them ever knew why – he lifted his machine toward the mountains and melted in the ragged cloaks of cloud and mist. For nearly half a minute after the drone of the engine had died away they must have remained standing where they were, their faces still turned skyward and with the pallor of dead lightning.

So vividly did he relive this moment that Gregory thought he could smell the dew on the grass and the fresh dankness of the newly ploughed patch of earth they had just tramped over when the plane appeared.

He felt a touch on his arm and started. Brassy wings fluttered and froze into a blade that burned icily through his brain.

"Are you feeling ill?" Olivia whispered.

He made no reply.

"You look as if you're seeing yourself stabbed in the mirror."

The trembling sound in his head gradually abated. A wintry hollow near his heart filled in and grew warm.

"Didn't you hear the bump upstairs?"

"No."

"It sounded in your and Mabel's room, Ollie," said Berton. "I believe it's nothing but a bat."

"Why should it be a bat?" frowned his mother.

"Mother is scared of bats," Olivia murmured to Gregory. "Garvey, too."

Gregory heard a soft thud on the floor overhead. One of the boards creaked.

"There again! Did you hear it?" said Berton.

Mabel glanced enquiringly at Olivia. "Is somebody upstairs?"

"Only the bats," said Olivia.

"Only the bats," nodded Berton.

Garvey fidgeted and snapped: "Why don't you stop all this silly fooling?"

Olivia raised her right hand and jabbed her thumb downward. Berton did the same.

Mr. Harmston, who was carving a chicken, glanced up and gave a grunt of amusement. Mrs. Harmston called to Ellen to come and remove the soup plates, and Ellen appeared at once from the pantry as though she had been awaiting the call. As she met Gregory's gaze, a sulky smile came to her broad Indian face. Her jet-black hair hung down her back, tied with a piece of green cloth as a makeshift for ribbon. She wore a calico dress with blue spots that had faded. It was not too clean, and where the nipples of her sharply jutting breasts protruded were two dirt-spots. To Gregory, it was as if two bristling eyes were hidden behind the cloth evilly focused upon him. The chill columns poled upward from his feet, but Olivia saved him. She said: "This is the first time you're seeing Ellen? She's cook and maid combined. You must be careful of her."

"Why?" asked Gregory, feeling better and better.

"She's a hater."

"Oh."

"She hates me and Logan especially. Sorry. Logan and me. You see, Logan is a servant like her – he's in Labour Squad – but as we adopted him as an orphan since he was eleven we don't like to make him feel too servile, and Ellen envies him because of that. With me, she hates me because Berton loves me. She's madly in love with Berton, even though he's only fourteen and she's a big creature eighteen years old. And Berton won't sniff on her. That makes her hate me more."

Gregory smiled, with greater and greater relief.

"It's so silly, because Berton only loves me in a brotherly way – not in an infestuous way. Is that the word? I heard Dorothea Buckmaster use it once. She said I must be careful not to love Berton in an infestuous way. Or it might be indestuous. Anyway, it means sex in the family."

"Incestuous," murmured Gregory.

"Yes, that's more like it, I think."

Shortly after Ellen had taken the soup plates into the kitchen, Gregory happened to be gazing in the direction of the door that opened into the sitting-room. More in the corner of his eye than not he thought he saw a shape move in the sitting-room. He centred his gaze full on the doorway – and saw nothing. Yet the conviction remained that he had seen a human figure pass across the other room. An oil-lamp had been burning in there when he had come downstairs; now the room was in darkness.

Olivia asked in a whisper: "What did you see in there?"

"A shape."

He felt her hand secretly on his knee.

"Any particular part of the chicken you care for, my boy?" smiled his aunt.

"The leg, thank you."

"Dad, didn't you light the lamp in the sitting-room?" Garvey asked.

"Yes. Why?"

"It must have gone out."

Mr. Harmston looked round with a frown. "That's odd. I don't see why it should have. There was a lot of oil in it." He gave Berton a suspicious glance. "Did you put it out, Berton?"

"No, Daddy."

"Nor I," said Olivia.

"One of you go and relight it."

"I'll do it," Mabel offered, rising.

Gregory knew, in a glow of intuition, that Berton and Olivia had told the truth. Neither of them had put out the lamp.

Another boat was going past on the river. This time Gregory heard a rhythmical wooden thud-thud besides the splash of the water, and Olivia murmured: "It's a woman paddling."

"How do you know?"

"Women always make that dup-dup noise with the paddle on the side of the boat. Men never. Nobody knows why, but it's so."

Boiled rice in loose grains went with the roast chicken – and yams and sweet potatoes. Gregory ate everything, and Mrs. Harmston, at the end of the meal – there was no dessert – complimented him. "I like to see my menfolk eat heartily," she smiled.

"Your illness," mumbled Olivia, "hasn't spoilt your appetite, eh?"

"No. I sleep well, too."

"What kind of illness have you got?"

"It's a complex one."

"It isn't only your nerves, then?"

"My nerves are only the instruments of response."

Mrs. Harmston laughed. "Ollie, what's it you keep whispering at the poor young man all the time? Don't let her plague you, Gregory."

"Mother, he's whispering back at me, too. You haven't noticed?"

Her father laughed. His face grew reddish and his thick, muscle-hard body vibrated as though a dynamo had got going inside it. Blebs of water were arrayed like dew in his small trimmed brown moustache. He put down the tumbler and said: "You're going to need a ton of patience and endurance to hit it off with these children, Gregory."

"Don't intimidate him, Gerald," gurgled his wife.

"Daddy's right, Mother," growled Garvey. "Berton and Ollie are like two ticks."

"You're a louse," said Berton.

"And a mouse," said Olivia. "A louse-mouse. You find them tickling people in pantries and kitchens."

"And in hammocks in *benabs,*" nodded Berton.

Garvey turned red. Mabel, too, her eyes twinkling in a knowing way.

"What compliments," she said.

Behind her, in Gregory's fancy, a fire burned, and stretched out near the coal-scuttle was his mother's grey Siamese cat, its blue eyes fixed meditatively on the orange spots on the tips of its paws. Peace and safety spiralled among the winter-bare silver birches seen through the window, and night made a gentle fade-in with fog and the veiling smoke of many coal-fires.

Mabel had changed the pink dress she had worn at the landing-place for one dark-green with black circles interlocked. Her great mass of brown hair was still piled high on her head like quiet, harmless serpents. As he watched her she rose and moved toward the sideboard with an ungraceful but primitively exciting stumble. She took something from a drawer, and a moment later had come round to his side and was holding out a greenish carton from which protruded three cigarettes.

"Don't you smoke?"

A holly hedge turned magically brown, and a fieldmouse burrowed into the loamy earth to evade the sniffing muzzle of the terrier. It took the straining of a tower of muscle and will to keep down the jelly that tried to topple and take him with it into the trickle in the ditch. He wanted to tell her of the song of a thrush, but managed to say in a whisper: "Thanks. But – yes, I do smoke. But not this evening."

"Sure?"

"Yes. Thanks. Thank you very much."

"We always keep some in the sideboard drawers," she said softly. "If you want any at any time just look in one of the drawers."

Gregory nodded. The singing of spring-green chestnut leaves fell in a shower upon his senses, and he found that he could stir in his chair and smile at her: "I have some in tins upstairs. Do you smoke? You could try one or two if you care?"

"No, I don't smoke, thanks."

When she moved off Olivia whispered: "See what I told you. She'd make you a good wife." Almost in the same breath she asked: "Would you like to play a game of chess before you go to bed, or you're tired?"

"I think I'm rather tired."

"I thought you might be, but I just asked. I'm glad you're ill."

"Why?"

"Because if you weren't you wouldn't have come to stay with us. You're going to have some exciting times here. Berton thinks so, too. He says he felt very worried and nervous when he saw you in the *corial*."

"Why?"

"You had a queer staring look on your face, he said. I saw it myself from where I was hiding. Berton said he thought you were an enemy. But now he's sure you're good. And you're a friend, he thinks. He's always right about people. He's got infruition."

"Intuition."

"Thanks. I read a lot, but I still get some words wrong." She put her hand on his knee. "You mustn't be afraid of anything in this house. Berton and I will protect you from the evil things."

"Are there evil things here?"

"Another boat is passing on the river. Hear it? No dup-dup noise with the paddles against the side of the boat, so it's a man paddling. I wish I could mother you. When you go upstairs look out of your window and you'll see how lovely the bush looks. It was New Moon on Saturday – and today is Wednesday. We have young moonlight tonight."

About a quarter of an hour later, he smiled at the jungle from one of the two windows in his room and remembered what she had said. "We have young moonlight tonight." The moon, a thickening curved blade, weak red in hue, shimmered low above the tops of the trees. In a few minutes it would vanish behind the fretted silhouette that the treetops made against the mauve-grey sky. Its light lay in long limbs in the clearing where the house and church stood, and shadows of the trees blended with the black masses of the two buildings, the shadows of the buildings, in turn, blending with, and merging away into, the black water of the river in which stars were reflected. But the stars seemed dim with death in contrast to the fireflies that flickered unendingly against the background of the water on the one hand and, on the other, the wall of trees that enclosed the clearing. The fireflies flickered without sound in the darkness – several at a time, sporadic and unstable. They could have been semaphoring danger or trying to show the way to some secret track that led to treasure. The moon put a velvet glimmer on the leaves of the trees on the other bank, and now and then, when something disturbed the water, a ripple would reveal itself as a line of tinsel that attracted other tinsel lines, and all would suddenly subside again into the star-dotted liquidity of mirrored sky as though the accident had never happened.

The air was laden with the leafy scent of dew on decayed vegetation, and came to him in slow drifts as if borne on the waves of insect-shrilling – but just before he turned away from the window, the empty measuring-glass in hand, he caught a musky-sweet aroma that must have come from a flower concealed where neither moon nor sun ever made shadows.

When he was pouring from the bottle and carefully watching, by the light of the lamp, the level of the liquid rise in the glass, he kept thinking of this flower and trying to imagine its colour and the shape of its petals, the nature of the gloom in which it dwelt, and the kind of bees that must buzz about it, the thin prancing creatures that sometimes peered at it…

And drinking, he thought he could see it dripping incredibly blue porcelain petals in a gloom purpled with honey too pure to be tangible. The tension that was its stalk curved with the softness of a young vine and was no more a stalk but a circle of song…

Under the mosquito-net he heard it. A song of limp perfume and undulating love, it lulled him swiftly to sleep.

VII

The corridor ran from east to west and divided the upper storey into two equal sections. The southern section was divided into two bedrooms of equal size, Gregory's being the southwestern one and Mabel and Olivia's the southeastern. Two-thirds of the northern section went to form the large bedroom occupied by Mr. and Mrs. Harmston, the remaining third – in the northeastern angle of the building – the bath and toilet.

The bed Olivia and Mabel slept in was, like Gregory's and the one in their parents' room, an old-fashioned mahogany four-poster with tester. Olivia had a particular fondness for the tester. Not only did it combine with the mosquito-net to create a shut-in security but it provided a place on which things could go plop in the dark. Many a night before falling asleep she would lie and listen for the plops. Some nights there would be none, but some nights – plop! Followed by the dotted patter of puny feet… She would huddle up against Mabel and shiver and choke in an ecstasy of cosiness. From the loudness of a plop and the nature of the succeeding patter she could tell whether it was a full-grown six-inch-long centipede or a youngish one, or whether it was a black Hercules beetle, or one of the smaller black beetles. Or a hairy spider. Beetles and hairy spiders went plop and stayed still for a few seconds before moving, but centipedes began to run at once with a quick itchy swishing noise. There were nights when together with the plop would flare a wad of fire, abrupt and frightening, and she would watch the wad flare its way along, showing up the dust on the tester-top in black splotches like a silhouette-map of islands. Then it would vanish and leave her roving-eyed with suspense. But not for long. In the mid-darkness of the room a small lantern would suddenly come into fuzzy flame… Over the washstand… Over the chest of drawers… Over the chair where she and Mabel had piled their clothes… Now, alarmingly, right beside her head outside the net.

Fireflies and beetles and hairy spiders were friends. Centipedes and scorpions – scorpions were noiseless – enemies. Hairy spiders looked terrifying with their fat bodies and thick, long legs tipped with crimson, but they were harmless; for them she and Berton felt love and pity. And fireflies they regarded as friendly jumbies who knew the hiding-place of the Green Bottle in which the Genie lived (one day, at twilight, she and Berton hoped, a good, kind firefly would guide them to the spot).

Not twenty minutes after Gregory had retired the family decided to follow his example. It was a rule laid down by Mr. Harmston that they must all retire together; he did not believe in late-hour stragglers reading or playing chess downstairs.

As Olivia lay and watched Mabel undress she thought of Gregory in the next room, and wondered whether he had fallen asleep already, for she had heard no sound from him since she and Mabel had come in.

"Do you think he's smoking in the dark, Mabel?"

"Why should he be smoking in the dark? He must be asleep. He looked as if he was tired." She spoke in a murmur, her face toward the picture of Jesus as a boy over the dressing-table (a gecko lived behind this picture, greyish-brown like the wall boards). She had taken off the green dress with the black circles and was in her petticoat. She took up things from the dressing-table and put them down in her usual indeterminate way, as though she had lost trend of what she had been doing. Then as though remembering, she pulled off her petticoat and began to pat and smooth it. She placed in on the chair and yawned, then looked leisurely about the room. Meditatively rubbed the back of her fingers up and down her long, flat stomach. She was freckled from throat to navel, and the freckles were of all sizes and shapes, from pinpoint dots to paw-prints of midget beasts (Berton had once said: "I believe Mabel's chest-and-belly freckles are a jumbie code-map. If we could shift them and put them together it might show us the spot where the Green Bottle is buried.")

"Ollie, where's my dressing-gown? Have you seen it?"

"No. Isn't it hanging up behind the door?"

"No. I don't see it."

"But it ought to be there. That's where I saw it before we went down to dinner."

"I saw it there myself."

"I haven't touched it. I suppose Mother must have borrowed it."

"But she always tells me when she wants it."

"She must have forgotten to. Hurry up and come into bed. I want to listen for the plops."

Mabel, however, continued to rub her stomach and scratch. She scratched a pink-brown nipple with the back of her thumb, then her navel with a forefinger. The perplexed look which had come to her face when she asked about her dressing-gown faded, and her eyes grew large and began to take in the room in slow, drifting glances. It happened every night like this, and every night Olivia thought: If only I could find out what's going through her thoughts!

It would have been useless, Olivia knew, to ask her. She would simply have smiled and said: "Nothing. Why?"

To Olivia, Mabel was a mystery. Her very simplicity and lack of whims and passionate outbursts made her so. No one, Olivia reasoned, ought to be so normal. Every human body possessed a spirit, and a spirit was a wreathing thing – like a genie; wreathing with good or with evil: sometimes with both. People who appeared quiet and sweet and nothing more must be hiding the passions that were in them. Purposely. What could Mabel's purpose be in wanting to hide her passions? She never expressed hatred for anyone or any creature. Nor love. She very seldom got angry, and she never said spiteful things. Nor got excited. She was mild and sweet and easy-going, thoughtful on other people's behalf. But surely there must be something behind all this. Lovely fires, ugly devils. Why did Mabel not want other people to see her fires and devils?

Watch her now. She was smiling slightly as at some memory. But what memories could she have that were exciting? She had grown up from babyhood at Berkelhoost, and except for a day, or a week at the most, in New Amsterdam, once in about a year, she knew nothing of town life. Of course, like the rest of the children, she was well-informed and well-read; their father's educational system had seen to that. She knew a lot about the world and people, from books and hearsay. She had been friendly with one or two of the Indian young men and she liked lovemaking. There were nights when she sighed and tossed in her sleep, and sometimes she would fondle Olivia's cheek or hair. In her sleep Mabel did this. One night she had murmured: "My dear. Oh, my dear!", in a voice sobbingly rapturous. But this was nothing abnormal. Everybody liked lovemaking and daydreamed or night-dreamed about it when they were not doing it in actuality.

With a slight start, Mabel moved toward the bed, fumbled her nightgown from under her pillow and shook it out. It was a habit they all had, this shaking, for the mosquito-nets were bunched up around the tester during the day, and you never knew if a scorpion or a centipede might not have crawled into the bed and hidden itself under the pillows.

"I must remember to tell Gregory he must search under his pillows and shake out his pyjamas before putting them on," said Olivia. "Just as a percussionary measure."

Mabel smiled. "Try not to lead him a dance."

"I told him how nice you are. I said you'd make him a good wife if he wanted to get married."

"You never did!"

"I did."

"How could you have told him such a thing! You're mad, Ollie."

"Don't you like him? When he gets well he ought to be good for marrying. He's long and tall like you. You'll suit each other."

Mabel stared at her. And then laughed. Her eyes gleamed secretly. She bent and blew out the lamp on the dressing-table and got into bed. Olivia listened to the whisper of the net as Mabel tucked it in carefully. "You've forgotten to let down your hair, Mabel."

"Oh, Lord! So I have. Do it for me."

Olivia did it, collecting the hairpins which she tucked under her pillow. Almost every other night this happened.

"You have nice long hair. I can imagine how he's going to enjoy running his fingers through it."

"Why don't you stop this silly talk, child."

Olivia kept stroking her sister's long tresses. It was very dark in the room; even the starlight made no difference.

"I wonder what he'll be like when he comes."

"Who?"

"Gregory."

"But isn't he here already?"

"Only his shadow."

Plop!…

VIII

In his sleep, Gregory heard a voice. "Remember…"

He tried to stir, but the fireflies seemed to flicker too densely in the dark, and the dark allied itself to the painless flames and pressed upon his lids so that his lids, like his body, would not move.

"Remember Osbert!" cried the voice.

Gregory struggled.

"Oh, heavenly fadder! Remember Osbert!" flamed the voice out of the flickering dark that gradually undarkened to let in the light of the already dawned day… The grey, Gregory saw as he looked through the mosquito-net, had given place to pink and pale orange.

He sat up. He had had a refreshing sleep. A gap in the perpetual peepshow. An interlude of immunity. But morning never failed to come. And with morning the pestiferous panorama to the right and to the left of him. Before and behind – and beyond… And the shiver that was a herald of the deeper tremors to come in the day before him. The tick of the pole, the crack of the icicle, tensed to rise. Up, and unless arrested, up…

"Oh, heavenly fadder! What I see last night wid me own two eyes! Oh, iniquity! Remember Osbert!" cried the voice in the tone of "Remember Lot's wife!"

Gregory untucked the mosquito-net and got out of bed. He went to the window that faced south – the other one faced west – and saw a short olive man in dirty khaki pants and an old rusty-brown waistcoat pacing up and down on the stunted grass that grew near the side of the house. It was Logan. Gregory heard him giving forth low groans. As he paced he kept his hands clasped behind his back, his gaze on the ground. He came to a halt and looked up at Gregory, recoiled somewhat as if in surprise, then recovering, cried: "Remember Osbert! Oh, heavenly fadder! What I see last night wid me own two eyes! Ow! Shame upon you, sinner! Shame!"

Gregory smiled, entertained to such a degree that tulips rose red around his toppling spirit and rendered smooth-petalled support from the imminent fall. The air came damp and refreshing into his lungs, weighted with scents from the jungle of many matted leaves in decay and many dew-dripping ferns. On the surface of the river floated flimsy kerchiefs of mist, as if the last surviving evils of night were dissolving out of the black water and yielding to the love and peace in the softly-coloured sky.

Gregory saw Logan begin to pace again, and withdrew from the window. The door had opened – the door had no means of being secured – and Mr. Harmston, in shorts and shirt and rubber-soled canvas shoes, stood smiling at him. Strong and healthy and with an air that gave instant confidence.

"So you're up already."

"Yes. I heard the voice."

"Voice? Oh, you mean Logan. What's all that noise he's making out there? Did he disturb you?"

"He's calling upon his heavenly father. He woke me."

"I can shake the life out of him sometimes." He strode to the window and looked out. "Logan! What are you doing down there? What's the matter?"

Logan stopped pacing and looked up.

"Oh, heavenly fadder! Remember Osbert! Remember Osbert! What I see last night –"

"Shut up! Stop that racket and get away!"

"Parson, listen to me. If you know what I see –"

"That will do. Be off with yourself!"

"Awright, sah. Ah will go in peace. But you standing in a room wid sin, parson. Remember Osbert!"

"Get away! And don't let me see you hanging about here again!"

"Who is Osbert?" asked Gregory.

"He lives on the Indian reservation. A half-breed. If Logan goes on this way any longer I'll have to chain him. It's the only punishment that does him any good. What sort of night did you have?"

"I slept soundly."

"Glad to hear that. I thought I'd come in and wake you so we

80

could get one or two things cleared up properly before the day is much older. We all wake at six o'clock."

"Is it six o'clock now?"

"Nearly half past. Think six too early an hour for you to get up every morning?"

"Yes. But I can discipline myself into it."

"Good. Discipline is the keynote of our lives here. I've always insisted on it." Mr. Harmston smiled and seated himself on the edge of the bed, pushing back the mosquito-net as he sank down. "What I'm anxious to find out is how severe is this illness of yours and what form it takes."

"Yes."

Gregory stood with his back to the dressing-table. He began to be aware of the chilly floor, for he was barefooted. In a moment there might be thunder in the mirror, and the toilet articles on the dressing-table would assume volcanic qualities. Outside himself, he watched himself and his host.

"In your letter you said it was your nerves."

"Yes."

"I've read somewhere that most neurotics need only a bit of firm handling to put them right. Half their ills are imaginary. Is it that way with you?"

"No."

Mr. Harmston seemed to consider. He stroked his chin; his chin was smooth and looked freshly shaven. From his person came a smell of soapy cleanliness.

"Now, tell me. How do your nerves affect you? You feel agitated about something you can't define? You feel disillusioned about living? You lack confidence in yourself? Or is it a kind of depression you can't rouse yourself out of?"

"All those – and more."

"More?"

"I'm watched."

"Watched?"

"By eyes."

"What eyes? You suffer from hallucinations, you mean?"

Gregory saw himself about to shrivel. Behind him the mirror contained a frozen land. And when he shrivelled the flesh would give sound as it contracted. It would whimper out of its desiccating valleys, and a shroud would wrap it round. Already the shroud lay in ambush, rigid with cold, in the arctic mirror.

Berton appeared at the door which his father had left wide open when he had entered the room. "How wide is the world – oh, you're in here with him, Daddy! I didn't know."

Gregory smiled. The boy had rescued him. He stepped back into himself.

"Now, Berton my boy! I'm having a word with Gregory. Cut along!"

"I only wanted to give him the password and hear him reply," said Berton. "Gregory, how wide is the world?"

"How broad is the bush?" smiled Gregory.

Berton threw up his arms and crowed. "Friend!" he cried. "Advance, friend!" And went. His footsteps receded like amiable iron balls in a bumping rapture on the bare floorboards of the corridor. Gregory heard him calling his sister's name. "Ollie! Ollie!"

"These children," chuckled Mr. Harmston. "As we were saying. You suffer from hallucinations, my boy?"

"From your point of view, yes. From mine, no."

"Um. Naturally, I suppose. H'm. And what are you doing about it? Taking medicine of some sort or just trying to will yourself better?"

"Both."

Footsteps came from downstairs. And voices. The house seemed to rear up gently as though the day's quota of living stirred it into new vibrations. A magic-sword from the sun slashed softly past Gregory's blue-striped pyjama sleeve and buried itself through the mosquito-net to the other wall. A boat was passing on the river, a woman paddling.

"The Government Dispenser is at Ida Sabina, about two hours up-river."

"Do you measure distance here in hours?"

Mr. Harmston laughed. "As a rule. Strikes you as a bit odd, eh? Yes, we generally speak in terms of the time it takes from one place to another. All travel here is by boat. We have no roads, and no tracks that run parallel with the bank. At least, not for any distance."

"I'm interested."

"To get back to what I was saying. If you need your prescription renewed at any time you can let me have it and I'll get Buckmaster to take it to Ida Sabina in the launch. He's the manager of a charcoal grant ten minutes up-river. Dabbles in timber, too."

"Thanks, but I think I have enough medicine to see me to the end of my cure. Eight bottles and part of a bottle."

"Eight bottles!" Mr. Harmston's eyes wandered to the wash-stand, and appeared to rest on the measuring-glass that stood near the large enamel-ware mug. "I see your measuring-glass, but – is it patent stuff?"

"My medicine? No."

"Some kind of bromide? Where do you keep it all?"

"There. In the expanding suitcase."

"Why don't you unpack it? Not afraid it may leak out and make a mess of the things in your suitcase?"

"No. The bottles are well corked and sealed. Except the one I'm using at the moment, and I generally take care to cork that securely after use."

"Um." Mr. Harmston stroked his chin again. "I was going to suggest that you put yourself in my hands – if it's simply a matter of nerves. What I mean is if you care to submit to my system of treatment I think I'd be able to knock you into shape. We live more or less a Spartan life here. I don't think a neurotic could stand up to the Spartan life – and remain neurotic."

"Yes."

"You mean you agree? You'll let me take a shy at curing you?"

"Yes."

"You can go on taking your medicine, of course."

"I will."

"Um. Get dressed and come down to breakfast, then. It's at seven so you'd better hurry. By the way, thanks for that cheque you sent in your letter to Joan. It was perfectly adequate."

"At the end of three months remind me to let you have another."

"That's all right, my boy. Wish we could afford to board you for nothing, but our resources are limited. As you must have noticed, the house isn't even painted."

"I noticed."

On the point of rising, Mr. Harmston gave Gregory a long stare. "Not that the unpainted state of the house troubles us very much," he said quietly. "It's the soundness of the wood rather than the appearance of its surface that concerns us."

"I understand."

"I wonder if you do."

Gregory trembled.

"Stop that trembling."

The trembling stopped.

"Um," said Mr. Harmston. He rose slowly, with a smile, and gave Gregory a pat on the shoulder. "Now, hurry up and get dressed and come downstairs. I don't like late-comers at the meal-table."

After his departure, Gregory shut the door and dressed. He put on white drill shorts and shirt, white stockings and tennis shoes (this had been his attire during most of his stay in Barbados). Then he opened the expanding suitcase and took out the bottle of medicine in use. He poured exactly six and three-quarter ounces into the eight-ounce measuring-glass (the night before the quantity had been six and seven-eights ounces).

He placed the glass on the washstand and put away the bottle, after making sure that it was tightly corked. He locked the suitcase and stood erect, his manner suddenly brittle. He looked about him with an air of drama, expectant and even a trifle anxious.

He snatched up the glass and drank the contents at one gulp, and began to smile. Colour crept into his cheeks. He felt at ease – but only physically. His mind and spirit remained ill. The surrounding vigilance abated – but did not cease. For about an hour he knew he would experience a relief that would produce the illusion that he was normal. Anxiety would be less acute, the inclination to step out of himself and shake free not so strong…

…The mirror and the bed merging into the webbed mist of the net… Stamp, trample on it – a wet, red, raw, pumping human heart overflooded with blood. Hurt! Crush it so that it went splosh-gnash!

With thumb and forefinger he caught at his throat and stifled back the scream.

The fit passed as it had come – always came and went – in a flash.

He rinsed out the measuring-glass, and put it down beside the mug on the washstand. He washed his face and brushed his hair, and when he was regarding his chin in the mirror of the dressing-table and telling himself that he need not shave this morning he noticed that something pink-striped and feminine lay in a heap under the bed. He frowned in wonder, considered an instant, then decided not to investigate. He left the room at once.

In the sitting-room he encountered Olivia who had just come out of the screened-off section in which Berton and Garvey had slept last night in camp-cots. She came close to him and whispered: "I'm glad you remembered the password. Berton is very pleased, too."

"I'm glad I remembered," he told her gravely.

"You've been drinking whisky. I smell it in your breath."

"Johnnie Walker's Gold Label," he nodded. "It's my medicine."

She held his hand. "Let's go in to breakfast."

IX

Breakfast, which consisted of cocoa, bread and butter and soft-boiled eggs, was well on the way when the quarrel began in the kitchen. Ellen's voice filtered through to the dining-room as a haggling, mournful whine and Logan's as a hollow prophetic baying. No word or phrase of Ellen's could be made out, but many of Logan's came through clearly.

"It's something to do with sinning," said Olivia.

"Did you hear him outside the house a little while ago?" asked Berton.

"Yes. He kept walking up and down under our window," said Mabel. "I wonder what's got into his head now?"

"Perhaps he saw a bat in Ellen's hammock last night," Berton hazarded.

"Are you still with that silly joke, Berton?" Garvey growled.

Gregory saw Mabel blush.

"Ellen sleeps in a hammock in the kitchen," Olivia explained in a murmur to Gregory. "And Logan sleeps in the gallery on a mattress."

"Have they mosquito-nets?"

"No. The bad-biting insects don't bother them. They have cuts."

"Cuts?"

"Yes. The centipede-cut and the scorpion-cut. Centipedes and scorpions can't bite them. You've never heard of cuts?"

"Now you mention it, I think I've heard of the snake-cut."

"Yes. Berton has that. An old Buck man gave it to him secretly. Daddy doesn't know. Daddy won't let us have cuts. He doesn't like the idea."

"Ho! Haw!" bayed Logan in the kitchen. "Anybody can look at you and see you is a dog-bitch!"

Gregory glanced at Mr. Harmston and noticed that the reverend gentleman's face remained untroubled. Mrs. Harmston, however, looked slightly worried. She mumbled something to her husband, and he nodded.

Olivia stiffened, and Gregory saw her eyes grow bright.

"But, Daddy, she *is* a dog-bitch. You can't put him in chains for saying that!"

"He's a pest," Garvey drawled. "He deserves to be in chains."

Their father made no response. Helped himself to a slice of bread and buttered it. There was cocoa on his moustache.

A damp thump of bare feet sounded in the pantry, and Ellen appeared.

"Mistress."

"Yes, Ellen?"

"Logan cussing me off in de kitchen."

"Very well, Ellen. The master will attend to him after breakfast."

"Beat 'e good, parson. Beat 'e and beat 'e till blood come. 'E been saying bad t'ings 'bout Miss Mabel."

"About me?"

"Yes, Miss Mabel. Dat's what start up de quarrel. 'E say you is a sinner."

"Get back to the kitchen, hater! Get back before I throw some hot cocoa in your ugly Buck face!"

"Now, Olivia!" frowned Mr. Harmston.

"'E say 'e see Miss Mabel sinning last night in Mister Gregory' room, mistress. 'E's a lying-tongue man."

Mabel stiffened and coloured. "Did he say that?"

"Yes, miss. He say dat. 'E say 'e hear a noise in Mister Gregory' room midnight last night and when 'e go upstairs soft he peep in de room and see you in bed wid Mr. Gregory, and you was sinning."

"Did he really say that, Ellen?" said Mrs. Harmston.

"Yes, miss. And 'e call me a dog-bitch and a stink-puss girl."

"He was right! Get back to the kitchen and hate yourself to death!"

"Olivia, leave the table and go upstairs."

"All right, Daddy, I'll go. I don't mind. But Logan is right. She is a dirty beast. A dog-bitch girl and a stink-puss girl!"

"Come here."

She rose and approached him. He slapped her face. Left the imprint of his hand on her cheek. She trembled but not a tear came. Her eyes were marbles of hate. She went.

In the silence she left behind her Gregory could hear the breath in him like nettle leaves being brushed against.

"Remember Osbert!" bayed Logan in the kitchen. "Oh, iniquity!"

"Go back to the kitchen, Ellen," said Mrs. Harmston quietly.

Ellen looked at Berton and smiled – then went.

Berton's face was pale. His spirit, Gregory thought, had gone out of the room; it had alighted on a lonely rock around which the sea surged with savage boisterousness.

"I wonder what could possibly have prompted him to say such things about me," said Mabel. "He must be going off his head." She gave Gregory a swift, perturbed glance.

But the influence of Gregory's medicine had not yet worn off and no tension rose in him. On the contrary, he felt elated and at ease. He finished his egg with relish.

From where he sat he could see the belfry, a slim, unsteady-looking wooden structure topped by a small, pointed roof under which hung the green-tarnished bell. The bell-rope seemed stout and strong but grey from age. Nearby stood a thick-trunked palm with a robust plumage of dark-green fronds; but beneath this plumage, pressed close against the upper part of the trunk, drooped a dense, sultry thicket of dead fronds in which, Gregory was sure, innumerable bats and insects must have their home.

He would have liked to know what variety of palm it was, and of a sudden grew keenly aware of Olivia's absence. Had she not been sent upstairs he could have asked her. A quaint flitting child. In his fancy he saw her as a milky shadow upon a veil of evening dusk. Unlike Mabel, she would not have fitted into a Surrey setting. Berkelhoost was her proper background: jungle and black water, jumbies and strange-scented blooms. He tried to compare her with Brenda, his dead wife, and in this instant knew that tension was brewing within him again; the effects of his medicine had begun to wear off; the walls warned him of their peephole possibilities.

With a brittle click-clack Mr. Harmston put down his cup and rose. He asked to be excused and moved toward the pantry, his manner unhurried.

If the pictures on the wall were to have been pushed gently aside...

Gregory finished his cocoa at a gulp. Without himself, he watched the pallor of his face as he rose and pushed in his chair. He tried to be controlled in his movements, but a jelly of urgency congealed around the aureole of his detached self. He asked to be excused, too, putting emphasis on the "too". He felt uncertain whether his voice had penetrated the fragile phantoms massed around him, but did not wait to observe the expressions on the faces of the others. Later he could explain to them why he had to go, why it was imperative that he should witness what was about to take place in the kitchen. They would probably not understand even when he explained, but never mind. Oneself came before other selves. Oneself was a balloon swelling, soaring... brightening...

In the pantry the boards of the floor were loose and yielded under his weight, adding to his sense of insecurity on the plane of actuality.

Logan was a whimpering ball on the kitchen floor, and over him towered the Reverend Mr. Harmston, colossus-like, a benevolent smile on his strong face. He was telling Logan to get up and come outside with him.

Ellen stood by the soot-blackened iron cooking-stove on which a pot and a kettle sent up little twisted ghosts of steam. Her coffee face was distorted by a smile of satiated hate-hunger. At sight of Gregory, the smile dulled slightly from surprise.

Mr. Harmston showed no surprise, however. He did not even turn his head to acknowledge Gregory's advent. He had an air of quiet concentration on the matter in hand.

"Come, Logan. Get up. Let's take a trip to the workshed."

"Beat me if Ah do wrong, parson," pleaded Logan, "but don't chain me up. Please, sah. Na do dat to me. Ah beg you wid all me heart."

"Up," smiled Mr. Harmston. "It's for your good."

"Ow, parson. Ah didn't mean to do wrong. Only de spirit move me, and Ah had to talk out. Remember Osbert, parson!"

"Up!"

"Ah witness sinful doings last night, parson, and God mek me talk. Don't chain me up, sah. Please!"

Ellen tittered. She started to rub one hand leisurely over the other, and her black eyes were feverish-bright. Hate rolled in invisible molasses rivers down her short, shapely body: streams that seemed to have their source in her smooth, jet, glittery hair; this morning it was not tied with green cloth and hung loose down her back.

"Please, sah! Please, parson!" Logan looked up and saw Gregory. "Ow, Mr. Gregory sah, you come to beg for me? Plead wid parson to spare me."

"He talk bad t'ings 'gainst you, Mister Gregory, sah. Don't beg for 'e. Let parson chain 'e up and beat 'e. You must beat 'e hard when you chain 'e up, parson. And let de red ants bite 'e backside."

"Quiet, Ellen."

Logan, still in a ball at Mr. Harmston's feet, threw her a glance of ferocity and hissed a shower of spittle at her ankles.

"For every minute more I have to wait I'm going to add a quarter of an hour to your punishment, Logan. As it is, you've earned an added hour already." The reverend gentleman took from his shirt pocket a large briskly ticking Westclox watch. "I'm timing you," he told Logan.

With a despairing whine, Logan crept toward the doorway that gave on to the stairs. Slowly he rose from his grovelling posture and began to descend the shaky treaders. Ellen uttered husky chortlings.

"Yes, go down let parson chain you up. Nasty, lying-tongue man."

"Quiet, Ellen."

"Yes, parson," said Ellen, cowering back as though expectant of a blow.

Mr. Harmston followed Logan down the stairs, and Gregory went after him, Ellen coming close behind Gregory, in a shudder of gloating. As they got to the foot of the stairs she fell into step beside him and said in an excited husky voice: "'E don't like de chain, Mister Gregory. 'E always afraid de parson might lose de key dat padlock 'e hands and 'e will lie down chain-up till darkness when de jumbie-man come."

A choking mossy cluck of laughter circled in her throat, and Gregory caught, in a whiff, the exciting, musky femaleness of her.

About fifty feet from the house, on the northern side, stood a crude wall-less shed (a *benab* Gregory afterwards learnt it was called), roofed with dry palm-fronds. Just beyond it the jungle parted in what was evidently the beginning of a track.

"Where does that track lead to?"

"De Indian risvation. Me mudder and fadder live dere."

"Were you born there?"

"Yes. And Logan, too. He born dere same as me."

A short distance past the track-opening, and right against the dense-looming jungle, stood a smaller shed, this one walled in all round with rusty sheets of corrugated iron and draped from palm-leaf roof to ground with the tendrils of a vine that bore clusters of tiny pink flowers.

Gregory heard a jingle and saw that Mr. Harmston had taken from his hip pocket a bunch of keys; the pocket had come out and jutted like a short sideways tail on his muscular rump. He was unlocking the door of the shed, and Logan, hands clasped together, besought him to relent.

Attacked by an urge that came from the surrounding plasmic sieve, Gregory glanced toward the house, and at the tiny bathroom window saw a face. It was Olivia. But she did not seem to be looking in the direction of the shed. She had the appearance of being interested in an event nearer the house – perhaps in the vicinity of the two large water storage vats that swelled fatly on low concrete blocks not far from the kitchen. She could have been watching the movements of someone who glided in easy spectral speed around one of these vats.

At an urgent whisper from Ellen, Gregory gave his attention again to the shed. Mr. Harmston had opened the door and gone inside. Now he was emerging with a heavy length of chain at each end of which was attached a pair of old-fashioned manacles.

Gregory had a sensation of having drifted back on a ripple of time to the eighteenth century. The youth of Middenshot gazed on a Hogarth print in Middenshot Manor and magically was amid the rowdy crowd and the grime and cruelty; the low-bosomed slatterns howled, and clawed his shins, the gamecocks bled and fluttered in combat, a femur cracked on the wheel to the cheering of the crowd....

As though Ellen fathomed his fantasy, he heard her mumble: "Dem chains you see, they come from Dutchman times, Mister Gregory. Dat's why Logan frighten dem so bad. 'E afraid one day Dutchman might come back and choke 'e to death when Dutchman find 'e chain up."

She was shaking and humid with delight, and gripped his arm. "Come. Come quick. Parson taking 'e round behind de shed to chain 'e up."

Gregory moved round to a point where they could see. Ellen moaned, as through a rusty iron ring fastened to the back of the shed Mr. Harmston threaded the chain. Smilingly the reverend gentleman caught Logan and dragged him near. The manacles made an unmusical clank-clank. It was very dark with tree-shadows behind the shed. The padlocks went tuck-clock as the key turned in them. And Logan howled and beat his forehead against the corrugated iron wall. Ellen seemed to echo the sound of the key in the padlocks. "Tuck-clock!" she went in her stomach. She was clinging now to Gregory, pressed limp against him, her skin roughened with a gooseflesh of ecstasy, her nipples like stiff fingertips pushing out the calico, her face in a lachrymal grimace of pleasurable pain. Laughter whirled in her throat like round pebbles rolling in a goblet.

"Back to the house, Ellen!" frowned Mr. Harmston.

"Yes, sah," she panted. "Yes, parson." She echoed the padlocks again. "Tuck-clock! Tuck-clock!" Deep in her stomach, as though her rapture of hatred had fermented into big bubbles inside her.

She detached herself from Gregory and began to move off. All the way to the house she kept looking back and smiling and taking quick grabbing squeezes at her thighs.

Mr. Harmston approached and held Gregory's arm with paternal affectionateness. "One of the jobs I don't like doing, my boy," he said. "But I have to do it. Part of my programme of discipline. He'd get completely out of hand if I didn't punish him."

"Do you have occasion to punish him often?"

"Not the chaining. He gets that once in about three months,

on an average, when he indulges in really disgusting behaviour. But hardly a week goes by that I don't have to give him a flogging. He's an intractable, perverse fellow. Distinctly abnormal, too, in many ways." He frowned and amended in a mutter: "Or perhaps I should say subnormal."

"I thought Ellen, too, not very normal."

Mr. Harmston smiled. "She's in her glee. It's a big day for her when I chain Logan. Yes, she isn't normal herself. The local influences have had an unusually powerful effect on her."

"Oh."

"Joan and Mabel are about the least susceptible. The rest of the family have high-voltage personalities, and this environment, coupled with our religion, tends to stimulate our imaginations to unorthodox behaviour. Do you believe in psychic phenomena?"

"Up to a point."

"This place is full of psychic phenomena."

"You mean it's haunted?"

"In a manner of speaking. Let's sit here." Strolling toward the house, they had come to a rough wooden bench that stood near an arbour covered with a tangle of vines and situated under two of the dining-room windows.

"Honeysuckle, coralita and bougainvillea," smiled Mr. Harmston, noticing Gregory's interest in the arbour. "The big, thick-stalked vine is bougainvillea. It's not in bloom at the moment. It's the dark-red variety. The coralita is the one with the small pink flowers. Same as on the workshed. Cosy little arbour. Dark and shady under there. Olivia and Berton call it their Cavern. They go under there for 'conferences'."

"I see."

As they sat down Mr. Harmston took out his watch and said: "Twenty to eight. We can have a little chat until eight. The business of the day begins at eight. I don't suppose you know much about the history of British Guiana. Ever heard of the great slave insurrection of 1763?"

"No."

"Um. Berkelhoost was in the thick of it. Some bloody massacres took place here."

"Who massacred whom?"

"The negro slaves ran amok and massacred their Dutch masters. All this jungle was cultivated land in the eighteenth century. Berbice was a flourishing colony. But the Dutch were cruel masters."

"The eighteenth century was a cruel century. It wasn't only the Dutch who were cruel."

"Exactly. Anyway, there were bloody doings in this little colony. Two or three thousand slaves took charge of affairs practically overnight and the few hundred whites were slaughtered right and left. Very few escaped. Later on, when the Government gained control again, the rebel leaders were burnt at the stake and broken on the wheel. Berkelhoost teems with passionate, cruel spirits. The whole neighbourhood bristles with the residual effluvia of past violence. Before long you'll sense it."

"Yes."

Mr. Harmston chuckled and patted Gregory's knee. "I don't say it will necessarily have a harmful effect on you."

"No."

"Don't think I'm trying to scare you."

"Has it affected you?"

"At first, very much. But I struggled and mastered myself."

"How long have you been here."

"Twenty-four years. I met your aunt at Middenshot in February, 1913. We were married in the summer, after I'd graduated at Oxford. We sailed for this colony in early October – a week after the Brethren ordained me. We still have the autumn leaves we gathered in the woods near your mother's cottage. We keep them in a trinket-box."

Mr. Harmston jingled his bunch of keys reflectively, his gaze on the arbour. They sat in the shadow of the house. Now and then unexpectedly a tiny dark spot would circle into Gregory's vision, and he would feel a tickling on his eyelashes that would cause him to brush at his face. He learnt afterwards that it was an eye-fly. It was an annoyingly persistent creature.

After a silence, Gregory produced a small silver cigarette-case and held it out, but Mr. Harmston shook his head.

"I limit myself to three cigarettes a day. I smoked one on

getting out of bed. I mustn't have another until after lunch. Discipline."

"Oh."

Gregory lit one.

"But for discipline I should have succumbed to the spirit of this place. We can achieve anything if we discipline ourselves."

"I agree. Do you mind if I ask your age?"

"Forty-six last March."

A flock of birds flew past low overhead, chattering noisily, and vanished amid the trees in the vicinity of the *benab*.

"Parrots," said Mr. Harmston.

They heard Logan howling.

"Joan is forty-four. Think we look our ages?"

"Just about. You've kept well."

"We both feel younger than our ages. Is your mother alive?"

"No."

"What happened to the cottage at Middenshot?"

"I sold it after Mother's death."

"When did she die?"

"A little under two years ago. Cancer of the stomach."

"A pity she had to behave as she did."

"Yes. She never forgave Aunt Joan for marrying you."

"She never replied to any of Joan's letters."

"I know. But she kept them. I found them in her escritoire. That's how I knew your address here, Mother could be very bitter."

"She had a weakness for trying to manage other people's lives."

"That's quite true. Did you know my father?"

"I met him only once – a Sunday afternoon in Camberley. Shortly before he died. I took a liking to him on the spot. You were about seven then, I think?"

"Yes. I remember him only vaguely."

A mooing came from far up-river. Cool like the arbour. Peaceful.

"The steamer," said Mr. Harmston.

"On its way back to New Amsterdam."

"Stop that trembling."

Gregory tried to and stopped it.

"Haven't you any letters to send off?"

"Yes, two," nodded his host. "And a box of vegetables for the Pastor in New Amsterdam. Berton will take them out in the *corial*. That's one of his duties."

They heard Mrs. Harmston's voice in the dining-room. It sounded upset. She was saying something to Mabel, and Mabel replied with a protest.

Gregory glanced enquiringly at Mr. Harmston.

"He died," said Mr. Harmston, "trying to put out a heath fire, poor fellow."

"That's right," Gregory nodded. "An old lady's cottage was threatened, and he went to help hack away the trees in the vicinity to keep away the fire, but he stepped into a deep rut and broke his leg. It was too late when they rescued him. The flames had swept upon him already. He died of the burns the same night."

"I remember his moustache. The colour of Garvey's hair."

"I, too, strangely enough. It's the only thing about him I can say I recall."

A shower of rain was approaching. Gregory heard it swashing softly through the bush, leisurely crashing its way toward them in a hush of remote menace. Then miraculously it was gone and a breeze shook the foliage of the trees on the edge of the clearing and touched his face so that he knew that it was wind he had heard and not rain.

Mabel's voice sounded in the dining-room raised indignantly. "Something is wrong in the house."

"Um. One day we must have a long chat about yourself and the Old Country," Mr. Harmston smiled. "Or have you come here to forget?"

"I was married, by the way."

"You were? What happened? Divorced?"

"She died – in Barbados. Accidentally drowned at a place called Martin's Bay on the north coast. Just a week or two before I arrived in the island."

"Were you going there to join her?"

"No. To kill her. She was evil."

"Um."

"Gerald!" called Mrs. Harmston.

"I'm out here, Joan!"

Her face appeared at one of the dining-room windows.

"Gerald, could you come at once?"

Mr. Harmston took out his watch. "In about four minutes," he smiled up at her. "Having a chat with Gregory."

"Very well, dear."

"She seems very upset," said Gregory. "Shouldn't you go?"

"Nothing urgent. Some little domestic trouble."

From where they sat they could not see the river, but Gregory heard the splash of oars or paddles accompanied by a rhythmical thud-thud.

"The Buckmaster girls. Susan and Dorothea," said Mr. Harmston. He rose. "They come to school here. We hold school in the *benab* over there." He took another glance at his watch. "We have two minutes to spare. Come and meet them."

They went past the water-vats, skirted the kitchen and made their way to the landing-place where Garvey, seated in the *corial* with a crate of vegetables, was about to push off into the stream. Another *corial* was drawing alongside the logs. Its occupants, two olive-skinned girls – one about fifteen, the other about thirteen – stepped ashore with shy smiles. The younger secured the *corial*. Mr. Harmston waited until she had done so and then introduced her to Gregory as Susan. She held out her hand with a quiet: "Howdy do?"

"And this is Dorothea."

Dorothea's hand was clammy in the palm. Both girls were fat but not short. They had features more negroid than European. Dark eyes. And dark, wavy hair well greased, and plaited into pigtails tied with ribbon. They wore cotton dresses with blue spots, and carried exercise books and textbooks secured with leather straps. Gregory noticed the title of one book: *Children's Cyclopedia Volume Three.*

"Run along now and get your stools and boxes ready, girls," said Mr. Harmston.

"May I say something to Mr. Hawke first?" asked Dorothea.

Gregory gave her a stare of surprise.

"Say on," said Mr. Harmston, without surprise.

"I saw you in a dream last night," said Dorothea, with a demure smile.

"Me?" said Gregory.

"Yes. But you had pink horns. And a green something else."

Susan sniggered and exclaimed: "Ow, Dorrit!"

Mr. Harmston laughed and patted Susan's head. "That will do. Run along now like good girls."

They went.

"Delightful youngsters," smiled Mr. Harmston. "Very much under the local influences. I must be leaving you to your own devices now, my boy. The business of the day. How do you want to occupy yourself this morning? A bit of reading?"

"I think I'll stay here and watch the steamer go by – and just laze for awhile."

"Excellent plan. During the afternoon, if I have a moment to spare, I'll take you to see the ruins."

"Ruins?"

"Yes. We have some quite near here. Dutch ruins. And tombs."

Logan howled.

And, as if in echo, the steamer mooed. Not so far off now.

"We won't be seeing it again until next Wednesday," said Mr. Harmston.

"Oh."

"The steamer I mean. You'll find," he said, lowering his voice, "that this is a safe place to hide when you're wanted by the police."

He hurried off before Gregory, rigid like a pillar of salt, could make any comment.

X

Olivia felt no ill feeling against her father as she stood at the bathroom window and watched him take Logan to the workshed. Her cheek still burned from his slap, but she knew she had deserved it; he would have fallen in her esteem if he had not slapped her. Nor did she consider him harsh because he was going to chain up Logan. Logan's behaviour had called for severe punishment. This did not prevent her, however, from being sorry for Logan nor from hating Ellen.

When she saw Ellen and Gregory come into view from around the kitchen the hate in her became so intense that she had to bend her head and look at the patch of blackish-green moss low down on the side of the smaller of the two water-vats. After a moment the moss took on the nature of her hate, and it moved and swelled into an ugly shape. It slithered off the vat and stood humped and demon-like, fat with evil and furry with venom. She had only to tell it and it would have glided off to do her bidding, a thing hoarse and slimy.

The scent of honeysuckle from the arbour came up to her and she smiled. A memory unravelled in her: Berton and herself eating a green mango with pepper and salt in their Cavern, and talking about the things they would do when they grew up: the houses they would build in the jungle with cosy rooms and passages and secret doors… "when we find the cache of rubies and emeralds and sapphires…"

Hate melted out of her, and the demon turned back into the harmless moss on the side of the vat. Her gaze moved toward the arbour, and love made a waving in her like delicate plants under quick, clear water. When she heard her father order Ellen back to the house his voice might have come, from a long way off down-river, and the words meant nothing to her.

Out of the corner of her eye she saw him with Gregory approach the house and sit down on the bench near the arbour.

Then she heard the wind coming through the jungle, mysterious like waves on the beach of Crusoe's island. Man Friday had just seen the footprints in the sand and was hurrying to Crusoe to tell him... When it touched her face she shut her eyes and breathed deeply and listened to what seemed like powder moving in cool grains down tunnels that were veins in her.

She turned away from the window, and knew the loveliness of life. She opened her eyes and looked slowly around the bathroom, and could feel the familiarity of it in her bones: its woody, soapy smell.

In the corridor she heard her mother call Mabel, her voice upset. Alert, she listened and heard Mabel answer from downstairs in the dining-room. Heard her steps on the stairs.

"Calling me, Mother? What's it? Have you finished making up the beds already?"

"Mabel. Child." She spoke in a lowered voice.

"What's the matter?"

"This. Look. Your dressing-gown."

"Yes. I was looking for it last night. Did you borrow it?"

A silence... In her fancy Olivia saw her mother's eyes on Mabel.

"But... I don't understand, Mother. What are you staring at me like that for?" Mabel laughed.

"Do you have to ask me why?"

"What are you getting at?"

"I found this under Gregory's bed."

"Under Gregory's bed? How did it get there?"

"That's what I want you to tell me. Did you go in there to him last night? Look, we mustn't talk here. Come into your room."

Mabel began to speak in a protesting voice but what she said faded with the shutting of the bedroom door, and Olivia, a cold hand on her chest, a bottle of tears about to splinter behind her eyes, left the bathroom and hurried downstairs.

She found Berton in the sitting-room. He sat at the centre table with its carved mahogany legs, writing in an exercise book. He glanced round and smiled: "You're down? I've got your egg." He fumbled out an egg from his pants pocket. It was the one she had been about to eat at breakfast when her father sent her upstairs.

She took it and thanked him, and asked him what he was doing; couldn't he put it aside a minute?

"It's my French anecdote. Something has happened?"

She nodded.

"Logan?" He closed the exercise book. "Let's go to the Cavern."

"No, we can't. Daddy and Gregory are on the bench talking. It isn't Logan. It's Mabel. Her flesh threatens my spirit."

He began to speak, then stopped. They heard Mabel and their mother coming down the stairs. They looked and saw that Mabel's eyes were angry and their mother's face set and pale. They watched them go into the dining-room. Their mother said: "My God! I don't think I could stand it."

"Mother, please! Don't be ridiculous!"

Berton whispered: "Was Logan right about what he said? I thought he was lying as usual."

"I hope he was. My spirit would burn with jealousy if she's really invaded his flesh. Mother found her dressing-gown under his bed."

"Gregory's bed? But Mabel isn't like that."

They heard their mother calling their father.

"I should hate her and hate her," said Olivia, her eyes bright.

Mabel came into the sitting-room.

"What ails thee, Maby?" asked Olivia.

"Ollie, don't you remember I asked you if you'd seen my dressing-gown? Last night before we went to bed?"

"Yes. I remember. I recall it with clarification."

"Clarity," nodded Berton. "Maby, did you have any dreams? You know what kind I mean."

Mabel nodded.

"You had?" said Olivia and Berton in chorus.

"Yes," said Mabel. "I did have sexy dreams. What about it?"

"You dreamt of Gregory?"

Mabel blushed and nodded, trying to frown impatiently at the same time. Berton gave a whistle, and Olivia's eyes grew brighter.

"Can you remember the dream, Maby? All the details?"

"I don't want to be questioned."

"But it's important."

"Remember," said Olivia, "we live under strange influences. Dreams, in Berkelhoost, sometimes merge into actual deeds, and what we may think shadows can prove to be pillars of substance with eyes of fire."

"And brimstone," nodded Berton.

Mabel laughed.

"It's nothing to laugh at, Maby."

"You're not," said Olivia, "sneering at our religion are you?"

Mabel said nothing.

Their mother called Mabel, and Mabel tripped awkwardly back into the dining-room.

Olivia said to Berton: "We'll have to intertorrogate Gregory."

Berton nodded. "Interrogate," he said.

"Maby doesn't really respect the local influences."

"I know," said Berton. "She'll regret it one day."

"I hate this place. It's beastly, beastly! You hear me? Beastly!"

"Ollie! How can you say a thing like that!"

She unclenched her bands and her eyes lost their glint. "You know I don't mean that. I said it for passionate effect. Berkelhoost is lovely to live in. Our fairy-jumbie jungle home. I don't want to live anywhere else. Do you?"

He touched her wrist and said: "Of course not. It's too magical here. Especially with a sweet, queer girl like you moving about. You mustn't vanish and leave me, though. You hear? I don't know what would happen to me if you do. I wouldn't want to go on living."

She pulled his ear. "I won't vanish and leave my knight-errant."

They heard women in a boat.

"Susan and Dot. It must be eight o'clock."

He went to the door that gave into the dining-room and looked at the clock on the shelf over the dinner-wagon. "Two minutes to eight," he said.

Mabel was standing at one of the windows that looked out on the river. Mrs. Harmston must have gone into the pantry, for she was not in the room, Behind Berton, Olivia watched Mabel.

"I love her and hate her," she whispered. "Maby, come!" she called.

Mabel came, a troubled frown on her face. She followed Olivia and Berton into the sitting-room and asked them what they wanted.

"Don't let what's happened get you down, Maby," said Olivia. "You're so sweet and good. Berton and I are going to see what we can do."

Mabel gave a slight enigmatical smile.

"Not *all* dreams mean something. I've had funny ones myself."

"I, too," said Berton. "With you – and that nasty thing Ellen."

They heard the steamer's siren. Olivia, watching Mabel's smile, said: "Maby, you don't mean to tell us you went in to him in a waking state?"

Mabel laughed. "And what if I did?"

"But that would be probitchousness! Rank probitchscrewity!"

"Promiscuousness," Berton amended, with a solemn nod. "Promiscuity."

"Suppose I say I'd fallen in love with him at first sight," Mabel mooted, and Olivia replied: "Well, that would be all right. But I'm sure you haven't fallen in love with him."

"I haven't. That's why mother is so upset."

Olivia grunted. "Are you sure you didn't sleepwalk and sleep-act?"

"I'm quite sure I didn't," said Mabel.

"But how can you be sure?" said Berton. "The shadows move in mysterious ways."

"Shadows don't trouble me," Mabel assured him.

"Mockery. You've told Mother you had a dream about Gregory?"

"Yes. That's why she thinks it must have happened in reality. I'm surprised at Mother, that's the truth. Such thing's don't really happen to people. She ought to know that."

"But they can – at Berkelhoost. We live among phantoms here."

Mabel shrugged. "At heart, I've never believed in all that."

"Remember Osbert."

Mabel was silent.

"Daddy thought he'd done it in a dream."

Mabel turned off with a click of her tongue. "What I can't

understand is the dressing-gown. How did it get under his bed? If even I had gone to his room last night I wouldn't have worn my dressing-gown, because I didn't have it in my room before I got into bed. You're there to confirm that, at least, Olivia."

"Yes, that's odd. I've got to investigate that."

"Daddy's calling you. It's time for school."

"Yes, I must be off. And above all, don't worry. I'll fix up everything for you. And please don't think evil or herebetical thoughts. Our religion is nothing to go making fun over, you know."

Mabel smiled and told her to go.

Olivia came upon her parents in the pantry. They were standing by the little table with the burnt-earth water-goblet and the tumbler, and seemed in conference, her mother on the point of tears but her father smiling and unconcerned. He frowned round at Olivia: "Didn't you hear me calling you, Olivia? It's time for school." Then he turned back to her mother and patted her shoulder. "A normal sleep-fantasy, my dear," he said. "Such a thing won't happen to Mabel She isn't the type to fall under the spell of this place. She's taken after you in that respect."

Her mother looked a trifle mollified and murmured that she hoped he was right. She gave a sniffle.

Olivia approached them and said: "Daddy, I wonder if I couldn't have an hour off from school this morning. I want to ask Gregory a few things. It's very important."

"To do with Mabel?"

"Yes."

"Don't question him about it. I'm just telling your mother there's no cause to worry. I'm certain nothing happened."

"I feel pretty certain myself, but we have to make sure. The shadows are sometimes perverse."

Her father nodded gravely.

"I've given Maby a serious talking to," said Olivia, "but she's inclined to treat the matter lightly."

"Excellent," congratulated her father. "Mabel can always do with a talking to, my girl."

"Mabel is a steady child," said Mrs. Harmston. "She's no wanton."

"Uncomfortably steady, I'm sometimes inclined to think, my dear." He chucked Olivia affectionately under the chin. "Not as richly imaginative as our Olivia."

Olivia, flattered, but trying to keep a solemn face, said: "Anyway, Daddy, why I want to question Gregory is because I'm not so sure she mightn't have gone to his room last night. Sort of sleep-walked and tried to get into bed with him. From what I grasp, she had a very vivid dream."

"Um. Most of our dreams in this place are vivid. Nothing new in that. No, I don't like the idea of your questioning that young man. In his present condition it may have a damaging effect. We want to do all we can to get him better. I tell you what you can do, my girl. Ask Logan a few questions on the quiet. See if you can get out of him what he was doing while we were at dinner last night. I have a feeling he can solve the mystery of this dressing-gown."

"You think so? Yes, you may be right. Remember somebody put out the lamp in the sitting-room while we were eating? Gregory said he noticed a shape move. Can I go now and question Logan?"

"No. At recess time. Go to the *benab* at once and see after the children. I'll be there in a minute."

"Yes, Daddy."

She found Dorothea and Susan already settled on their folding-stools, their books arranged before them on the soapboxes that served as desks. They had set up the stools and boxes for the other children, but, to Olivia's surprise, only two of them were in their places: Brownie and Jane, the twins of Benab Number Eight on the Reservation.

"Hallo, Dot! Susan! Where is everybody else this morning?"

"Haven't you got ears?" said Dorothea.

"Don't you hear the singing?" asked Susan.

"You don't mean…" Without finishing her sentence Olivia sprinted off toward the workshed. At the back she found the rest of the children. There were nine of them, four boys and five girls, all of them Indians from the Reservation, short and black-haired with coffee-hued skins, and between the ages of nine and thirteen. They had ranged themselves in a half-circle around Logan who, huddled grotesquely against the wall of the shed, uttered prolonged moans, head sorrowfully bent. The children kept chanting at him two lines from *The Tempest,* several passages of which they had been made to memorize during the past few weeks.

> "'*Ban, 'Ban,*" they chanted. "*Ca-Caliban!*
> "*Has a new master: get a new man!*
> "'*Ban, 'Ban –*"

"Children!"

The chanting stopped. They turned, startled.

"Aren't you ashamed of yourselves! Mabel would be disappointed if I told her what use you'd put her Shakespeare lessons to. Away from here! Back to the *benab* this minute. You'll get two bad marks for this!"

Two of the boys giggled defiantly, but the others looked ashamed. They scampered off toward the *benab,* their bare feet swishing softly in the damp grass. The girls wore cotton dresses, the boys khaki pants and shirts blotchy-grey from much washing.

Olivia watched them go, the frown still heavy on her face, then turned and bent and stroked Logan's head. She told him not to trouble; the time would soon pass and he would be free again.

He groaned louder, and beat his forehead against the rusty corrugated iron wall, and Olivia could not help thinking that he did look a little like Caliban. Perhaps it was because he could be so half-animal in his looks and ways at times that she had such a deep compassion for him. He was a creature that needed protection – like the bush-spiders that strayed into the house or into the church.

"At recess time I'm going to come and bring you something to eat. And some water. Did you have any breakfast?"

"Yes, Miss Ollie. Ah had lil' bread and milk before de master come in de kitchen. Ow, miss! Tell de master careful not to lose de key for me handcuffs. Please! If night come and find me here Dutchman' jumbie will break me neck. Ah dream Ah see de Dutchman' jumbie two nights ago."

"Daddy won't lose the key. And no jumbie will trouble you."

"Ah hope not, miss. Ow!"

He kept his legs hugged against him and stared mournfully at the manacles around his wrists. His face was shiny with sweat and tears, and his eyes bloodshot. His stiffish black curls were flecked with bits of reddish gravel and small twigs, and his forehead had a smear of blood from the bruised spot made by his continual beating it against the wall.

Yet, she noticed, despite his apparent misery he seemed to guard within him a sly contentment; she could tell from the strained squint of his eyes and the way his lips curved down spasmodically at certain instants. He was suffering bodily discomfort but enjoying his suffering. When he howled it was only because of the terror he felt of being left here until after dark. Could he have cast off his unreasonable fear that her father would lose the key for his manacles, his secret happiness would have been unmarred.

She smiled in wonder at his oddity and told him to stay well, then ran back to the *benab* where the children were settling down on their camp-stools and slapping down exercise books and textbooks on the boxes before them.

"I'm very annoyed with you," she frowned at them. "And you of all girls, Katey! I'm really surprised at you doing such a thing."

"It was Mary who say we must tease him," Katey mumbled.

"No, it was you who say we must do it," Mary contradicted.

"John! Correct their sentences!"

"It was Mary who *said*," said John. "Past tense."

"Very good. I hope you heard that, Mary and Katey."

John, who sat behind Katey, put out his foot and prodded Katey's leg. Katey turned and growled: "Don't do that, John. Ollie, you see what John did? He kicked my foot."

"Did he? You deserved it, anyway. John, don't do that again."

The Reverend Mr. Harmston approached with long strides, a smile on his face. He had to bend slightly to enter the *benab,* but once under the roof he could stand erect without fear of his head touching. He heaved a great breath of vitality, but his voice was even and soft as he bade them good morning.

"Good morning, parson!" the children chorused, keeping their seats, for Mr. Harmston did not believe in too much ceremony.

"Everything in order, Ollie? How have they been behaving?"

"Not so well, parson. I had to correct them a bit."

"Um. That doesn't sound too good. Anything serious enough to merit bad marks?"

"Yes, parson. Two bad marks each for nine of them."

"Good. Remember to enter them down in the Bad-mark Book at Recess. Very well, my girl. You can take your place now."

Olivia made her way round to the stool placed behind the class. She had no box nor books, for though a pupil herself she was considered a sort of lieutenant. Her function was to stand by to take the class should her father, for some reason, be called away, or to assist him in illustrating some aspect of the lesson when illustration was called for, or to run to the house for any book or appliance that might be needed. Her status, however, did not give her the right to be inattentive to the lesson. Often her father fired an unexpected question at her and to be guilty of inattention at such a moment would have constituted an act of disloyalty to him, for he depended upon her to show a good example to the others.

This morning, with her mind on the situation which had developed around Gregory and Mabel, it was not easy to concentrate on the lesson. She kept seeing Mabel's smiling, secretive face. And the suspicion she felt about Mabel would merge with the compassion she felt for Logan, and swirl inside her like different waves of heat getting tangled. She wondered where Gregory could be at the moment. Had he drifted off into the jungle, a whisky-scented ghost, or was he stalking Mabel, a murder-glint in his pale blue eyes? Why did he call whisky his medicine?

To make things worse, her father chose to begin the day's lesson with a talk on personal hygiene, a subject on which she deemed herself very well informed and which, therefore, held little interest for her.

She heard the steamer go past (the river was not visible from the *benab*). Its siren sounded down-river to warn other homesteads and outposts of its approach. The morning, too, proved a distracting influence. The sun shone on the still dew-wet grass, and the grass shimmered like satin, in patches. Not far from the *benab* – a little way down the track that led to the Indian reservation – some parrots kept up a squawking and paraded with precarious deliberation along the delicate, feathery fronds of a clump of manicole palms. And then, without warning, now and then, the wind would make that faraway rushing swash in the jungle…

"Katey! You! You tell us why!"

With a jerk her attention came back to the lesson. She saw Katey stand, a thin girl of twelve in a pink cotton dress. Katey was one of their brightest pupils – and, as a rule, the quietest.

"Because of germs, parson," she answered.

"Right. Because of germs. Germs breed in dirt, and if we fail to get rid of the dirt that gathers on our skins we harbour germs on our bodies, and one day we wake up and find that we've contracted some terrible disease. Thanks, Katey. Sit down. Now, John! You! Tell us why you think we ought to see that fleas don't breed in our bedclothes."

John, ten years old, sheepish-smiling, rose with an air of uncertainty; he was good at grammar and syntax but lacked imagination. After a moment's hesitation he said: "Because fleas can bite, parson, and they might keep you from sleeping at night."

"An idea. Yes, certainly an idea. Loss of sleep can result in bad health. But there's another reason. Ollie! You! Tell us the danger in fleas."

Olivia, glad that she had been paying attention, rose and said: "A certain kind of flea spreads a disease known as the plague. We don't get it in this country. Mostly in India you get it. But you never know what kind of flea might stray into your bedclothes so it's just as well to be careful. If it's a plague-flea and it bites you you'll get the disease. Big hard balls called buboes will come out in your groins and swell out and hurt you, and you'll get hot fever and die off in a few days."

"Excellent! Sit down, Ollie – and thanks. Now, children, you've heard why fleas are dangerous. You might be bitten by a plague-flea – and then whoo! One day you find yourself feeling giddy and weak. Your head aches, and you vomit. And worst of all, you come out in black spots." His arm shot out – but not dramatically; with an easy briskness – and his forefinger pointed at Brownie, a plump girl of eleven. "Tell us another name for this disease, Brownie. Let me see if you have a good memory."

109

Brownie rose and bit her upper lip, then her lower. She smiled and shook her head. "Ah can't remember, parson."

"Eh? What's that? What did I hear? *Ah* can't remember!"

"*I* can't remember," Brownie amended.

"That's better. All right, Brownie, sit down. David, you! Can you tell us another name for the plague?"

"Blackwater fever, parson."

Mr. Harmston laughed good-naturedly. "Very good try, Dave my boy, but you're mixing up your diseases. Blackwater fever is a bad kind of malaria we get in this country. Don't forget what Ollie said. We don't get plague here. Very well, Katey, you're itching to tell us. Let's hear."

"The Black Death."

"Good girl. The Black Death. And now that you've told us, I think we'll go straight on to our history lesson. As you've suggested the theme, in a manner of speaking, Katey, I'll deal with the Restoration period in English history. No, no! Close your history books. I'll tell you when I want you to refer to anything. In what year was the Great Plague?"

Half-a-dozen voices cried: "Sixteen sixty-five."

"Good work! Splendid! And quick! Who can tell me the name of the man who wrote a famous diary around that time?"

"Pepper!"

"Samuel Peeper!" called Katey.

"Getting warm! Any other tries?"

"Samuel Peppees!" amended Katey.

"That's it. But it's pronounced Peeps, Katey. Spell it, let's hear."

"P-E-P-double-Y-S."

"Wrong. Dorothea – yes?"

"P-E-P-Y-S."

"Correct. Write it down in your exercise-books. Wait! Not on the pages with your history notes. Do it on the calligraphy pages, and put 'peeps' in brackets after it, so you'll remember the pronunciation. Now, go ahead. Do a nice fine piece of writing!"

He stood with folded arms waiting for them to get it done, and Olivia knew that he had given them this task in order to catch his breath before starting his talk on Restoration England. She watched him with admiration, seeing him as a hero-giant in whom she could put her trust without fear. Not only was he physically strong but he was wise and clever. It was not easy to fool him over anything. He could be harsh when the occasion called for discipline, but he had a kind heart. She got fits of spite against him when he thwarted her in something she had set her mind on, but underneath her love and respect for him remained steady.

After they had shown him their efforts at fine writing, he began his lecture on the Restoration, and was well into it when Olivia, whose attention strayed, for there was little about the Restoration period she did not know, became aware that Gregory had appeared from the direction of the kitchen.

Her heart seemed to shrink slightly with excitement. She watched him. He stood not ten yards away, behind her father, listening to her father's lecture.

He was smiling – a sure sign, she had come to learn, that he was entertained.

XI

"But," Mr. Harmston told them in conclusion, "I don't want you to go away with the impression that only the English were loose in their conduct. The French were just as bad. Probably a good deal worse. And that reminds me! Ollie, run to the house and see if Berton has completed his French anecdote. If he has, tell him to come at once with it. And while you're about it, my girl, bring the gramophone and Album Three. No. Album Four. We had Three the day before yesterday."

"Very well, parson. Parson?"

"Yes?"

"You have a spectator," she said – and set off for the house at the double.

Mr. Harmston turned without haste or surprise, and smiled upon Gregory. "Morning lessons, my boy. Usual routine. Come and let me introduce you to them."

Gregory did not move. He stopped smiling, for abruptly the outer circle wavered then closed in upon the inner – without a crackle or a lisp. And as the sun emerged from a cloud the jungle pulsed, and pullulated a multitude of new and threatening points of light.

Mr. Harmston approached him.

"Enjoying yourself? Did you watch the steamer pass?"

"Yes."

"How are you feeling now?"

"Yes."

"You mean not too good?"

"No."

"Don't think about it. How do you like my class? I take a pride in these children. I want them to grow up into men and women with rich minds. And I want them to live full but quiet, natural lives in this their jungle home. My aim is to teach them to be civilized without cynicism."

"Do you do this all day? This teaching?"

112

"No. At ten-fifteen Joan relieves me until noon. Mabel takes over after lunch, and I have the older children from three to four. Space being limited, we can't teach juniors and seniors at the same time."

"Oh."

"Would you care to sit down at the back of the class with Olivia?"

"Yes."

"You wouldn't like me to introduce you to the children first?"

"No."

When Olivia returned she found that her father had set up another stool beside hers, and on it Gregory was seated. He smiled at her.

"Going to keep me company?" she said, as she placed the portable Columbia gramophone and the album of records on the ground beside her stool.

"Yes. For a while."

"Eyes front, please, children! Ollie, what of Berton and his anecdote?"

"He's on the last paragraph, parson. He'll be here with it in about five minutes, he says."

"Um. Very well. In the meantime we'll have a record or two."

From his shirt pocket he took a notebook and pencil and began to write, and the children opened their exercise books and got their pencils ready. Olivia whispered to Gregory: "He's jotting down their names."

"Oh."

Olivia put on a record, and after the first few bars of the *Moonlight Sonata* had rippled out of the machine, which had a fairly good tone, Gregory noticed, Mr. Harmston raised his hand and Olivia stopped the record.

The children bent over their exercise books and wrote. "They have to put down what piece it is and who is the composer," Olivia whispered.

She played in succession the opening bars of the *1812 Overture*, Chopin's *Fantasie impromptu*, the *Ride of the Valkyries* and the overture to the *Bohemian Girl*, and was about to put on the waltz from the Nutcracker Suite when her father told her to desist.

Berton had come, exercise book in hand.

"That will do, children. We'll resume after the anecdote. Let's hear the results of what you've just done. Dorothea!"

Dorothea rose and read from her open exercise book: " 'The Moonlight Sonata, Beethoven. The 1812 overture, Tchaycowsky. The minute waltz, Chopin. The ride of the Valeries, Wagner. The Bohemian Girl.' I can't remember the name of the composer of that, parson."

Without comment, the reverend gentleman jotted down her marks and told her to be seated. "Susan, let's hear you, my child."

When he had heard them all, he announced that Katey and Joseph, a ten-year-old boy, had tied for first place with eight marks out of ten. He announced the pieces and their composers, thanked Olivia for her services and told Berton: "We're ready for your anecdote, my boy."

Berton went round to the front of the class, and while his father stood aside with folded arms, the boy read out his anecdote.

"He's marvellous at French," Olivia whispered to Gregory. "He composed it between breakfast and now. Can you understand French?"

Gregory nodded. He seemed to get paler and paler as he listened to Berton.

"…et les feuilles commençaient à tomber. Une… deux… trois çi et ça… Et puis l'homme s'arrêtait. Il avait entendu le son d'un oiseau – un petit chant… Le chant s'approchait. D'abord doucement, doucement – puis tout-à-coup –"

Berton broke off.

Gregory had slumped sideways off his seat in a faint. Mr. Harmston hurried round to Olivia's assistance. She was trying to support him. Berton threw down his exercise book and ran round to help.

The children rose, and a murmuring began among them. "Keep your seats, please, children," said Mr. Harmston, his manner unflustered.

Behind the workshed Logan howled mournfully. Gregory opened his eyes.

"I'm afraid I…"

"It's all right, my boy. Nothing at all to worry about."

"I seem to have fainted."

"Yes, just a little giddiness, I suppose."

"Yes."

"Olivia, I think you'd better take him for a walk around the yard. The sunshine will do him good."

"Very well, parson."

She took him toward the church, her hand on his arm. He trembled.

"I'm afraid I owe your father an apology."

"You needn't bother about that. He'll understand. You're not well."

"It was the French."

"You're allectric to French?"

"Allectric? You mean allergic. In a way, yes. Brenda – my wife spoke it – and wrote it – fluently. She once wrote a little tale in French. One evening she read it for me in our flat. Berton – his voice reminded me –"

"It's all right. I understand. She's dead?"

"Yes."

"Mother knows French, too. She can write and speak it as she can English. She went to school for four years in Belgium. A French marquis once proposed to her. He saw her when she was in a little village near Antwerp. She was very pretty then."

"She's still pretty."

"Let's sit here."

They had come to the three concrete steps that led up to the west door of the church. It was shady here, but a few yards off the belfry, with the robust palm nearby, stood in the full bright sunshine. He asked her the name of the palm and she said: "It's a *cookerit* palm. You'll like *cookerits* when they begin to bear. About September the season should be on."

"What is it like – the fruit?"

"It's lovely. Sort of pear-shaped, and it has a hard outer skin and a cap where it joins up with the stem. Hard almost like a nut-shell. When you peel off the cap and the skin you come to the seed, and the seed is covered with a sweet, oily pulp that you have to scrape off with your teeth. Once you start eating them you can't stop. My mouth is watering."

They watched the belfry in silence for a while. About fifty feet away – beyond the belfry and the palm – loomed the jungle, a mixture of spreading-limbed trees and palms: palms of all varieties. They could not see the river from here, but once they heard a tinkling plep as though a berry had dropped into the water. After that, the only sound was the voice of Mr. Harmston from the *benab,* muffled by the bulk of the church. Now and then the gramophone sent a thread of music through the air. Something all of a sudden went tick… tick… amidst the trees – and stopped.

A grey dot hovered into Gregory's vision, but before the eye-fly could tickle his lashes he brushed it away.

"A nuisance, aren't they? Eye-flies."

"Is that what they're called?"

"Yes. Have you noticed anything? We have no mosquitoes up here."

"Yet you have mosquito-nets."

"That's for scorpions and centipedes – and tarantulas."

"A mosquito-net can keep out mosquitoes only."

"Is that a mysterious saying?"

He was silent.

"I think I know what you mean. You mean it can't keep out shadows."

"You're very understanding."

Out of the silence came a throbbing. It faded but returned, and after a moment developed into a regular beat. Gregory recognized it as the outboard engine of a motorboat. It lasted for several minutes, then died away as though enticed into some sleeping alcove in the depths of the jungle. The sound of a violin came from the house.

"That's Garvey. He's not too bad. Mother taught him. She can play."

"Do you play any instrument?"

"Only the harmonium. I want a piano badly. Daddy's been saving for years to buy one."

"And Mabel?"

"She plays the flute and the harmonium. Berton can play the flute, too. Do you play anything?"

"No. Brenda played the piano."

"Were you happy with her?"

"Only for the first few months. She was evil."

"What work did you do in England?"

"The theatre chiefly. I've produced one or two plays. And I painted and wrote."

"You're trembling. Don't talk about it."

He watched the trunk of the *cookerit* palm. Wary. Though he knew that the keyhole in the door behind them held far more danger.

"Everything I did she did – and did better. Always better." He was panting softly.

She rose, searched for and found a pebble, and shied it up into the dead fronds of the palm. A bat flew out and began to flit about the clearing like a torn-off piece of black skirt.

He stood up and smiled, and relief sank through him like heavy oil.

She came back and sat down on the steps, and he sat down again, too.

"It will find its way back before long. Let's watch it."

They watched the bat. It continued to flit about, lonely and blind in the sunshine. Abruptly it made a dart at the palm, and with a crisp rustle wriggled and vanished among the dead fronds. They heard it squeak, then it flew out again, and another one emerged with it. The two of them tilted and tumbled silently around the clearing, vanishing off and on past the angle of the church. Then one returned to the fronds, and a few seconds later, the other followed, and after rustlings and a squeak or two silence settled on the palm once more.

"Can war wound your spirit?"

"What?"

She repeated the question.

"Yes, it can. You mean… no. It wasn't war that wounded my spirit. It was she. Brenda did that."

She touched his knee and his hand stopped shaking.

They looked round them at the morning. The three palms that stood between the church and the house seemed, after a moment, to hold his attention. He might have been waiting for a bat to fly out of one of them. She told him that the two shortish ones with

117

sharp spindles jutting from their trunks were *awara* palms, and the tallish one a *cookerit*.

"The *awara* bears a fruit you can eat, too. It's not as nice as *cookerit*, and it makes your tongue bright yellow, and the pulp has hard strings that get between your teeth. It has a nice hard, black seed, though. We used to make tops with them when we were younger. Was your wife a lymphomaniac? Is that what broke up your marriage?"

"Nymphomaniac. No. I never had reason to believe that she was promiscuous in any way. But she was evil." He spoke without tension now, and she told herself that she had discovered the knack of putting him at ease.

"In what way was she evil?"

"She went out of her way to diminish my spirit. She was more talented than I, and she maliciously outshone me. In 1934 – the spring – I held a one-man show of my paintings – and in the autumn she put on a show, too – of some of her own works. She'd taken many of the subjects I had treated and done them better – supremely better. Deliberately to prove to me her superiority. If I produced a play she produced one similar – and made a more clever job of it, and invariably scored a big hit. Once I wrote a novel and had it published. It was well received by the critics, but it didn't sell. She wrote one, using the very theme – almost the very plot – and it wasn't only a tremendous *succès d'estime* but it went into three impressions within five weeks. Everything I did she went one better. Deliberately."

"You were separated, of course, when she did all this?"

"Yes. We separated eleven months after we were married." His hands kept clenching. "She watches me continuously – from a thousand unseen peepholes. She's with us now. Everywhere I go her eyes follow and surround me. She's still waiting to outdo me."

"But didn't you say she was dead?"

"Not she herself. She's imperishable. Only in sleep I'm safe from her vigilance. I'm perpetually in dread of the instant when she'll decide to manifest herself visually – and strike at me."

After a thoughtful silence, she asked: "Why did you go to the war in Spain?"

"Brenda was there. She was doing work as a war correspondent for a literary weekly. I went ostensibly as a correspondent myself – free lance. A French painter, a good friend of mine, accompanied me. Raoul Bijou. We were genuine sympathizers with the Government cause. But actually I went because I was after Brenda. I thought I might run into her. I had made up my mind to kill her. Kill her not only in body but in essence. I meant to get her alone somehow – kidnap her if possible and take her into the mountains, and – and humiliate her, and by a gradual process convince myself irrevocably that she was only human and not so much my superior as I thought. And then I'd kill her."

"And you didn't run into her?"

"No. She'd always just left any place I went to. Then I heard she'd gone back to England, so I went home, too. But when I got there I heard she'd gone to Barbados for a rest-cure; she'd done too much in Spain and was suffering from nervous exhaustion. So I followed her to Barbados, but when I got there I learnt that she had met with a drowning accident. They didn't find her body."

"Wasn't she a good swimmer?"

"Very. But it appeared that she bit off more than she could chew this time." He was smiling, his eyes a-glitter with triumph. He moistened his lips. Then she saw him grimace as though he wanted to cry. He put his hands to his face, and mumbled: "My mind. My mind. It isn't fair to tell you this. I seem to be cadging for your pity. My God. I'm not sane."

"Don't be an ass. Go on telling me about her. How did she drown?"

"A fisherman told me how it happened. It was at a place called Martin's Bay on the north coast. The villagers had warned her not to bathe at a certain point. A number of submerged rocks lie very near in to the shore, and there are sunken reefs about there, too. At one particular spot there's a sort of crevasse where the water is continually sucked down, forming a dangerous whirlpool. If you stand on the beach and look out you can see it. The water just at that spot looks bluer than the surrounding water, and you can see the swirl and foam. It's called the Well Pit. Even fishing boats have been known to be lost there, Finlay told me. But Brenda must have thought she could create a record by being the first human to swim across it and survive. One morning two fishermen saw her strike out for the Well Pit. They ran along the beach and called to her to come back, but she just waved at them and laughed. She was always an exhibitionist. She swam on right into the Well Pit, and was immediately sucked down – and she never came up. She hasn't been seen since."

Tick… tick…

He stood up.

She held his elbow and told him to sit down. "It's only a beetle. Its wings go tick, tick like that."

He sat down.

"If only they could have recovered her body."

"She must have been trapped in some submarine cave among the rocks."

"Yes."

"It must be lovely and purple-blue down there. I can see it. And a lot of green and red sea-weed must wave about."

He began to look stealthily around.

Tick… tick…

Far away surf seemed to hiss on a beach and slowly surge nearer…

"That's the wind in the jungle. It sounds like a shower of rain coming, doesn't it?"

"Yes. And sometimes like the sea. I saw the Well Pit."

"Do you drink whisky to – to sort of drown your unhappiness?"

"No. I'm trying to cure myself of delirium tremens."

"Delirium – I've read… That's what they call D.T.'s, eh?"

"Yes."

"But how are you going to cure yourself by drinking whisky?"

"I take it in gradually diminishing doses every day. I hope that by the time the stock I've brought is exhausted my craving for it will have ceased entirely."

"I see. Then you mean that half your nervous illness is due to D.T.'s?"

"Yes. And half to Brenda's perpetual vigilance. She watches and wishes I'd fail in my attempts to master my craving for drink. But I mean to foil her. I have the will to do it."

"I'm sure you have. Quite sure. I can see it behind your shadow."

"You can?"

"Yes. Behind your shadow you're a man. I sense it. I'm infruitive."

"Brenda imagined I had no will. She didn't think much of my character. But I'll do it. I'll master all my weaknesses."

"Is that why you've come to stay with us? To cure yourself of drink?"

"Yes. Of drink – and something else."

"Of what else?"

"The flesh."

She gave him a startled look. "But –"

"Yes?"

"Nothing. I – is that one of your weaknesses? The flesh?"

"One of my worst."

She was thoughtful, then asked: "You weren't faithful to Brenda?"

"No. The very night after our wedding I slept with another woman. I've been promiscuous from my adolescence."

"And you've come now to realize it doesn't pay?"

"Yes. Lust is clinker. It glows entrancingly when it is hot. It fascinates you. Then it cools and reveals itself as clinker."

"But clinker was once coal. Good coal." She patted his knee. "All right. Don't tremble. Let's go on talking. You think being with us here will have a good influence on you and help you to cure yourself?"

"Yes."

"Daddy isn't an ordinary goody-goody parson, you know."

"I've already begun to suspect so."

"I suppose you thought there'd be not so many temptations here?"

"Yes."

"Well, we haven't much whisky, but we have plenty of flesh."

"Yes."

"Are you rich?"

"I'm very well off. Brenda left me all her money, and there was a lot of it. Several thousands. And before that I was comfortably off."

"But how's that? You mean even though she persecuted you so much she still left you all her money?"

"Yes. I was surprised myself. They found a will among her things at the hotel in Bridgetown where she was staying. She bequeathed everything to me 'with all the deep love I've carried, and will forever carry, for him.' I've quoted her exact words."

"You really believe she was evil?"

He began to tremble and look about him in a panic. He was very white.

"Never mind. Look. There's a spider crawling on the trunk of the *awara* palm. The one over that way!"

The crisis dissolved within him.

They sat in silence for a while.

A black, shiny, tailless lizard darted swiftly past their feet and vanished into the tapering, red-veined leaves of some plants that grew wild at the side of the steps.

"We have plenty of those lizards here. They are friends – not enemies. You must never injure them."

He asked her the name of the plants, and she told him: "Dragon's blood."

"I rather like it. I was fond of wild plants and flowers as a boy."

"Do you think it's just your nerves that are bad? Couldn't it be that you're suffering from dementia peacocks?"

"Praecox. No. I thought it might be paranoia, as a matter of fact. But a psychiatrist told me not. Personally, I'm still doubtful, though."

"What's paranoia?"

"A mania that takes the form of delusions. Especially if you believe you're being persecuted by someone better than yourself."

Plep!

"What was that?"

"A berry. It dropped into the river." She touched his cheek and said quietly: "I believe you're mad, but I'm going to try to get you better. Do you trust me?"

"Yes."

"You don't think me silly and precocious?"

"No."

"If I try to help you you'll cooperate?"

"Yes."

122

"You won't try to stab me in the back with a stiletto when I'm not looking, and hide my body in a trunk?"

He smiled and tapped her wrist.

"I think I've got the hang of your little tricks."

"I'm convinced you have."

"I must go now. It's nearly recess time, and I've got to take some water and food for Logan. And I have to question him about various things."

"What things?"

"I won't be too long."

He watched her run off and disappear round the house. A dark speck circled slowly toward his eye. After he had brushed it off he sat and watched a large black ant that was crawling leisurely along the step on which his feet rested. It tried to climb on to his shoe, but before it could do so he shifted his foot and made to crush it, then spared it. It stopped, waggled its feelers, then ambled away toward the dragon's blood.

Tick... Tick...

He was looking toward the house now. Looking to the right. He heard a light step – on his left. He turned his head quickly but there was no one. He sat on waiting. Then Olivia appeared around the angle of the church and giggled. She came toward the steps and said: "I was spying on you. I wanted to hear if you were talking to yourself."

"Oh."

"I still love and pity you," she said – and went. At a sprint. And left him shudderingly at peace.

Tick...

Plep!

XII

After dinner, that evening, Olivia asked Gregory if he would like a game of chess, but, as on the evening before, he did not show any enthusiasm. He said he thought it would be better if he went to bed. Olivia did not insist, and after he had gone up she looked round the table at the others and said: "I think we've got to have a conference before we go to bed."

Berton stuck up his right thumb, a signal of agreement.

Mr. Harmston, who had just lit his after-dinner cigarette, the third and last for the day, nodded and said that she was right; a conference was necessary. "We'll give him a chance to get into bed," he added, "then we'll gather in the Big Room." The bedroom he and his wife occupied was referred to as the Big Room.

Mabel uttered a sound of disappointment. "I was hoping we could have held a concert this evening," she said, "and invited Robert and his sister."

"Yes, I was going to suggest that myself," said her mother. "Garvey is doing very well with the new Paganini study he's learning."

"Um. I was looking forward to hearing him, too," said Mr. Harmston, "but the conference must take precedent. We're up against a delicate situation. I realized it this morning."

"What sort of delicate situation?" asked Garvey.

His father raised his hand. "We'll discuss that upstairs, Garvey."

"You mean Greg –"

"Quiet, please!"

Garvey shrugged and shut up. He began to whistle softly.

Silence came upon them for a while. They listened to Gregory's steps upstairs in his room. From the kitchen came the clink of a pot or plate, and the occasional thump of Ellen's or Logan's bare feet on the floor. Some way off down-river a baboon roared gruffly, and after an interval another one answered. And once, for a brief moment when there was no sound either upstairs or in the

124

kitchen, they heard the river's secretive lapping. A drift of air, not quite a breeze, moved into the room through the southern windows and brought with it the dank smell of water mingled with the mouldy scent of the century-rotted leaves and twigs that carpeted the jungle: the scent of a myriad ancient deaths. In a second it was gone, and close upon it followed a strong and prolonged aroma of musky blossoms.

Berton was the first to speak. "I don't hear him anymore. He must be in bed now."

"Give him another five minutes," said his father, glancing at his watch.

When the five minutes had elapsed, he broke another long silence that came upon them and said: "We'll go up now." And they all rose.

The Big Room was big only in relation to the size of the other rooms; it was no more than twenty feet by twelve and with its four-poster, chest of drawers, dressing-table washstand, towel-horse, two tall bookcases, rocking-chair and two easy chairs it certainly gave no impression of spaciousness. On the other hand, it did not seem overcrowded, for the heavy furniture had been arranged so as to save every possible square-foot of floor space, and there were only two pictures on the walls: one a small watercolour depicting a young, striped tapir against a fallen palm and – in the farther background – dense trees; the other an oil, about eighteen inches by twelve in a grey frame, showing a bunch of bananas and two *sawari* nuts resting on a table. In a final survey, the Big Room succeeded in being both roomy and cosy.

Olivia liked its smell. She was certain that no other room in the world could have concocted a smell like it. It was a mixture of old clothes, books, vegetation and creosote (her father regularly painted the insides of the bookcases with creosote against insects, and her mother was intensely fond of wild ferns and flowers, a selection of which, fresh or wilted, could always be found in the two vases on the chest of drawers). Sometimes the creosote predominated, sometimes the old clothes and books – these two generally went together – and sometimes the ferns and flowers alone in all their perfumed rankness saturated the room.

Tonight, the flowers and wild ferns held full sway (the water in the vases was brownish with suspended vegetable matter in advanced decay); the paraffin lamp on the dressing-table was not enough to keep them down, smoky though it was inclined to be.

Berton wrinkled his nose and said: "Time you put some fresh bush in those vases, Mother."

His mother smiled and said: "Why didn't you gather some for me this afternoon after lessons. And don't you call my lovely flowers and ferns bush. They're not just bush."

"You can't very well say they're lovely now. They're in a state of decomposition."

"Out of that chair, you devil! You know I like the rocker."

"Only teasing you," he laughed, springing up and giving her a quick hug. "I'm taking the floor, as usual. You can't fall down from the floor."

"What a clever and original *bon mot!*" drawled Garvey.

"Very, very clever and original," nodded Berton. "Give me some applause." He clapped his hands.

"I've got the agenda made out already," said Olivia, seating herself on the floor beside Berton. "I did it since this afternoon."

Her father had taken one of the two easy chairs, and Mabel and Garvey, after a brief argument, had squashed themselves both into the other.

Olivia unfolded a sheet of exercise book paper. "Item One," she said, reading from it, "is 'Logan. Results of investigations and Interrogations'."

"I thought this conference had to do with Gregory," said Garvey. "How does Logan come into it?"

"If you shut up, Gorgon-face, you'll hear," snapped Olivia.

"Yes, we want to hear what Logan told you," said Mrs. Harmston, leaning forward in the rocking-chair, her face serious.

"Stop boring your elbow into my side, Garvey," Mabel complained.

"Well, if you keep shoving against me how can I help it!"

"Now, Garvey! Now!" frowned Mr. Harmston.

"Why don't you sit on the floor with your brother and sister, Garvey?"

"How could you expect the Grand Knob of Ramham-bonepore to lower himself like that, Mother!"

126

"I sat here first. Why can't Mabel sit on the floor?"

"You didn't sit here first," Mabel contradicted. "I was just going to sit down and you wriggled yourself quickly and slipped down past me."

"Nothing new in that. He's always been an expert wriggler."

"Now, Berton! Now!"

Olivia folded her arms with an air of elaborate patience and began to hum the Triumphal March from *Aida*.

"Wait, I hope you children realize," said Mrs. Harmston in a lowered voice, "that these wails are thin. If you speak so loudly you'll wake Gregory – if you haven't done so already."

"I bet anything he's at the keyhole listening," grinned Garvey.

"Enough foolery," frowned Mr. Harmston. "Let's hear you, Olivia."

"Well, I questioned Logan at recess time," said Olivia, "and he told me everything. The mystery is solved, He did it as a practical joke. He crept in through the front door when we were eating last night and went upstairs, and he took down Mabel's dressing-gown from behind the door and went and put it under Gregory's bed. And this morning he set up that racket under Gregory's window to fool us he'd really seen something during the night. It was simply another of his bawdy pranks."

"But what's all this about Mabel's dressing-gown?" asked Garvey. "I didn't hear about that."

"You couldn't," said Berton, "because when Mother made the discovery this morning after breakfast you'd already hopped off to the Reservation farm to help the Buck girls dig up cassava."

Mabel blushed and laughed, and Garvey snapped: "You're as bad a liar as Logan. After breakfast I went out to the steamer."

"And after that where did you vanish to?"

"Order, please! Order!" frowned their father.

"Any vital questions arising?" asked Olivia.

"Did he tell you whether he had any dreams, Olivia?"

"No, he said he didn't have any, Mother."

"I believe he's lying," said Berton. "Logan has dreams every night – and he sleepwalks and sleep-acts in them, too."

"No, I feel pretty sure he's telling the truth about last night, Berton," said Olivia. "I'd have known if he wasn't."

"I think he is," nodded Mr. Harmston. "A chaining up never fails to bring the truth out of him. Very well, Olivia. Get on with Item Two."

"Item Two," said Olivia, consulting her paper, "is 'Gregory. Results of morning investigations and cross-examinations. Results of afternoon observations and Recointering'."

Her mother gave a gurgle of mirth, and the reverend gentleman threw her a reproving glance. "Let's try to keep this serious, Joan."

"I am serious, Gerald. It's only the way she expresses herself!"

"'Recointering'. I must note it," sniggered Garvey. "New word coined by our Mrs. Malaprop."

"Tell the class what it should be, then, Mr. Clever," said Olivia.

Mr. Harmston smiled and asked them if they had forgotten their vows of discipline, then told Olivia to proceed.

Olivia described in detail her chat with Gregory on the church steps. They listened to her without interruption, their eyes (save their father's) getting wider with interest. At length, as though unable to restrain herself, Mrs. Harmston cut in with: "No! But he *must* be insane!" This broke the spell, and the others (except the reverend gentleman) piled in with comments and exclamations. Mabel wanted to know more about his wife; did he say if she was lovely: was she fair or dark? Mrs. Harmston asked about his mother; did he speak of her? Berton was interested in the Well Pit; how deep was it? Did he tell her? Did he see any octopuses among the rocks at Martin's Bay? "But where," Garvey asked, "does he keep this stock of whisky he's brought for his D.T.'s?"

"In his expanding suitcase," Mr. Harmston unexpectedly answered – and all eyes turned on him. He sat cross-legged and quietly amused, watching them with an air of paternal affection.

"Have you been searching through his things, Gerald?"

Mr. Harmston shook his head. He told them of the chat he had had with Gregory before breakfast. "I guessed it must have been whisky or gin when he said he had eight bottles and part of a bottle."

"But this is terrible!" said Mrs. Harmston. "If I'd had any idea he was addicted to alcohol I'd never have agreed to have him here."

"Oh, Mother! What an unliberal thing to say!" Mabel reproved.

"'Illiberal'," said Garvey. "No such word as 'unliberal'."

"I prefer 'unliberal'," said Mabel.

"But it's not in the dictionary –"

"Discipline, please! Yes, Joan, I'm inclined to agree with Mabel. If he's addicted to alcohol, all the more reason why we should want to have him here. He's in need of our ministrations."

"And we're in need of his money," said Garvey.

"Now, Garvey! Now!"

"Isn't it the truth?" Garvey persisted. "If he's rich why shouldn't he give us a helping hand? Look at the things we want in this place. The Delco electric plant we've always been talking about, and some paint for the house. And an outboard motor boat."

"And the piano," said Olivia. "Yes, I agree with Garvey, Daddy. He can make life much pleasanter for us up here with his money. And after all, he'll be benefiting, too, for he'll be living with us."

Mrs. Harmston said: "Yes, that's true. I don't see why he shouldn't help us along. Edith was well provided for when Garvey died, and after her death all her property must have gone to him as the only child. You did say Edith was dead, didn't you, Gerald?"

"Yes, so he told me when we were chatting near the arbour this morning. Cancer of the stomach."

"Pretty awful," said Berton, grimacing. "I was reading about it the day before yesterday. I wonder if there was any metastasis."

"Discipline, please, Berton!"

"His wife must have been very rich, too," said Olivia, "if she was a writer and a painter and a play-producer. And she left him all her money."

"Personally, I'd say we're in clover," said Garvey. "We've just got to stroke him the right way, and the next thing we know he'll be shedding bank-notes like feathers."

His father shook his head slowly and grunted. "Don't you think it would be a great pity," he said, "if after all the sermons I've hammered into you about the evils of money you begin to develop a hankering after this young man's wealth?"

His wife flushed. "Don't be absurd, Gerald! Who said anything about hankering after his wealth! We're only trying to face the matter in a spirit of common sense. And as Olivia rightly puts it, he'll be sharing in the benefits as much as ourselves."

"I see your point, my dear, but I simply mention what I do because I want to prevent you from indulging in over-dazzling visions of ease and splendour. Always remember: we have vowed to live the lives of Spartans. We're not ascetics; no one can accuse the Brethren of Christ the Man of severe restraints or rigorous self-denial, but there must be discipline – both of conduct and as to the extent of our comforts. Nothing can damage the soul more than the contemplation of money within easy grasp. Half the happiness we've achieved in this wilderness – and we have been happy – is due to our not having had enough money to enjoy all the amenities of civilization. Discipline and austerity sharpen the pleasure of small comforts. We wanted a modern toilet, and after years of saving we eventually were able to lay down a septic tank and have the bowl and fittings installed. We weren't unreasonable in desiring such a convenience. Nor can electric light or a piano or a motorboat be looked upon as an excessive comfort. We're saving for the piano and the Delco lighting plant, and in two or three years' time we'll get these things – and we'll appreciate them all the more for having had to wait for them. But if they drop into our laps like manna from heaven you'll find we'd value them less – and worse still, we'd yearn for more and still more. Whenever a man reaches that state when he wants more and more his soul has begun to disintegrate. Decadence has set in. And you can't say I haven't impressed upon you the ideal I aim at in my work in this jungle: the ideal that every missionary of the Brethren of Christ the Man strives after. Civilization without cynicism."

He spoke calmly and in an even tone, nothing preachy in his manner, and when he stopped a silence came upon them. They had a rebuked air.

After a while, Mabel mumbled: "Daddy's quite right. And in any case, I think it would be disgusting to try to make capital out of the poor fellow just because he's not too right in his head."

"Nobody suggested trying to make capital out of him," grumbled Olivia. She gave a significant grunt and added: "And if you imagine he's loony you're making a serious mistake."

"What do you mean?" said Garvey.

"What I say."

"But didn't you tell us he talked about eyes watching him? That his dead wife follows him everywhere and spies on him? Isn't that insanity?"

She gave a sly smile. "It sounds so, I know, but you take it from me, he's far saner than you think. What he's suffering from is – well, I've diagnosed it as a mixture of D.T.'s and – and a tame kind of madness that isn't really madness."

"What on earth are you trying to say?"

Mr. Harmston regarded her seriously and asked her to explain herself.

"I mean he's mad but not mad in a clin – in a clin –"

"In a clinical sense, I suppose you mean," said Garvey.

"Yes. That's the word. I've been observing his behaviour and taking note of various things he says, and I'm sure I know what's wrong. There's a word for it, but I won't bother to mention it."

"Why?"

"Well, for one thing, it has an indecent sound."

"Oh, stop pretending you're so modest and spout it out," said Garvey.

She pinkened a trifle, looked up at the rafters and said: "I believe he's a mild case of shittsophrenia."

Garvey pressed his hands to his stomach and leant forward, attacked with such sudden laughter that when Mabel, seeing her opportunity, gave him a push he went toppling out of the chair. He did not mind, however, but lay doubled up on the floor shaking and gasping. He infected the others, and Olivia herself had to join in.

"I think it has a 'z' in it somewhere," she smiled, "but that's how it's pronounced. I looked it up once in the medical dictionary. It means dual personality or split mind – and that's what Gregory is. He's two people. One of him is a kind of shadow; that's the him we know now. He's hiding the solid him from us, but I feel before long I'm going to find out what he's really like behind the shadow him – and then I'll know exactly how to go about curing him."

"I've already promised him to do my best to effect a cure," said her father.

"What are you going to cure him of? His nerves?"

"Yes. And of his dipsomania."

"He's not a simple case. You saw how he fainted? You think it was a real faint? He didn't fool me. He didn't faint one bit."

"How do you know?"

"That's my secret."

Berton wagged his right thumb before his nose, and Olivia responded with the same sign. It meant that she would tell him all about it later on in one of their Cavern conferences.

Mr. Harmston smiled and said: "We won't ask you to divulge your professional secrets." He sat forward and went on: "I think we've strayed a bit, though. Let's get back to where we were. Tell us about your observations and reconnoitring activities during the afternoon."

"Yes, that's right," said Olivia. She straightened up and assumed an air of ceremony. "I kept an eye on him as per your suggestion. Garvey, what's the matter?"

Garvey was spluttering.

"Now, Garvey! Now!"

"I kept an eye on him as per – as you suggested. As soon as we'd finished lunch he began to moon about the compound. He examined the wild plants near the edge of the bank, and he looked at the church for a long time as if he was planning an act of incen— as if he was trying to think up the best way to burn it down. But he didn't talk to himself as I thought he was going to do. I was a little disappointed. Then when you set Logan free at around half-past two he was looking on, and he smiled. He wasn't in the compound anymore now. He'd gone upstairs, and I perceived him at the window of the bathroom. He was watching from there as you and Logan came from round the back of the shed. At three o'clock I came upstairs to him and found him still in the bathroom looking out. I think he was watching Mabel teach the children their drawing. I entered the bathroom, and he turned and smiled at me, and I told him I had a moment to spare and if he liked I could take him to see over the Reservation, but he said no, he just wanted to be quiet for the rest of the day. I said: 'You're

132

sure? Well, what about the ruins and the tombs? I could take you to see those,' but he said: 'Tomorrow, perhaps. I want to get my bearings in the house and in the clearing first before I venture elsewhere.' So I came down and did my daily hour of reading in the dining-room. Garvey and Berton were doing their hours, too, and after a time we heard him come downstairs. He went out through the front door. Berton and I thereupon left off our reading for a minute and went – Garvey, if you don't stop behaving like a spitting cat I'll shut up!"

Mrs. Harmston gave a muffled gurgle.

"Now, Garvey! Now, Joan!"

Garvey and his mother disciplined themselves, and Olivia continued.

"Berton and I left off our reading and went to the window, and we saw him going toward the landing-place. Berton thought he might be contemplating suicide, and he said: 'Better let's go after him,' but I retorted: 'No, let's watch him from here. I don't think he wants to do anything like that.' So we watched him from the dining-room window, and we saw him go and sit down near the logs, and he began to stare at the water as if he wanted to go into a trance. Then suddenly he turned his head and he looked back as if he was listening to you hammering and sawing and doing your carpentry work in the workshed, Daddy. I alone was watching him when he did this, because Berton had gone back to his reading. He was reading about gallstones in one of the medical books, and you know how he likes medical subjects. He couldn't resist going back to devour the book. I don't say this to reflect any blame upon him. I only note it in passing.

"Anyway, I was wrong in my conclusions. Gregory wasn't listening to you doing your carpentry work. What he was really doing was looking at Ellen. Ellen was in the kitchen. I knew it was she he was looking at because after a minute I saw him give a smile, and he waved his hand. And I heard Ellen give a little laugh in the kitchen – her sex-heat laugh. Then after a while, he got up and came up to the kitchen. I hid so that he couldn't see me, and he walked up the kitchen stairs. The next minute I heard him talking with Ellen quietly in the kitchen. I couldn't hear what they were saying because they were talking softly, and I couldn't risk going into the pantry because the boards go bup-bup, dum-dum when you walk on them, and that would have given away my presence. Anyway, after a few minutes he came into the dining-room, and he smiled at us, and I asked him how he was enjoying himself, and he replied: 'Admirably. I was talking to Ellen.' And I said: 'Be careful with her. She's fleshy. She might tempt you.' And he said: 'Yes. She's been doing that.' And I asked: 'You didn't yield, though?' And he gave his head a shake and said: 'No, but I could have.' And I asked him: 'What stopped you from yielding?' And he smiled and said: 'Brenda. I had to defy her and prove I'm strong.' Then Garvey asked him if he'd like to have a game of chess, and he said yes, certainly. So Garvey told him he was just finishing off his reading and he would call him in twenty minutes. Gregory said: 'Very well. I'll be in my room. What are you reading, by the way?' And Garvey said: '*Time Magazine.* We go halves with Mr. Buckmaster and subscribe to it. We don't get newspapers here, you see, so we have to read *Time* to keep in touch with the outside world. It's part of our general education.' He gave Garvey a stare as if Garvey was a freak, and then he smiled and said: 'I'm interested,' and went upstairs. And later on, as soon as Garvey had finished his hour of reading, he went up and called him and he came down and played two games. He played one with Garvey and one with Berton. He beat Garvey, but Berton beat him. He's a good player. Berton only beat him because he managed to take that knight when –"

"I think that will do, my girl," interrupted her father. "An excellent report. I think we have enough to go on now to be in a position to formulate our plan of action for the immediate future. It seems clear that if he's insane his insanity isn't of the dangerous type. I mean, he doesn't appear to have any homicidal tendencies."

"How can you say that, Gerald? Didn't Olivia give as her opinion that he might be a schizophrenic? Most homicidal maniacs are schizophrenics, if I've read aright."

The reverend gentleman nodded. "Yes, there's always that possibility, of course, but personally I don't believe he's suffering from any acute form of schizophrenia. The sanest of us often possess schizophrenic traits. Myself, for example, as you ought to know. No, we'll run the risk of regarding him as a tame lunatic who needs our care."

"If we succeed in curing him don't you think he'll do splendidly as a husband for Mabel, Daddy?"

Mr. Harmston tilted his head and said: "Oh, yes, it's an idea. Just as well an English as an Indian husband, Mabel my girl."

"No English wife for me," said Berton. "I'm marrying an Indian."

Mr. Harmston rose. "Time for bed, I think."

"But we haven't discussed our plan of action yet!" said Olivia.

"I know." Her father spoke quietly and glanced toward one of the three windows – the one that faced west. "But it's time for bed."

"You mean... Did you...?"

"You saw something, Daddy?"

He nodded.

They looked at him expectantly. Mrs. Harmston had paled.

"Mynheer?" asked Olivia.

"Mynheer," he said, his voice low.

They continued to look at him.

"At the window," he told them, after a silence. "Over there."

A drift of air, leaf-chilly and aromatic, entered the room, settling about them as though heavy with the residue of once-enacted dramas.

"Yes, we'd better turn in, then," Olivia mumbled.

"Wait. Listen!" said Berton in a whisper.

They stood still.

"Is it downstairs?"

"No. In the corridor."

XIII

Under the canopy of tangled foliage the dusk was warm and dense with vegetable vapours, and Gregory's tennis shoes sank deep into the white sand. Little cracklings at long intervals failed to frighten him, for he knew that it was only the tailless, black lizards wriggling quickly on the sand from one twig or dry leaf to another. The humid, palpable air did not oppress him, nor create in him – as it should have done – a feeling of terrifying solitude. On the contrary, it seemed to weave continually about him, out of its moist miasma of decay, a protective web so that he could view himself as the life within a cocoon, secure from billed foes.

After a few minutes, the sand on the track gave place to a spongy mat of damp leaf-mould. He came upon a fallen palm, and stopped to examine its rotting trunk and fronds. Cotton-white spider-webs were wrapped like winding-sheets around many of the fronds, and in the catacombal-dark spaces between leaf and web he could sense the stir, as though it were an aerial tremor, of the hairy monsters that dwelled within. He could imagine the sparkle of star-dust gazes that must be focused on him, alert for any act of aggression on his part.

Yet he was not afraid. This morning he felt more confidence in himself. It was Saturday, and he had had two days and three nights in which to inure himself to the stress of his new life. The sound of the river and the noises of insects and lizards no longer caused him to stiffen and tilt his head. And save for Olivia, he had got the measure of the household. He liked them all, including Logan and Ellen, for he could detect no evil in them. They were passionate but not poisonous. He felt at ease among them; they refreshed him. The reverend gentleman's strong stolidity and his subtle airs of mystery amused and intrigued him. For his aunt and Mabel he felt a quiet affection, as though they were two ponies he had acquired as pets. Berton appealed to him as a rare porcelain vase; there was something fine and fragile about him, and often he emitted fascinating lights. Garvey seemed a sulky demon, but he was capable of a yapping sarcasm; Gregory sometimes saw Garvey in his fancy as an aloof dog of high pedigree. Logan was a frog whose clumsy antics and croakings could be most entertaining. Ellen, grotesque but dynamic, writhed with healthy hates and lusts; she excited him, and her grotesquery only added zest to the victories he had already begun to score over her fleshly temptations.

Olivia…

As he moved on along the track, he found that he wanted to shudder in wavering ecstasy at the thought of Olivia. What could she be? Shadow or memory-mirage? Friend or ghoul in the offing gloom? She comforted him, steadied him – and upset him in her he seemed to sense security and peace – or infinite catastrophe. She was the brink. The blue valley in the morning. Lupins and ragwort. And the muffled cough when the heart falters.

Olivia…

He was skirting some plants with long, tapering, razor-sharp leaves. Each leaf jutted straight from the ground, four or five feet high, and might have been the tongue of a wicked dragon buried beneath the damp leaf-mould. In the centre of each cluster a spider had woven its web, and out of the dark tunnelled opening two blue-black legs protruded.

Olivia…

Lizards, she had said, were friends – not enemies. And spiders, were they friends, too?

Something crackled. Not a lizard.

He halted and assumed a listening air.

Not an insect shrilled, but in some coffined vacuum the dusk seemed to distil a swaying whine that touched the hearing off and on: a noiseless noise that was close partner to the silence. A silence so real that once he was certain he could sense it wreathe up into his nostrils like the ceremonial incense of entombed blossoms, and at any instant he expected to start round at the cool tolling of a bell and see a beam of sunshine make a hatpin hole in the foliage above and settle a red coin of mystery on the spot where a queen of orchids fell, some centuries of midnights gone.

"Indeed, indeed…"

A female voice, it came as though out of a submarine cave. It was lovely and purple-blue down there…

"Indeed, indeed, repentance oft before
"I swore…"

Out of the swirling foam. Bluer than the surrounding blue…

She appeared from around one of the sharp-leafed clumps. Smiled at him and said: "You ought to have answered: *But was I sober when I swore?* Don't you know your *Omar?*"

He said nothing, half in and out of himself.

"Did you think I was Brenda?"

He nodded.

"I saw you slip away after breakfast and go off on your own, so I followed you, but I took a shorter track. If you'd looked around you carefully when you reached the fallen palm you'd have seen that another track branches off to the right. This one you're following is a longer one."

She turned and smiled around and took a deep breath. "Lovely jungle, isn't it? So silent and mouldy. I don't want to be anywhere else. You can taste the silence if you have a nose to smell. To smell is to taste."

"And to taste is to be entangled."

"Yes, it's not easy to escape from this jungle."

"Would you want me to escape?"

She smiled: "Daddy has taught us many little secrets. One of them is never commit yourself finally on anything that's vital."

He began to tremble.

"Look," she said, "do you know what these are? They're wild pines. They can slice you like a knife if you're not careful."

"I was wondering what they were," he said, feeling better.

"My friends live in them, have you noticed?"

"The ubiquitous arachnida," he murmured.

"Are you swearing at me in Arabic? Look." She pulled up her skirt and showed him a pink birthmark high on her thigh. "This is the Scar of the Hissing *Kanaima.* When I was four years old a *kanaima* bit me."

"What's a *kanaima?*"

"It's a who. He's a terrible Indian man who stalks through the jungle looking for people to attack. Before he attacks he gives a long hissing whistle, and when he gets you he sticks a poison-arrow into your throat and sucks your blood. Luckily he only managed to nip me here. Daddy rescued me before he could stick the poisoned arrow into my throat."

"Who is the author of the *kanaima* legend? Your father?"

She gave him a long stare, suddenly tense. Then, recovering, she said quietly: "No, it's an Indian legend. This is the first big shock you've given me."

"I know. Shall we go on to the ruins?"

"Yes. Come." She held his hand. "We'll take this track as we're on it already, but on our way back we can go by the shorter one."

"You're determined to be my guide, it seems."

"Only until you stop being your shadow."

"Do you think there is any hope for me?"

"I'd know that if you could tell me something."

"What's that?"

"Did you murder Brenda?"

He was staring at a clump of palms they were passing on their right. Palms with small, fine-leafed fronds and that bore bunches of purplish berries the size of a walnut. They cast a great gloom, and one or two had pushed their plumes above the tangle of foliage overhead.

"What palms are those?" he asked.

"*Ada* palms. The core of the wood is very good for stropping razors. Was it a razor you used to cut her throat? Or did you just shoot her and throw her body into the Well Pit so that it could never be found?"

"There's a word I must remember to tell you about."

She gave him a keen look and shook her head in a puzzled way. "You're getting more shadowy. What word is that?"

"The pronunciation of it. Later on I'll tell you. Here are the ruins."

Immediately ahead of them the track opened into a small clearing in which crumbling brick walls, creeper-grown and mossy – walls of what must once have been a smallish house – loomed against the background of jungle. The sky could now be seen, but in patches only, for the foliage-roof, though thinner, still persisted. Tall palms grew singly within the clearing, their fronds linked together by rope-like vines. A pale, greenish-brown twilight pervaded the scene, as though the moss and creepers that covered the broken walls exuded a dim radiance of their own. Rusty-red sand showed between the twigs and dry leaves that thinly carpeted the ground so that a lake of blood, thought Gregory, might have subsided and left behind its ruddy hue. The silence had an ethereal, intelligent quality. There was no vacuum here, but a vibrant, replete livingness: a world of voices on the verge of sound, a shadow-crowd shifty just beyond the edge of vision. Death and life seemed to whirl with equal strength in the elusive aromas that continually smote the senses.

"Are you afraid?"

He shook his head. But his manner was alert and listening.

All about them was a whispering. Or a breathing. It might be insects invisibly on the move in the undergrowth, and it might be…

He saw stone steps, and what looked like a large copper basin, green with mould, half-buried. A length of rusted chain protruded from under a clump of ferns; the links seemed as though they would crumble to dust at the touch of a finger. To the left of him, not many yards away, a purple-green slab lay at a slant, partly buried. He had a glimpse of a skull and crossbones and words… *Hier leyt begraven*… Leaves and moss… *1764*…

"All the tombs around here," she said, "have skulls and crossbones engraved on them."

They stood for a while longer, looking about them silently.

In Gregory the sensation increased that they were not alone.

"Come," said Olivia, and led him round to where a barred window was visible amid dense festoons of creepers. "Down in there," she told him, "is a cellar, and if you went in you'd find bones. Human bones. It's down there Daddy found the manacles that he uses for Logan."

"Not the chain, too?"

She hesitated, and gave him a suspicious look, but his face was emotionless. "Yes, the chain, too," she said. She suddenly smiled as though something had brushed her sense of humour. "So Daddy told us."

"I've had one or two enlightening chats with your father during the past few days. A remarkable man."

"Yes, remarkable. He's my hero – and I'll kill you if you try to destroy my faith in him. Do you hear me?"

"Is it known who lived here?"

"A Dutch family called Schoonlust. Mr. Buckmaster is one of their descendants. He knows a lot about the history of Berbice and the old Dutch families. It's his hobby. The Schoonlusts were all murdered by the slaves in 1763, except two children, a boy and a girl named Hendrik and Joanna. Joanna was Mr. Buckmaster's great-great-grandmother. The old Berkelhoost plantation belonged to the Schoonlusts. Are you paying attention to me?"

"Yes."

"Mevrouw Adriana Schoonlust was a very lovely woman, and her sister Luise was living with her in 1763 when the slaves revolted. Luise was lovely, too. She was seventeen. The slaves raped them both, and kept them prisoners in the cellar down there. But – please listen to me carefully – Luise didn't mind being raped. She liked it. Mevrouw resisted – she didn't like it at all – and as soon as the slaves had got tired of her they killed her. But they spared Luise, and one of the leaders took her as his mistress – and she liked being his mistress. She told him she had seen him in a dream long before the insurrection began. She gave him silver buckles for his shoes, and kept house for him and the rebels, and she wrote letters for him to another rebel leader farther up the river. He was the big leader, and his name was Cuffy. He couldn't read or write, either, and he had to get white prisoners to do his secretarial work for him, too.

"When Governor van Hoogenheim and the soldiers that came from St. Eustatius in the West Indies launched an attack on Berkelhoost the slave-leader cut off Luise's head rather than have her captured. He used a sabre. Mr. Buckmaster has it still. It hangs on his sitting-room wall. The bones of Luise and Mevrouw Schoonlust are down there now in the cellar, and you might think I'm talking nonsense but the ghost of Luise is standing behind you now, smiling at you. No, please don't look round," she murmured. "Stand still and keep on looking at the cellar window as if nothing were the matter. Yes, that's right. I must say, you have presence of mind. The reason why I don't want you to look round is because Luise hasn't got on a stitch and it would make me jealous if you saw her. She's terribly tempting. A real knock-out all round – face, fanny and figure. I feel certain you're going to dream about her tonight – and the Lord help you if you sleepwalk and sleep-act. Yield to her and your soul is lost forever. You hear me talking in this quiet voice? It's because I'm a little frightened. I can't stand female ghosts. It's a good thing she can't see or hear me. She's blind and deaf to women in the real world; that's because she died wanting men so badly. You should see the indecent gestures she's making to try to attract your attention. A filthy creature! I believe Dorothea Buckmaster has inherited some of her lewdness, though Daddy says it's only the local influences that make Dorothea so hot. Did you know," she whispered, still watching Luise, "that Daddy has a crush on Susan Buckmaster? He dreams about her, and we're all afraid that one night he'll sleepwalk and take a trip in the *corial* to the Buckmasters' place and try to get into bed with Susan – all in his sleep, of course, so he won't be to blame. It's only his strength of character that has saved him so far. But, in Berkelhoost, the Flesh is powerful, and the Devil lurks in the shadow of every twig. Are you paying attention to me?"

"Yes."

"Years and years ago – before I was born – Daddy had a dream about a pretty Buck girl on the Reservation, and nine months later Osbert was born. Mother nearly left him it upset her so much, but he managed to persuade her that he was blameless; it was the local influences that had caught him napping. I don't mean that as a pun. It's all right for you to look round now. Luise has just vanished. By the way, you mightn't have noticed, but you're standing on a stone slab. It's the tomb of a Mynheer Ruijsdael. If you scrape away the dry leaves you'll see his name and the skull and crossbones, and the dates. He died in 1734, and Mr. Buckmaster thinks he might have been the owner of Berkelhoost before the Schoonlusts came on the scene. Mynheer Ruijsdael haunts the whole neighbourhood. He's very fond of our house."

"Is it he who brought your conference to an abrupt end the other night?"

She gave him a stare. "Did Daddy tell you?"

"No."

"Then how did you know?"

"The pronunciation of that word is skizzofrennic. You don't pronounce the 'sch' and the 'z' as in German."

"So that's it, eh?"

"Yes. I happened to dream I was listening outside the door of your parents' room. A most entertaining dream."

"I see. Which means that that sound we heard in the corridor…"

"Was me going back into my room," he nodded. "All in a dream, so I'm entirely without blame. Shall we go now?"

A bitterness against him simmered in her. All of a sudden he did not seem a friend anymore. He had stepped out of his shadow and revealed for an instant the real him, and it was a detestable him. An eavesdropping him.

"I don't know whether to hate you or what," she said.

"Yes."

A feeling of despair came upon her. She said: "You want to end it all for me? Strangle me and throw my body into the cellar there. I can show you how to find the trap-door. It's just under those swizzle-stick trees over there."

He smiled, but she noticed that his fingers moved slowly like rain-chilled worms coming to life before a wood-fire, each worm with a purpose of its own. But she was not afraid – only full of despair as at something about to dissolve; something precious in the process of being shown up for a fraud. And she felt anxious, too. In her fancy she saw his teeth in a flour-white fence of laughter ranged above Mabel as he pressed the wind out of her body. Would he count the freckles on her chest and belly? Or would he spread her long tresses out on the pillow and weep into them?

"Why are they called swizzle-stick trees?"

"Come and I'll show you."

He followed her round some clumps of shrubs and ferns into a sort of cavern formed by vines that linked the trunks of three young palms. They had to bend low, and amidst the vines he heard the tick and click of insects. For an instant he paused, rigid and humped forward, his face upturned with fear. But he saw that it was only large black ants crawling in lines along the vines. He moved on after her, picking his way cautiously because the ground was slippery with loose, moss-covered bricks. In a moment they had emerged among more ferns and shrubs, and after a few paces to the right – over more mossy bricks – came to the copse of trees she had pointed out when they were standing near the cellar-window. They were not tall trees – the highest was about seven feet – and their trunks were straight, slim and bare, with branches that shot out horizontally near the top. They were overgrown shrubs rather than trees.

"See," she said, "each branch has only three off-shoots. If you're very lucky you'll find one with four. Well, you cut the branch off about a foot long, and then you trim the off-shoots so as to form three prongs jutting out at the end, and after you pare off the bark and smooth down the little knots nicely you have a swizzle-stick. You use it for swizzling up milk and eggs into a coag or making a rum-swizzle. Now," she murmured, "is your chance. Look over there! See the trap-door? It isn't quite closed. There's a brick keeping it ajar, and you can pull it up by the iron ring in it. You can't see the ring now because it's covered with leaves and moss."

She came close to him.

"You can do it now. Choke me as you choked Brenda. And drop my body through the trap-door. It's mossy and slushy in the cellar, and I'll rot quickly because this is a hot climate – and hardly anyone comes this way in weeks, so they won't smell me out. Only the crows will do that. Vultures. We call them carrion-crows here. They have pink heads. They'll find their way down into the cellar and eat me up in less than two days, and my bones will lie side by side with Luise's and her sister's – and I'll be a legend. I'll haunt the whole jungle. Don't you want to kill me?"

He stood very still and peered past her through the dusk of the swizzle-stick trees at the dark opening in the ground – a mouth mysteriously ensconced between mossy bricks and damp twigs and leaves. He could hear a sizzle as though some beetle were working a windmill of hard wings in the dank blackness down below.

"I'll try to struggle, but you'll be too strong for me, especially as you're a madman. Does that hurt you? If it does I'm glad. I mean it to. You'll see my tongue lolling out, and I'll be clammy and dead – like poor Brenda. Go on. Do it. You mightn't get the chance again. I'm a spiteful person. I can spite even myself if I think it would spite you as you deserve, you eavesdropping murderer of a loving wife."

He smiled. "Let's go."

"Are you entertained?"

"Highly."

She stared at him keenly, then said: "All right. Let's go."

When they were passing the cellar-window she asked: "What was it you and Daddy have been talking about in your chats with him?"

"About life and religion chiefly."

"Are you coming to church tomorrow?"

"Yes."

"Do you believe in Christ the Man?"

"Yes."

"But not in Christ the Son of God?"

"No."

She stopped. "I'm still not sure about you. Do you think you've begun to understand about us up here? Did Daddy explain anything definite?"

"Listen. The wind."

"Yes. Like rain, only it isn't rain."

"Like Martin's Bay, at a distance."

"Poor Brenda. Poor thing."

"All day and all night without cessation the waves snarl in Martin's Bay."

"She wasn't evil. I believe you lied to me. Admit it."

"You're crying," he said.

She took his hand, and they went on.

XIV

At the bottom of the Ibi Creek it was maroon-dark, and dim, deathly plants uncoiled tongues to lick at you as you squirmed by looking for the Green Bottle in which the Genie lived. Fiery fish-eyes hovered, and faded like lamps snuffed out, and a monster with aardvark ears gave a snouty grin from its cave, wanting to be friendly, so you stopped to ask it if it knew anything about the Green Bottle, only to see it squiggle back down into the venom-ous gloom of its home, no more a friend but an enemy poised to pounce. You wriggled on, and presently a bottle blinked amber on the bed of the creek, but when you plunged slowly toward it it melted into the ruddy haze, and the grisly plants quaked with a serene, slithery laughter… "Rare rum," a mauve snail mur-mured behind your ear. "Only rare rum."

On her way to the surface, the bubbles rolled in rings around her, each sounding a note of its own, and the dark grew lighter red. The water whirled and drummed, but the bubbles still plonged an alarm… The aardvark was coming after her, its snout sucking close on her heel, tasting in anticipation the sago-softness of her Achilles tendon, and the bubbles and bells bong-banged in warning, so loud now that they woke her.

She sat up and found that Mabel was awake, too.

"What's happening?" asked Mabel. "Who's ringing the bell?"

The grey light of the Sunday dawn struck through the mos-quito-net upon them, and Olivia, now fully awake, untucked the net and got out of bed. She went to the window and looked toward the belfry.

A short figure with wild, trailing black hair kept bending in two and bobbing up as it tugged at the bell-rope.

"It's Ellen. She must be out of her mind."

Mabel joined her at the window.

Footsteps thumped in the corridor, and their parents, bare-footed and in night-clothes, came in.

"Who is it, children?" asked Mrs. Harmston. "Who's that ringing the bell?"

"Ellen. She's either mad or she's had a terrible dream. Yes, it must have been a dream. She looks as if she's still in her nightgown."

"Um. Olivia, you'd better run down and deal with her, my girl. She'll have all our people from the Reservation swarming along here in a minute. They'll think it's a fire."

Olivia was off. In the gallery she saw Logan on his mattress, and heard him grumbling sleepily. She encountered Berton and Garvey in pyjamas at the front door on the point of going out. "I believe it's a gnome," said Berton excitedly. "Remember Daddy used to tell us of gnomes that rang church-bells 'in the dark thunder-hours of the morn'?"

"It's no gnome," said Olivia. "It's that hateful creature Ellen. Come on. Let's go and spank her bottom as she deserves. This is the chance I've been waiting for for months."

"Oh, good," chortled Berton, and the three of them went hurtling out of the front door and down the steps, their bare feet thrumming deeply on the wooden treaders like the reverberant echo of jumbie-guitars.

Olivia was an easy first. She arrived at the belfry with such speed that she barely prevented herself from colliding with the still bowing, bobbing Ellen. Ellen uttered low bumblebee moanings as she tugged at the bell-rope; she might have been in a trance after eating honeycomb and the drippings of blue fungus. Olivia caught her by her hair and tried to drag her away from the rope, but Ellen kept her grip on the rope. Berton came to the rescue and wrested the rope out of her hands. And all at once Ellen's moanings merged into a sigh of ecstasy as she reached out and snaked her arms around Berton's body.

Garvey gave a gulp and began to bite his lower lip, in a shiver of jealous heat-hunger.

Olivia slapped Ellen on her bottom, but Ellen seemed not to mind; she kept on clasping Berton tight and sighing. Berton struggled to free himself; but in vain, and Olivia told him to bite Ellen's ear.

"I can't," gasped Berton. "Her hair keeps getting in the way."

He and Ellen collapsed, Ellen behaving like a boa-constrictor with Berton her victim. But Garvey now took a hand in the fray, seating himself on Ellen's rump when Ellen's rump, for a brief second, happened to be just in the right position to be sat on. Ellen, pinioned down unexpectedly, was compelled to slacken her hold on Berton, and Berton squirmed free and got up.

"That's right. Sit on her, Garvey," he panted. "I'll go and get the whip."

Before he could run off, however, his father, who had hauled on an old pair of khaki trousers, came hurrying up. "What's the meaning of this fantastic behaviour, Ellen?" he demanded. "Get up from there at once, Garvey!"

"I was just going for the whip, Daddy," said Berton.

"Then change your mind," said his father.

Garvey rose – with evident reluctance – from Ellen's rump, and Ellen sat up, her hair in a tangle about her cotton nightgown.

"Parson, me too frighten," she said. "Ow, parson!"

"What frightened you?"

"Murder happen, parson. Me wake up sudden from me night-sleep and me so frighten me jump out me hammock and run out de kitchen and come ring de bell. Murder happen."

"Where has it happened?"

"On de kitchen steps, parson."

"She's been having filthy dreams, that's what it is," said Olivia.

Logan, red-eyed with sleep, in a yellow nightshirt badly frayed at the hem – it was an old petticoat of Mrs. Harmston's converted into a nightshirt – came ambling on the scene. "Man can't get lil' sleep even on a Sunday marning," he grumbled. "Nasty Buck girl waking up everybody like dis wid 'er wicked-ness. Oh, gawd!"

"Now, Logan! Now! No abuse, please. Proceed and tell us what happened, Ellen. I'm waiting."

But Ellen, sitting on the ground, arms hugged around her drawn up legs, had switched her attention to Berton. She smiled and said to him: "Come sit near me here, quiet me down."

Berton sniffed and said: "Didn't you hear the parson speak to you? Tell us how the murder happened."

"Yes, go on," urged Olivia. "Who was the murderee and

where's the murderer? Give us the facts or you're in for the soundest walloping on your miserable bottom."

Ellen gave her a hate-charged glance, and pulling her hair round to hide her face, told them how it had happened. She had been asleep in her hammock in the kitchen when a scream and "a batter-batter sound as if two people was fighting on de kitchen steps" woke her. She sat up, frightened, and waited, then heard a man grunt and walk down the steps. "De footsteps move about in de yard, and sudden me so frighten me begin to trimble-trimble. Den me get up and open de door soft and look out – and wha' me see, parson! Wha' me see!" She pulled more hair round to the front as though the better to curtain her face from the terror that menaced her.

"Well, what did you see? Go on, tell us."

"Don't keep edging up so close to her, Garvey," said Berton. "She doesn't need you to keep her warm."

"Who's edging up close to her!" said Garvey, reddening and edging away.

"Discipline, please, boys! Continue your narrative, Ellen my girl."

"Parson, me see blood," said Ellen in a low gasp. She whimpered and rocked herself from side to side.

"Blood?"

"Yes, sah. Blood." She rose and wrung her hands, turned and took a few staggering steps towards the belfry, grabbed the rope and began to ring the bell. "Blood, blood all over de steps," she wailed.

Garvey held her and wrested the rope from her.

"Ow! Blood, blood! Murder happen. Murder!" she screamed.

Olivia darted off toward the kitchen stairs.

"Calm yourself, Ellen!"

Garvey gripped her arm and told her to sit down. He shivered ecstatically and moistened his lips, though red in the face from bashfulness. Berton gave her a slap on her cheek when she reached out to embrace him. With a rapturous croon, she sank down again and shook her hair round to hide her face.

Olivia, from the kitchen stairs, sang out: "She's right, Daddy! There's blood on the steps. Big patches of fresh blood. Wet, thick and very slushy. A murder has been committed."

"Oh, whoops!" exclaimed Berton, and ran off toward the kitchen.

Mabel, in her pink dressing-gown, was coming toward the belfry, but seeing Berton running toward the kitchen and her father moving more sedately in the same direction, she changed course and made for the kitchen, too.

Garvey, with a swift breath of passion, settled himself beside Ellen and told her in a shaky voice not to be upset; he stroked her hair with a trembling hand, but she made no response – only pulled more hair round to protect her face from lurking horrors.

Mr. Harmston, unflustered, surveyed the blood on the kitchen steps and said: "H'm. Most peculiar. Where could it all have come from, I wonder!"

"From the wounds of the murderee, of course," said Olivia.

"This is exciting," whined Berton. "A murder mystery literally on our doorstep."

"New lil' nancy story-tale," croaked Logan, who had just come up. He grinned with his bluish, decayed teeth, his manner mollified, as though the sight of blood and the rumour of murder compensated for the loss of sleep he had suffered.

Mabel, pale, murmured: "Daddy, have you seen Gregory anywhere about?"

All eyes turned upon her.

"What do you mean?" said her father. "Isn't he in his room?"

"No," said Mabel. "Mother and I peeped into his room. He isn't there. His pyjamas are on his bed, as if – as if he got up early and dressed and went out."

"Oh, gawd! Oh, lawd!" said Logan, clapping his hands and bopping in delight. "Must be Mr. Gregory is de murder-man!"

"Be quiet, Logan," frowned Mr. Harmston. "Mabel, are you certain he isn't in the house? Did you and your mother look everywhere?"

"Yes, we searched in all the rooms upstairs. He wasn't anywhere about."

"What about the dining-room?"

"I don't know," said Mabel. "We didn't look there."

Olivia, picking her way between the small lakes of blood on the steps, ran up and disappeared into the kitchen. Her footsteps could be heard on the loose floorboards in the pantry. They stood in silence, waiting. Then she returned, and from the kitchen door told them: "No. He's not in the dining-room or in the sitting-room. It must be one of our people from the Reservation he's done in."

"But why should he have brought the living body to the kitchen steps here to murder it?" posed Berton.

Mabel shivered. "It's chilly out here. Better let's go upstairs."

"Logan, get this blood cleaned up, please," said the reverend gentleman.

"Yes, sah. Right off," said Logan. "Oh, Almighty! Oh, iniquity of man! Look trouble dis good Sunday marning!"

"But, Daddy, shouldn't we leave the blood as evidence for the doctor and the police to examine and analyse?" said Olivia.

"H'm. That's a point. No, let Logan clean it up. I can take a specimen on a glass-slide for the authorities."

"Shall we form a search-party, Daddy?" Berton asked.

"What for?"

"To search for the body – and the murder suspect."

"Not immediately, no," said his father. "I'll think it over, though."

In the house they heard Mrs. Harmston calling.

"Gerald! Mabel! Where have you all got to?"

She appeared at the kitchen door beside Olivia, looked down at the steps and said: "Oh, but, Logan, how could you have been so careless?"

"Me, ma'am? How me careless, ma'am?"

"Why did you have to kill that cock on the steps here?"

"Cock, ma'am? Dis na cock. Dis is murder, ma'am. Iniquity."

"Murder? What are you talking about? Gerald, what's happened here?"

"Yes, it's murder, Mother," Olivia said quietly. "Gregory's committed a gruesome murder."

"Oh, nonsense! Don't be silly." But she paled somewhat. "Where's Ellen? Why was she ringing the bell like that?"

"She did it in a panic when she saw the blood. She was awakened by a blood-curdling scream and the sound of a violent struggle."

"She was nearly an eye-witness," said Berton.

"Wait. Sssh!" said Mabel. "What's that? Listen!"

They fell silent.

"Footsteps," whispered Olivia.

Gregory appeared from round the kitchen, a plucked rooster in hand, blood on his clothes and a smile on his face. He bade them good morning. "I heard voices," he said.

"Not the bell, too?" asked Olivia.

"But – ah – that bird in your hand, my boy – could you explain —?"

"For our dinner," said Gregory. "But I have a little problem, I fear."

"A problem?"

"Yes. The head."

"What head?"

"The bird's. I don't quite know what to do with it. I left it with the feathers near the chicken-house on the other side of the kitchen, but surely it ought to be disposed of in some way, oughtn't it?"

"Inturgidment, you mean?" asked Olivia.

"Inturg – oh – ah – interment, yes. That is a possible solution."

"But look here," said Berton, "do you mean you killed this rooster and plucked it for us? It wasn't a human victim, then?"

"No, not a human victim. Only this bird. I heard your mother mention yesterday that we were going to have roast chicken for our Sunday dinner, and as I chanced to wake this morning with an inclination to kill something I thought I'd do you a good turn."

"Oh."

"Oh," said Olivia, too, glancing from her father to her mother.

"I had a strong whim to see blood," said Gregory.

"You had?" said Olivia.

"Yes. The urge sometimes comes just after taking my medicine. I have the desire to squelch a nice fat throbbing heart and see the blood squirt."

"Oh," said Olivia and Berton in chorus.

"Um," said Mr. Harmston.

"But why," asked Berton, "did you have to kill the cock on the steps here? Why not near the chicken-house?"

"It escaped soon after I'd taken it out of the chicken-house, and gave me quite a chase around the compound," Gregory explained. "Eventually I caught it on the steps here, and thought it wise to slash its throat on the spot. I'm sorry I had to make a mess of the steps but it couldn't be helped."

"What did you use to slash its throat with?" asked Olivia.

"My razor." He drew from his hip pocket a black-handled razor of the kind used by barbers. "I much prefer this type to the modern safety-razor. It makes a longer, cleaner and more elegant gash."

"Are you speaking from experience?"

"A delightful morning, isn't it?" said her cousin.

Logan began to snigger, and Mr. Harmston frowned at him.

"How did you leave the house, my boy? By the kitchen door?"

"Yes. I walked very quietly so as not to disturb Ellen in her hammock."

"Why you didn't tickle 'er throat wid you' razor, Mr. Gregory?" Logan sniggered, and Mr. Harmston said sternly: "Now, Logan! Now!"

"I think perhaps it might be as well to begin with yours, Logan," said Gregory, and with a smile took a step towards Logan, razor poised.

Logan, uttering a quarking hiccup, turned and fled toward the church at a stumbling run, his nightshirt flapping behind him with the sound of pallid thunder back of a haunted stage.

Gregory laughed. "You see how much better I'm feeling this morning," he said to the others. "I feel full of activity and laughter."

"You mean your medicine is doing you good, then?" said Olivia.

"Yes. But chiefly, I think it's this environment. It seems to have set something ticking in me."

"I told you it would, my boy," smiled Mr. Harmston. "It's the psychic influences."

Mabel and her mother shuddered. Mrs. Harmston frowned: "Gerald, I do wish you wouldn't refer to that sort of thing openly."

"We must look upon Gregory as one of us now, my dear."

"Quite right," nodded Berton. "It's high time we initiated him into our Deeper Secrets."

The sun had risen above the jungle on the opposite bank. Its mild rays pierced the scarves of mist that wreathed a wraith-like ballet over the water. The river looked unreal: the remnant of a dream left over from the night before and reluctant to yield to the actuality of daytime. Here and there, through the shifting mist, golden maps of *mora* blossom could be seen drifting slowly on the tide.

"A lovely morning," Mabel murmured, breaking a silence that had come upon them.

"All our mornings are lovely," said Olivia.

In this moment it was as though a spell closed in around them. The blood on the steps and on Gregory's clothes did not matter, nor did the absurdity of his standing here, a plucked rooster in hand. The air smelt of mist and night-damp bush, and the river groped reminders of its presence into their senses: they could hear its stealthy lapping along the bank and, now and then, a small gurgle as though some miniature monster had emerged and then quickly gone under again.

"All our mornings have magic," said Berton.

From the other side of the house came the sound of voices, and Mr. Harmston said: "Just as I thought. That bell has brought out some of our people. I'd better go and speak to them."

He moved off round the kitchen, Berton accompanying him, and Olivia and her mother turned from the kitchen door and went back into the house. Mabel was about to follow her father and Berton when Gregory smiled and said: "Could you spare me a moment, Mabel?"

She paused, surprised – her manner a trifle nervous. "Yes?"

"Could you help me with my little problem?"

"Your little – what problem?"

"The question of the head."

"Head? I'm afraid I – I don't understand."

"The head that was once on this bird. I left it on the other side of the kitchen perched on a heap of feathers. Couldn't you suggest how I might dispose of it? Olivia mooted interment, but I wonder if that would suffice."

She gave a shaky laugh. "It's all right. Logan or Ellen will see after it."

"Yes." He smiled at her – not blankly but with a kindling intelligence, almost with a sly humour. "You've relieved my mind. Could I say something?"

"Of course."

"You look charming."

She averted her face, colouring. "Thanks. I – could I take the chicken up to the kitchen for you?"

"You could. I should be grateful." He held it out and she took it – gingerly.

He murmured: "You're not too afraid of me?"

"No. No, not at all."

"I'm glad. Shall I tell you something?"

"Certainly."

"A little buffoonery can be extremely salutary."

"Buffoonery?"

He nodded and winked.

"But I don't – oh. Yes, I think I see what you mean now."

"I thought you would. You're intelligent. Shall I tell you something else?"

"Please."

"I believe I'm on the way to recovery."

"You do? That's good."

"This morning, for several weeks, I feel less watched. You know what I mean?"

"Not – no, not quite."

"I mean the ceiling has lifted. The celestial array of points is not so menacing in its impressiveness."

"Oh."

"Are you going to church?" he smiled.

"Yes. Aren't you?"

"Yes. I'm looking forward to saying the creed."

She giggled. "Are you really?" She coloured – not with shyness now; with amusement.

"Could I sit next to you?" he asked.

"Would you like to?"

"I would. Very much."

155

"Of course you can." She spoke with more confidence, and in her eyes appeared a swift light of excitement.

They stood looking at each other.

"Have you ever been in love?" he asked.

"In love?" She nodded. "Once or twice. Nothing really serious."

"With whom? Indian young men?"

"Yes."

"I understand you mix freely with them."

"Oh, yes. We have no prejudices at all."

"Do they visit your home?"

"Certainly. But the truth is, we're all so tired in the evening that we can't do much entertaining. Every month we have a big party and throw the house open to everybody, but during the rest of the time anyone can drop in to see us and be welcome."

"Have you a current boy friend?"

She laughed. "I had, but just the week before you came we called it off – though we're still good friends. You'll meet him before long."

He was silent a moment, then said: "I shall make a request of you after church."

"Why not now?"

"The moment is not strategic."

"Very well. After church, then," she laughed – and went.

XV

Rain came down unexpectedly at about ten o'clock. It fell in dense, coarse drops and with a crashing savagery, and ceased an hour later when the sun came out with dramatic abruptness and shone from a clear blue sky, the rain-clouds vanishing over the jungle in the south-west. Steam rose from the roofs of the church and the house, but quickly dissipated as the corrugated iron dried. The trees, however, dripped and plip-plepped for a long time after the shower. Throughout the service (which began at half-past eleven) Gregory listened to the sound of water dropping. It was a peaceful background, and went well, he thought, with Mabel's pale green dress and the smell of the perfume on her person.

All the pews, save two at the back, were filled. The Indians from the Reservation came, attired in cotton and khaki; the women in cotton and the men in khaki. They brought their children with them: those between eight and sixteen or seventeen; they all looked very clean and well washed, the girls with neatly plaited pigtails, the boys' hair brushed flat and shiny with water or vaseline. The Buckmaster family was present (they came in a launch), old Mr. Buckmaster – Gregory judged him to be about sixty-seven or - eight and not pure white – in grey flannels and a white shirt; he wore no tie. Mrs. Buckmaster, about forty-five, a shortish, coffee-complexioned woman with an intelligent face, evidently of mixed bloods, wore a dark-blue dress and a small black hat trimmed with pink berries. They sat with Dorothea and Susan, hatless like the Harmston girls, in the pew under the pulpit.

The Harmstons' pew was the one immediately behind. It could only accommodate four people with comfort, so Gregory and Mabel had had to sit in the pew in line with it on the other side of the aisle. With them sat an Indian and his wife and their very thin child of eight or nine, a girl with large black eyes which kept looking up curiously at Gregory.

Logan rang the bell five minutes before the service started, and then entered and seated himself in the rearmost pew and the one nearest the font. He wore white shorts (no shirt) and a cocoa-brown waistcoat that seemed far too big for him.

Wearing a dark-green gown under which white drill trousers showed, the Reverend Mr. Harmston emerged from the vestry, and taking his stand before the lectern, smiled round upon his congregation. In an even, conversational voice he announced that they would begin the service with Hymn Number Two hundred and twenty (only the English Hymnal, Gregory had learnt, was used).

Mabel found the place and shared her hymnal with him.

Olivia, at the harmonium, played faultlessly, but the congregation did not sing in tune. However, Gregory found it delightful. He listened to Mabel's voice. Himself, he made no attempt to sing. Once Mabel gave him a twinkling sidewise glance that contained enquiry, and he smiled and nodded, and felt certain that he had managed to communicate to her that though he could not sing he was interested and entertained, and appreciated her sharing her book with him.

When the hymn ended, Mr. Harmston said: "Perhaps we can now spend five minutes or so in pleasant reflections on past dreams and fancies." His tone was half-interrogatory, and at once a murmur of approval came from the congregation. There was a general shuffle and scraping of feet, and some resumed their seats and some kneeled.

"Shall we sit or kneel?" Mabel asked, with a cautious glance at Gregory. And Gregory smiled: "Sit, if you please. I think it would be more comfortable."

So they sat down. And after a moment – Olivia played voluntaries; Gregory afterwards learnt that they were improvisations of her own – Gregory whispered: "I like your hair."

"Do you?" she whispered back.

"Yes. And your perfume."

She averted her face, trying to suppress a shy smile.

From all over the church came whispers and murmurings. And outside, amid the trees, water dripped, each drop seeming a hushed echo, a stealthy mimicry, of the voices within the church.

"Have your past dreams and fancies been pleasant?" Gregory asked.

She nodded slightly, her face still averted.

"Have I been in any of them?"

"One or two," she murmured, after a hesitation, her voice barely audible.

"You," he whispered, "have been in many of mine."

In her lap she began to squeeze her fingers, one by one.

The harmonium rose in a shrill, vivid crescendo, and this might have been the signal for which the Reverend Mr. Harmston was waiting, for he got up from the chair near the lectern where he had seated himself, and in a deep, mellow voice said: "I believe…"

"In what I can sense," the congregation responded.

The harmonium had stopped. A silence settled through the small building. It might have been a segment of the heat gathering in the day outside which had seeped in upon them.

A bat squeaked in the rafters.

In the distance, some parrots were going past, and their unmusical chatter sounded like the tinkle of little jam-bottles breaking in the bush.

"And I believe…"

"In the reality beyond the shadows…"

"The shadows that move among us," intoned Mr. Harmston.

Olivia began to play a soft, indeterminate tune on the harmonium, and the notes moved in a blurred thread through the church, cunning and tinted with mystery. At one instant it was a mere throbbing in the lower register; at another such a breath-like staccato murmur that Gregory could not be sure whether it came from the harmonium or from the rafters: the furry thump and whirr of a bat fluttering a wing as it squirmed.

"Verily, I believe…"

"In God the Father of all Myth…"

"Himself," intoned the reverend gentleman, "the most wonderful Myth."

"And in Jesus Christ," chanted the congregation.

"Born of Joseph and Mary," continued Mr. Harmston, "in natural union."

"In natural union," confirmed the congregation.

"Jesus, among men, the King of Dreamers…"

"Creator of many beautiful parables…"

The harmonium wheezed out a series of high, trilling notes, and then trailed downward in a rather weird, but soothing, melodic scale.

"And I believe in the Bible…"

"But only as a book of lovely legends…"

"And a few true tales of long, long ago."

"Oh, enchanting book of literary jewels!"

"Oh, enchanting book!"

The harmonium trumpeted an emphatic pàean of joy, and grew still. An ecstasy of whispering and murmuring broke out over the church. Gregory saw the Indian and his wife sitting next to him smile and nod at each other, a light of bliss and secret communion in their eyes.

"I do believe…"

"In a life of cultured simplicity…"

"In comforts but not in vain extravagances," droned Mr. Harmston.

"In dreams and fancies; in fairies and phantoms…"

"In hard work, frank love and wholesome play…"

"Always spiced with make-believe."

"And I believe," prompted the reverend gentleman.

"In the basic Christian way of living…"

"Love thy neighbour; pity thine enemy…"

"Walk in humility, seeking no power; revel in the day…"

"But hope for nothing," chanted Mr. Harmston solemnly, "beyond this life…"

"For in this life is the Kingdom of Heaven…"

"And after death only shadows…"

"Oh, nothing – nothing but shadows, shadows." It was a deep chorused murmur uttered in a spirit of intense sincerity and accompanied by a low rumble of notes on the harmonium that created, Gregory thought, a most impressive effect. For an instant it shattered his neutrality.

During the pause that followed he could sense the elation and almost quivering spirit of freedom that flickered through the congregation. He felt a buoyancy within, and for no reason wanted to laugh and dance.

Mr. Harmston announced another hymn. Number One hundred and eleven.

While it was being sung Gregory whispered to Mabel: "Does your religion accept that Christ died to save the sins of the world?" And Mabel shook her head and replied: "No." Gregory gave her a glance of enquiry, and she understood and whispered: "You mean this is a Passion Week hymn, eh?... We only sing it because it has a sad, haunting tune. We don't bother with the meaning of the words." Gregory smiled his comprehension and touched her hand.

When the hymn was over, Mr. Harmston went up into the pulpit, and began in a quiet, unrhetorical voice to tell them of the activities planned for the coming week. "On Tuesday afternoon at four we'll hold an intelligence test for children between the ages of six and ten – our usual half-yearly test. Bring them to the *benab* where school is held. The summer holidays will soon begin, and I want to make sure that Labour Squad is still up to the mark in outdoor skill only. From one or two little rumours I've been hearing, there may be a child here and there in Labour Squad whose intelligence might have developed during the past six months sufficiently to merit his or her inclusion in School Squad. You know how anxious I am to transfer children from Labour Squad to School Squad if I discover signs of bookishness. So just bring them along and let's see... And now here is some good news – especially for all those of you particularly interested in music. On Thursday night at eight there'll be a concert in the church here. Mr. Buckmaster is bringing his radiogram and a selection of records to entertain us for two hours. We haven't quite made up our programme yet, but you can look out definitely for Beethoven's Seventh Symphony and Rimsky-Korsakov's *Scheherazade,* and possibly we'll have an item or two by Debussy. You may all come to this concert – there are no restrictions as to squad-rating. The first four pews, though, will be reserved for Music Squad, as it's only fair that our music-lovers should have the best seats. And by the way, I know Book Squad must be wondering when we're going to get started on our rehearsals for our annual Shakespeare Night. Well, don't think I've forgotten you, Book Squad. As soon as the summer holidays commence I'll get things going for you. I think we'll do our readings from *Macbeth* this year, so, in the meantime, you can devote yourselves to refreshing your memories by reading over *Macbeth*…"

The announcements over, Mr. Harmston clasped his hands together and seemed to take a deep breath. After a pause, he said: "Our sermon-tale this Sunday is taken from a book called *Selected Tales of Terror and the Supernatural*. It is in the best spirit of our kind of myth, and I hope you enjoy it."

He paused again, and Gregory noticed that an air of pleasant expectation came upon the congregation; there was a lisp and shuffle of feet and clothes, as though everyone was settling back more comfortably in his or her seat. Mr. Buckmaster lit his pipe, and glancing round, Gregory watched a match here and there flare and a wisp of cigarette smoke curl upward.

"Our man's name," began Mr. Harmston, leaning gently on the bookrest in the pulpit, "was Harry Moordaunt. Moordaunt was spending a holiday in Cornwall. A friend of his had allowed him the use of his cottage which stood on a cliff. You have all seen pictures of the Cornish coast, so you know the kind of scenery around the cottage. Rugged, big rocks, and steep paths, and down below a narrow shingle beach. Plenty of coves. And the sea rumbling and roaring day and night…"

Nods and grunts of comprehension greeted this description, and Mr. Harmston smiled and continued. He described the interior of the cottage in detail and mentioned that Harry was something of an eccentric; he liked his own company… "Rather bookish sort of chap – and very matter-of-fact. Note that. He certainly never gave a thought to anything supernatural when he entered the cottage. Yet strange and horrifying events befell him before many days had elapsed…"

During the next fifteen minutes Mr. Harmston proceeded to convey, in a remarkably successful manner, the strangeness and horror of the events that befell Harry Moordaunt. He was an accomplished raconteur, Gregory realized. His elocution was superb. He created atmosphere: lowered his voice and observed silences with a nice feeling for dramatic effect. At no time was he sensational or melodramatic. While he spoke the church ceased to exist; it became the cottage on the cliff in Cornwall. Everybody in the congregation was Harry Moordaunt, and everybody listened to the monotonous rumble of the sea and the humming of the wind. Everybody waited in tense dread for the click and tap of spectral footsteps on the pathway that led up to the cottage – and for the instant when the footsteps would pause outside the door of the cottage. Everybody chilled at the thought of the sighing presence about to enter...

During any particularly harrowing silence Olivia would play soft trickling notes on the harmonium which, in their unexpectedness and weird discordance, would evoke gasps from various parts of the church. Out of the corner of his eye Gregory saw Mrs. Harmston shudder frequently. Mabel sat very still, hands clasped in her lap, gaze on the lectern. It was obvious that she, too, was very much affected. Indeed, Gregory himself often found it difficult to suppress a startled exclamation, and could well sympathize with the wife of the Indian, in the same pew, when on one occasion she clutched her husband's arm and whimpered.

When Mr. Harmston – after what seemed more like an hour than fifteen minutes – brought the tale to an end he was perspiring. He dabbed at his forehead with a large handkerchief and smiled round with an air of satisfaction and affectionateness in acknowledgement of the rumble of stamping feet and murmurs of appreciation.

"I'm glad you enjoyed it," he said. "I trust it will stimulate you to weird and exciting dreams tonight. Next Sunday's sermontale, I can promise you, is going to be a *very* shivery one. It's called *The Smiling Fair Presence*. Hymn Number Two hundred and seventy-four."

While Mabel was engaged in finding the hymn, Gregory murmured: "You recall what I mentioned this morning? About the request I had to make of you after the service?"

"Yes."

"I think I'll make it now. This is a strategic moment."

"Is it?" she smiled. "Very well. Let's hear what it is."

"You whisper delightfully. You'd make a wonderful conspirator."

She averted her face and nearly dropped the hymn-book.

"I wanted to ask you if you would be so good, when the service is over, to show me over the Indian Reservation."

"You haven't seen over it yet, have you?"

"No."

"Of course. I'd be only too pleased," she said.

"Shall we slip out by way of the vestry the moment the service is over?"

"Why such stealth?"

He tilted his head. "Can you hear the drip of water in the jungle? Listen."

She made an uncertain sound – and gave him a quick, curious glance.

He had a smile, fixed and spectral. "Think," he whispered, "how alarmed they'll be when they miss us."

She frowned at the book and did not sing.

"They'll assume I've taken you into the bush and murdered you."

She fidgeted – and tried to smile.

"Tell me. Don't you hear the drip-drip deep in the jungle?"

She made no response.

"This morning, first thing, a bird. This afternoon, you."

After a pause, he chuckled and murmured: "That eternal little problem." And she took a swift breath and recoiled. For he had just withdrawn his hand from his trousers pocket, and cupped within it for her to see was the head of the rooster he had killed.

XVI

"I send you home in love and friendship, and commend your spirits throughout this day and throughout the coming week to many very pleasant thoughts and fantasies. Amen."

The Reverend Mr. Harmston lowered his hand, a quiet, benign smile on his strong face. He had pronounced his benediction as though he meant every word he uttered; he had made it sound sincere and not a mere ritualistic, parrot-like pronouncement.

Gregory glanced at Mabel, and she gave an uncertain smile and then frowned. He detected something new in her attitude toward him: a certain suppressed resentment. "I seem to have earned your disfavour," he said. "Must I assume that you no more trust me?"

"Trust you?" She shook her head and murmured: "It's not a case of trusting you. But if you want to know – well, it seems as if you have a rather perverted sense of humour."

"Perverted... oh. You think so? But, surely, when one is in Rome..."

She said nothing, but her manner grew colder.

"Shall we go now?" he asked.

She nodded stiffly and said: "Very well – if you wish. But not through the vestry door."

Her father's voice arrested them as they were about to move along the aisle toward the west door.

"Gregory, meet two of my dearest friends and co-workers."

Gregory turned. A rain of grasshoppers fell from the rafters and held him, dizzy and precarious, in space. Each with its winged eye, green and venomous. Each with a hooked clip to clamp a segment of his spirit.

"Yes?" he said.

"Mr. Hendrik Buckmaster and Mrs. Sophie Buckmaster."

Pale, on the verge of trembling, Gregory regarded the leathery-faced old gentleman with curly white hair who smiled mischievously and winked with solemn lewdness as he gripped the hand Gregory held out. The smile and wink put Gregory at ease immediately, and he felt some of the astral pressure lift. The grasshoppers recoiled to take off into upper space.

"New member of our distinguished flock, eh?" said Mr. Buckmaster. "Must say you do look like a bloody ghost yourself. Ought to say 'bloodless' really but 'bloody' sounds more indecent." He winked again.

Mrs. Buckmaster held out her hand and said in a quiet voice: "How do you do?", her manner easy and cultured... Perfectly normal, thought Gregory. Too normal. The pressure lowered...

"I heard about the fowl-cock," said Mr. Buckmaster.

"You have?" smiled Gregory – abruptly at ease again.

"Yes. Your Uncle Gerald has just told me. He thinks you're going to do splendidly among us. What he means is that you have the right spirit – and that's no frigging pun."

"Hendrik! Please! No obscenity."

"That's all right, Sophie love. It wasn't premeditated. It wasn't even me who said it. It was my confounded Doppelganger."

"Your what?" asked Gregory.

"Doppelganger," said Mr. Buckmaster, winking. "I've got an oversexed Doppelganger, my boy. It does nothing but father illegitimate children. Every night I get a lurid dream." He tapped Gregory on the chest. "I'm king of sleepwalkers in this neighbourhood – my Doppelganger, I mean. And as for sleep-acting – well, you ask some of these Buck women and hear what they tell you."

"Hendrik, I think that's quite enough for now," said Mrs. Buckmaster – but in her eyes there was a twinkle of humour. She took her husband's arm and smiled at Gregory: "Let me hurry him away from you, Gregory, before he annoys you anymore."

"He doesn't," said Gregory. "On the contrary, I'd like to see him often. I find him most refreshing."

Mr. Buckmaster waved his hand. "Even men can't help falling for me, by Christ!" he guffawed – and was led off by his wife toward the north door, full of quips and chuckles.

"A regular fun-stick," smiled Mr. Harmston. "Most likeable old chap."

166

"I agree," nodded Gregory.

"A great scholar," said Mr. Harmston seriously. "His obscenity is only a pose, I can assure you."

"Daddy, I'm taking Gregory to see over the Reservation."

"You are? Excellent plan. See and be back in time for lunch."

At the west door, they were intercepted by Olivia. "In your place, Mabel," she said, "I wouldn't go with him until I'd made sure he hasn't got his razor on him." And she was off at a dart.

Gregory looked amused. "Do you wish to make sure about my razor?"

"Please let's be going," said Mabel stiffly.

They said nothing until they were entering the track that opened near the school-*benab* when he asked: "Why are you annoyed with me?"

"It ought to be obvious, I think," she said.

"Not to one ill in body and in mind."

"You're no more mad or ill than I am. All you're doing is having a good laugh at us."

"You're so intelligent," he smiled, clasping his hands together as though trying to suppress his glee. "That is exactly what I am doing."

"You have a nerve to admit it."

"But," he said, "you're wrong in your conclusion about my mental health."

"I'm quite sure I'm not. Mad people don't know when they're mad."

"I used to think so myself. Until…"

A look of contempt came to her face.

The track was composed of white sand, and the land rose rather steeply so that their pace was perforce leisurely.

"Until I murdered Brenda."

She stumbled to a halt, and seemed to balance herself in the loose sand, then gave a short laugh and went on. "I may look silly but you can't fool me so easily," she said.

He stopped smiling, and the blood left his face. "You don't believe me, then? You don't think me dangerous?"

"No. I don't think you could harm a fly." Her manner was challenging, her shyness of a while ago entirely gone. Her lips

167

were firmly set together, and her eyes, formerly so docile in expression, had a hostile gleam.

He began to smile again; the blood returned to his face in a rush. "You interest me," he murmured. "More and more. It may be you who are the schizophrenic and not me."

"I'm no schizophrenic. I'm a perfectly ordinary person. But I can't stand being laughed at. It always rouses my blood."

He caught her arm and pulled her round to face him. "I'm going to kill you. Cut out your heart and tread on it."

"Release me, please."

Behind them, round the bend in the track, they could hear voices. People from church were on their way home. But he continued to hold her, watching her face, his body as rigid as hers.

A lizard – or an insect – rustled in a clump of ferns at the side of the track, near the base of a palm, and his head gave a barely noticeable tremble as though he were attacked with an impulse to glance at the ferns.

The voices sounded nearer. She made a half-step back in an effort to pull away, but he acted. He drew her to him and kissed her. By a misjudgment the kiss landed on her nose, but swiftly he kissed her again – this time on her mouth. She trembled, and parted her lips to say something, trying to strain her head back to avoid him, but no sound came from her. He had her arms pinned to her sides, and her strength was not equal to his, so she had to stop resisting. He looked at her white face, then smiled and suddenly released her and began to move on up the track – and, after a second's hesitation, she moved after him, awkward of gait and like an intoxicated being, her eyes round and bright.

The people had not yet come round the bend.

The track made a sharp turn to the right, and they came out into a wide, cleared tract of land, cultivated and with rows of *benabs*. A broad pathway, almost a road, for it was well built up with gravel and pebbles, divided the cultivated patches from the section where the *benabs* stood.

He pointed to some shrubs with thin, bare, knotty stems and asked her what they were, and she replied: "Cassavas," in a shaky, breathless voice, the blood coming briefly to her face.

After they had taken a few paces along the pathway, he came

to a stop, staring into one of the *benabs,* at the moment unoccupied.

"Not really!" He gave her a look of incredulity. "Penguins! Look!"

She made no reply.

"Penguins," he repeated. "In an Indian *benab!*"

"What's so extraordinary about that?" There was more confidence in her manner now. She had lost her dazed look.

"But can they read them – and appreciate the contents?"

"Yes, they can. Because they were educated."

"I see. So your methods do succeed sometimes?"

"They do – every time. They're Indians, but their brains are as much human as the brains of the people who live in Surrey."

"The only difference being that their background is the jungle."

"So is mine. I was born in the jungle the same as they were. Yet I don't think I find it so difficult to read a Penguin novel and appreciate what's in it. And I'd like to bet anything that quite a good many of your Surrey peasants probably can't even write their own names, let alone read a novel."

He nodded, as though a rain of reverie had begun to fall in his awareness. "Book Squad," he murmured, and might have been addressing himself. "And Music Squad." He glanced into another *benab* when they moved on and saw a portable gramophone. "I take it," he said, "they're all perfectly familiar with the Queen's Hall repertory."

"Perfectly. Because we've brought them up from childhood on good music. Reproduced music, it's true, but Beethoven is Beethoven whether in the Queen's Hall or on a gramophone."

"Or on Mr. Buckmaster's radiogram."

"Yes, laugh at him, too, if you like. He might seem a fool, but he's written and published two fine books on the history of Berbice, and he can speak and read two or three languages."

"Did he garner all this learning in the jungle?"

"He was educated at Cambridge and Amsterdam."

Every now and then they would be greeted by one of the *benab*-dwellers who were mostly at ease and reclining in hammocks. Every *benab* was equipped with at least two hammocks; many with three or four: there were no beds. In some were rough tables on which lay combs and brushes – and books. In more than one Gregory saw unframed canvases of still-life and landscape studies, and watercolours in passe-partout. In one a young man of about twenty-two was at work before an easel. He smiled and greeted them, and Gregory halted and said: "May I have a glance at what you're doing, Mr. Rubens?"

"Certainly," he replied. "But you won't find it anything like Rubens. Hallo, Mabel!"

"Hallo, Robert! This is my cousin, Gregory Hawke."

"Yes, I heard he'd come." Robert adjusted his easel so that Gregory could see the painting. It depicted, against a background of palms and shrubs, what looked like a ghostly snake with brown and green spots, its head raised as though to strike at the sketched-in form of a nude girl.

"What is this supposed to represent?" asked Gregory.

"It's more or less a fantasy," explained Robert. "I'm calling it 'A girl's nightmare'. My sister is posing for me, but she's at church, so I'm just touching up the ghost-snake and the background until she comes back."

"Why didn't you go to church?"

"I didn't feel like going today," he smiled.

"Won't the parson be annoyed with you for such remissness?"

Robert glanced at Mabel. "Haven't you explained to him about our church-going?"

"We haven't explained a good many things to him yet."

"No compulsion about going to church here," smiled Robert. "We go because we like going and really enjoy the service. But when we happen not to feel in the mood for it we just stay away, and we're not considered awful sinners for being absent. We have no Hell to be afraid of, you know."

"Thanks for explaining, Robert," Mabel said, and she and the young man exchanged a glance of amused irony.

Gregory, his teeth almost chattering, smiled: "An odd religion."

"Yes, but a most effective one," said Robert. "Our religion doesn't make us miserable with fear and remorse. We treat it lightly, you see, as if it were a kind of recreation, and because of that we get from it genuine upliftment – an entertainment.

Singing hymns and listening to sermon-tales for us is as good fun as listening to a symphony or a concerto, or looking at a fine picture. We enjoy being in church because we know there's no compulsion in being there. And we enjoy our religion because we know no one will frown on us if we make fun of it. And we all believe in God, but we don't have to shiver in awe at the thought of him. We take him casually – even have a good laugh at him sometimes. And if he's a God who's worth his salt I'm sure he can appreciate a joke as well as we can. We look upon him as a good jumbie-friend. We don't fear him. Why should we be afraid of our friends? Especially our mythical friends?"

"Yes," said Gregory, stiffening inwardly, his fingertips cold. "Your drawing, if I may remark, is excellent."

"Thanks," said Robert.

"I suppose you belong to Art Squad?"

"That's right."

"Does that mean you spend every day doing nothing but paint?"

"It doesn't. I only paint in my spare time and on Sundays. During the week I'm engaged in basket-making and farming."

"To whom do you sell your baskets and farm produce?"

"To the people on the coast. The Pastor in New Amsterdam is our business manager. He handles all our transactions, and does all our selling – and buying."

"Hasn't he a church of his own in New Amsterdam?"

"No. He's only a sort of agent who acts for us in civilized areas. Our kind of church wouldn't thrive in civilized places. Cities and towns contain too many cynical and contaminating influences."

"Then you mean you don't want to gain converts?"

"Converts are always welcome, but we don't try to proselytize anyone. Our Pastor in New Amsterdam – and our Pastors all over the world, for that matter – do their best to tell people about our religion and our way of living, but only in a passive spirit. Who chooses to come into the wilds and join us we welcome, but we never try to persuade anyone to our ways because, for one thing, we're not so foolish as to believe that everyone would like this kind of life, and, for another, we don't care to have a pack of silly tourists always plaguing us."

Gregory noticed that on Mabel's face was a look of great satisfaction, as though she were having her revenge on him. The tautness within him momently worsened.

"Shall we move on?" he said.

"By all means," Mabel nodded.

"Have you taken him to the Ibi Creek yet, Mabel?" asked Robert.

"No. I'd better take him there now."

"What is the attraction on the Ibi Creek?" Gregory asked.

"Nothing of attraction," she said. "Only a few things of interest." She led the way past the last of the *benabs* into one of three track-openings that branched away in different directions.

"Where do the other tracks lead to?"

"One goes to the coconut plot, the other to the baths and toilets. I'll take you there another day, and show you how we dispose of the sewage. Ronald Buckmaster planned it and carried it out."

"Is he a son of Mr. Buckmaster?"

"Yes. He's in the timber business with Mr. Buckmaster. He spends most of his time topside."

"Topside?"

"Yes. It's a term used up here. It means any point very far up-river – say, sixty or seventy miles beyond here. That's where most of the timber grants are. The logs are brought down in rafts."

They had not far to go, and in a few minutes emerged into another clearing – this one on the bank of a narrow stream. Three large *benabs,* stacked with what appeared to be crates and boxes, stood by the water's edge, and along the bank were moored at least two dozen *corials* and skiffs.

"This," Mabel told him, "is a sort of port. Our people store their produce in these *benabs,* and every Wednesday they take to Mr. Buckmaster's place whatever they have to send to New Amsterdam. There's a wharf at Mr. Buckmaster's place, and the steamer comes alongside it on Thursday morning to take in cargo."

"Yes," he said, trembling inwardly.

"If you follow me I'll show you something more," she said. She went past the *benabs* and entered upon another track. The land

172

rose steeply, and was sandy, and the jungle consisted of a profusion of spreading-limbed trees – wild cacao, *wallaba* and *mora,* he afterwards discovered they were – but very few palms. They passed a little spring of clear water that oozed from the side of the hill and trickled away amid the undergrowth. Then the land descended again – not so steeply – and they came out into a stretch of territory on which grew regular rows of trees with narrow, tapering leaves. They could see the Ibi Creek again.

"This," she told him, "is our mango orchard. When the season is on we reap thousands of mangoes of all varieties – from the common ones you squeeze and suck to the rare spice ones like the Julie and the Bombay. We send a lot to New Amsterdam and get a good price for them, but we always take good care to satisfy our own needs first. We aren't simply out to make money. Money doesn't dazzle us."

"It only tempts you on occasion."

"What do you mean by that?"

"Nothing," he said, smiling a secret smile, for he was remembering the conference in the Big Room. He began to clench his hands which were cold now, and it was with difficulty that he prevented himself from trembling visibly.

"The coconut plot is on the other side of this hill."

"Yes." He pointed to the creek. "What log is that spanning the creek?"

"It's a sort of improvised bridge. It's a *mora* tree that fell in a thunderstorm. Berkelhoost ends on this bank of the Ibi, but we go over into the jungle on the other side sometimes to explore."

"Shall we?"

"Shall we what?"

"Shall we go over and explore?"

She hesitated and gave him a cautious glance, then in a tone of amusement said: "Very well, if you'd like to. But we can't go far," she added in a mumble, as though suddenly a little fearful despite her convictions.

He followed her toward the log-bridge, and as they were crossing said: "Aren't you afraid to venture over there with me alone?"

"Why should I be?"

"Suppose I try to kiss you again?"

"If you do I'll slap you. It was only because you took me by surprise that I didn't a little while ago. And to be honest, I forgot that it was the conventional thing among civilized people like yourself to slap a man who tried to be fresh."

"Isn't it the custom among you here to slap a man who is fresh?"

"It isn't," she replied, though she was blushing as she said it. "We have our inhibitions, I admit, but we don't make sex the dreadful thing you make it in England. We try to treat it as a normal and pleasant function and nothing to be ashamed about and to discuss in whispers."

"You're blushing delightfully."

"Because I happen to be me, that's all," she snapped.

They were over on the other side of the Ibi now. A seemingly little-used track led off through dense bush – wild cacao and swizzle-stick trees and ferns and sparse grass that grew out of reddish sand. The land rose gradually, but, without warning, they came to a point where it climbed with almost perpendicular steepness. They could hear a sound of running water, and she said: "Over there is a spring – under that tangle of vines and dragon's blood. Do you want to climb to the top of the hill, or shall we turn back here?"

"What is at the top of the hill?"

"Only more jungle. But if we follow the track we'll come out eventually into open savannah."

"We won't go, then. We'll remain here."

She turned her head and looked at him. He was paper-pale, his eyes like fixed glass marbles. "What's the matter?"

"Yes."

She giggled. "Are you trying to put on another insane act? Don't bother. It won't impress me."

"Nothing," he said, "I have done has ever impressed you."

She regarded him with a frown.

"You have always gone out of your way," he continued, "to make me look foolish and inferior."

"I haven't done anything of the sort. You've been laughing at us up your sleeve ever since you arrived here. All I've been doing during the past hour or so is trying to show you something of the good work our mission has achieved."

"You could always find excuses for your conduct."

She laughed – but with a note of uneasiness. "I don't intend to stay here and argue with you, anyway," she said – and turned to go. But he gripped her arm.

"You're not going." He spoke in a choked mutter. "I have you in the spot I've wanted you for years. I trailed you all over Spain to get you alone like this. I followed you to Barbados – and you tried to cheat me by getting yourself drowned. But I knew I'd catch up with you in the long run. This is the moment."

"Take your hands off me, please. You – you don't deceive me one bit. You know who I am. You're not mad."

"You've said so innumerable times. At the Graves' party you laughed at me when I suggested that I was going off my head. And the evening you met me at the Barringhams in Staines and offered me a lift home – I wept trying to convince you I wasn't well, but you simply smiled and said: 'Poor dear, why will you insist on feeling you're insane'." A tear ran down his cheek. "You never want to believe me, but it's true. I'm mad. Genius and madness go together, but you won't admit my madness because you feel I have no genius. Today I'm going to prove you wrong. You can't go on overshadowing me forever."

His hold on her arm did not slacken, but he was trembling as though in an ague. He seemed fighting to stifle back the sobs that threatened him.

"Release me – or I'm going to scream for help," she said – and from her pallor it was plain that she was now alarmed in earnest.

With his free hand he drew from his hip-pocket the black-handled razor.

"If you scream," he said, "I'll cut your throat – and afterwards mine. When help arrives we'll both be disinterested. I mean it. I'd do that." He could not keep back the sob now.

She gave a soft gasp.

"You're frightened. At last. You were never afraid of me. But today it's different. Sit down. You mustn't stand in my presence. You're beneath me now – on a lower plane of achievement. Sit down."

After an instant's hesitation, she obeyed. Sat down on the reddish sand, her pale green dress blending with the ferns and the grass.

"How beautiful you look now. But crystalline underneath. I told you so once – that morning on the platform at Virginia Water station, remember? You smiled – contemptuous, as usual. Superior. Though you kept pretending you loved me still. It was during the second week of *The Harrowed.* You were so elated because the critics were all yelping their praises. But don't forget what I told you about Eugene. I knew – Charles told me – Eugene didn't think so much of *The Harrowed,* but he had to join the chorus because he was in love with you, and he wasn't sure how you might take adverse criticism. He hated me – that's why he slated *The Raider.* And he had the impudence to refer to *The Raider* in his review of your thing – to my detriment, of course. I admit *The Harrowed* was a better play, but I can't forgive you because you used my theme – don't try to deny it. You know you did – deliberately to prove how much better you could handle it. It was the same with my show at Ramier Fils in the spring of 'thirty-four. That show you put on in Grosvenor Street – you took many of my subjects and treated them more effectively, remember? The silver birches. And the field near Frimley. And you got the Bewlay's gardener to pose for you – because you knew it was he who posed for that study of him I exhibited at my show. You made a much better job of it, I admit – but it was cruel of you to try to show me up as your inferior. My book, too. You stole my theme and plot and gave yours a slightly different twist to disguise it. But Charles agreed with me that you'd done it deliberately. You said I was talking nonsense when I challenged you, but Charles saw it, too. You fooled the critics, of course, because you gave my theme a wider significance, and your characters were more sharply drawn, but…"

Something crackled in the bush, and he broke off and glanced about. He was panting, his head in a continuous tremble. His hands looked purple-grey.

"I've lived so long for this moment you won't realize how moved I am. I can't help telling you this."

He began to glance about again. "Did you hear a noise?"

Her hands were pressed hard on the sand, her eyes bright as she stared up at him.

"Undress," he said. "Quickly. We might be disturbed. I must humiliate you before help comes. After this you'll admit I'm your equal. Your better, you may say. Yes, you may want to confess that, who knows. Undress."

She made to rise, but he waved the razor and croaked: "No, no! You mustn't try to get up. Your plane is beneath mine. You have to sit and undress. As a symbol of lowliness. You're much less than I now. Much."

She had begun to tremble. She murmured: "My God."

"You're frightened. I'm so glad. If you really are afraid of me I won't harm you. I mightn't even laugh at you down the chasm. But you must undress so that I can demean you. Quickly. You were always sensitive about revealing your body – even to me, remember? This is an excellent way to crush you into the dust. Begin. At once – or I'll have to rip your things off you."

She made no move to obey.

He bent over her, his face distorted and twitching. Tears ran down his cheeks and fell on her dress. "You're pitying me, aren't you? I can see it on your face. It always touches me when you pity me. Please don't do it. But you must be quick and get this over. I don't want to harm you. Undress. I'll have to slash you with this if you don't. Begin. Please."

She murmured: "Oh, my God," and began to undress. She half-rose to pull off her dress, but he warned her again not to stand. "No level. No par. You mustn't even kneel. No equality of plane whatever. You must sit and do it. That's it. Lowly. Lowly. Think of yourself as very humble. Filth, if you can."

Trembling – and awkward because of her sitting posture – she struggled to get off her clothes.

He made soft whining sounds, and once his knees knocked together. He mumbled incoherently to himself, and his eyes were shiny and harrowed.

She was nude to the waist when he started and uttered a blubbering cry. He stumbled, and she thought he would have fallen over her. She winced as though to avoid the razor.

"Please stop," he said. "Don't take off anymore."

He was staring at her, a baffled, utterly despairing look on his face.

"Freckles. You have so many. She had none. None at all. You're not – I've fooled myself again. I've…"

The razor fell from his hand. He pressed his hands to his face and sobbed. His knees gave, and he collapsed in a shaking mass.

She dressed again with agitated hurry, skipped past him and was about to run off; but suddenly the panic in her died and she paused and looked back at him. She took a pace toward him, stooped and picked up the razor and threw it far into the undergrowth, then bent and touched his head and said: "Get up and let's go back. Come on."

His whimpers ceased, and he raised his head and looked at her, and the expression on his face was such that she had to bite her lip hard, her eyes getting moist.

Still shaking, he got up and accompanied her along the track back toward the creek.

Crossing on the log was a precarious business. She had to hold his hand and lead him slowly step by step. His hand was cold and he trembled without cessation.

When they were safe on the other bank, he said: "Thank you," with a smile.

PART TWO

I

Gregory was assailed by three successive sensations. First, it seemed to him that a lump of grit had detached itself from some section of his mind and dropped away so that a vast, immediate relief spread through his system like a serum in his blood. Then, on their way back to the house, he kept glancing about him with the feeling that he had just emerged from a glass tank in which the air had been dense and oppressive. The trembling gradually left him and the third sensation surged upon him in the form of a sudden strong curiosity; he had the notion that a momentous event, the details of which eluded him, had recently occurred and it was imperative that he should know what it was. "Would you think me silly," he said to Mabel, "if I asked you a question?"

"What's that?"

"Did I act in any way strangely a little while ago?"

She gave him a keen glance, and after some hesitation shook her head and murmured: "No." He noticed that her face had a strained look.

"Are you quite sure?"

"Yes." She said it without meeting his gaze, the colour coming to her cheeks.

"You needn't spare my feelings, you know. Tell me. Didn't I even say anything that struck you as – as odd or absurd?"

She smiled. "But surely you would know if you had. Is your memory as bad as all that?"

He looked uncomfortable and mumbled: "Yes, I suppose it is a foolish thing to ask. Just forget it, then."

An awkward silence fell between them. Presently, as though out of sheer perplexity, she broke it by saying: "You honestly don't remember anything at all?" Her voice was kindly.

He shook his head and said quietly: "Nothing out of the ordinary, no. After we crossed over on to the other side of that creek I have an idea I must have drawn into myself a bit. I have a vague memory of talking to myself, that's all."

"But why do you feel something out of the ordinary took place?"

He hesitated. "It's just a notion. When we were returning – when you'd helped me over that log – I felt a sense of shock." He gave a grin and said: "It's as if I was in a black mood of depression and all of a sudden somebody gave me a shaking and I found myself cheerful again. I can't describe it any better than that, I'm afraid."

Nothing more was said between them. A troubled look settled on his face, and lasted all the way to the house.

For the rest of that day and for several days after he was quiet and kept to his own company. After every meal he would go up to his room and read (before Sunday he had done no reading at all). He spoke only when addressed, but spoke amiably and without any vagueness, though he was noticeably shy whenever he came in contact with Mabel; it was as though he suspected her of having an advantage over him.

"I believe Maby worked some kind of *obeah* on him," said Garvey, "when she took him over the Reservation on Sunday."

They were at lunch on Tuesday, and Gregory had just gone upstairs after asking to be excused.

Olivia and Berton exchanged secret signs, but Mabel said nothing.

"He's certainly seemed much different during the past day or two," said Mrs. Harmston. "Yesterday morning I saw him reading in his room and asked him if he'd like to look over the books in the Big Room and he said yes – and he spent nearly an hour in there going through the cases."

"Yes, I've noted a decided change," nodded Mr. Harmston.

"Don't you know what has happened?" said Olivia, with a mysterious smile. "Can't you guess?"

"Guess what? What has happened?" asked her father. She looked across at Berton and waved her thumb before her face, and Berton returned the sign, solemn-faced.

"Oh, stop all that hanky-panky," frowned Garvey. "What's the big mystery now?"

"Explain, Olivia," said Mr. Harmston seriously.

"It's very simply explained. The him we saw before noon on

Sunday was his shadow, but what we've been seeing since then is he himself. In other words, he has arrived among us."

"And what caused his arrival on Sunday at noon?"

She fanned herself. "Isn't it hot? I believe we're going to have a thunderstorm this evening."

"I heard distant thunder a little while ago," nodded Berton gravely.

Mrs. Harmston glanced at Mabel. "Mabel, what happened on Sunday?"

"How do you mean what happened? What could have happened?"

Her mother broke into a gurgle of mirth. "Come to think of it, you yourself have seemed a little strange of late. There's something on your mind, child. Has Gregory been making love to you?"

Mabel laughed, very pink. "Please don't be silly, Mother."

Garvey grunted. "I don't know about silly. Mother's right. You've had a distinctly foggy look these past two or three days. Since Sunday. I believe you're trying to hide something."

"No harm if you think so," murmured Mabel coldly.

"Didn't you have a dream about him the very first night he arrived here? And your dressing-gown – didn't Mother find it under his bed?"

"Don't be a fool!" Mabel snapped. "You know very well we proved there was nothing substantial in that."

"I don't know anything of the sort. Isn't it part of our religious belief that dreams and actuality are often one? How can we swear you didn't sleepwalk into his room that night and get into bed with him?"

"She didn't, Garvey – that's enough!" intervened his mother sharply. "Please end this discussion at once."

Garvey gave a sneering snigger. "I thought Daddy always stressed that it was salutary to discuss matters relating to our religious myths."

Mr. Harmston glanced at his wife and said: "Let him have his say, Joan. It can do no harm to thresh the matter out again."

But Garvey said nothing more. He whistled softly to himself.

Mrs. Harmston and Mabel both looked tense.

183

Thunder sounded in a low booming far away in the south, and after a moment they heard it echoing in the jungle.

"Hear that?" said Berton. "A storm is coming over."

"I don't think it will come to anything," said his father, lighting a cigarette. "We've been having a lot of distant thunder of late."

Outside, the day vibrated with heat. The palms – their fronds – glittered like spiders of metal against the grey-blue haze of sky. The river was without a ripple, and looked tensed as if it might break into terrible laughter if only troubled by a fallen pip. Such silence and immobility, one felt, could not last. Some ghastly scythe would mow through it before long, releasing whatever waited in the dormant breathless spaces of the air.

Mr. Harmston, however, proved right. No storm came over. Not that day, nor the next, though the heat continued to be intense and thunder rumbled in the far south. It was hot even at night, and mosquito-nets became blood-warm barricades that thickened the heat within the cubed pockets of their protection. The river ebbed and flowed in japanned sleekness, seeming to hold beneath the skin of its surface innumerable unheard, yet momentous, crepitations.

Thursday it was the same, but the thunder did not make itself heard until late afternoon when the sun hovered above the tortured trees, a blob of liquid brass. The thunder came from the east, a barely audible mutter.

The temperature in the house was at least a hundred, and though Mr. Harmston and the boys moved around in nothing but shorts, their bodies streamed continuously with perspiration. Olivia put on a green bathing-suit, threadbare from age and with many darned patches.

At about three o'clock, she and her brothers were in the dining-room doing their daily hour of reading – Olivia with Darwin's *A Naturalist's Voyage,* Berton with Gray's *Anatomy* and Garvey deep in Byron's *Childe Harold* – when a croaking shout split the silence of the hot day.

They sprang up and went to the windows that looked out on the river. They saw Logan, completely nude, lumbering toward the house at a limping trot. His brown body glistened wet in the fierce sunshine and his mouth opened and shut like a gnome's cavern to bellow in fear and pain.

Olivia whistled. "It looks like his foot – it's bleeding. The silly ass must have gone swimming too far out and a *perai* got him."

Berton hurried into the dining-room to the sideboard to get the first-aid box, and by the time Logan had reached the kitchen steps Mr. Harmston, who had been engaged in carpentry work in the workshed – he was making a bookcase for the dining-room – had come hurrying round to enquire what was the matter.

"Look at the mess," said Olivia, examining Logan's left foot. "He's had almost his whole heel lopped off. Give me a wad of cotton-wool, Berton."

Logan howled.

The treaders of the kitchen stairs were red with small pools of blood from the wound.

"You ought to be soundly whipped for this, Logan," frowned the reverend gentleman. "How many times haven't you been warned not to bathe in the river!"

"Ow, sah! But de wedder! De wedder so hot, and Ah didn't feel like teking de long walk to de creek. Na punish me, parson. Ah beg you! *Perai* punish me bad enough." He threw back his head and bellowed.

"What is a *perai*?"

They glanced up to see Gregory at the kitchen door. There was a strained frown on his face. In his hand he held a book with a coloured jacket, his forefinger between the pages to keep the place where he had evidently broken off in his reading.

"It's a fish, my boy," smiled Mr. Harmston. "Something like a small shark. Swordfish variety. Very fierce. The river abounds with them."

"He seems to have got an ugly wound."

"He's lucky," said Garvey. "He could have had his toes or fingers lopped off at one slice."

Olivia, all her senses on the alert, saw Gregory glance past them at the steps and give a slight shudder. The sight of the blood appeared to upset him.

Ellen, who had been asleep in her hammock in the kitchen, awoke, roused by the voices. She sat up and gasped: "Oh, Jumbie-

God!" in a frightened voice. Only Gregory at the door was visible to her from where she sat in the hammock, and, still dazed with sleep, she smiled at him and said: "Was you talk to me while me sleep? You come to me for lil' quick-quick sweetness?" She made a graphic circular motion with a finger.

"No, I'm afraid I haven't," Gregory smiled. "Logan has met with an accident."

"Accident?"

Berton showed his face round the door-post and said: "Lie down and go to sleep again, Ellen, and stop your sexy suggestions. It's hot enough without your making it hotter with your heat."

"Now, Berton! Now!" frowned his father.

Gregory gave an amused chuckle and went back into the house. In the dining-room he encountered his aunt who had just come downstairs; she had been having her afternoon siesta in the Big Room.

"What's happened, Gregory? What is Logan yelling like that for?"

He explained, and she sighed: "Logan is so stupid and disobedient. I really don't know what we're going to do with him." She was about to move off in the direction of the kitchen when he touched her arm. "Just a moment, Aunt Joan."

"Yes, my boy?"

He was frowning. After a slight hesitation, he said: "Did anything – was anyone hurt during the past day or two? Near the back stairs?"

"Hurt? Not that I know of. Why?"

"Oh, it's possibly just a notion of mine, but…" He gave an uncomfortable laugh. "Well, for some reason, the sight of Logan's blood on the kitchen stairs seemed to remind me of a similar sight not very long ago. It's no doubt my imagination."

She laughed and said: "But don't you remember? The rooster you killed for us on Sunday morning. You spilled the blood all over the steps."

"Rooster? Did I kill…?" A look of complete dismay came to his face. "Oh, I see," he said hurriedly, flushing. "Yes, of course."

"But you really don't remember?"

"Not very clearly, to be truthful – but I'm sure I must have done it if you say so." He laughed confusedly and began to move off. "I'd better go up and finish this book. Very nasty wound Logan has got. Go and have a look at it."

Back in his room, he did not resume his reading at once but seated himself by the window in the one easy chair the room possessed and bowed his head in thought. An eye-fly circled slowly into his vision, and he brushed it off automatically. He put his hand to his temple, his head aching slightly from the heat and the glare but in his spirit an invincible restfulness. Once he looked at the river, and the sight of it gave him a feeling of safety. It's so much more pleasant, he thought, to be able to look out of a window and see river and jungle instead of traffic in a street. I never wish to see traffic again.

Some greyish birds were twittering in the *cookerit* palm near the belfry – sackies, Olivia had told him they were. He had seen blue ones, too… He remembered the thrushes that used to sing in Middenshot, but he felt no nostalgia. He smiled and thought: Birds are birds wherever they are, thrushes or sackies. They bear no malice…

He was still in his room at about five o'clock when the thunder boomed far away in the east. He looked up from his book and nodded, his eyes narrowing reminiscently. There had been a scene in his play that called for distant thunder… Even the theatre, he thought, I don't miss.

Olivia came in with a cup on a tray. "Tea," she said. "It's specially for you. Mother got it from New Amsterdam yesterday with our weekly provisions."

"Very thoughtful of her," he smiled. "I can do with it."

"Can you? I'd have thought ice cream would be much better in all this scorching heat."

"Quite. But tea is tea. It's always welcome."

"We knew you'd look at it that way. You had to, being English."

"But aren't you English, too?"

"Only by blood – not in spirit."

"Is that why you never have afternoon tea here?"

"No. That's because we can't have more than three meals a day. We have to observe our vows, don't forget."

"What vows?"

"Our vows of discipline. Every member of our faith has to take vows not to eat too much or indulge in an excess of pleasure, or behave in an unrestrained manner on occasions that call for order and formal conduct."

He sipped the tea and regarded her with slight wonder.

"Don't look so cynical."

"I'm not *feeling* cynical. Do you always keep your vows?"

"We try to, but we slip up now and then. We're human, you see. We never try to fool ourselves we're divine creatures. That's one of the great merits of our religion. It always takes into consideration the fact that we're human beings."

"Who was the founder of your religion, by the way?"

"Daddy and a group of his friends at Oxford founded it. One of them, Geoffrey Banningham, financed the project. An aunt from Westmorland came to see Geoffrey at Oxford, and he told her of his religious beliefs, and she was very impressed. She settled five thousand pounds on him, and willed all her money to him. She was a bit flighty, I admit – so Daddy says. She died during Geoffrey's last term at Oxford, and Geoffrey said that he'd use the money she left him to found the Brethren. He ordained Daddy, and Daddy ordained him. There were eight of them, and they ordained each other and organized missions to various parts of the world. The money Geoffrey's aunt left him wasn't so much but it was enough to get things comfortably started, and as the Brethren and their families live modest, Spartan lives they've managed to keep going, and they've made a success of the project, too. We exchange reports every year with the other Brethren in Africa and Malaya and Burma."

"Your father did mention that, yes."

"Didn't he tell you how we came to be founded? Didn't you ask him?"

"No, it really slipped me to ask him," he said.

"Anyway, I've told you. You know now. Well, I must be off."

"Stay if you like."

She shrugged and seated herself on the bed.

"You're an odd little girl."

"Don't be trite."

A dark tremor penetrated the building and trailed like a troubled groan far into the jungle.

"Hear it? In the east today. It's going to come over."

"I wish it would. This heat is unbearable."

"Why don't you dress like me?"

"It's an idea," he smiled. "Perhaps tomorrow. I have bathing trunks." He glanced toward his suitcases as he spoke.

"By the way?" she said.

"Yes?"

"Did you take your medicine as usual today?"

"My what? Medicine? What medicine?"

"Your Johnnie Walker's Gold Label."

"Oh. Why, no. I don't think I've touched it for days. Why do you ask?"

"Nothing. I just felt like asking. You stopped taking it since Sunday, didn't you?"

"I – yes, I believe so," he murmured, looking uncomfortable. He sat forward, his gaze on her, as though eager to ask her something, then leaned back again, evidently changing his mind. She gave him no encouragement, whistling softly and slapping her hands idly against her thin thighs.

"Are you coming tonight to the concert?" she asked suddenly.

"No, I don't think so," he said.

"Aren't you fond of good music?"

"Extremely. But I'm not in the mood for it this evening."

"Do you know something? I'm clairvoyant."

"Are you?"

"Yes – I can foresee events. Not all the time – but sometimes."

He grinned. "What a wonderful little girl you are!"

"Why will you insist on calling me 'little'! I'm not so little. I'm twelve going on to thirteen – and I have cogrizance of lots of things many grown-up people haven't got. Haven't you discovered that yet?"

"Oh, quite. I'm not attempting to cast aspersions on your cogri – on your cognizance."

"Careful how you lead me on. I can be a tigress."

"Can you?"

"Yes. I foresaw something about you the very first night you arrived here – I mean, the first night your shadow arrived here. I was in bed undoing Mabel's hair for her when I foresaw it, and part of it has already come to pass."

He leant forward a little. "What's that?"

She began to hum a tune from *Rigoletto*. She got up and said she must be going. At the door she paused. "Thunder again." She smiled at him and said: "Some day I'll give you back your razor."

"My razor?"

"Yes. Or I might kill you with it instead. I'm terribly jealous."
She went.

Such a plurality of greens, Gregory thought, watching the jungle from his window... Shadows were lengthening, but the heat persisted; it trembled above the roof of the church... The difficulty, he thought, lies in segregation... Breathing deeply, he smelt the weathered wood of the windowsill... If I could probe into the green it's possible I'd find reality glinting like a jewel within the chlorophyll. Crystalline rivers of living spirit in leaves and branches... In my forearm I can see rivers, but these are blue because they're glutted with filth: impure with the sewage of a human cerebrum. Soundlessly in a cranium the mire swirls, and now and then a formula is thrown up and a symphony or a poem takes shape – though sometimes it's a skyscraper or a deadly gas to kill armies; there's no telling what might be cast up from such a cesspit. Anything from sapphires to stinking chaff... Again, you see, it's a question of segregation. Probe into the muck, separate filth from gems...

The heat breathed upon his neck.

The river. Yellow maps of *mora* blossom drifted slowly on the tide.

Trees, he reflected, are different. The achievements of trees arise unwittingly out of the mystery of morning and through midnight ministrations of dew. Trees don't reach to the sky for power, or flame in conscious vanity. Yet I mustn't forget the parasite that sinks sap-drinking suckers into a tree's flesh and feeds on the other's substance. A parasite is as much a tree-thing as the tree it sucks. I wonder, then, if trees merely sham passive benignity. Could it be that enclosed in their static awareness is the poison of competition? Am I to believe that in their noiseless cores they pant with a desire to over-top each other – to strangle each other and win selfish magnificence?

I know I shouldn't be doing this. With a temperament like mine, I have no right to indulge in introspection; in this environment it's doubly dangerous because of my idleness and security; here I have no audience to struggle to please, and no one to question my talents or speak belittlingly of my creations. Even that chap Robert doesn't bother me, because he's so obviously unspoilt; his remarks on Sunday contained no malice; nor did Mabel's, though her sarcasm hit me hard – almost threw me off balance. She spoke to me as Brenda might have done. Made me feel wormishly inferior. At one point I very nearly had the illusion that she was Brenda... It's malice I can't stand: the venomous kind that oozes out of the sick souls of over-civilized people. People like myself – and Brenda – and Eugene... My God, but I still can't believe that Brenda's cheated me by dying...

He shut his eyes and shook his head, and felt as if white-hot grains of pollen were moving in his brain, searing the slow-swirling mire so that it bubbled and formed a pewter scum...

After a moment, the burning in his head rationalized itself into a mere burning; it passed, and his brain appeared to his fancy a brain and not a mire. He fell into a doze from sheer nervous exhaustion, and when he awoke darkness had fallen. He assumed it must have been the distant thunder that had roused him. He could hear it echoing in the jungle. A bat darted by with a crape-like flutter, and he heard it squeak... The thunder had died away soon after Olivia had left the room, he recalled, as though the storm had by-passed them as the others yesterday and the day before had done. Now another one was making itself heard; in the south-east. He looked and saw the clustered domes of a cloud-pile showing above the jungle on the opposite bank; even as he watched lightning grinned evilly.

The house vibrated with footsteps, and he could hear splashings in the bathroom as if someone were having a shower.

Fireflies flashed their own small lightnings in the deep dusk, and the smell of sun-warmed vegetation came in whiffs to his senses, pleasantly stifling and charged with the sting of many overheated blossoms. Night-time insects wheezed their early evening runes, elusive as usual and seemingly in league with the inmost essence of the jungle's silence, thickening the sultry air with reedy forefingers of menace, more terrible because un-seen... More sinister because mere symbols of my morbid fancy.

Lightning again... One, two... He counted up to twenty-one before the thunder came grumbling on the air.

Olivia appeared at the door, naked save for a towel draped around her waist. "We're having dinner in fifteen minutes," she said. "It has to be earlier this evening because of the concert."

Before he could thank her for the information she had gone.

He got up and lit the lamp, intending to spend the fifteen minutes before dinner in reading, but had hardly seated himself again and opened the book when Berton, also naked except for a towel around his waist, looked in and said: "I hear you're not going to the concert. That means you'll be alone in the house with the shadows. Doesn't the prospect frighten you?"

"Not particularly, no," Gregory smiled. "I don't mind shadows."

"You must know best. But if I were you I'd come to the concert."

He was off, and the next minute Gregory heard the spatter of water in the bathroom, and the voices of Olivia and Berton chanting the Liebestod from *Tristan.* Shortly after, Olivia was at the door again, clad as before, her hair lank and dripping.

"I've just had a quick shower with Berton. Are you shocked?"

"Shocked? Not at all, no. Why should I be?"

"Doesn't it even shock you to see me like this?"

He grinned. "Not in the slightest. You're still a little girl."

Her eyes gleamed. "In another year or two my chest won't be as flat as this, you know."

"We can only trust not – but it's possible it could be."

She was quiet a moment, then took a pace toward him and said in a lowered voice: "You want to betray me. I can see infidelity in your heart. Take warning. Something dreadful is going to happen. Very, very dreadful." Her thin body suddenly shook with sobs. She turned and rushed out of the room. Almost at once lightning flashed.

He had to give up trying to read. He went down into the gallery, which was a kind of closed-in veranda with windows and jalousies, and settled himself in an easy chair provided with long projecting arms for resting one's outstretched legs (a Berbice chair, he had heard it called). Despite Olivia's outburst and the

193

nagging uncertainty at the back of his mind concerning his actions during the past week, the restfulness in his spirit remained. It seemed as invulnerable as the dark silhouette of the jungle. His only worry was that forces outside himself might try to destroy it – either unwittingly or purposely.

All life is conflict; nothing was meant to be at rest or at peace. Vitality results from friction and action; that which is static declines, atrophies and eventually ceases to be… Vicious, vicious circle…

His head began to burn again, and he stopped himself before his thoughts got out of hand.

It was a relief to hear his aunt call out: "Dinner is ready, everybody! Hurry up and come down!"

He went in and took his place at the table, and presently the others joined him. Garvey sat at Gregory's right, as usual, but Olivia, instead of sitting at Gregory's left, which was her place, took Berton's place on the other side of the table, and Berton took her place. She looked pale, Gregory noticed. And Berton had that sensitive, remote air that sometimes came upon him.

"Why have you two changed places?" their father frowned as he took his seat.

"Just a whim," said Olivia with a quick smile.

Berton's face twitched slightly, and his breath hissed. Mabel gave him a frown and asked him if anything were the matter.

He made no reply.

Mabel glanced at Gregory, and his gaze met hers and shifted off…

Thunder throbbed through the room. It had no sooner died away when the chug-chug of a motorboat became audible, and Garvey remarked: "That sounds like the launch."

"Or the outboard motorboat," said his mother.

"No, it's the launch. I can tell by the beat."

"It's not the only thing coming," said Olivia, with a snigger.

"What?"

"I said it's not the only thing coming."

"She means a thunderstorm is coming," said Berton in a voice barely above a whisper.

"And a very bad one, too," said Olivia.

"Oh, I think it will pass off like all the others," said her mother.

Olivia gave a snigger again but said nothing.

I wonder what's got her into this strange mood, thought Gregory. A really most unpredictable child.

Ellen came in with a dish of steaming yams and eddoes. In placing the dish on the table she rubbed the tips of her breasts against the back of Gregory's head, doing it so that it appeared an accident. She uttered a clucking gluey giggle before she returned to the kitchen, and Gregory saw Mabel frowning at her retreating form.

Olivia asked to be excused and rose.

"Not finished already, surely?" said her father.

"No. Something I have to attend to upstairs. I'll be back in a minute." She hurried away, and Gregory noticed that Berton's gaze followed her anxiously. Berton lowered his knife and fork to watch her go.

"I wonder what prank she's up to now," Mrs. Harmston smiled. "Help yourself to some yams, Gregory."

"Thanks," smiled Gregory, and was about to help himself when he glanced at Mabel. "What of you? Can I help you…?"

"No, thank you," murmured Mabel, her gaze meeting his and moving away, the blood coming to her face.

"Olivia is in danger," said Berton in a breathless voice.

"What's that?" asked Mr. Harmston.

"I say Olivia is in danger."

"What from?"

"From the lightning – and herself." He seemed on the point of sobbing.

Mabel gave him a troubled stare.

In the kitchen Logan was singing "Jerusalem my happy home."

"There's lightning in everything tonight," whispered Berton.

His mother laughed. "You and your sister are far too imaginative."

Mr. Harmston, however, took Berton seriously and asked him to explain.

"I swore by the Green Genie I wouldn't divulge anything," Berton replied. "But I know what I'm saying when I tell you she's in danger."

Garvey grunted. "I'm afraid it's a case of too much myth hath made thee mad, young fellow."

"Are you making fun of our religion?" Berton blazed out.

"And why not," said Garvey. "One of the tenets of our religion is that we are at liberty to make fun of it. Am I wrong or right Dad?"

"Quite correct, my boy," nodded the reverend gentleman. He seemed unperturbed. "It is always very important that we should never let ourselves become slaves to rigid doctrine. If religion is to be a joy to us we must keep it elastic, by which I mean we must be able to laugh at our most sacred precepts without feeling we've committed a wrong. Religion without a sense of humour to dilute it can only result in being an awful bore."

"That's sound," said Gregory. "I agree."

Olivia appeared and resumed her seat. Her eyes had a glazed brightness.

The beat of the launch was very clear now. It cut through the still air in separate dull plaques of sound, steady and rhythmical, shutting out the insect hubbub, itself now a part of the night-time stillness.

A brilliant, forked flash of lightning caused Gregory to look out of the window. He saw the *cookerit* palm near the belfry greenishly a-glimmer in the rays of a nearly-full moon, and, as he continued to watch, a bat moved across the view with a jet flicker, like lightning lapsed into mourning. He heard the bat squeak almost in the same instant as Berton gasped.

Berton was staring at Olivia.

"What's the trouble now, Berton?" frowned Mr. Harmston.

Berton did not answer but continued to stare at his sister.

Mabel took a quick breath and exclaimed: "Olivia! What's happened to your arm?"

"Did you meet with an accident upstairs, child?" said Mrs. Harmston.

"It was no accident," shrilled Berton, dropping his knife and fork. "This is the beginning of the dreadfulness."

Thunder came, filling the room with a muffled vibration as of an organ's larger bellows responding to a passionate surge of air.

Down the upper part of Olivia's arm the trickle of blood slowly ran. Soon it would reach her elbow.

"Did you cut yourself or what, Olivia?" asked Mr. Harmston.

"Yes," said Olivia. "I cut myself. On purpose."

"On purpose?"

"Yes. I used a razor to do it."

"What razor? Have you been meddling with my shaving things?"

"No. It's Gregory's razor. The one he used to kill the rooster on Sunday morning."

Gregory stopped eating.

"Where did you get it from?" asked Mabel, erect and staring.

"*I sometimes think that never blows so red*," quoted Olivia, "*The rose as where some buried Caesar bled*."

"Oh, she's off her pins," laughed Garvey. "Clean loony."

"Shut up, you filthy masturbating jackass," snarled Olivia.

"Olivia! Up! Leave the table!" said Mr. Harmston.

Olivia made no move.

"At once, Olivia."

"I won't."

Mr. Harmston rose – unhurriedly and calmly – and moving round, grasped her by a shoulder and jerked her to her feet. Her chair fell backwards to the floor with a clatter. The knuckles of her hands whitened as her grip tightened on her knife and fork. But her father, alert, caught her wrists and twisted hard and the knife and fork fell clinkingly to the floor.

"Upstairs," he said, very softly, his face emotionless.

She obeyed. Her feet, as she went, made hardly any sound on the floor.

She might be a wraith, thought Gregory.

III

The lightning had shifted round to the south-west… That means, Olivia told herself as she lay on her back in bed, that the storm has given us the go-by. The thunder is getting farther off. A few minutes ago when the lightning flashed I counted twenty-three before the thunder came. Now the count is twenty-seven, and the flash wasn't as bright as the last one. The very weather balks me. Miserable me. Don't worry, though. I'll get even with everything and everybody before long. Genie, if I could only discover where you are in your Green Bottle. I'd just have to go and rub your bottle as Aladdin rubbed his lamp and you'd rise out of the bottle like smoke and I'd tell you my wishes. You would help me to spite people who thwart me – I know you would… A woman scorned. He called me a little girl. Just because my chest is flat… He wouldn't call Mabel little because she isn't flat. Two ripe, freckled fruits Mabel has… I'm so jealous my head is swaying like a tower…

Mabel came in.

"Ollie, why haven't you lit the lamp?"

"I prefer the darkness."

"Why did you have to behave like that at table?"

"A maroon jinx is sitting on my shoulder."

Mabel lit the lamp. "I've brought up some bread and butter for you."

"Have you? Thanks. I'm hungry." She got up and helped herself to one of the pile of slices on the plate Mabel had placed on the washstand. Then she took two quick steps and kissed Mabel's cheek. "You're a sweet, nice, tall thing. I like you so much – that's why I'm sorry I have to hate you."

"What's all this you were saying about Gregory's razor?"

"What about it?"

"Have you really got a razor belonging to him?"

"I have." She began to hum a tune from *Carmen*.

Mabel regarded her curiously. "How did you come by it?"

"You threw it at me. It just missed cutting my shin by that!"

Mabel watched her in silence as she skipped about the room humming and eating.

"Take your mind back," said Olivia, "and see if you don't remember something making a slight noise in the undergrowth. It was just before you began to undress."

"You don't mean… were you there?"

"Armed with Egbert's Winchester point two-two. I had it trained straight at the maniac's head. I was just waiting to see how far he would go. If he'd attempted to cut you I'd have pulled the trigger."

"But – what possessed you to follow us?"

"I preceded you. I didn't follow you. I was expecting something like it. You ought to know what a good promnostigator I am." She took up another slice.

Mabel was blushing. She turned off and began to undress.

"Aren't you going to the concert?"

"No. I don't feel like going."

"Oh. Interesting."

They heard voices outside. The launch had arrived with the Buckmasters.

"I don't suppose he remembers anything that happened, eh?"

"No," said Mabel, pulling off her dress. It was the dark-green one with black circles interlocked, and there was no petticoat under it because of the heat. Olivia's face twitched. "Every time," she said, "you're half-naked like this you must think of him, eh?"

Mabel said nothing. She pulled on the mauve dress she had worn during the day.

"That storm," said Olivia, "has bypassed us. And I could have sworn it was going to come over. I'd planned to do something dramatic. Everything and everybody keeps frustrating me." She flung the half-eaten slice out of the window. "Mabel, I hate you! I don't want to. I love you because you're good and I like undoing your hair at night in the dark – but I hate you like chicken-gall!"

She rushed out of the room, her breath rasping in an anguish of emotion. She nearly collided with her parents in the corridor.

"Olivia," said her father, "go down and have something to eat and then run across to the church and help Mr. Buckmaster with the gramophone records. And see that the Dietz lanterns are lit – the red ones."

"I'm not going to the concert, Daddy."

"Not going? Why?"

"I've decided to stay at home – like Mabel."

"Indeed!"

"Isn't Mabel going?" said Mrs. Harmston.

"No. The heat is keeping her in. She's burning and burning."

"Anyway, you are going," said Mr. Harmston.

"I'm not, Daddy. I'm a little girl, but I can feel heat, too. My heat is in my spirit."

"No argument. Go down and eat something and go across to the church."

"I'm not obeying."

"Don't say that again."

"I'm not obeying."

He caught her arm and slapped her twice across her face.

"Gerald! Oh! That was too hard!"

"Going now?" asked the reverend gentleman of Olivia.

"Yes," said Olivia.

"Excellent," smiled her father, patting her shoulder. "Run down and have a little snack and be off, there's a good girl."

She went downstairs, her face afire but a smile on her lips.

Now, she thought, I'm suffering in body as well as in spirit.

She touched the dried trickle of blood on her arm, and her spirit surged upward like a scarf leaving her body… Vain, miserable me, she thought. But being miserable makes me happy. I'm going to enjoy being at the concert. I'll weep all through it, but they won't see the tears because the tears won't run down my cheeks but the walls of my heart…

She went into the kitchen. "Ellen, do something for me."

Ellen was washing up the dinner things, and turned from the sink with a scowl of surprise and annoyance. Her hair was tied with green cloth, and hung in two pigtails down her back… Snakes with poison-green fangs, thought Olivia. That's what her hair looks like. One day they'll strike at me and kill me, and I'll turn green when I die…

"Wha' you want me to do?" asked Ellen sulkily.

"Slap me hard and then kick me in the behind."

"Eh-eh!" said Ellen, gaping. She sucked her teeth and turned back to the sink to continue washing up.

"I'm serious. I beseech you. I'm a worm wriggling before you. Slap me and then kick me, Ellen. I want to feel pain."

Ellen ignored her for a few seconds, then turned again, and with her wet hand slapped her face – and a hard blow it was, stinging with the strong-distilled spite that went behind it.

Olivia sobbed. "Thanks. Now – now kick me. As hard as you can."

Ellen, with a whine of hate, moved round behind and kicked her – so hard that Olivia stumbled toward the door and had to clutch at the door-post to prevent herself pitching forward down the steps.

"Thank you, Ellen. Now I *am* suffering."

She ran down the stairs out into the darkness, and Ellen, roused, uttered a chuckling cluck and followed her. Caught up with her at the foot of the stairs and hit out at her, and Olivia, not expecting the attack, gasped and staggered and fell. Ellen, a dim, grey, trembling phantom of hate, kicked her in the chest, in the face; the darkness whirled with her female musk, and in the sound of her panting gurgles was malice, long pent-up, foetid and turgid.

Olivia lay quiescent and took the punishment. Shivers of elation ran through her, and she thought, even as stars spattered the gloom behind her shut eyes: I know now how Logan feels when Daddy beats him. This is joy.

Ellen desisted, and Olivia heard her whimpering softly with satisfaction. Opening her eyes, Olivia saw her squat shapely form foreshortened above her against the moonlit sky. Here near the foot of the stairs they were in deep shadow, and the shadow seemed to Olivia to rustle and hiss... I'm dazed, she thought, and shut her eyes, for she saw the shadow lowering above her face... And now the hiss could not be mistaken, for the hot shower stung her cheeks, and when she buried her face into the sparse grass the shower continued on the back of her head and on the nape of her neck and tickled its way down her back. She bore it – even the sharp, ammonia-like aroma of it... The last few drops landed on her left ear, and she heard the rustle again.

201

With a growl as though there were curds and treacle in her stomach, Ellen rose and adjusted her clothes and ran up the steps into the kitchen. And Olivia, with a sob, got up and stumbled away toward the church.

From his window, Gregory watched her but did not know it was she, for the figures of many people were visible, moving about the clearing: going into and coming out of the church.

He stood for some minutes at the window. The lightning was less vivid now and not so frequent, and the thunder came very rarely, and, when it did, faintly. In the house the bustle of footsteps gradually died down as one by one the members of the household left and went across to the church.

When, at length, all was quiet, he seated himself and thought: Now I can be at solitude with my reflections.

But the lamplight fell on Mabel in her mauve dress standing in the doorway.

"Haven't you gone? I thought I was alone in the house."

"No, I changed my mind. I don't feel like going," she said, stammering.

"Oh."

After she had looked about the room a moment with an air of discomfiture, she murmured: "I preferred staying with you."

"I see. Please come in, won't you?" He rose. "You can have this chair. I'll sit on the bed if you like." He spoke quickly and with confusion.

"No, I'll get the chair from my room."

"Do let me," he said, and hurried past her, and in a moment returned with the easy chair from the next room. They seated themselves in silence, half-facing each other, he near the window, his arm resting on the sill.

After an awkward pause, he said: "Do you – is there something you want to discuss with me?"

"Not exactly – yes, one or two things. Would you mind if we put out the lamp?"

"You'd prefer it out?"

"Yes. The moonlight is bright enough, and – and I'd be more at ease."

"By all means, then." He gave her a quick grin as he rose,

and said: "You prefer me not to see you blushing – isn't that it?"

She laughed: "Yes, you've guessed right. It is silly of me."

They were both uncomfortable for an interval, listening to the sound of voices and the thump and rustle of activity over at the church. Besides two gas-lamps, there were ruby-glassed Dietz lanterns at the western end of the church, and what with the blue-white pallor of the gas-light and the rich red rays of the Dietz lanterns, the effect, viewed from the house here, was weird in the extreme.

Gregory felt the restfulness returning; it moved over and through him like a soothing powder. He said: "I wish it were possible to extend this moment endlessly through time."

"What's that?"

He repeated what he had said, and added: "I mean, if life could continue to be nothing more than this room with you and me sitting in the half-darkness and looking at the church and the moonlight, and no necessity to eat or drink or move from our seats, and no need to take into account the impact of all the years before we arrived at this moment."

She gave a reflective grunt.

After a silence, she said: "You're sure you don't mind me being in here? You didn't want to read or anything?"

"I did want to – but not badly. I much prefer it like this."

"What are you reading?"

"Brenda's play. I think I mentioned to one of you that she wrote a play?"

"Yes. *The Harrowed.*"

He started. "But... I'm sure I didn't mention the title."

"Yes – to me. On Sunday."

The soaring powerful shriek of violins and woodwinds came to them from the church.

"Sibelius's Second," Mabel murmured. "I didn't know they were going to play that."

"Tell me. What actually happened on Sunday?"

She told him – quietly and with composure. In her manner, at this moment, there was something of her father.

"Good God! But how humiliating for you!"

"Humiliating? Why humiliating? Oh, you mean my undressing. Not at all. That was the least. We don't attach so much importance here to the exposure of our bodies, though, I admit, I am a little shy now and then. The truth is I was terribly frightened. I thought you meant to cut my throat after I'd undressed. I nearly ran off and left you, but – but I suddenly knew that you couldn't help yourself – that you weren't shamming as I'd thought at first – and – and I just wanted to help you."

"You mean – what you want to say is that you felt sorry for me. You needn't be afraid to say it." He spoke harshly.

"Yes, I was. I nearly cried."

He began to shift about in his chair and look from side to side.

"It's the worst thing you could have told me," he said. "Nothing upsets me more than to be pitied. It's the thing above everything else I can't stand – and that's because subconsciously it's the thing I yearn for most of all. Pity – and love."

"Have you been so starved of pity and love?"

He shook his head slightly and looked out of the window. The fireflies, in the moonlight, seemed pale and ineffectual… Tympani rumbled dramatically in the church, hurling ladders of triumph through the windless hot night… "I got too much of it," he said, without looking at her. "From my mother – and more from Brenda. I hated them both for it. All my life I've had pity and love dribbled on me. I've never been able to escape the shower. And the trouble is I revel in it and need it even though it embitters me when I get it." He began to squeeze his hands together. "I'm afraid I'm an awful mess. An awful mess," he repeated in a mumble as though to himself.

"I… you've misunderstood me a little. It was only on Sunday, for a second or two, I felt sorry for you. I don't feel so now." She laughed. "It's a good thing the lamp is out."

They listened to the music.

Lightning twitched weakly above the jungle. Up-river a baboon roared, and after a few seconds they heard the answering roar of its mate.

"You people are fond of talking about shadows here. Yours are ghosts – but mine are more tangible. As soon as I dodge one, another confronts me."

"Did your wife really die by drowning in Barbados?"

"Yes. I've mentioned it, haven't I?"

"Yes, you told Ollie."

He tilted his head thoughtfully and then nodded. "On the church steps there, yes. I remember now. We heard insects going tick, tick."

She watched him steadily.

"What exactly did I tell her? Do you know?"

She told him.

"Yes, that's what happened. I have a newspaper cutting about it. It happened a few days before I arrived in the island. It was the shock of the news that set me off. It came to me as the climaxing frustration. After following her around so persistently and always being cheated of meeting her so that I could humiliate her. I didn't really intend killing her. I wanted her to live and – and convince me that she was no more clever than I. I wanted…" He put his hand to his temple and was silent a moment. "She wasn't evil. You can ignore that part of what I told Olivia. But she did make me feel inferior. She did go out of her way to eclipse me."

Lightning.

"The great trouble with me is that I've never had to do any struggling. I've never known poverty, you see."

"Uncle Garvey was in real estate, wasn't he?"

"Yes. And it was a very prosperous firm."

After a silence he said: "Things fell into my lap too easily. The result was that what talent I had couldn't develop. Talent, like everything else, needs friction if it is to bloom richly. Opposition, struggle – rob any living thing of them and gradual atrophy follows. That's my chief tragedy – I've met so little resistance. It's made me conceited and complacent to the point of megalomania. At school I was brilliant in class – I won two scholarships, and I graduated at Cambridge with first class honours. I was a good cricketer and a good footballer. I couldn't do anything badly. At home my mother pampered me disgracefully. I was her little god. Then I married Brenda, and she pampered me, too. But the difficulty there was that she was more talented than I – and I couldn't bear the thought, so I left her. She did everything in her power to persuade me to come back, but I wouldn't. I insulted her on innumerable occasions when we happened to meet. At last, when she saw that it was hopeless she tried to spite me deliberately by outshining me at everything I did. Sheer pique drove her to it, that's all. Couldn't really blame her. Now I look back on it I see that it was a kind of illness we were both suffering from – the filthy sickness of ultra-civilized people. In that sense she was evil. We were both evil. But at heart she was good – and she really cared deeply about me."

The house creaked in the privacy of its concealed interstices, and about them the dark seemed to wreathe with subtle vapours breathed in from the moonlight. A firefly alighted on the windowsill, crawled an inch or two then hopped off into flight again, entering the room with silent white arcs thrust through the dark. They turned their heads to follow it about the room. It vanished above the tester of the bed, but they could see the outer aura of its glowing. Then it appeared like a swift comet and dived toward the pillows, illuminating the linen in one limp revealing flash before it shot past them and out through the window.

Mabel made a puzzled sound.

"Anything the matter?" he asked.

Without replying, she rose and crossed to the bed. She bent forward, and he saw her hand reach out and take up something from the pillows. A white square of paper. He heard it rustle.

"What's this?" she asked. "Did you put it here?"

"What's what?"

She brought it to the window, and they read what was on it. Even by moonlight they could tell that the words had been daubed in blood.

MY FLAT CHEST BURNS FOR YOU.

Mabel giggled. "So this is why she cut her arm."

"She has a most peculiar temperament. I don't understand her."

"I must try and get your razor back from her."

"Oh, it doesn't matter. I seldom use it. I have a Gillette set." He shifted about uncomfortably. "Do you know how she managed to find it?"

She told him.

"She witnessed everything, then?"

"Yes. But don't let it trouble you. It doesn't matter."

He said nothing, and she moved away from the window and resumed her seat, crumpling up the paper and dropping it on the floor.

An insect – a Hercules beetle in all probability – began to make a buzzing in the rafters.

"I've been wondering," she began.

"Yes?"

"Do you like it being here with us?"

"Very much."

"You – do you mean that honestly?"

"Of course. I have no desire whatever to see a city again."

The beetle buzzed right over their heads. She glanced up.

"You don't mind – the beetles and hairy spiders, and not having theatres and nightclubs?"

"No."

Her hands were restless in her lap.

"Why do you ask?"

"I just wanted to know," she mumbled, after a hesitation.

They heard applause in the church. A drift of air entered, dank and warm, and dense with verdure, like water from the river in spirit form.

"Are you – do you really suffer from delirium tremens?"

"Good Lord, no. I've never at any time been a drinker at all. What makes you – ?"

"But I thought –"

"Oh, I see what you're getting at." They spoke together in a confused babble. "The whisky I brought." He gave an uncomfortable laugh. "I must have developed a delusion that I was addicted to alcohol. I took it three times a day in diminishing doses if I'm not mistaken. I started that in Barbados after learning of Brenda's death. It was part of my self-pity neurosis. I had to have a serious 'ailment' that needed prolonged treatment, and delirium tremens must have seemed to me just the thing. I have an idea, too, I was trying to convince Brenda's ghostly presence of my strength of character."

After a silence of fidgetings, she asked: "Have you suffered often from delusions in the past?"

"On one or two occasions when life seemed particularly intolerable. The stress of things – my frustrations…" He broke off, but mastered himself almost at once and said: "I've been treated by a psychiatrist. He was of the opinion that only a complete change of environment would cure me. I never took his advice because of my obsession with Brenda. It's only the knowledge that she's dead that makes it possible for me to stay here."

"You mean if she were alive you'd have to go on following her about wherever she went?"

"Yes." He uncrossed his legs, then crossed them again.

"You think it possible you might have a relapse?"

"I oughtn't to – not living under these conditions. But one can never be sure."

"I… you mustn't think me inquisitive…"

He waited for her to continue.

"I wanted to tell you – no, I won't bother."

"What's it you want to say now?"

"I'm beginning to like you – a lot," she said.

"Oh."

During the prolonged silence that followed they heard the river whisper amidst the shrubs along the bank. The mooring ropes that secured the launch at the landing-place creaked off and on as the craft swayed gently in the water.

The air in the room was very close; the heat seemed to trail around them as though spun out in unseen but tactile threads from the ghostly cloud that was the bunched-up mosquito-net.

The languorous sustained wail of a violin twined its winding way through the night air.

"The *Scheherazade*."

"Yes," he said.

During another silence they heard footsteps downstairs, and tilted their heads alertly.

"Logan?" he suggested.

She shook her head. "He should be asleep by now. Ellen, too."

After an interval they heard the thud-thud again – this time on the stairs. It was someone barefooted.

"No harm if I investigated," he whispered, rising.

"No, please. I don't think – it may not be anyone real."

"What do you mean it may not –"

"Sit down. Please," she begged, touching him, and he sat down.

Presently, the footsteps sounded in the corridor. Then in the next room. They were stealthy. He rose at a bound, was at the door in two strides, his rubber-soled shoes noiseless on the floor. Three more strides brought him to the door of the next room. He looked in and saw a shortish figure moving furtively about the room, made a rush, and the next moment had the man firmly in his grasp, wrists pinioned behind him. The fellow made a few gasping sounds, struggled, then surrendered.

Mabel came in.

"Light the lamp," Gregory told her, and she stumbled nervously to the dressing-table and lit the lamp.

"Sigmund!"

The man gave a sheepish smile, shifty-eyed.

"The fourth time! Oh, my heavens!" There was such an intensity of emotion in her manner that Gregory gave her a puzzled stare.

"You see that! Daddy was right. You're hopeless."

Sigmund scowled and struggled ineffectually.

"You took advantage of the concert. I suppose you heard Gregory had arrived and you were just waiting for a chance to break in and see what you could filch from his belongings. Gregory, release him."

Gregory obeyed – with uncertainty and reluctance.

"All right, go. Get out of the house. Tomorrow the parson will come for you – and you know what it means!"

They accompanied him downstairs and saw him out through the front door. In the gallery Logan lay asleep on his mattress, flat on his back and naked, mouth open. His bandaged foot, a rugged, jutting monstrosity splashed white with moonlight from a window nearby, kept twitching. Their footsteps on the floorboards, one or two of which drummed loosely, did not disturb him. The house swam in a lake of heat, and the large planes of darkness humped about them contained the whirr of insect wings, a soft menace that persistently followed them and persistently failed to materialize. When they were upstairs again, she blew out the lamp and looked around the room as though expectant of some event or presence crouched within the shaft of an unknown dimension. The mellowed woody scent of the unpainted walls swirled strongly about them. Outside, the launch's mooring ropes creaked lazily.

"Is something bothering you?" he asked.

She fanned herself with her hand.

He watched her, and saw her profile abruptly silhouetted against the glow of a firefly at the window. The insect as suddenly vanished.

"I felt so sure he'd given up his thieving ways." She spoke as though she had forgotten his presence.

"How do you punish such cases here?" he asked.

She had the air of being reluctant to explain, but replied: "Our rule is not to punish them in any way – for the first three major offences. We caution them and do what we can to educate them out of the crime habit."

They went back into his room and resumed their seats. "What about the fourth major offence? You punish them for that?"

She nodded, staring before her, chin in hand, elbow on knee. She was perspiring from the heat and their recent activity; he could smell the perspiration – mingled with the perfume she used. He was perspiring, too; the steamy warmth of it seemed to seep into his spirit and produce a wavering anxiety allied to the buzzing of another beetle in the rafters.

She said impulsively: "I'll trust you. Eventually you'll have to know, anyway. He's got to die."

"Die?"

"Yes. I have to report him. It's my duty." She spoke agitatedly. "We have our own secret laws here, and anyone who commits a major offence for the fourth time has got to be – to be done away with, because it means he's an incurable criminal and a nuisance and menace to our community."

He only watched her.

"We've created our own set of values here – about human relations and living generally. You won't understand – they'll seem strange to you, but I can tell you, we honestly want to be a happy and healthy community – and to bring this about we have

210

to have a firm and practical policy in regard to the weeding out of all undesirable elements." She stretched out and touched his knee. "Please try to understand. Don't sneer, or condemn our ways." She was trembling.

He leant forward. "Calm yourself and let's get this straight. Who's going to try this chap and sentence him to death? Doesn't he come under British law? Isn't this a British country?"

"Haven't I just told you that we have secret laws of our own?"

"Secret laws?"

"We're over a hundred miles from the police. No one troubles about us up here."

"But if I remember, your father mentioned to me that this reservation exists only by permission of the government."

"Yes, that's true. When the mission was established here Daddy had to get permission to act as protector over the Indians on this reservation – and he's gained the reputation of being a very fit and proper protector, so the government leaves us alone. And we deserve to be left alone to do things our way. Look at the good we're doing for these people. We're giving them an education they could never have hoped to get from the government. We've developed their imaginations with our religious myths, and we've taught them to be disciplined and to be satisfied with a simple life and yet to be appreciative of the arts. Haven't we a right to form secret laws of our own if we feel the laws of the government unimaginative and ineffectual when applied to the affairs of our community?"

"I'm sorry," he said. "I didn't intend to get you worked up like this."

"It isn't you. It's – I'm upset because of Sigmund."

"But why should you be – if you consider he'll be getting justice?"

"Because I'm human, that's why!" she flashed. "I can't help my feelings, can I? Trust you to say something like that. It's typical of the civilization you've left behind you. In your modern world you never remember that people are human. You make your smug, rigid rules and expect people to conform with them as if they were machines. Here we teach that rules must be elastic, because human nature is elastic. We believe in discipline, but we don't let discipline enslave us. And we don't try to be hypocritical or sentimental about our duty. Sometimes we have to do certain things that pain us, and we admit they're painful, but we go ahead and do them because it's practical and sensible and necessary to our happiness to do them. And above all, we don't try to torture our consciences with moral issues."

"Please be calm. Please. Remember I'm not yet fully initiated into your ways here." He patted her knee, and felt her tremble.

She settled back in her chair and said quietly: "You must excuse me."

After a silence, he said: "Could I make a suggestion?"

"What's that?"

"Logan was asleep when we let Sigmund out of the house."

"What of that?"

"Only you and I know that he broke in here tonight. Why couldn't we simply forget all about it?"

She made a noncommittal sound and pressed her hands to her face.

"You could depend upon me not to breathe a word," he said.

She removed her hands from her face slowly.

Applause sounded in the church. A bird in the jungle made solemn, bell-like notes.

"It would be a breach of trust. Daddy depends upon us to do our duty. He would be very disappointed in me if he knew I hadn't reported the incident." She took a long breath. "Perhaps you've got the impression that he's superficial and insincere. To a stranger he would seem so – but in reality he's solid. We respect him very much."

He said nothing.

"A few years ago we had another case like Sigmund's – the only other one since our mission started here. I cried for a whole night after – after the man was killed. His name was Cedric. He was a buffianda."

"What's a buffianda?"

"A half-breed. Generally Indian and negro."

"Logan, for instance?"

"Yes. He's got Portuguese in him, too."

"How was Cedric killed?"

212

"*Curari* – an Indian poison. He was given a needle dipped in *curari* after he was sentenced – but he was too much of a coward to do it himself, so it was done for him – by a member of the jury who found him guilty. We select twelve of the most intelligent of our people to act as jury."

"Wasn't there an inquest?"

"Yes, but Daddy acts as coroner at any inquest up here, and in his report to the authorities he said that Cedric died from snakebite. Death by misadventure." She cleared her throat. "Daddy is Registrar of births and deaths. He's everything in one up here."

He watched her.

In the dining-room downstairs the clock struck the half-hour.

"I won't tell on Sigmund – since you suggest I shouldn't."

He put out his hand, smiling, and she put out hers. Their fingers touched. She gave a gasp and rose and bent quickly and kissed him, then turned and went stumbling hurriedly out of the room.

IV

… a complication I had not foreseen, though I ought to have, for it seems, now that I review the situation, an inevitable development. Nineteen and probably not once come into intimate contact with a sophisticated man of my type; it is natural that she would find me fascinating. My colourful past, too, must appeal to her imagination; she no doubt sees me as a glamorously wicked man of the world. A Lord Henry Wootton watered down somewhat by remorse – and neurosis. I probably seem to her ripe for conversion into the kind of husband with whom she could live happily ever after. A real pity, for she is a fine creature. I enjoy talking to her; her company is soothing – like a segment of the general restfulness this place has brought to me. How can I let her know that I have lost all inclination for sexual relations, that the calm which possesses me is the calm of the castrated? Let me be careful now. I am in no position to know whether a eunuch experiences calmness of spirit, for I am not one *in facto*. This may be a phase I am passing through; in a week or two my virility may begin to reassert itself; in fact, if I were deadly honest with myself I would foresee this as a certainty. The spirit may impose its jadedness upon the flesh – but not for long. My problem, then, will be to decide how to react toward this girl. To seduce her would be simple – but that would damage me irreparably; I should be attacked with a self-revulsion too intense to be borne, for I don't love her nor do I feel I ever could – and if even I could, marriage would be out of the question. After Brenda, married life with any woman would be ludicrous: I should find it impossible to reconcile myself to such a state; my mind would deteriorate from sheer self-ridicule. That isn't cynical. I am being honest… Trees, river, I do wish you could sing to me the formula I need. I wish you could tell me how to be at peace without disturbing the peace of others. And how does one achieve harmony between spirit and fevered flesh…

"Not a penny – half a crown for 'em!"

Gregory started and smiled. "Oh, nothing important, I'm sure."

The reverend gentleman sank down beside him on the ground and idly plucked a leaf of dragon's blood and flicked it over the logs into the water. "This seems to be your favourite spot of late, I notice," he said with a friendly smile. "Keeping an eye out for the police?"

"The police?"

Mr. Harmston fanned himself; he was attired in shorts only, and his hairy torso streamed in the mid-afternoon heat. He had just come from the workshed where he had been putting in his daily two hours on the now nearly completed bookcase.

"Wish I could keep as cool as you manage to," he said. "You made a similar remark on my first morning here about the police. On this same spot, too, if I remember."

"You do remember, then?"

"Yes."

Mr. Harmston gave an amused grunt. "A little joke of mine, that's all, my boy. I'm full of such trifling pleasantries."

They watched the swaying *corial* and skiff moored against the logs…

Thunder boomed in the south.

"Always distant."

"I beg your pardon," said Gregory, starting out of a reverie.

"The thunder."

"Oh."

"One day soon, when we least expect, one of these storms will come our way."

"I suppose they're pretty violent in these parts?"

"Extremely. Thunder can be almost continuous sometimes. We had a bad one only a few days before you arrived. June, July, August is the thunderstorm period here."

"In England, too. Have you forgotten?"

The reverend gentleman smiled. "No. No, I haven't forgotten."

They listened to the water lapping amidst the shrubs.

"We're generally lucky with lightning. Never once been hit."

He added as an afterthought: "A new *tacooba* or two in the creek is about the worst inconvenience we've suffered."

"What's a *tacooba*?"

"Indian word. Means a fallen tree or any sort of obstruction in a river or creek that constitutes a menace to navigation." He plucked a leaf. "Many such, I presume, in your stream of consciousness?"

"Many such… what do you mean?"

"Phew! Warm. Coming to church tomorrow?"

"Yes, I daresay."

"Sitting next to Mabel again?"

Gregory gave him a sharp glance. "It's possible. Why?"

"Just thought I'd ask. I recall you sat next to her last Sunday."

"Oh."

"It's Communion Sunday tomorrow."

"Will I be permitted to take communion?"

"Certainly. No formality about being confirmed."

"Do you go in for baptism and confirmation here?"

"No. The font you see in the church is purely decorative."

"Like the altar?"

"Exactly. As tomorrow is communion we'll light candles. Symbol of festivity and warm hearts – and of life: the flickering, ephemeral flame of life."

Gregory smiled.

"Beginning to get settled down among us?" asked Mr. Harmston.

"Yes – I think so. I find it very pleasant."

"Um. Quite cured of all your nervous troubles and what not?"

"I feel very well, thank you."

"Excellent. A remarkable recovery. Hardly here ten days and a new man. Speaks well for the local influences."

Gregory grinned. "By the way, what *are* these local influences?"

"Psychic," said Mr. Harmston.

Gregory grunted. "I do wish you'd come straight for a change."

"And destroy my whole philosophy of life?"

"Oh."

"Haven't you come to realize yet that the keynote of our

happiness here is evasion?" He brushed off an eye-fly. "The chief fault in the civilization you've left behind you is its obsession with conclusions. Nothing, my boy, creates greater disillusion than the arrival at a conclusion. Pardon me if I seem wantonly epigrammatical."

Gregory smiled.

"Look at this water," said Mr. Harmston. "Black and mysterious. Sinister. Leave it at that, and it's a thing of perpetual fascination. But take a specimen of it, analyse it and discover that its blackness is the result of the suspended vegetable matter it contains, and behold! it's no longer a thing of fascination. You've stripped it of its mystery. Forever after it's merely water. That's what's happening to your civilization. One by one you're reducing your myths to commonplace dust."

"But isn't it human to be curious about mysteries?"

"Yes. The human race suffers from an incurable curiosity, but there's no harm in that, surely. On the contrary, I should say curiosity is a healthy sign. It indicates the presence of dynamic factors: the will to develop, the will to create. But why can't we control it? Think of the pleasant paths our curiosity can lead us up; the thrilling quests it can set us on. Yet we deliberately spoil our fun by our insistence on finding the hidden treasure. A jewel chanced upon now and then is good; an odd jewel here and there imbues us with hope, inspires us to new dreams, new efforts. But no. That isn't enough. We must rush headlong up the path, greedy and ranting, and root out the whole bag of precious stones – and then what? The secret is out. The mystery is exploded. Our fun is over. Life, my boy, is an interlude between one mystery and another – the mystery that precedes birth and the mystery that succeeds death. It is only we who have imbued this gap between dark and dark with articulation and significance. Hence why so much importunacy?

"Life is quite pointless. There is no purpose in it. It is only we who give it importance and fret ourselves into wrinkles over big deals and national institutions, codes of morality and religious and political ideologies. We make it seem so sensationally momentous, don't we? But what? The end is always the grave; the ignominious worms. Nebuchadnezzar, Pericles, Attila, Julius

Caesar, Cicero, Beethoven, Napoleon, President Wilson – all in the grave. Shadows returned to the shadows.

"We ourselves, unwittingly, have created reality, my boy, and we have created it out of the dream-stuff of our own fancies. The birth of every infant is the birth of an empty cloud – a cloud that only time may fill, and shape into a vision of coherence and tangibility. We can exist in harmony with reality – which is to say we can be happy – only if we admit the tenuous quality of reality; if we perceive the close affinity between actuality and dream. Don't you agree that it is uncertainty that brings us our greatest delight, that stimulates our interest in our fellows and in our surroundings and gives us the incentive to work and create, to amuse ourselves? Suppose we knew in detail precisely how everything would fall out tomorrow and the day after to the end of our lives, do you think we would find much pleasure in being alive? No. It's the thrill of the unknown that keeps us excited and humming – the not being aware of what lurks in that dark corner over there – or around the next bend. Think, my boy. To sit in a room and know that you are with a chair, a table, a bookcase, two or three people and other known and predictable company – or to sit in a room with a phantom that never wholly reveals itself to eye or ear. Which do you say would be the more interesting situation?"

"In other words," said Gregory, "you're advocating that to be really happy we must lead a life that is a mixture of fantasy and reality?"

"You've summed it up crudely but clearly." The reverend gentleman smiled – and brushed off an eye-fly. "Just enough reality," he said, "to keep us fed, sheltered and tolerably entertained, and just not enough fantasy to have us certified insane."

Footsteps thudded on the gravel track behind them, and Olivia came up at a trot, a sealed envelope in one hand, an electric torch in the other. She was in the old green bathing costume.

Her father smiled round at her with enquiry.

"Missive from Gertrude, wife of Sigmund," she said in a formal voice, holding out the envelope.

"H'm," said her father, taking it. "Anything important?"

"I believe so, parson."

Gregory smiled at her, but she ignored him.

The reverend gentleman turned the letter over contempla-tively, then glanced at her and asked: "Whose torch is that, by the way?"

"It is the property of Eric of Book Squad, parson."

"What are you doing with it?"

"I borrowed it for a certain secret purpose, parson. I regret it cannot be divulged."

Mr. Harmston stroked his chin. "Anything else to report from the Reservation?"

"Gunther and his wife Rachel between them today completed three shirts, a dress for Mabel and a pair of trousers. It's a record, they say. But they state that the Singer machine needs some overhauling."

"Yes. I've ordered some new parts. What of the pair of shorts I ordered last week?"

"They finished those since yesterday. I've taken them home. They now repose on the bed in the Big Room."

"Excellent. Anything else to report?"

"A calf was born last night to Ethelred's cow. A bull-calf."

There was distant thunder.

Gregory glanced toward the south and saw the grey-blue cloud-pile.

Olivia stood waiting.

"Very well, my girl," said her father. "You can go off duty now."

Her manner relaxed. She began to hum a tune from *Samson and Delilah.* "Cooling off a bit, Daddy? Or waiting for the storm?"

"Cooling off a bit. I don't think the storm will come over. Not today."

"Always an optimist, eh?" She hummed another snatch of *My heart at thy sweet voice,* then said: "By the way, guess where Maby is at the minute."

"Where is she?"

"Having a swim in the creek with Berton and Garvey and Robert of Art Squad and Robert's sister."

"What's so odd in that?"

"Nothing. I just thought I'd mention it. Phew! Isn't it scorching!" She went off at a dart, and Mr. Harmston smiled and wagged his head affectionately. "Regular little sprite," he said. "Takes our doctrines very seriously."

"Yes, she's certainly a most mystifying child," nodded Gregory.

"Of course, you see what she was getting at in that remark about Mabel?"

"No, I'm afraid I don't."

"It was meant for you," chuckled the reverend gentleman, tearing open the envelope as he spoke. "She probably thinks you'll be tempted to find your way to the creek to watch Mabel and the boys besporting themselves in the water."

Gregory frowned. "Why should I be tempted to do that?"

Mr. Harmston was reading what was written on the slip of paper he had taken from the envelope. He grunted. "Not so nice, this," he said, folding up the paper and tucking it into his shirt pocket. "Oh, you were asking. Well, you see, we all bathe naked here. I suppose Olivia thought it would shock – and titillate – your civilized sensibilities to see Mabel swimming around in the nude." He sighed and rose. "Must be off to attend to a little matter, my boy."

"Oh."

"Rather serious report from Gertrude," Mr. Harmston murmured.

"Serious?"

"Um. She states that her husband Sigmund has vanished. She has seen nothing of him since Thursday night – the night of the concert."

220

V

…in time, I have, little doubt, I shall get accustomed to their antics and quirks. I must try not to be disturbed. Detachment of spirit is what I need to strive after – or perhaps I could modify that and say that if I joined my spirit to the passivity of this water and the trees I would achieve the peace I want. Yet, again, let me be frank and admit that without human companionship, without positive relations with my fellow beings, my soul would slowly mummify… Vivid flash, that. Strange that these storms should threaten but never come to anything. It is almost as though we were outside their notice: in a sector of contempt. Or a more lucid way of putting it would be to say that we are just without the circumference of the storm-circle and may watch the drama at near-distance. One day, by an isobaric vagary, the circle will shift, and then – assuming that it shifts in our direction – our roles will become changed from audience to persons of the drama… my soul would slowly mummify… I wonder if I shall ever feel again the urge to write a play. In such a conjecture lies terror. I know I have been purposely avoiding the issue. Evading it… "the keynote of our happiness here is evasion…" Will my creative energy reassert itself before long – and if it does am I to yield to it and write plays and paint pictures that will never be known to anyone beyond this jungle settlement? Would my vanity be able to stand such an eclipse?…

Thunder.

A punt was going past laden with rough logs. Behind it, in tow, moved a raft of more logs securely lashed together. The punt was provided with a palm-leaf tent under which hammocks were slung, and a negro and an Indian wielded the huge oars that propelled the craft.

Ten days of life moving at the pace of that punt, and I am much improved – but not yet cured. Could I stand ten weeks, ten months, of this kind of life… The sun is hot. I should not sit here bareheaded like this… Strange that these storms should threaten…

Footsteps…

He turned his head and saw Mabel approaching. She was in a pink cotton dress. Her hair hung down to her waist and was wet and limp. She smiled and said: "I saw you sitting on this same spot over an hour ago. Haven't you moved from here since?"

"No."

She settled herself beside him, and he smelt the creek-water smell of her, refreshing and wholesome.

"You've been having a bathe in the creek, I heard."

"Yes, who told you?"

"Olivia."

"Yes, I generally do on Saturday afternoons. In this hot weather I could go swimming every day if I had the time."

"There are no *perai* in the creek?"

"No, it's perfectly safe. You should come and bathe with us." In voice and manner she exuded exhilaration.

He smiled and said: "It would be a pleasure." Then he remembered and added: "But I'm afraid – well, I haven't yet taken to nudism."

She laughed, colouring. "It doesn't matter about that. You can wear trunks if it would embarrass you."

"And wouldn't you yourself be embarrassed – wearing nothing?"

"No."

He gave her a keen stare. "Are you serious?"

"Of course. You see, we've grown up accustomed not to be shy of exposing our bodies. When you first came I would have been a bit shy to let you see me, but not now that I know you better."

"But I'm still what I was when I arrived. I mean my views are still those of a man from the civilization beyond this jungle."

"I suppose they are, but you're no stranger now."

He smiled: "Do you honestly feel that your way of doing things up here is wholesome and sensible?"

"Certainly. Wholesome and sensible *and* civilized. We don't look upon you as civilized. We think you barbarous in many ways. Your views on sex and religion and clothes – they're what one would expect of savages. When I say 'you' I mean your civilization, of course."

He was silent a moment, then said: "But if you favour nudism why do you go about clothed as you do?"

"For the benefit of the authorities. We have to do many things for the sake of appearances. Imagine if some Government official paid us a surprise visit and found us all walking around in the nude. Why, before we knew it, Daddy would be denounced as immoral and no fit person to be a protector over the Indians here. The Government would shut us down." She smiled. "We have to be realists in spite of our belief in a – in a make-believe existence, and in spite of our codes of healthy living."

He regarded her reflectively for a moment, then murmured: "You've changed."

"I? Changed?"

"Yes. Within the past few days, I mean. You seemed so diffident and reticent when I first arrived."

She nodded, looking at the water. "I know I've changed. I feel it. It's you that's responsible."

"Me?"

"Yes."

He frowned. "Look here, I think you're being unwise."

"In what way?"

He hesitated, discomfited, then said: "I should prefer if you didn't become interested in me."

"But I am already. I'm in love with you."

He smiled and shook his head. "That's not being realistic, Mabel."

"You mean… You think I'm only infatuated? I'm not. I was in love with Robert of Art Squad. We were friendly – but it wasn't like this."

He shrugged.

"I thought it might be infatuation myself. During the early part of the week I thought so. But Thursday night I felt… I never felt like that before." Her voice sounded level and unimpassioned, but she sat very still.

"Shouldn't you go and dry your hair? It's very wet."

"Yes. I'm going to dry it and comb it. Thursday night I wanted you so much I nearly…" She began to squeeze her thumb. "Are you a wrestler?"

"I have done a bit of wrestling – and boxing. Not profession-ally, of course. At school. Why do you ask?"

"The way you caught and held Sigmund on Thursday night."

They heard a soft, distant swashing noise. It seemed to ap-proach, then died away. It was the wind in the jungle. An insect amidst the shrubs nearby made a steamy wheeze, thin and tweeting – and stopped. The sound was not repeated. They heard the lapping of the water.

"If only we could get some rain," she murmured. "You shouldn't sit in the sun bareheaded like this."

"Have you heard about Sigmund?" he asked.

"No. What about him?"

"Your father got a note from his wife. She says he's been missing since Thursday night."

Some of the colour left her face.

"I suppose he'll turn up before long," he said. She said nothing, her face troubled.

"If," he said, "a magician – or let us say Olivia's Genie in the Green Bottle – offered to bestow upon you some superhuman power of your own choice, what power would you ask for?"

She smiled. "I don't know. I'd have to think it over before I could decide. What would you ask for?"

"The power to be immune from the frustrations, anxieties and disillusionments that go with human passions and yet not to be divorced from the sensual pleasures they can bring me."

"In other words, to be able to eat your cake and have it."

"In a manner of speaking, yes. I'm a coward, you see."

"I know you are. It's partly why I love you."

He smiled and grunted. "Are you sure? Or is it because of the way I caught and held Sigmund Thursday night?"

"That, too." She pinkened and shifted about. "You're strong and weak together. I like the mixture." As though to cover up her slight confusion, she went on: "I suppose he must be hiding in the jungle, poor fellow. Afraid to face the consequences."

"The instinct of self-preservation," he murmured.

"He must have been sure I would have reported him."

"There lies," he said, "the snag in all our doings."

"What snag?"

"Compassion. It is the enemy of every human endeavour, yet we must cherish it, for without it we'd cease to be human."

"I feel very guilty for not reporting him, though."

He touched her knee. "The blame is mine, not yours."

"It isn't. It's very much mine. Brought up as I was, I ought never to have allowed you to persuade me away from my duty."

Thunder. It prattled like palm-seeds scattered on a roof.

She edged closer to him.

He mumbled something, and she asked him what he had said.

"Nothing," he replied.

"But I heard what you said. You said you like the smell of me."

He nodded, his gaze on the water, his hands twitching slightly. "My virility reasserting itself," he murmured.

Her breath came in swift long lisps.

And when the Angel with his darker Draught…

They started and turned their heads.

"Draws up to thee," continued Olivia, halting behind them.

"Take that, and do not shrink," finished Gregory, with a smile.

Mabel blushed and frowned. "What's the idea of creeping up so quietly upon us, Olivia?"

"The better to overhear you, my dears."

"I hope you liked what you overheard," said Mabel coldly.

"I like what I smell of you. You smell of creek water. Oh, lovely, hot thing! What nice, wet, long hair! Go and put it up so that tonight in bed I can take it down for you." She sank down beside Gregory and smiled at him: "Now you're between shadow and substance. I bet you won't guess who is the substance."

"It's too warm for betting or guessing, I fear."

"That sounds as if it might be a line from your new play."

He winced.

"See! I can hit you on your tender spots when I want. I've learnt all of them."

"Olivia, why don't you run off and leave us alone!"

"Because, sweet creature, I have as much right as you to make love to him." She leant her head against Gregory's shoulder. "Tell me. Haven't I, Gregory darling?"

"Oh, by all means," Gregory grinned.

Mabel made a sound of impatience and rose, but Gregory

caught her hand and said: "Please don't go," and she hesitated and then sat down again.

"Love knows no sense of humour," said Olivia.

"Nor do children, it is to be greatly feared," murmured Gregory.

"Some children are wiser than their years."

"And extremely annoying," nodded Gregory.

"Only when they know what grown-ups don't like them to know."

"I suppose you imagine you're being awfully clever," said Mabel.

"I think I am a little. Defend me, Gregory dear, won't you?"

"I won't, wicked child."

Olivia began to hum a tune, waving her head to and fro in time.

Gregory gave her pigtail a pull and said: "Where did you get this war-worn bathing suit from, by the way?"

"This? It belongs to Mother. She used to wear it in the days when she was too shy to go swimming without anything on."

"It suits you admirably," said Gregory, and glanced at Mabel and winked. Mabel gave a reluctant smile.

"I don't agree with you, fair sir," said Olivia. "It sags abominably, and should certainly not grace the person of a handsome maid like yours sincerely. From tomorrow I'm going around in panties instead, and I'll have this thing burnt at the stake. Fortunately I haven't got freckles on my poor flat chest and belly, so I won't be self-conscious."

"I have a partiality for freckles," said Gregory, "especially on the female chest and belly."

"You're making our poor Mabel blush. I bet she didn't blush on Thursday night when she kissed you. Ah! That makes you both blush!" She threw back her head and laughed wildly. "That was only a Palthian shot!" she cried, springing up. "Let me go now and do my harmonium practice."

"You're mad, child," said Mabel.

"Not *so* mad as somebody recently was. I wonder where Sigmund is. Daddy is forming search-parties to go and look for him."

Gregory and Mabel stared at her, Gregory abruptly serious.

"I told Daddy I have a theory about his disappearance, and he heeded my words, because he respects the spirit rather than the freckled flesh."

Lightning flashed brassily in the south.

"Did you see the fiery fork?" said Olivia. "Well, I must be off. Harmonium practice in the empty church with phantoms around me. See you in bed tonight, my hot sister!"

They watched her dart off. Saw her pause and look back at them and smile.

"*And when the Angel…*" She waved at them, laughed shrilly and went sprinting toward the church, her long legs lithe, her feet noiseless on the earth.

VI

"You frighten me, Ollie."

"I'm sorry, Berton dear, but sometimes I must frighten you."

"Did you see it in the red depths of the Ibi?"

"No, in the powder-blue mists."

"In the mists of the moonlight?"

"No, in the ghostly mists of twilight."

"You really saw blood?"

"Yes, and lightning. And a flashing weapon. A skimingtar."

"A scimitar, you mean. Did you see any freckles?"

"Yes. And myself in dank, scented danger."

"Were the freckles very menacing?"

"I saw evil heads doing a dance around them."

Berton winced. For a full minute they said nothing, looking out at the pale moonlight of evening spread like a spider-web counterpane on the grass. It touched them, as they squatted under the arbour, in patches shaped like coins, kites and handprints. Over the trees the afterglow of sunset had not yet faded. Now and then a firefly dived like a flaming wire into the gloom with them and turned their faces into brief ghosts before snuffing itself out amidst the tangle of vines overhead. They could see the school-*benab* and the workshed safe against the wall of jungle, silent with early night-shadows but fertile with insect-voices that rose higher and higher as the dusk deepened.

"Why were there evil heads dancing around the freckles?" asked Berton.

"Because I believe the soul of Luise has entered the body that bears the freckles. The heads were all male."

"You really think Luise has entered her?"

"I do. Why else would she be making such violent love to him?"

"Has she been making violent love to him?"

"Haven't you eyes to perceive?"

228

"Has she kissed him?"

"I feel sure she did – on Thursday night. I sensed it in the mists."

"The mists might be wrong."

"Mockery. How could the mists be wrong?"

He fidgeted. "But seriously, Ollie, you really think things are heading for a bloody climax? You think he'll try to kill you?"

"*Ah, moon of my delight…*"

"I hate when you have these premonitions."

"*The curfew tolls the knell of parting day.*"

"I'll kill myself if anything happens to you, Ollie."

"*Thou wast not born for death, immortal Bird!*"

"My soul would search for you forever."

"*Among the guests star-scattered on the grass?*"

"Stop being mysterious and be serious."

"*Tomorrow I may be myself with yesterday's seven thousand years.*"

"Mother's calling us for dinner."

"Yes, let's go. This cavern is slowly filling up with perverse shadows. *'Tis nothing but a Magic Shadow-show.*"

"You frighten me."

At dinner he was silent, nervous and sensitive, so that Gregory kept giving him curious glances and wondering what could have put him into this mood. He's almost as unpredictable, thought Gregory, as his sister Olivia.

Berton sat in his old place opposite Olivia, and Olivia sat on Gregory's left. She seemed very pleased with herself, and about halfway through the meal whispered to Gregory: "I'm overflowing with poetry tonight – especially Omar. It's a portembous sign."

"Is it?" said Gregory.

"Yes. It means that I'm in a clairvoyant trance. Remember that morning when I met you in the jungle going to the ruins? Remember I called out to you '*Indeed, indeed…*'?"

"I remember."

"I was in a clairvoyant trance then."

He grinned.

Mabel glanced at him and smiled.

Mr. Harmston was discussing the new bookcase with his wife.

"This evening I foresaw several things, too. At twilight in the grey ghostly mists."

"And what have you foreseen?"

"Blood and danger. And Luise."

"Luise?"

"Don't you know who is Luise?"

"Oh, yes, of course. The Dutch girl of the eighteenth century who delighted in being raped."

"You remember, do you? I thought your madness would have prevented you from recalling what I said that morning. You're a deep 'un."

He stirred in his chair.

"That makes you embarrassed. Good. You deserve a little punishment. Do you know that the soul of Luise is threatening you?"

A baboon roared up-river. Briefly and with a rough coughing note.

Berton glanced behind him, his face troubled.

Gregory saw the belfry in the moonlight.

"By night and by day you are being slowly invaded."

"I'm grateful to you for the warning."

"Don't laugh at me. Take heed before it is too late."

"What precautions would you advise me to observe?"

"Avoid being alone with Mabel. Luise's soul has taken possession of her."

He grinned.

"Don't keep showing your teeth like a Cheshire cat. Have a good loud un-English laugh for a change, can't you?"

"After dinner I will."

"You know," she said, "you've turned out a disappointment."

"Have I? In what way?"

"When you were mad you were much better. You fitted in with our religious myth. For instance, look how you killed that rooster last Sunday morning. That was good. We like things like that. They're unusual and shadowy. If you could have gone on doing more acts like that you'd have met with our full appo – approbation. But instead, you have to go and get sane and behave like an ordinary person from the world outside this jungle."

He did not know why, but her words disturbed him. Intuitively he felt that she had put her finger on something vital.

Beside him, Garvey abruptly asked: "What about Sigmund, Daddy? Have the search-parties reported yet?"

"Two of them have reported failure, my boy," said his father. "I'm awaiting word from the third." He spoke in a slightly worried voice. It was the first time Gregory had seen him in a not unruffled mood.

"But what on earth could have got into his head to cause him to run off like that," said Garvey.

"Olivia," Mr. Harmston told him, "has suggested that he might have committed a felony and is afraid to face the music. A feasible theory, though its weakness lies in that no one has reported losing anything."

"It would be his fourth offence, wouldn't it?" said Mrs. Harmston.

"Yes," said her husband.

A silence came upon them.

Gregory saw, on the opposite wall, over the picture of the Crimean War battle-scene, a hairy black spider. It was crawling sluggishly toward the ceiling; its fat body seemed to retard its movements, and at any instant Gregory expected it to fall to the floor with a soft plop.

In the jungle, a bird uttered bell-like notes, and on the river a boat rowed by a man was going past; the paddles swished rhythmically in the water, and one could even hear the tinkle of the little splashed blebs and the swift curling gurgle as the wavelets receded from the paddles.

"The fourth offence," whispered Olivia to Gregory, "means death."

"Yes."

"Yes? Aren't you surprised to hear it?"

He scowled in irritation.

"I've annoyed you. Funny. Very funny."

He could feel her eyes probingly intense upon him.

Mabel said: "Olivia, why don't you stop pestering Gregory?"

"Am I pestering him?"

Mabel frowned, and her knife and fork made an impatient jingle.

Something struck the side of the house with a sharp clack. "What's that?"

They heard padding footsteps in the clearing, near the house.

Mr. Harmston rose, but his chair had hardly scraped on the floor when a hard brown object whizzed past Berton's head, crashed on to the table, smashed a tumbler of water, flew past Gregory and bumped twice on the floor before coming to rest near the dinner-wagon.

"Sigmund!"

Garvey threw down his knife and fork and rushed round the table to one of the two windows on the river side of the house. Mr. Harmston was already at the other window, frowning out at the moonlit scene.

Mabel and Gregory kept their seats but exchanged glances.

Olivia dashed into the pantry, Berton following her.

Mrs. Harmston moved up behind her husband with an air of caution, her face strained-looking.

"I don't see a soul," said Garvey. "He must be hiding behind the church – or behind one of the palms."

"I think," said his father, "I see someone near the belfry."

"Yes, you're right," said Garvey. "He's there. I see him now."

At that instant they saw the figures of Olivia and Berton hurtling across the clearing in the direction of the church, Olivia toward the western end and Berton toward the eastern, Berton carrying what looked like a stick and Olivia with a smaller object. A cry sounded from the kitchen, and Ellen appeared, too, stumping her way frenziedly after them and calling out.

"Come back!" she cried. "'E might kill you, Berton lovesweet! 'E's a bad, bad man, petty-love!"

"Shall I go up and get the rifle, Dad?" asked Garvey.

"No, you'll do nothing of the kind," said his father, his voice steady but his face set. His hands were clenched hard. Gregory and Mabel had now joined Garvey at the window, and Gregory felt Mabel's hand touch his wrist. He could sense the fear and tension in her.

Berton, nearly round the eastern end of the church, heard Olivia call to him and changed direction. In doing so he caused Ellen to gain on him. She flung out her arms to grapple with him and succeeded in clutching the back of his shirt. He tried to jerk away but she held on, and he stumbled and nearly fell, his shirt flapping outside his pants. Ellen made desperate moaning sounds like a pigeon-choir ecstatic in an anthem.

"Leave him alone, you fool Ellen you!" shrieked Olivia.

"Shut you' mouth," Ellen spat at her, "before me pee 'pon you again!"

Olivia rushed up and struck her in the face, and Garvey yelled: "You idiots! He's getting away! Look, he's running!"

Solemnly in the jungle the bird uttered bell-like notes. "What bird is that?" Gregory asked of Mabel in a whisper.

"A bell-bird★," she replied. "It's a species of owl."

"Chase him! Hurry!" cried Garvey.

"He's got a bag with something," quavered Mrs. Harmston.

"Whoops! I don't think it's Sigmund, after all," said Garvey. "He's limping like Logan. Yes, it *is* Logan!"

Berton and Olivia, with Ellen in pursuit, went after the awkwardly hopping figure with sack on back. They overtook him with ease before he could reach the opening in the bush where the track that led to the ruins commenced. Berton sprang on him and bore him to the ground, a quarking bellow rising on the night air. Ellen, panting, piled straight on top of the two as they went down. Olivia pulled up in time, and with an exclamation, called shrilly to the house: "It's Logan, Daddy! Not Sigmund!"

They saw a ray of white light spurt from her hand and reveal the turmoil of tangled figures on the ground.

"He's got a bagful of *sawari* nuts!" She gave a shriek of laughter, and the beam of the torch swept erratically past the night-filled spaces of the jungle-wall near them, showing up the black shape of a bat as it swooped bellying past with soundless speed.

Garvey shuddered.

"Well, I never!" exclaimed Mrs. Harmston. "What else won't Logan do! He could have injured one of us with that nut he pelted in."

"Where did Olivia get that torch from, I wonder," Mabel murmured.

"She borrowed it from Eric of Book Squad," Gregory told her.

"Mabel, my girl," said the Reverend Mr. Harmston, "I should

★ Not to be confused with the campanero which is a daytime bird.

be glad if you would take your place and continue the meal. The same applies to you, Garvey."

Mabel and Garvey resumed their places, and Gregory followed suit.

As Mrs. Harmston, too, took her chair, she gave her husband an anxious glance. His face was blank, but his eyes held, thought Gregory, an ominous glint.

They heard the voices of Logan and Olivia and Berton in the clearing. Olivia and Berton appeared to be scolding Logan. Ellen made crooning love-noises – evidently directed at Berton. Once or twice Logan uttered a shout of laughter, a sound that wavered through the air, half-human, half-beast in timbre. Gregory looked out of the window at the belfry; its small roof gleamed green-white in the moonlight. Other voices joined those of Olivia and Berton and Logan, and Mrs. Harmston began to say something to her husband, then seemed to think better of it and broke off.

Mabel's manner was markedly nervous now. She looked at Gregory, and he returned her gaze and then looked away. It was as though a thundercloud, unseen, were drifting through the room. Gregory caught a whiff of the river, dank and herb-rank in the night air, and happening to turn his gaze upwards, saw that the hairy black spider was on the ceiling, almost immediately above the table; it paused in its crawling and curled a leg slowly inward, its gross body sagging precariously.

Olivia and Berton came in from the pantry, breathless, Olivia laughing. Berton, his mood of earlier quite gone, said: "It was Logan who threw in the nut, Daddy. He said he did it as a joke. He went off in the bush with one of the search-parties and found a lot of the nuts. He's got a bagful of them. He said the spirit moved him to pelt two of them at the house and he couldn't stop himself."

"He only did it in fun," laughed Olivia, though Gregory noticed that she kept casting slyly anxious glances at her father.

"All in keeping with our kind of myth," nodded Berton.

"Exactly," agreed Olivia. "Just the local influences, that's all."

"The third search-party has come back, Daddy," said Berton. "Harry of Music Squad asks me to tell you that they didn't find Sigmund. They searched everywhere you advised them to, but drew a blank. Harry says he thinks Sigmund has gone up-river.

Harry thinks he's making for topside. He says one of the *corials* at the Ibi depot is missing."

"Did Harry give you this as an official report, my boy?"

"Yes, Daddy. He would have come upstairs, but I told him we were at dinner. He said he might drop in later on to borrow a book and he'll give you any other details you want."

"Thanks."

"Did he mention how Kathleen's arm is now, Berton?" asked Mrs. Harmston.

"Yes, much better, he said. The cut is almost quite healed up."

"Daddy."

"Yes, Mabel?"

Gregory looked at Mabel. She sat very erect. She was white.

"I have a confession to make, Daddy."

Gregory stiffened.

"Yes?" said the reverend gentleman.

Olivia, about to resume her seat, hesitated and stared at her sister, hand on the back of her chair.

Berton had begun to say something else but stopped.

"I'm waiting, Mabel," said Mr. Harmston. "What's this confession?"

Mrs. Harmston threw Gregory a quick, anxious glance.

"Sigmund broke into the house here on Thursday night when the concert was going on." Mabel's voice was steady. "Gregory caught him in my room, but I told him to release him – and we let him go. I should have reported him, but I was sorry for him because it was his fourth offence."

Mrs. Harmston uttered a soft: "My God!"

Olivia shrilled: "What you mean is you failed in your duty! You've transgressed one of our major rules!"

"You're a traitor to our Code!" cried Berton, his hands clenched.

"Be silent, please, Berton and Olivia," said the reverend gentleman quietly. "Mabel, I take it that this is the truth. You surprised Sigmund after he had broken into this house on Thursday night, and released him, and then failed to make a report to me. Is that right?"

"Yes, Daddy."

"Very well, my girl," said her father. He looked at Olivia.

"Olivia, please take your place and continue eating. Berton, the same to you."

Gregory cleared his throat which, he found, had gone husky. "May I say something?"

"Yes, Gregory?" said Mr. Harmston, with a slight, polite smile.

"I think I ought to explain that Mabel had every intention of reporting the incident. It was I who persuaded her not to."

"It was?" smiled on the reverend gentleman. "Very good, my boy. I thank you for the explanation. Not, however, that it alters the situation in the slightest."

"But I should have thought it did," said Gregory coldly.

"Your thoughts don't matter," said Olivia. "You come from a world of barbarians."

"Barbarians and hollow sentimentalists," nodded Berton.

"Didn't your father order you to be silent, Berton and Olivia?" frowned Mrs. Harmston. "Gregory my boy, take no notice of them."

"I'm not," said Gregory. "And I should like to state again that so far as this Sigmund affair is concerned I am to be blamed entirely."

"I understand, my boy," murmured his aunt.

Mr. Harmston smiled and said: "Not entirely to be blamed, though, surely. Mabel has a will of her own."

Ellen had appeared at the pantry door. She stood listening to the conversation. The reverend gentleman looked at her and said: "Ellen, have this broken glass cleaned up, if you please."

"Yes, sah. Ow, parson! You should punish Logan bad for what 'e do. Beat 'e, parson. Beat 'e and beat 'e and put 'e to sit down in red-ants' nest. Ah can show you where to find a big nest."

"Shut your blabbering mouth, Ellen!" Olivia flared.

"Me na shut it!" Ellen snarled back. "Me must talk. Logan is a bad man. 'E want plenty beating."

Languidly Mr. Harmston rose. He moved round and slapped Olivia once across her face. Then he turned and clouted Ellen on the back of her head. Ellen stumbled forward with a gasp. A slight smile on his face, the reverend gentleman returned to his chair. Ellen collected the fragments of the broken glass and took them away. They tinkled shiftily in her hand. Logan, in the kitchen, gave a bellow of laughter, and they heard Ellen speaking to him in an angry whining voice. Olivia, her eyes shining, mumbled something to herself. Mabel made a pretence of eating, but Gregory's appetite seemed unaffected. A warm shawl of air stirred its way through the room, dry and silken against the cheek and smelling uncertainly of garlic and the perfume of freshly opened flowers.

"Daddy."

"Yes, Olivia?"

"You're not going to punish him, are you?"

"Yes, I'm afraid I am, my girl."

"But he only did it in fun. He didn't mean to cause any damage."

Her father made no response.

"Are you going to beat him with the balata whip?"

"Continue eating, Olivia."

Gregory looked up and saw that the spider had crossed the ceiling and was coming down on the other wall – just above the clock on its shelf. It still moved very slowly. At the moment it had paused, and stood with all its eight legs spread out wide as though arrested in a suspense of expectancy and unable to move on until something happened.

Berton said: "Daddy, what about Mabel? Are you going to punish her?"

"Yes," said his father, without looking up from his plate.

Mrs. Harmston breathed deeply, and her face twitched.

"How are you going to punish her?" asked Berton.

"Continue eating, Berton."

"She deserves severe punishment," Berton mumbled. Gregory turned his head and saw that Olivia's cheeks were streaming.

Garvey mentioned, as they were rising from the table, that he wanted to do a little practice on the Paganini study before bed, and his father crushed out his cigarette and nodded slowly. "Excellent, my boy. I'm thinking it might be a good idea to call upon you to play it for us some time during the service tomorrow."

Garvey made an uncertain sound. "Not so sure I could bring it off before a crowd. All depends upon how I feel tomorrow morning."

"You can do it if you try. Just a matter of having a little confidence." Mr. Harmston touched him affectionately on the shoulder and moved toward the pantry.

His wife and Olivia and Berton, who had been watching him tensely for the past minute, followed him, Mrs. Harmston after a slight hesitation.

In the lamp-lit kitchen they found Ellen on a stool near the iron stove, eating out of the cover of a saucepan. Logan squatted on the floor by the dresser, eating out of a large iron pot. He looked up, a spoon of rice and fish poised before his mouth, a look of mild wonder on his face. He seemed quite innocent of impending trouble. Even the squeal of pleasure Ellen gave did not appear to give him a clue.

"You hear about de nuts Ah find in de bush, parson?" he said, his black eyes glinting with childish friendliness in the reddish light from the oil-lamp.

"Yes, I've heard, Logan," smiled Mr. Harmston.

"Ah get a whole bagful, parson. You must lend me you' hammer so Ah can break a few."

"Very good. Tomorrow."

"They all good nuts, parson."

"Um. *Sawari* nuts, eh?"

"Yes, parson. Look dem over dere in dat bag." Logan pointed to the sack that lay in the corner with Ellen's rolled-up hammock. "You must tek some. Tek as much as you want."

"Thanks. I'll take a few tomorrow. All good nuts, eh?"

"Oh, Gerald, Gerald!" exclaimed Mrs. Harmston, a sob in her voice.

"Yes, Joan?" said her husband, turning toward her with an air of surprise and enquiry.

"Why draw him out like that!"

"Um," said Mr. Harmston.

Logan, chewing vigorously, glanced with a curious, squirrel-like expression, from one to the other of them. He suddenly tittered and said: "Wha' wrong, ma'am? Lil' nancy-story game?"

"No. No game," smiled the reverend gentleman. "I'm just waiting for you to finish eating."

"Yes, parson. Ah nearly done. Just two-t'ree more grains o' rice. You got a lil job you want me to do?"

"No. No job. Just waiting for you to finish eating."

"Oh. Ma'am, you must tek some nuts, too. Tek all you want."

"Thanks, Logan," murmured Mrs. Harmston, her eyes moist. She smiled and averted her face.

Ellen laughed and broke out: "But you so stupid, Logan, you ain' know wha' de parson come in to do! 'E come to punish you for pelting de nut in de dining-room window. Parson going to beat you' tail bad and shove you in red-ants' nest."

"Please be silent, Ellen," murmured Mr. Harmston. "Logan, finish eating."

Logan put aside the pot and dropped the spoon inside it. He got up, his eyes now full of fear. His mouth gaped twistedly, his thick lips shiny with food-grease.

Ellen began to moan, her body in a tremble of pleasurable anticipation. Olivia glared at her.

"You vexed wid me, parson? Ah only pelt de nut for fun, sah," Logan pleaded. "Ah didn' mean no harm, parson."

"Have you finished eating, Logan?" smiled the reverend gentleman.

"Yes, parson, Ah finish. Ow, sah, don't punish me. De spirit move me, dat's why Ah pelt de nut. Moonlight so bright me spirit feel good, and me pelt nuts wild. Lil' nancy-story fun, parson, dat's all."

"Pelting is always dangerous. Nancy-story fun can be carried too far. Come outside with me."

"Parson, de spirit move me, Ah tell you."

"The spirit can be controlled. Come."

"Where we going, parson?"

Olivia gasped: "But Daddy!"

"Yes, Olivia?"

"You – oh, you don't mean to chain him up! You can't! It's night-time. Mynheer will appear and frighten him."

"Gerald! Not that! He would die of fright behind that shed. Please, dear, anything but that!"

Without a word, the reverend gentleman took a pace forward and caught Logan by the arm. Olivia rushed up and held her father's elbow restrainingly. "Please, Daddy! I beg you. Flog him but don't do that."

Unheedingly, silently, calm of face, Mr. Harmston dragged Logan out through the door and down the steps. His wife moved after him, entreating him to desist, and Olivia sobbed, but Mr. Harmston took no notice. Logan's yells almost drowned Mrs. Harmston's voice. Ellen whimpered and whined as if she were in harrowing pain. Gregory and Mabel and Garvey had appeared now, and they all followed Mr. Harmston out into the moonlit night.

Logan refused to rise or use his feet, so Mr. Harmston was forced to drag him, a stiff, huddled ball, all the way to the workshed. His mournful howling echoed through the jungle, returning upon them like clay wet and warped, as from a gnashing sorrow, and muddying the moonlight.

Ellen came last in the procession, a crouched figure retarded by the web of her emotional reactions. She came to a stop every second or so to hug herself and shudder, gibbering gutturally in the passion of delight that possessed her.

Throughout the whole business of Logan's chaining up Ellen kept up a moaning or a whining. Once Olivia struck her a blow in the chest, but it had no effect whatever; she merely retreated a pace, and leaning against the trunk of a tree, watched the parson, in the half-gloom behind the shed, turn the key in the padlocks of the manacles and secure the chain to the ring in the wall.

Logan's voice had now become a gasping wail, hoarse and tremulous. As Mr. Harmston straightened up and left him behind the shed he began to sob and strain at the chain in a vain effort to break free.

Mrs. Harmston and Mabel and Gregory had already turned away and were moving back toward the house, but Garvey and Olivia and Berton lingered near the shed. Garvey had approached Ellen. He held her arm, and seemed trying to persuade her to return to the house with him; she appeared to yield, for she began to lurch reluctantly forward away from the tree. Garvey led her off in the direction of the kitchen, and as they went Ellen kept on making noises of ecstasy.

Olivia and Berton intercepted their father as he was about to go past, and Olivia said: "Daddy, have mercy on the poor fellow. You know he's not all there in the head. He'll die if you leave him here all night. He won't be able to survive the fright."

Her father smiled and patted her head. "I don't intend to leave him behind there more than half-an-hour, my girl. I simply want to give him a quick but thorough frightening – something he'll remember, and that will cure him once and for all of throwing things at the house."

"Oh, well, that's a relief," said Olivia. "Poor fellow, he can't help himself, really. Would you mind if Berton and I stayed around here until the half-hour is up?"

"If you wish. But don't reveal your presence to him or it will render the punishment useless."

"No, we'll keep near the front part of the shed. It's just in case he should fall into a fit or something, you know."

"Um. But I don't think he'll fall into a fit,"

He chucked her affectionately under the chin and went off toward the house. On the kitchen stairs he found Garvey sitting with Ellen. His arm was around her and he seemed to be murmuring something into her ear. He made no move to alter the situation as his father mounted the stairs. Mr. Harmston chuckled as he went past them and said: "Don't forget that Paganini study, Garvey my boy."

"No, Daddy. I'm coming in presently to work on it." He spoke a trifle shyly, but, the instant his father had gone inside, proceeded to address himself once more to the business of fondling and exploring Ellen's still shudderingly ecstatic person.

In the sitting-room the reverend gentleman found Mabel and Gregory playing chess. Mrs. Harmston was just settling down into an easy chair with a book, her face still rather strained-looking from the events of the evening.

"No sign of Harry yet, Joan?"

"No, Gerald. Not yet."

"Did you have a look at his wife's arm yesterday?"

"Yes. It was coming round nicely."

He approached her chair and began to stroke her hair, bent and frowned at the book in her lap. "T. S. Eliot again, eh?"

She nodded. "I always find him soothing when I'm upset."

"Mm. So I've noticed." He chuckled. "Oh, by the way, Mabel!"

"Yes, Daddy!"

"I should be glad if you won't leave your room in the morning, my girl, until I come in and see you."

"Very well, Daddy."

Mr. Harmston fanned himself. "This heat. Phew! Joan my dear?"

"Yes, Gerald?"

"Think you could leave Eliot for a bit? I'd like to have a word with you in the Big Room. Won't be more than a minute."

"Certainly."

She rose and went upstairs with him.

"Your move," Gregory murmured.

"Is it? Sorry. So it is. I'm dreaming," laughed Mabel.

VIII

Every now and then a creak leapt from the marrow of the timber, and in the dark that pervaded pantry, dining-room and bedroom lurked the drone or whine of many a minute creature – a drone or whine too low or too high to be heard by human ear yet undoubtedly there. Intangible like the warm wind that flooded in through the window unhurried like a funeral, night moved within the arc of time, and the jungle waited, brewing imperturbably, out of dew and dead leaf and mould, the aroma of dawn. The river flowed in the moonlight, and the moonlight dimmed and went out, but the river flowed on without a grunt of comment. When early morning fog began to wreathe and turn the air grey and honey in the light that grew like a cloud over the jungle the river kept on flowing, never for a moment moved to cry out a yea or nay. And not a leaf or limb in the whole jungle winked or nodded in recognition of the event.

Today or tomorrow, Gregory reflected, watching the honey brighten to orange, July or October, the river and the jungle care no more than an idol of granite. The river and the jungle don't dream. And being unable to dream, they live without fear of tomorrow's thunder. I should have been the river or the jungle.

Daydreams and sleep-dreams, thought Olivia in the next room, watching the sky, too. I wish I knew what's the difference between them. I've had as many nightmares imagining things during the day as I've had at night in bed when I'm asleep... bad sequence... when I was asleep... *the hunter of the east has caught the Sultan's turret...*

She giggled.

Mabel stirred in her sleep.

Where, Olivia wondered, can the dream-land be where Mabel is smiling now and sighing with love, or stumbling and screaming at the edge of a nightmare cliff? Is it in this room only I can't see it? Or is it boxed away like a small-size solar-system in her brain

243

so that whenever she falls asleep she turns into a midget ghost and goes adventuring about in it?

She raised herself, and with chin cupped in hand, her elbow resting on her pillow, regarded her sleeping sister. Long and slim and pink-brown Mabel's body looked in the early daylight, the freckles red-brown. Because of the hot nights she slept with nothing on. They had both been sleeping naked during the past week. Mabel's hair lay spread out like a forest of dark vines on her pillow, her face half-hidden.

Olivia smiled, and shifting her elbow, lifted the corner of her pillow and glanced at the black handle of Gregory's razor. Above the pillow lay the torch she had borrowed from Eric.

If only Mabel could know why I borrowed it – and why I have this razor under my pillow...

Her gaze moved from her sister to the chair beside the bed. On it lay the old green bathing-suit... Today I'm going to burn you, bathing-suit, as I told him yesterday I'd do. I'll shed a few tears for you, but I must do it. He must see that I never speak in vain...

A frown came to her face.

...funny. Didn't Maby leave her clothes on the chair there with my bathing-suit? We both undressed together last night...

She felt as though a worm were crawling on a dew-wet leaf inside her chest. Her eyes rested once again on her sister, and this time they were bright. Her hand crept under the pillow and closed on the razor...

The bitch, she thought. She must have gone into his room during the night and left her clothes there...

The worm suddenly turned warm, and the dew melted away into her blood, leaving a laughing relief in her limbs.

How silly of me! She wouldn't have taken her clothes into his room with her. She would have gone in naked just as she is now. What foolish things jealousy can make people think!... Yet it's funny. Her clothes ought to be on the chair there. Her panties and the blue dress with green and red leaves and lines...

She looked all round the room but could see nothing of her sister's clothes... Could it have been a jumbie that removed them?...

Mabel opened her eyes. Olivia smiled into them and said:

"So you're awake. What didst thou dream, lovely creature? Tell me."

Mabel frowned, as though memory of the events of last evening had just loomed up like a wall and blotted out the memory of her sleep-dreams. She made no reply.

"Tell me quickly," whispered Olivia, "before the curtain descends. Did you dream you were in his arms cuddly and snuggly? Did you like the feel of his chest-muscles pressing down on your two breasts which are 'like two young roes that are twins which feed among the lilies'?"

"Stop being foolish," Mabel murmured. She saw the torch and said: "What's that torch for?"

"I knew you would ask. It's for a secret purpose. A fell purpose."

Mabel said nothing, her face troubled.

"You must stop being friendly with him, Maby. I'm very jealous."

"What?"

"You heard me."

"I wish you'd stop making yourself a nuisance to him."

"Do you feel you're in love with him?"

Mabel said nothing.

"Tell me. Go on. It's important."

"I am in love with him," said Mabel.

"So you admit it, eh? What about Robert of Art Squad? Weren't you supposed to be soft on him before Gregory came? Weren't we even speaking of your marrying him?"

"Robert," Mabel told her, "is in love with Edith of Music Squad."

"Oh. Is that why he stopped coming to the house here?"

"Yes."

"You're a deep 'un. You never breathed a word. We were all thinking it was you who had turned him down. You've fallen out of love with him very conveniently, I must say."

"I was never really in love with him. I was just fond of him. He knew it. We discussed it at length."

Olivia regarded her for a moment and then said: "I have a theory about you. The local influences are beginning to work on you, at last."

245

Mabel gave an amused smile.

"Don't sneer. I believe the soul of Luise has taken possession of you. You see this torch? It's in bed with us because of you. I have a weapon, too. If Daddy hadn't said that he was going to punish you I'd have done something to you when you were asleep last night. I'd meant to perform a slight but serious operation on you."

"Stop talking nonsense."

"It isn't nonsense. I'm a jealous woman. I can be a leopard when I'm jealous. Gregory's making the same mistake you're making. He's not taking me seriously."

"What were you going to do to me last night?"

Olivia hesitated, then said: "I'd meant to slice off your breasts."

"To what?"

Olivia's eyes became tearful. "Oh, you know I wouldn't have done it. You know I wouldn't have done it, Maby. But I really am mad with you for setting your cap at Gregory. He's insulted me because I'm not grown-up like you. He called me a little girl because my chest is flat."

Mabel laughed.

Footsteps sounded, and their father came in. Like themselves, he was nude. Over his arm he carried what looked like a crumpled old dress of their mother's. He was smiling.

"Heard your voices," he said cheerfully.

They sat up.

"What ails thee, sire?" asked Olivia.

"Brought you something, Mabel," he said, draping the old dress over the back of the chair that stood near the bed.

"Something?"

"Mm. An old discarded dress of your mother's we fished out of the clothes-basket before going to bed. Something for you to wear during the next fortnight."

"That thing! I've got to wear…"

"Yes, my girl. Just for a fortnight."

"But, Daddy…"

"Yes?" smiled her father, raising his brows in gentle inquiry.

"Surely… You don't expect me to wear that to church, do you?"

He stroked his chin reflectively. "Not a nice prospect, eh? But I'm afraid there's no help for it, my child. Your mother and I have taken charge of your complete wardrobe. We came in here while you were asleep. I can see it's going to be a trifle awkward for you, but discipline is discipline."

"I see."

"I thought you would." He glanced out of the window, smiled and took a deep breath. "Another fine, hot day ahead of us, it seems."

"With thunder in the offing," said Olivia.

"Um. There may be a bit of thunder," agreed her father. He pulled up the mosquito-net, pushed in his hand and patted them both affectionately on the head. "See you later," he smiled, and went out.

Mabel, rigid, kept staring through the net at the brightening sky.

"I'm sorry, dear-heart," Olivia murmured.

Mabel said nothing.

"It smells frowsy, too. I can smell it sitting here."

The tears began to run down Mabel's cheeks.

"You'll have to keep far from him for the next fortnight wearing a thing like that, won't you?"

The sound of a whimper came from downstairs.

"Poor Logan. He hasn't yet recovered from his fright. Hear him downstairs? Berton and I almost had to lift him back to the house when his half-hour was up. He was one trembling mass. But it was good for him. He'll always remember last night and never again throw hard objects in at the window. Discipline. We can't be happy without discipline."

IX

At breakfast, Garvey, about to take his place, recoiled. He was staring at Mabel who was just seating herself. "What the devil is that thing you've got on, Maby?" he asked.

Mabel made no reply.

Berton, already seated, glanced at his sister, and he, too, recoiled. "But... is it a joke or something? That's one of Mother's old dresses!"

Mabel still said nothing.

Olivia came in, and in a voice of doom told them what it was about. "Behold!" rumbled Olivia. "She suffereth for having transgressed against our Secret Code."

Gregory, who came in in time to hear her words, glanced at Mabel and grasped the situation in a flash. He assumed a polite mask of impassivity and watched the belfry.

Presently, Olivia murmured to him: "This is the end of the flaming romance. She's got to wear that horrible thing for two weeks."

He made no response.

"It smells. I can smell it from here. Can't you?"

After breakfast, he touched Mabel on the shoulder as she was on her way out of the room. She turned, the blood reddening her cheeks. "Yes, what's it?"

"Could I have a word with you by the landing-place?"

"A word with me? I – I don't know. Later perhaps." She hurried away.

Mrs. Harmston and Garvey, who were still in the dining-room, smiled. Mrs. Harmston took a step toward Gregory and said in a voice of conspiracy: "It's terrible, my boy, but it can't be helped. We have to be strict in matters like this."

Gregory nodded. "I can see that," he replied.

"A great pity, poor child."

"But tell me something, Aunt Joan. Do you really subscribe to all this – to this way of living?"

His aunt's face took on a look of surprise and resentment. "Most decidedly I do," she said. "What made you think I don't?"

He hesitated, then said: "Well, to be truthful, I was rather left with the impression that you were – not quite as abnormal as the rest of the family, if I may so put it."

Garvey bent in two, choking with silent laughter.

"However could you have gained such an impression, Gregory! Not quite as abnormal… But I should hope we're all normal here!"

"Oh, don't be purposely dense, Mother," said Garvey, recovering. "You know perfectly well what he means. He means you give the impression that you're not one of us – and that is the truth. Admit it and stop hedging. Things aren't always what they seem, Gregory – especially in Berkelhoost. Mother isn't actively affected by the local influences – nor Maby, come to that – but she's as much a staunch believer in our myth and codes as any of us."

"It's very kind of you to take it upon yourself to explain to him for me, Garvey," said his mother huffily, and was about to stalk off. But Gregory smiled and caught her arm.

"Keep your hair on, Aunt Joan. I only wanted to get things into their proper perspective. To go back to Mabel, don't you think you're being a bit rough on her – forcing her to wear that disgusting garment?"

"No, I don't. She's guilty of a grave defect of conduct and must be punished."

He gave her a long stare. "You do honestly feel so?"

"Most decidedly I do." Her manner softened abruptly and she went on: "I don't tell you I'm not upset, my boy. Mabel is such a dear, sweet child. It hurts my heart to see her punished. But discipline must be observed."

"Precisely," said Garvey. "And Maby knows she deserves what she's got, so don't waste your compassion on her, Gregory. I say, what's the trouble? Are you in love with her, or what?"

Gregory ignored the question. "I must apologize," he said to his aunt, "if I seem officious, but I got her into this hole, that's why I'm concerned."

"I understand how you feel," she said, her face troubled. "But

I think her father has really let her off lightly. Gerald is not as hard as you might be led to think. He's good and kind, Gregory my boy – and he's no fanatic. Mabel herself will tell you that, I'm sure."

"If you remain here long enough you'll find out a lot of things about Daddy you wouldn't have dreamt. He behaves like a charlatan, but it's only a pose. Under it he's sane and strong – and gentle. He's no dictator like your Hitler and Mussolini."

"I'm afraid your trouble is that you're so fresh from the outside world, my boy," smiled Mrs. Harmston, "that a truly civilized community like ours has flummoxed you."

"I haven't the slightest doubt you're correct," murmured her nephew.

About ten minutes later, he was sitting at the landing-place in the mild early morning sunshine when a step sounded behind him, and turning his head, he saw Garvey approaching. The boy seated himself beside him and stretched out his bare feet toward the logs.

"Don't get down-spirited," he said, his manner sympathetic. "You'll get the hang of things before long. Once you become accustomed to us you won't find us so unusual. Why don't you start doing some creative work?"

"Creative work?"

"Yes. You write plays, don't you? And you paint. Get busy if you don't want to go dotty again. Idleness encourages introspection. Introspection eats away the mind. Before you know where you are you'll be developing another attack of melancholia or whatever it is you were suffering from when you arrived."

Gregory smiled. He was watching the jungle on the opposite bank. It was reflected in the water with leaf-detailed clarity. It seemed very safe in its inarticulation. No matter how long he watched it it would never talk back at him or advise him how to keep sane. He remembered how he lay in bed this morning and watched it growing clearer in the mist and brightening daylight, how he wished he could have been it instead of himself.

"I like you," said Garvey, plucking a leaf and chewing it meditatively. "You're a decent sort, and you're no fool. Even when you were supposed to be not all there in the top-storey you didn't seem a fool. I say, tell me. Were you really mad, or just shamming?"

250

"Nice morning, isn't it?"

Garvey laughed. "Picking up our little habits, eh? Good for you. But seriously, I'm still a bit baffled about your case. This explanation you gave about your wife doesn't convince me. Sounds tall."

"Things," said Gregory, "aren't always what they seem."

"Is it true, then? You really went funny because of your wife?" Gregory nodded.

Garvey regarded him keenly. "And how do you feel now? Quite normal again? You don't think you could have a relapse?"

Gregory shrugged. "I suppose it's possible I could. I don't know."

"You've been treated by a psychiatrist on one or two occasions, eh?"

Gregory nodded.

"I'm interested. Mental cases interest me." He fidgeted. "I feel a little guilty talking to you like this. Seems heartless – but I don't mean to be. You're the sort of chap that evokes one's compassion. I say, Ollie is making herself a nuisance to you, eh?"

"Now and then she can be a bit tiresome."

"I know. You mustn't bother with her. She's only doing it for myth-pleasure."

"Myth-pleasure?"

"Yes. She's exercising her creative imagination and amusing herself in accordance with our basic code of make-believe. Ollie's a very promising girl. She has drive – and a rich fancy."

Gregory made no comment.

"You find our way of life absurd, I suppose?"

"Somewhat," Gregory murmured.

A raft of timber was going past.

"As absurd as we find your way. A case of values. You," said Garvey, "are a good example of the misery and emptiness of your pseudo-civilization. Look at you! Rudderless, unhappy, cynical. And look at us in contrast. We're full of life and fire. We're positive in our approach to living, even though our philosophy has much in it that is negative. We're happy – and I mean when I say happy that we're not burdened with a sense of world-guilt as you are, and we know what we want out of life; we don't exaggerate the importance of *homo sapiens* on the earth, so we have a saner and more balanced outlook on ourselves in relation to our achievements. We don't want to be powerful and to dominate anybody, or to own vast tracts of territory. We just want to live and be tolerably comfortable and tolerably entertained while life lasts." He plucked another leaf. "You beyond this jungle take life so seriously, and estimate human nature at so high a rate, that you have no time to enjoy life; most of your time is spent boosting your egos, trying your best to convince yourselves how much superior you are to the baboons and the chimpanzees. We don't suffer from such egotism, you see; we take life with a big pinch of salt, because we know it has no purpose beyond today; that's why we can throw ourselves into it with such heartiness and extract all its richness. But you beyond this jungle – you're so confoundedly conceited that you have to conceive of yourselves as being fashioned in the image of a God that you yourselves, out of your superstitions, created. And not satisfied with that, you have to see yourselves leaving your bodies after death and continuing to exist in a 'higher' sphere. And, of course, with all this on your minds, you have to invent things like morality and piousness – sorry, piety – to keep you pepped up and to prepare you for the Afterlife. Your sentiments and conventions are all coloured by your morality and piety, and so you have to deny yourselves most of the things that really give you fun. We here create our myths and conventions day by day and discard them as easily as we create them. We develop and trip along with carefree haphazardness. But you – you have to be content with the stale gods your forefathers forced down your throats. We get life at first-hand; you get it at second or third. We don't have to nail ourselves down to any set philosophy or flat conventions. We're fluid and dynamic. We – damn! Excuse me a minute. I think there's a flea in my pants. Worst of getting too chummy with that Ellen. Her hammock simply teems with fleas. Poop! Here's the beggar! Got him!" He cracked the flea between his thumbnails. "See it! Big female. Got an egg. Where were we again? Something to do with dynamic… I say, am I boring you or anything?"

"No. Not at all," said Gregory.

"I'm really sorry for you. I understand how you feel. You think you'll be able to stick this kind of life much longer?"

Gregory smiled. "That's a problem I'm still considering."

Garvey regarded him. "That first afternoon when I saw you in the *corial* I was scared stiff."

"Why?"

"Well, you were the first genuine savage I was about to meet, and I didn't know what to expect. I was shy and nervous."

Gregory grinned.

Garvey laughed, hugging his knees. Suddenly he grew serious. "You're all in a mess, I know. And you're going to be worse if you don't get down to some creative work. Write a few one-act plays and we'll produce them. Or paint a few pictures. Or volunteer to give Art Squad lectures on art, or something like that. *Do* something or you're lost. And what about sex? Don't you feel the need for a woman?"

Gregory fidgeted.

"Aha. Your inhibitions. You see how your barbarism keeps revealing itself? Now, what's there in sex to get fidgety about? Isn't it a natural function? If you were really civilized you wouldn't look upon it as a dirty subject. Only a savage puts up taboos against things that are natural. It's the same with your body. What's there to be ashamed of in showing your body? If the weather is cold I can understand you keeping yourself warm with clothes, but in high summer you have to walk around wearing clothes – cheating yourself of the good sunshine. If one of your women is surprised in a room naked by a man she behaves as if she's seen a ghost. If you know how absurd all *your* little funny ways seem to us you'd think twice before sniffing at our set-up here."

"Did you hear me sniffing?"

"You're doing it in effect, anyway. There's a macaw! See! Over there on that cluster of palms! Lovely, eh? Have you read Clive Bell's *Civilization*? You should. There's a nearly-civilized chap for you. If you had more like him then you'd be on the way to being genuinely civilized. I agree with him about religion and patriotism. No really civilized man can be religious or patriotic. There's nothing that limits your range of thought – and your enjoyment of life, as a result – more than religion and patriotism. Oh, you don't know what a laugh we get when we read about your statesmen in *Time Magazine*. Their mentalities are little better than the mentalities of cavemen. And the way they succeed in fooling the people! And your religious leaders who keep spouting stuff about God and morals and advocating a back-to-the-church movement and talking about Christianity as a means of saving the world and creating new spiritual values! Of all the hollow, idealistic tommyrot! Why they're no better than the African witch-doctors who fool the tribe they can work magic with juju charms and what not. I seem to be amusing you."

"Considerably," Gregory nodded.

Garvey laughed. "At least, you show some signs of hope. You have a sense of humour. That's another prerequisite of the truly civilized man."

"How old are you? Fifteen?"

"That's right. Sixteen in December. I sound precocious, eh? I'm not really. Just the books I was made to read and the way I've been educated. And I have a natural knack for reasoning."

Three *corials* came into view from down-river way and swished past at high speed, each with a single occupant. In the leading one Gregory saw a young man who looked distinctly more fair-complexioned than an Indian.

"Some of our people," said Garvey. "They're practising for the quarterly regatta."

"Do you hold a quarterly regatta?"

"We do. See the fair-skinned chap in the lead? Know who he is?"

"I'm afraid I don't."

"Osbert."

"Oh."

"He says 'Oh'. What have you heard about him?"

"Isn't he supposed to be a child of your father's – outside wedlock?"

"You've heard about it, then, eh?" Garvey grunted and looked slyly amused. "He's a first-class paddle. I'm backing him for our next regatta. Interested in outdoor sports?"

"Not very – no."

"I'm not myself. I prefer books. According to our basic codes, I ought to be interested in all healthy games and activities outdoors, but, of course, I just happen to be not keen, so Daddy doesn't insist. That's what I mean about fluidity. We have our rules but we can break them and not be horrified. All within moderation, naturally. So long as breaking a rule doesn't endanger our physical safety we never make a fuss. In Mabel's case she has to be punished because the rule she's broken does endanger our safety. This fellow Sigmund can easily become a menace to us if he isn't disposed of. She was foolish not to report him."

They were silent for a while. They saw the *corials* passing back.

"I say, about Daddy! I don't think if you lived here ten years you'd get to know him as he really is. He'd always seem an evasive, elusive figure. Look, I'm going to confide in you. I can trust you to keep it mum – and you must keep it mum. Osbert is not his son."

"Not his son?"

Garvey shook his head and smiled mysteriously. "Mr. Buckmaster is his father. Only Ollie and I know. At least, I think Ollie suspects – I won't be too sure. Osbert's mother died in childbirth, and Daddy purposely started the tale going that he was Osbert's father. Do you know why? Because he wanted himself to appear as one who had been capable of an act of human weakness. Osbert remains as a sort of living symbol of Daddy's human qualities. I'll tell you how I came to know all this. About a year ago I had a terrific row with him. I went shooting *labbas* – a *labba* is a species of rodent, something like an agouti. It makes a wonderful pepper-pot. Eric of Book Squad and Peter of Labour Squad were with me. We got two *labbas*. I shot one myself and Peter got the other one. But it took us all day and we didn't get back until eleven o'clock at night. I'd promised to be back in time to play a Mendelssohn piece at a concert that same night, and, of course, the concert was over when we arrived. Daddy was put out, but he understood, and everything would have been all right if it hadn't been for a black *marabunta* – that's a kind of wasp. While I was out hunting a black *marabunta* stung me on my leg, and it's a poisonous thing, I can tell you. You wait until one stings you and you'll know. My whole calf was swollen and I was in a very touchy mood. Daddy, instead of praising me for shooting the *labba* and sympathizing with me because of the *marabunta* sting must go and throw out a sarcastic comment about the concert. He said: 'We enjoyed your contribution this evening, young man.' I flew into a hell of a temper and told him he could kiss my bottom. Naturally, he landed me a clout, and that got me madder and I let loose some more lurid language at him. He took me into the kitchen and gave me a walloping with the balata whip and that brought me to my senses. But while he was beating me I called him a tyrant – said he was no better than a dirty Mussolini. He stopped beating me and said: 'We'll discuss that later,' and went on beating me. Then when he thought I'd had enough he laughed and said: 'Let's have a little talk, young man.' It was a moonlight night, and we went and sat on the kitchen steps and talked. He told me that I'd touched on his tender spot when I called him a tyrant. He said of all things he couldn't stand being looked upon as a tyrant. Then he told me about Osbert. He said he'd deliberately had himself framed up as the father of an illegitimate child because he knew it would put him on a plane of equality with the ordinary man. The Indians – and Mother – had looked up to him as though he was a god. In their eyes he was a hero who could do no wrong, who could never perform any act except a splendid and noble one. Fleshly things were not in his province. Well, he wanted to let them see he wasn't anything of the sort. He wanted them to see that he was as human and ordinary as anybody else, and could indulge in natural acts. Of course, he wouldn't have got away with the deception if Osbert's mother had lived, and he had to take Mr. Buckmaster into the plot, too. Anyway, he managed to get Mother and everybody else to believe that he was responsible. Mother was so shaken she threatened to leave him and go back to England, but he says he persuaded her to forgive him. He convinced her that though he had been guilty of a breach of discipline, he was not really to be blamed. The local influences had taken him unawares; he was as much vulnerable to the local influences as anyone else. Oh, he's an interesting chap, Daddy. You never know where you are with him. But that's in keeping with the essence of our myth. Evasion. Hedging. Make-believe. Shadows dodging shadows. Never commit yourself finally." He rose. "Have you seen the baths and toilets on the Ibi? Let me take you there."

Gregory rose with a slightly bewildered air.

"I say, Mabel isn't happy," said Garvey, as they made their way toward the track that led to the Reservation. "I left her in the bathroom washing that stinking old dress she's got to wear. She's going to put it in the sun when she's washed it and see if it will dry in time for church. She's in love with you. It's the real thing, I think. I've seen her going goofy over one or two of our chaps on the Reservation, but it wasn't like this."

Gregory made no comment.

After an interval of silence, Garvey said: "I really wish I could get you to think along our lines. If you're a playwright you ought to understand our approach to life without much trouble. Our idea is that life should savour of a sort of play – a perpetual minute-to-minute play. We believe that the only way to achieve true happiness is to forget reality – forget that we're serious, intellectual, noble creatures – and just *live* our lives: enjoy the sunshine and the trees, and anticipate rain and thunder as the necessary shading in the picture. Do just enough work to keep our minds and bodies healthily occupied and to provide ourselves with food and shelter and entertainment. Don't aim at bossing it over your fellow-men, or dressing better than your neighbour or puffing yourself up like a sick frog. Just be natural and create fun out of the stuff of life. Believe in fairies and ghosts and jumbies and goblins and build up myth around them – but always in the spirit of play-acting. When you see a man shot or stabbed on the stage you're thrilled and elated by the tragedy surrounding his death, aren't you? Good. But you don't get up and go and 'phone the police, do you? You take it seriously as a work of art, but you retain your sense of balance because you know it's all make-believe produced for your entertainment and elation. Well, it's the same with us. We believe in our ghosts and things, but in the same spirit as we'd believe in the actors in their roles on a stage. We deliberately frighten ourselves because it gives us a thrill. Don't you think this a much better way of living than hoarding money in a bank or boasting what a grand thing it is to be an Englishman or an American or a German, or punishing yourself by not having a woman just so that people can say you're a highly moral and righteous fellow, or getting stomach ulcers over stocks and shares and high finance so you can be known as a tycoon? What's in that? See how absurd *your* ways can seem to us! Here we are! The baths and toilets!"

They had emerged on to the bank of the Ibi Creek. Gregory saw what looked like a long ditch bestraddled with palm-roofed huts. He counted a dozen of these. The ditch was wide and seemed deep, and was filled with water evidently fed by the creek. At the point where it entered the stream stood what seemed to be a sluicegate.

"That's the *koker*," said Garvey. "It's a Dutch word which is still used in this country. The sewage matter drops into this ditch, and just before the tide reaches dead ebb the sluicegate is opened and all the befouled water in the ditch here rushes out into the creek and is swept straight into the river. The mouth of the creek is just beyond the next bend – about thirty or forty yards from this spot; so the upper part of the stream is never polluted by the sewage. The *koker* is left open so that the tide can rise and fill the ditch again with fresh water. Then at high tide the *koker* is shut. Quite a simple arrangement. Nothing complicated and ultra-civilized, you see. And look there! See past that hut there's a concrete drain? Well, that leads to the cow-pens. All the stuff from the pens is washed into that drain and is brought down into the ditch here to be disposed of along with the sewage."

"Very interesting," Gregory nodded.

"Very. Oh, by the way, let me give you this." He took from his pants pocket a folded slip of paper and held it out.

"What's this?"

"Little love-note from Mabel. She gave it to me to give you before I left the house, but my sense of the dramatic prevented me delivering it until now." He grinned and winked. "Let's go back if you've seen enough."

X

By twenty past eleven the church was nearly filled. Gregory sat in one of the front pews with his aunt and Garvey and Berton. He was in his usual attire – shorts, shirt, tennis shoes. Before leaving the house he had been presented by Olivia with a wild flower. "This is a gay occasion," she had said. "You must wear something to look gay. Do you mind if I put this on your shirt front?" He had raised no objections, and she had pinned the flower to his shirt. A white flower, bell-like, with a long stalk, and emitting a strong, sweet fragrance. He kept smelling it, and it took on the quality of a symbol of his immediate mood. Idly fingering the slip of paper in his pocket, Mabel's note, he turned his head frequently to glance toward the rear of the church, and every time he did so the piercing fragrance of the flower would surge upward into his senses. The bell began to ring, and the flower, in his fancy, rang, too – a silent nodding that produced waves of scent instead of sound. Waves that rippled inward through his chest, causing a warmth around his heart and in the pit of his stomach. At any instant he would start up and shout – but shout what he was not certain. He knew his aunt and Garvey had noticed the way he kept turning to glance back, but he did not care. What was brewing in him was too important to bother about what they thought.

At last, he saw what he was on the look-out for. Mabel entered by the west door and seated herself in the last pew with four other people who smilingly made room for her. A shower of relief came upon him.

Garvey gave a grunt and muttered: "It must be still a little damp in the seams."

Gregory looked at him sharply and asked: "What's that?"

"Don't pretend you don't know what I mean. Her dress, of course."

The bell stopped ringing. They heard Logan give a raucous quark of mirth. Then the bell began to ring again – with a wild, frolicsome frenzy.

"Are you playing the Paganini study, Garvey?" asked Mrs. Harmston.

"No. I've decided not to. I told Daddy."

At the harmonium Olivia, wearing only panties, sat waiting, her fingers caressing the keys idly but with an itching eagerness.

The church droned with voices in low and loudish conversation, and now and then laughter spattered up like invisible fireworks. Astral rockets and Catherine-wheels, thought Gregory, smiling to himself. He had stopped glancing round now. A spirit of gaiety pervaded the congregation. Coloured shirts among the men and bright, flowered dresses among the women added to the air of festivity as much as the lighted candles on the altar and the vases of wild flowers on and in the vicinity of the altar. In the pew in front of the one in which Gregory sat, Mr. Buckmaster was telling an anecdote featuring three characters called Burroo Goat, Burroo Tiger and Bill. A pretty Indian woman, who sat squeezed close beside him, listened and smiled or laughed, and every now and then Mrs. Buckmaster would interject a monosyllable of admonition in a playful voice. Dorothea and Susan giggled continuously.

The bell stopped, and Logan entered by the west door, grinned and did a clumsy jig, and then squatted on the floor near the font.

The Reverend Mr. Harmston, in a gown of washed-out red, entered and mounted to the pulpit. He smiled around with an affectionate, indulgent air while he waited for the voices to die down, then announced that the service would commence with a reading from *Isaiah*.

"I feel sure," he said, "that we shall appreciate the beautiful passages in Chapter Three, and I think our enjoyment would be definitely assured if I asked Ethelred of Drama Squad to read it for us. Ethelred my boy! Come!"

An Indian in a pink shirt – a young man of about twenty – rose and came toward the lectern, a shyish smile on his face.

Low applause broke out. Mr. Buckmaster uttered an encouraging bark.

"He's one of our finest actors," Garvey whispered to Gregory. "You should hear him recite some bits from *Hamlet* when Book Squad put on their literary evenings!"

Ethelred certainly made a good job of the reading. Gregory thought his elocution excellent. He had a feeling for the music of words.

"...the chains and the bracelets, and the mufflers... The bonnets and the ornaments of the legs, and the headbands, and the tablets, and the earrings... The rings and nose jewels..."

Ethelred lingered over the phrases, giving each word a rich, full tonal value. His head swayed gently in rhythm.

The warmth in Gregory's chest began to spread downwards then outwards. A scarf of spirit-steam might have been wreathing within him, trying to decide what shape to take, trying to achieve stability. In his fancy he saw Ethelred in a dim twilit corner of a stage murmuring lines that he Gregory had written... He heard Garvey's voice by the landing-place... "Why don't you start doing some creative work?... You write plays, don't you?... Write a few one-act plays and we'll produce them... *Do* something or you're lost..."

Ethelred was returning to his pew. Vigorous clapping began, and Gregory joined in it... "Good boy!" called Mrs. Harmston, pink in the face, shining-eyed... "Bravo!" bawled Mr. Buckmaster.

Mr. Harmston clapped loudly, nodding with an air of pride. "I told you Ethelred could do it," he said. When the applause died down he announced a hymn – an Easter hymn – and Garvey whispered: "Have you noticed anything? Our services don't take any regular form. Some Sundays we start off with a hymn, some Sundays with the creed, or a reading, or meditations on past dreams and fantasies. That prevents our services from getting monotonous and repetitive. Nothing," he added, "like the element of surprise."

The hymn – sung with a light-hearted fervour, and sometimes out of tune – was followed by the announcements, and as these began Mrs. Harmston and Berton left the pew and went into the vestry. Mrs. Buckmaster and Dorothea and Susan followed them. Garvey whispered: "They're going to get the communion things ready. Buns and limeade. We don't drink wine or any kind of alcoholic beverages here. It's against our health codes."

"...school vacation," Mr. Harmston was saying, "begins from Thursday this week, and the vacation will last four weeks, but I shall expect parents to keep their end up and see that the children glance through their notes now and then, and do a little reading in the afternoons or evenings, and practise their writing and drawing. The usual prize for the best holiday sketch will be offered. Adult classes will be resumed in a fortnight's time for all literate members of the community, and Olivia will hold a class for illiterates of Labour Squad who wish to improve their speech. These classes will be held on Tuesdays and Thursdays at four o'clock in the church here, beginning with this Tuesday. On Friday evening at eight Mr. Buckmaster will come with his projector to give a show in the church here. Travel and educational films will be put on, and I should be glad if you will all come, all squads and all the older children. On Wednesday of next week our monthly chumming-up party will take place in my home, and, as usual, we anticipate a rollicking time together. Mr. Buckmaster tells me he has learnt a few more conjuring tricks, and he'll trot these out for your entertainment together with whatever else he might have up his sleeve to amuse you…"

The reverend gentleman paused to join in the smiles and to acknowledge the applause that greeted this announcement.

Gregory, happening to glance out of a window, noticed that the sun seemed to have gone under a cloud.

Continuing, Mr. Harmston said: "Our monthly consignment of goods is due by this Wednesday's steamer. I have had word from our Pastor to say that he's sending among other things a new selection of Penguins and gramophone records and some paints and canvas. Those of you who have placed orders for these items will be notified during the course of the week and can come to the house to take delivery on Friday morning by which time I should have got everything sorted out. By the way, a fresh shipment of contraceptives and contraceptive appliances is expected by this same opportunity, and any of you who might find yourselves running short can call whenever you like to replenish your supplies…"

"We issue contraceptives free," Garvey whispered. "It's Item One on our list of basic necessities."

"…which brings me to a piece of good news," Mr. Harmston

was saying. "Our finances now permit of a new clearance scheme and the erection of several more *benabs* in the residential area. As a result, I'm glad to tell you that at least ten couples will be given permission to have babies. Their names will be announced shortly. We'll probably have a get-together, as on the last occasion, and discuss how these couples should be selected – that is, whether you prefer to draw lots or whether you prefer to let those who are first on the waiting list have the preference. Perhaps some of you who applied first might have changed your minds. We'll see. Oh, and before I forget. Our Pastor has informed me that the doctor and dentist can find it possible to come up by this Wednesday fortnight's steamer for the quarterly examination. All those of you who have cavities that you think can be filled must give in your names as early as possible…"

"Extractions are very, very seldom done here," Garvey whispered. "We never let teeth reach such a stage of decay that extraction is necessary."

"What about Logan?"

"What about him? You should see what happens when the dentist tries to examine him. He creates such a hell of a stink that we've had to give him up as a bad job. You won't find anybody else with teeth as bad as his."

"…and now I think," Mr. Harmston was saying, "we'll go on to our sermon-tale which, as I promised you, is an extraordinarily shivery one. It is entitled *The Smiling Fair Presence*."

Mr. Harmston clasped his hands lightly together and looked slowly around. Olivia played soft, breathless notes on the harmonium. The day had become intensely close. Gregory looked outside and saw the jungle unmoving in the breezeless air. The leaves had lost their glitter. The sun was still under a cloud. The eyes of everyone were on Mr. Harmston. Not the rustle of a garment sounded anywhere in the small building. Gregory marvelled at the discipline which made this possible.

"At the beginning of this century, in a mansion off Grosvenor Square, London, there lived a certain Mrs. Emily Bridesmoor and her daughter Noeline…"

Mrs. Buckmaster showed her face at the vestry door. She was fanning herself with what looked like an old *Time Magazine*.

"This lady and her daughter were attended upon by one servant –"

With a flick like that of a whip, a chunk of incandescent metal seemed to shoot in and out of the building, and something banged on the roof with the force of a tremendous barrel shattered in collision with the up-hurling fragments of an already shattered stone.

"Good Christ!"

A swift acrid smell fumed through the air, and a sharp scattered stammering followed that suddenly multiplied itself into a crashing roar.

Garvey sprang up. "I'm on duty – whoops!" He gripped Gregory's arm. "Come and help me! Quick!" The church seethed around them in a wailing babble of voices trying to triumph over the pandemonium on the roof; though Gregory noticed that it was more a pleasurable excitement than alarm that possessed the crowd.

Without question, in a spinning agitation, he followed Garvey out the north door and hurried after him through the dense drops toward the house.

"Round by the back! This way! Come on!" called Garvey – and Gregory moved blindly after him. In a few seconds they were drenched to the skin. Lightning swished between the shining drops like fiery teeth snapping at them, and thunder roared after it without even a second's interval.

They had hardly rounded the angle of the building when out of the welter of wetness a voice called: "Leave it to Garvey and me, Gregory! You're getting wet. Get in out of the rain."

It was Mabel. Like them, she was making for the back of the house. Her hair partly fallen down and indeterminately lank, the old, misfitting dress clinging wetly to her, she had a wild, unreal look as though she might just have sprung up, a fantastic product of the savage pelting rain and all the flickering and drumming that raged about the grey-looming house.

All three of them converged in the vicinity of the water-storage vats, and Gregory would have rushed on past them but Garvey yelled: "Here! Stop here! Bend over! Let me get on your back!"

"Get on *my* back, Garvey!" Mabel gasped, and standing herself close against the larger of the two vats, humped her back and rested her hands on her knees. Garvey muttered: "Oh, good!" and Gregory, bewildered, watched him mount on her back and climb on top the vat. Mabel straightened up and bawled something at him, but the lightning and thunder crashed it out.

A new spatter of water sounded, and Gregory discovered what Garvey had done. He had disconnected the water-pipe that conducted the water from the gutters that bordered the roof; so that instead of running into the vat the water now tumbled straight down in a jagged dirty-grey column beside the vat. When the water grew clear he would probably connect the pipe again. Mabel jumped aside just in time to avoid a fresh sousing.

"Much didn't get inside!" Garvey shouted down.

"What about the strainer?" Mabel called at him. "Get it cleaned!"

"I'm going to do that now. Give me a chance, can't you?"

Gregory watched the column of water. Bits of dry leaves, the dung of birds, pollen dust, dead insects, all must be mixed together in the turgidity of this water – the accumulation of a week of dry, blazing days… It could be the dross of my own spirit I'm watching being washed away… He laughed, turned abruptly and hurried away. He moved off at a trot. He heard Mabel call something after him – something about going into the house and getting his wet things off. But he ignored her. He slowed down to a walk as he came round to the front of the house. The rain seemed to fall not on but into his head… A round copper disc lay fixed to the floor of a cave, and the rain pattered on it like separate little voices loaded with a stuttering spite until, attracted, the lightning ribboned down and danced upon the red metal, dissolving the gloom in the cave… His head felt clear. The rain fell outside it now, stuttering still but less a part of the pattern of his disorientation. He stopped as the lightning cracked past him. This flash seemed to hurtle under the grass like a burrowing dragon. He clapped his hands to his face, the thought in him that if he looked around he would see clumps of broken metal falling, mingled with bits of himself in a floating powder of disintegration. As he dashed water from his nostrils he failed to hear the sniffle his breath made because of the cacophonous prattle of thunder that broke out overhead. He walked without being aware of what direction he was taking, and nearly collided with one of the three palms that stood in the space between the house and the church.

He chuckled and looked up at the dense clump of dead fronds. He heard squeaks, and a crisp rustling. The rain ran down his face and body in cool dribbles. His shirt and shorts clung closely to his skin. Olivia's wild flower was missing; a vague regret moved in him; he looked about the ground, felt he should retrace his steps and search for it; the warmth he had felt around his heart in the church returned, and a great bubble of sentiment began to swell up in him so that he knew in a minute he would cry. He had to laugh to stop the tears, imagine himself a reptile. He shut his eyes and saw in his fancy a two-chambered heart pumping blue rivers of poisonous blood. He opened his eyes and saw the sky ripped across by a network of fire, and the air shook with a bang. Rain came down with new force, new vengeance, the grass about his feet hissed as though alive with unseen snakes. He heard laughter in the church, heard Mabel's voice on the other side of the house. Suddenly he saw point in things. He felt a sense of direction. He identified himself with the weather, and saw the rain as possessed of a tremendous immediate purpose: a passionate perseverance that was almost human. The lightning, too: its swift vivid spite. And the ramming impact of the thunder. Yes, he thought, I can see shape here. It gives me shape. I'm a top spinning. The element in a gyroscope. He listened to the rain; it gave him a feeling of exultation. He could hear a continuous hushed drone in the nether depths of the deluge. Concealed voices seemed trying to communicate secrets to him, always just without success; but he felt no frustration: they were not secrets he should know.

An impulse caught him, and he fumbled his hand down into his trousers pocket and felt around for Mabel's note. He wanted to see it again. He must stand here, in the midst of this fury, and read over the pencilled words. See them washed by the rain and know that it was they, and not the weather, that were responsible for the turmoil in his spirit.

The paper nearly tore across as he pulled it out, for it was soft with wetness… "Please don't mind if I don't talk to you for a few days. I'm terribly embarrassed wearing this thing and I'd feel awful being near you. I'm trying to wash it now. Please understand. I still feel the same way about you. M."

As when he had read it two or three hours ago, he was so moved that he felt as though a stove had come alight within his chest. Compassion was not an emotion he could cope with when it was he who was experiencing it. In the past, other people had felt it on his behalf; now, virtually for the first time in his memory, he was feeling it on behalf of another fellow human. It bewildered him, because it brought into being new, unfamiliar values.

At this instant, however, he could see it without confusion. Something had happened within the past minute or two. The last remnants of the fog that had blurred his spirit were gone; he could see himself clearly. An illusion? It could be, but he preferred to think not. Better to let him say that a wheel had ticked over. The mechanism was functioning as it should.

As the lightning made a sizzle and the thunder tumbled down he suddenly remembered that it was dangerous to stand near to trees during a storm. He stuffed the paper back into his pocket and moved toward the church. He went up the three or four steps and paused on the threshold of the north door. Laughter and voices hit him like a palpable cloud, and seemed to billow past him out into the hubbub of the weather.

Olivia came up and said: "You're dripping wet! Why did you go out? Come in and break a bun with me."

"Is this the communion ceremony?"

"Yes, but we don't call it a ceremony. Or a sacrament. It's just an informal event. It's done like a love-feast. Have you heard of a love-feast? The Moravian Church does it, too. Water is pouring from you, but never mind. Come in and break a bun with me." She held his hand and he let her lead him toward the harmonium.

Mrs. Harmston saw him and exclaimed: "Good gracious! But he's drenched! You'll get chilled, my boy! Why don't you go and get those things off at once?"

"Have some limeade," said Berton, approaching with an enamel cup.

Dorothea and Susan laughed, and Dorothea called out something to Berton that Gregory did not make out. It was lost in the laughter and a grinding clatter of thunder. Somebody said that a tree was down in the clearing. A girl in a blue and pink dress held out a bun to Gregory, and asked him to break off a piece. He did so automatically. Then Olivia held out one, too, and he pinched off a piece from that. He put both pieces into his mouth and laughed for no reason at all. He felt uncomfortable in his wet clothes, but tried to forget it; nothing mattered but the clearness in his head, the freedom from doubt. He looked round him with interest. Somebody was saying that what a pity the sermon-tale had to be called off. Somebody else was expressing a hope that they would be among the ten who could have babies… "I'm twelfth on the waiting-list…" The church vibrated in another onslaught of thunder. The windows rattled from the force of the hurtling raindrops. Purpose and drive, thought Gregory. Orientation not chaos.

Abruptly he turned and hurried toward the north door. Olivia caught up with him just before he reached the steps.

"Where are you rushing off to? What's happened?"

"I'm going to walk in the rain."

"Oh." She gave him an incredulous stare, then said: "I see. That's good. That's a hopeful thing to say."

He left her and went out, moved in the direction of the landing-place. The river was pocked with rain, but it did not seem to flow any faster. It was too wide and deep, he supposed, to be affected by this downpour. He could barely make out the jungle on the other bank. It looked like a lotus-land.

He remembered the many times he had sat on this same spot in the blistering sun and watched the distant storms. Now one of them was here – without warning, without preliminary rumblings. It seemed impossible that only an hour ago the sun had been blazing down from a clear sky.

The lightning made him flinch. He glanced up at the sky and a sense of danger surged upon him. He remembered Spain. The plane that dived out of the mountain mists when he and Raoul and his company were crossing the field. The vacuous pause weighted with heightened consciousness. The incredible singing moment of imminent death.

The rain blinded him and he brushed the water from his eyes. As the thunder trailed away into mutterings the danger-feeling passed. A slow security began to move in him. He grew aware of the coolness of his body – and of the smell of the earth and the rain. He sniffled to dispel the trickles that ran down from his forehead, but it was a pleasant sniffling, water-tanged and exhilarating. He would not take a cold from this wetting. He looked back at the hazed house, and such an excitement leapt in him that he had to utter a whine and hug himself.

He began to fumble again for the note in his pocket, but desisted because he knew he would have torn the paper this time; it must be pulpy. So he shut his eyes and read the words in the pink darkness that the lightning in a jerk turned silvery... A wheel of ridicule whirled redly and dissolved like a fading nebula... Illusion, illusion, the rain began to hiss – but he silenced it. Forced it to say instead: Compassion, compassion and love... The wheel again whirling... But that, too, he defeated; grasped its coiled hysteria by the tail and pushed it into the distance, far into the lotus-land... Tomorrow he would watch the jungle again – and the river – and restfulness would drift through him like mist, but mist blown down from new heavens and charged with power – not with sloth but with livingness. With love and compassion... Or compassion and desire?... Desire, desire, the rain hissed. He did not try to stop it. What was wrong with desire? he wanted to ask it. Was desire obscene? Christ! The dirt in men that turned everything they thought upon unclean!... What if he went into the house now and said to her: "I feel compassion for you. And through compassion love and desire have taken root in me"? Hell! The filth in men! And how clean the rain, how unhypocritical the lightning, how sincere and deep the voice of the thunder!

PART THREE

I

The heat came back. Once again, day after day, the sun flamed in a clear sky, the jungle glittered and the river flowed by in serene silence. Toward afternoon, thunder rumbled in the south, and in the evening the rumble died away, and the stars and the fireflies struggled for the soul of the dark. The heat was no illusion: no shadow dodging behind another shadow; it was real – so real that the memory of Sunday's downpour, the large cooling drops, appeared to Gregory a fantasy that had arisen out of the turbulence of his imagination. He could smile at the thought, however, for the confidence he felt in himself at the moment was like a tower of granite; to his spirit had come a calculating calm in which the unreal and shadowy had no place. The clarity of mind with which he had emerged from the storm on Sunday had not only survived but even gave promise of being able to withstand indefinitely the corroding monotony of weather and scene. He was convinced that the hysterical explosion he had suffered while walking in the rain had resulted from issues far from superficial. Mabel's note, it could be said, had set up the first smouldering hiss, and the thunder and lightning and rain had added the final igniting spark, but the combustible material had been piling up in him since childhood: his gentle upbringing in Middenshot, the pampering he had got from his mother, his brilliant scholastic years, all the several effortless conquests over the women to whom he had taken a fancy, the equally effortless winning of Brenda and the ready acquiescence of his mother to the marriage… An acquiescence that had shocked him into rage so that he had nearly struck her… "But I expected you to make a hell of a scene, mater…" She had smiled: "I know. That just shows you how much you've misjudged my motives. I want only to see you happy, Gregory…" "Happy? Yes, but happy with you. Happy because of *your* ministrations. Oh, I don't understand you. One day you behave as if you'd like to put my soul in a jar and seal it up as your own property, and the next it's as if – as if you wanted

273

to surrender me up to the first woman that drifted along. Christ! I wish I could understand people! I wish I could understand life…"

All that and more like it. He could remember the night in bed with Brenda when, after a frenzied bout of lovemaking, he had looked at her face wincing with the anguish of unbearable pleasure and had said: "I wish you wouldn't go on calling yourself my slave. The next time you do it I'll push you from me and walk out of the room. All right. Don't say anything. Just listen to me. I'm tired of being flattered by women. You hear me! Sick like the deuce! Humiliate me for a change if you can. Do anything, but for Christ's sake don't behave as if I'm a god."

An intelligent, perceptive woman, Brenda had discerned the illness in the souls of all her acquaintances – but not in his. To her he had been the perfect being – a little puzzling and tiresome at times, she would have conceded "but that only makes you more perfect to me, darling." In her eyes he was the profound intellectual, the diverting wit, the talented artist – and the lover whose night-time feats had turned her into a whining slave… "I wish I could make myself into dust so that you could spit on me and grind me down with your heel. If ever you leave me I'll kill myself. Really I will."

And when he left her four months later she had actually attempted to take her life; he had heard about it through his brother-in-law, Charles Cadman (Charles the one friend whom he could talk to without fear of hearing himself described as a figure of gold.) And she herself had shown him the scars on her wrist one morning at Sunningdale when they met accidentally; she had done it with a penknife, she had said… "I think I'll do something like it again if you don't come back to me, Gregory – but I'll be more thorough about it this time." Her face looked pale and lined; ten years older; he knew she was not putting on an act. Inside him, as he had watched her, he had felt a contraction: an anguish of discomfiture and confusion. Something had fought hard for expression, but it was as though the accumulations of the past were too much for it.

Now, here in the jungle, he understood what it was that had been struggling to manifest itself. He had wanted to be sorry for her; he had wanted to feel compassion. Compassion had been a hard knot in him that would not untangle. It was his incapacity to untangle it that had built up the tinder-like tension of frustration in him; the psychiatrists who had treated him had never diagnosed that. He had had to come all the way into this wilderness to diagnose it himself.

He felt like a human being now – warm and flexible and easy. The core of his ego had softened; the alloy of conceit had been purged out of it. Now he was able to think more of others and less of the importance of his own destiny; he could feel a pulsing sympathy for his fellow-men.

On Thursday afternoon, he sat on a stool by the Ibi sketching the *benabs* and *corials* and boats at the port – or depot, as it was more often called – when Olivia appeared and approached. She stopped behind him and said: "Just look at that. Sketching again. The whole week you've been sketching. Some big change always seems to come over you on a Sunday. We'll have to watch you. Sunday must be your cruxial day."

"Run away and play or this will be your cruxial moment."

"Have I used the wrong word? You've got very cheeky, too, all of a sudden. Why are you doing all this sketching?"

"To keep myself occupied and prevent me from losing my temper with silly little plaguing girls."

She laughed. "You think you can taunt me so easily? It won't work. Did you see me burning the old bathing suit on Monday?"

"I did. I think you're a young goat." He laughed and put his arm about her and gave her a quick squeeze.

"This is the fourth hug you've given me for the week. You've got very affectionate. You weren't like this before last Sunday. Have you fallen for me, at last?"

"In a moment I'll fall *on* you. Run off and play and leave me in peace."

She regarded him and smiled. "You baffle me. From a raving lunatic to a sane, handsome young man doing sketches – all in three weeks. Shall I tell you something? I heard Maby talking in her sleep last night. She said: 'Oh, my darling! Oh, my darling!' And she huddled up against me. I had to wake her and tell her it was me in bed with her and not you."

"Has it occurred to you that you have a knack of saying the most embarrassing things?"

"I won't say you *look* very embarrassed at the minute. Have you spoken to Maby since Sunday?"

"No. She keeps avoiding me whenever I try to say anything."

"Yes, I've seen you trying. I've seen you eyeing her, too. You're in love with her, aren't you?"

"Shut up and run off."

"You're blushing. This looks serious. You know what I came here for? Daddy sent me to search for you. He's heard about your new sketching craze, and he says I must ask you if you'd like him to order any painting materials for you. He's making up his list of orders."

"He is? Yes, I could do with some canvas. I'd intended to ask him to order some for me."

"I'll tell him. What about paints?"

"I've got enough to last me for some time."

She looked at the black and white sketch he was working on. "You seem to know what you're doing. Are you going to make an oil from this?"

"Yes. When I get canvas."

"We can let you have some until yours comes. I'll ask your dearly beloved. She paints, too."

"Excellent."

"She'll be delighted to prepare it for you. Well, I must be going. It's nearly four o'clock. I've got to take the illiterates' class."

After she had gone, he sat staring at the sketch and reflecting. She had brought to the surface of his awareness a question that had been troubling him off and on during the past few days. He had tried to put it aside, but it came upon him now that it must be faced and threshed out. It was the question of how he felt about Mabel. He knew for a certainty that she attracted him physically. But so did one or two of the Buck girls he had seen on the Reservation. If he let himself he could become very fond of her, but should he let himself? The failure of his marriage with Brenda had left in him a sediment of guilt which would take a long time to sift out of his system; looking back on his life, he had no doubt about who had been at fault: he had treated Brenda shamefully. Could he risk another marriage? Would it be fair to subject another woman to the hazards of his uncertain temperament? Mabel was young and, in many respects, green and unspoilt. What would happen when he grew inured to the mysteries of her body, when the initial heat of physical passion cooled? She might seem to him dull; he might tire of her. Especially living in this environment. He could envisage her frank eyes suddenly one day growing hurt as the realization came upon her that she no longer appealed to him, that he was merely tolerating her out of a sense of duty. The picture made him squirm... To hurt her would be unbearable; he couldn't stand it.

The alternative, then, was to return to civilization: leave this peaceful refuge and go back to the muck he had run away from. The surface of his new-found calm began to grow furrowed. A terror arose within him so that he trembled and nearly dropped the lap-board with the drawing... No. There must be no return. He must never leave here. Rather than resume his old existence he would drown himself in this dark river.

Life on this settlement with these relatives of his had its distinctly absurd aspects, but, at least, it had a simplicity and freshness that was a soothing change from the complex and diseased world he had left behind. The very sight of the jungle and the river gave him reassurance and a sense of peace he had never before experienced; he was sure he could never grow tired of this setting: he could settle here for good and be happy. He knew himself well enough to be certain of this. The mere thought of city life gave him a feeling of panic. Just to contemplate a scene of traffic and orderly buildings stirred up anger and nausea in his spirit. From the commencement of his sojourn on this settlement he had begun to be subject to nightmares, and they all took one form: he was in London or New York or Paris in the company of people who talked politics or art or money, people who prattled insincerities or pretentious nonsense and drank cocktails with a casual, bored air. For a while all would seem perfectly easy and as it should be; he would be quite at home: he drank like them and talked like them, laughed with them. But gradually a sensation of fatigue, a lassitude and depression, a slow panic, came upon him; he tried to ask for an excuse, but he could not: he was tongue-tied.

They were all looking at him and laughing. They loomed tall around him: tall and elongated; they formed a fence around him… "You're trapped, don't you see?" they jeered. "You're trapped, Gregory!" Their eyes turned yellow and demoniac: their laughter spiralled around him like so many ribbons intent on binding him… and then he would wake. For a second or two after waking he would stare around the room, believing himself to be in his London flat or in a hotel room in some big city. Then sight of the mosquito-net brought him abruptly to the realization of where he actually was, and such an immense relief and joy engulfed him that he had to bury his face in his pillow to stifle the sigh or whine that tried to force its way out.

He knew that he would have to be realistic about the situation, however. It was all well and good to talk of his settling here permanently, but he must not blind himself to the snags. First, the set-up was a most unusual one: this highly unorthodox religion his relatives practised and the odd philosophy they had formulated, their antics and eccentricities. Except for Mabel and his aunt, they irritated him not a little sometimes. He tried not to take them seriously – to be amused at their oddities – but would he always be able to keep up this indulgent attitude? Of course, he had to admit that there was a lot in their methods that met with his approval; under their clowning lurked much that made one ponder. The efficient way in which the settlement was run – the system of education, birth-control, sanitation, the temper of the people and their interest in the arts – was certainly impressive; you couldn't in fairness brush that aside: it stood out as a distinct achievement. Yet…

He fidgeted on the stool.

And to return to Mabel… Now and then the thought of her aroused in him a deep throbbing of emotion: the new emotion of compassion that had been released in his system. In such moments he was caught in a trance of wonder and would stare inward at himself as a child would stare at some quaint insect new to its ken… Mabel clad in an old, misfitting, threadbare dress of her mother's, doing penance for having taken his advice not to report the incident of Sigmund's breaking into the house… It was not the actual punishment so much as the way she bore up under it that moved him. Mingled with his compassion was admiration and… yes, and something else that he could not yet decide about. On Sunday, walking in the rain, hysterical and distracted, he had diagnosed it as desire and love, but viewed now in a spirit of sane calculation, that seemed like sheer tommyrot – at least the "love" part of it. Could he ever love any woman? Had he loved Brenda? With a shock it occurred to him that he had not; she had never given him a chance to. No woman had ever allowed him to love her; she had always swamped him so completely with her own love that before he could respond contempt had already taken possession of him.

He fidgeted again. Looked about him feeling dismayed. The jungle across the Ibi shimmered with an aura of revelation. A sense of panic stole upon him, but in a minute his calm had prevailed.

He rose and folded up the stool, began to make his way home. In him was a feeling of something unresolved… He recalled the words of his uncle-in-law that day by the landing-place, and smiled dryly… "Nothing creates greater disillusion than the arrival at a conclusion…" It sounded spurious, and yet… Was it any use trying to clarify the problems in one's life? Was it humanly possible to arrive at a neat and foolproof conclusion concerning one's attitude to people and living or the course of action one should take for the future?

He felt himself overwhelmed by an aching impotence and futility.

II

After breakfast, on Monday morning, he was in his room doing a study of the church and belfry when his aunt came in to tidy up. She uttered a sound of approval and remarked: "It's so nice to see you busy like this. Is that the canvas Mabel prepared for you?"

"Yes," he said, without turning his head.

He could feel her gaze on him as she moved around the bed pulling and straightening the sheet. His back tingled sensitively.

"I'm glad you've decided to discard your shirt. In this weather I can't see the sense in wearing a shirt."

"Quite."

"I do wish we didn't have to be on our guard against surprise visits from Government officials. We could have done away with clothes entirely. In a hot climate like this! It's so absurd wearing clothes."

"That's so."

She gave a soft mirthful gurgle.

Amidst the fronds of the palms in the clearing coconut sackies kept up a gay twittering, their feet and wings and bills making a lisp-lisp as they busily explored the dead fronds for insects. His brush seemed to transpose the sounds onto the canvas: thin, nervous strokes of rose madder. His back tingled unbearably.

"I have some news that might please you," said his aunt as she appeared to be on the point of leaving the room; her voice took on a note of conspiracy. "Would you like to hear it?"

Still without turning his head, he said: "Naturally."

She shut the door carefully, approached close and said: "Gerald told Mabel this morning after breakfast she could have her own clothes back. The punishment is over."

He glanced round. "I'm certainly pleased to hear that. But the fortnight isn't up yet. Why this generosity on the part of the authorities?"

"That should show you Gerald isn't the monster you think him, my boy. He has a very good heart."

He laughed. "You all appear inordinately anxious to convince me of his virtues. I can't remember ever having questioned his integrity – and good-heartedness."

"You haven't done it openly, but your manner has suggested that you consider him something of a tyrant and a sham. You see, my boy, Gerald does *give* that impression sometimes. And he purposely lets people think him a hypocrite; that's the role he's chosen in our make-believe life-drama here. But he's in actuality very earnest, and he's not dictatorial."

Gregory made no comment, and his aunt smiled and said: "In many ways you remind me a lot of your father. Garvey often assumed that air of silent irony. What a pity he had to die. He wouldn't have let Edith pamper you. You would never have had need to see a psychiatrist."

He glanced at her and saw that her eyes were moist. She brushed an imaginary speck of dust from the front of her dress and smiled with a too sudden cheerfulness. She looked at the canvas and said: "I can see the influence of that new German school in your work. *Die blauer Reiter*, I think they call themselves. The Franz Marc group."

"You've heard of them, have you?"

"I've read of them."

She made no move to leave the room. He heard her pottering about behind him. He almost started round when she said: "Have you been sleeping well of late, Gregory?"

"What?"

She laughed. "You needn't scowl so!" The colour came to her face.

He tried to look apologetic. "I'm afraid I'm inclined to be a little jumpy when I'm painting. What's it you asked? If I'm sleeping well? Yes, perfectly, thanks. Why?"

He could detect some discomfiture in her manner. "You're sure you've never been disturbed at all?"

He lowered his brush and palette to his lap. "Disturbed? By what? Ghosts?"

"No, I'm not talking about ghosts – though it's possible Mynheer could have manifested himself in your room. I mean disturbed by dreams. Have you had any passionate dreams?"

"Passionate dreams? What are you hinting at?"

She patted his back in a conciliatory manner and said: "Never mind. I shouldn't have asked you. I ought to have realized you don't think along our lines."

"Wait, don't go. Let's straighten this out on the spot. Cut the mystery and tell me what you mean. Why are you interested in my dreams?"

She smiled, her self-possession returning. "What I mean is if you've been having dreams of Mabel – intimate dreams."

He grinned. "Oh, is that all you wanted to ask me! No, I can't say I've had dreams about her – or about anybody else, as far as I can remember. The only dreams I've had since I came here have been nightmares – and nightmares of a special kind. They won't interest you."

"I can see you're being purposely dense. You don't want me to embarrass you by asking you outright, do you?"

"Asking me what outright?"

She sighed. "I'm afraid it will always be difficult saying anything to you. Our standards are so different. What I mean in simple language, then, is have you and Mabel been sleeping together recently?"

"Sleeping together! Are you off your pins?"

The whole of her began to shake with mirth. "I'm perfectly sane, my boy. And please don't look so shocked – though I can understand how you feel. I'm not trying to censure you. I'm only interested, that's all."

"Interested?"

"Yes, I'm her mother, after all. Don't you think it's natural I should be?" She laughed. "Oh, please, Gregory! Don't *look* like that!"

"But can I help it? I mean –"

"Yes, I understand. But, you see – well, she's in love with you. We've all noticed that, and it would be the natural thing if she slept with you. That's why I asked."

"Oh. Oh, I see." He grinned again. "Awfully obtuse of me, I admit. No, we haven't slept together. Sorry to disappoint you. And since we're being so candid, it might interest you to know that I haven't slept with a woman since I left England three months ago."

282

She wagged her head. "You say that as if you're proud of your periods of celibacy. Why? Is it so disgraceful to have sexual indulgence as a matter of regular habit?"

"Did I say it was?"

"No, but your manner implies disgust. Oh, but this is horrible of me! I shouldn't tease you like this, poor fellow. I keep forgetting you're not fully civilized."

"Quite so. You must be indulgent with me."

She laughed. "You have a sense of humour, though. That's fortunate. But to be serious, my boy. Please don't let any foolish ideas of morality prevent you from associating with Mabel if you wish. I was rather upset the morning after your first night with us, because I thought she'd gone into your room during the night. That would have been shameful wantonness, and we frown very much on that sort of thing. Nothing would break my heart more than to see her going after men in a wanton spirit. But so long as she's in love with you and you respond – well, that's quite all right."

"I see."

"We have no cramping, barbarian taboos here, Gregory. I mean it seriously. We're very sincere in wanting to live sane and healthy lives. We train the children to be restrained when restraint is called for, but we want them to be free in such things as involve their natural urges. That's how we've trained all our people here. We believe that natural urges must of necessity be normal and healthy or they wouldn't be natural, so why should we stifle them and turn ourselves into warped, unwholesome personalities?"

"Why, indeed!"

"You've seen something of the Reservation, haven't you? Have you witnessed any orgies of licentiousness? No. Our people work hard. They aren't obsessed by sex. They treat it as an ordinary everyday function, and enjoy it when it's time to indulge in it. They make jokes about it as they make jokes about eating and swimming and going to church. They're not dirty jokes as you know dirty jokes, because we don't look on sex as a dirty subject. Oh, there's a lot you'll learn about us here, my boy, that you'll come to see is sound. We're not perfect. Nothing human can be perfect. We don't hope for perfection. On the contrary, we're always discovering some new defect in our pattern of life. But we do our best, and we're earnest. Always remember that. Don't judge us by our antics."

She smiled and grunted reminiscently. "When I first arrived here with your Uncle Gerald I looked at things just as you do. I was very shocked at Gerald's theories, and I didn't think them practicable. If I wasn't so much in love with him I would have left him and gone back to England. In fact, something occurred that caused me actually to pack my things and go to New Amsterdam preliminary to leaving the country – but he persuaded me to give him a chance, and I did. Nor did I ever regret it."

Gregory saw that her eyes were moist again.

"Gradually, my boy, I began to understand that one's morals are only the result of an attitude – an attitude that we ourselves, through ignorance or superstition, build up. Who can decide absolutely what is right or what is wrong about an action? Who can say that to behave in a certain way is correct or incorrect? It's all so obviously absurd that it's a wonder people can't see it – and in this age when we're supposed to be enlightened. That's why we keep pulling your leg, my boy. How could we help looking upon you as other than a savage. What passes for civilization in the world you've come from seems, in our eyes, just laughable barbarism – at least, it would be laughable if it weren't so pathetic – and tragic. Millions and millions of people all being bamboozled by sentimental moralists and pious charlatans. It's no wonder that your politicians can make such a mess of things for you."

She sighed. "You don't know how much I long to see our dear England again, Gregory. Gerald, too. We've spent many a sad night reminiscing in the Big Room. You think we don't miss England? Of course we do. But this work must go on – and we're happy here. Happy because we're achieving something. We're making two hundred-odd people happy as human beings should be happy – that's our consolation. And when we read *Time Magazine* and the *Daily Mirror* overseas edition, which Mr. Buckmaster takes sometimes, I can assure you, we get even more consolation. England! Look what England has come to! A cringing, shillyshallying England playing up to a Hitler and a Musso-

284

lini. Ah, but I mustn't say that." She sniffled and blew her nose hastily in her apron. She smiled brightly and asked: "What about Middenshot, Gregory? Has it changed much? Is Carp's Bun Shop still flourishing? And the Ram and Cross?"

"Still going strong. Middenshot doesn't change. Old man Carp is dead, but his nieces run the place. It's called a tea-shop now. The Ram and Cross is the same as I knew it when I was six."

She laughed. "You see how sentimental I can be when I get going!"

"I see," he smiled.

She regarded him a moment and then said: "I like you, Gregory. I think you'll get along with us. We aren't desperate characters. By your standards, we may be eccentric, but in time you'll see us as plain and ordinary people – and you'll feel as we feel: that Nature can't be wrong. You'll know that if you follow Nature you must go right. Don't smile. Wait and you'll see. I'm not telling you that it's right to *abuse* Nature. Don't misunderstand me. But so long as we work in harmony with Nature we can't be on a crooked track. In fact, I don't think anything calls for more restraint and discipline than a real down-to-earth, natural existence. Why, look, just take Mabel as an example. You wouldn't say from what you've seen of her that she's a dissolute character, would you? Answer me!"

"No, I wouldn't say so."

"Well, there you are! And Mabel's been having lovers since she was sixteen."

"She's been *what*?"

"I said she's been having lovers since she was sixteen."

III

"Yes, it's no untruth," said his aunt.

The sackies... Busy bills and wings and little feet...

"Her last lover was Robert of Art Squad. She was very fond of him, and we all thought she would decide to marry him, but it seems something went wrong and they called off the friendship. A year or so ago she was in love with Waldo of Drama Squad. They had a sweet, joyous affair. We used to let her sleep with him some nights in his *benab*."

"I see," he said, listening to the sackies still.

"If the whole of your civilized world followed our system there'd never be any of these poor tragic old maids going to their graves soured and dried-up from frustration."

A boat was passing on the river. A woman in it. The thud-thud of the paddle sounded clearly. Parrots were in the treetops across the stream; they uttered occasional squawks. Impersonal and equivocal: a part of the pattern of the scene. His aunt was saying something again. It took all his restraint not to turn and shout at her: "Oh, get out of the room! I don't want to hear anymore! Get out and leave me in peace! Keep your philosophy! I'm sick of philosophy! I'm sick of you and sick of mankind!"

"Why, you're trembling, my boy. What's the matter?"

Mabel's voice sounded in the corridor calling: "Mother! Where are you?" She pushed the door open and said: "Oh, you're in here." She was in a pale green dress – her own. She blushed slightly and said: "What's going on in here? A discussion on art?"

"Not exactly," smiled her mother. "Did you want me?"

"Daddy is having the new bookcase brought over from the workshed. The boys are helping him lift it across. He asked me to let you know."

"Yes, yes. I was forgetting. I must go down and help. We're putting it where the dinner-wagon is and shifting the dinner-wagon nearer the window." She ran her fingers affectionately through Gregory's hair and said with a laugh: "Get on with your painting. Let me see it when it's finished," and went bustling out of the room.

Mabel hesitated near the door, gauche and uncertain. She smiled and said: "Has she told you that the punishment is over?"

"Yes. Yes, she mentioned it. I'm glad." He smiled stiffly, and turned his attention to the canvas.

A puzzled look came to her face. "Am I interrupting?"

"No. Not at all." He glanced round briefly and said: "By the way, I mustn't forget to thank you for the canvas."

"It's nothing." On impulse she came close and rested her hands on his shoulders. "I've missed you. I've missed you terribly."

He said nothing. Only sat very still.

"You don't know how much discipline it called for – having you so near and always within my sight and not letting myself talk to you or sit with you anywhere."

He still said nothing.

She withdrew slowly and murmured: "Are you annoyed with me?"

He shook his head.

"What's the matter, then? You seem so… you don't seem glad to have me talk to you again."

"Sit down, will you?"

She made no move to comply.

He got up from the stool and crossed to the dressing-table and took up his cigarette-case, lit a cigarette. He looked at her and said: "Don't take any notice of me. I'm just angry with myself."

"Why?"

He shrugged. "Perhaps because I'm not civilized. I…" He laughed. "You're looking very lovely, Mabel."

From downstairs came a few thuds and the voices of Mr. Harmston and the boys. And Logan's raw, unrestrained laughter.

"Couldn't we go for a spin on the river?" she said.

"On the river? But – haven't you any duties to perform? I thought –"

"No, I'm not on official duty until after lunch. During school vacation I always have a lot of spare time."

"I see. Yes, I don't mind."

"That isn't enough. Say you want to."

"Yes, I want to."

At the landing-place, they encountered Ellen seated on the logs, her clothes off and resting in a careless pile on the ground behind her. She was leisurely soaping herself, her feet dangling in the water. She looked up at them with a smile and uttered a creamy chuckling sound. Gregory, instantly excited, averted his gaze. Mabel kicked off her shoes and said: "Ellen, take these back to the house for me, will you? And if the parson or the mistress asks for me say I've gone down-river in the *corial* with Mr. Gregory. We won't be long."

"Awright, miss," smiled Ellen. "Tek care and paddle good."

She helped with the mooring-rope when they had got in, and gave the craft a push off for them. From compulsion Gregory's gaze returned to her, and she winked and made a quick circular motion with her finger. Mabel saw, and smiled: "She thinks of nothing but sex." It was an offhand remark uttered in the same spirit as she might have said: "She's crazy about jam-tarts."

After they had proceeded about a hundred yards – in complete silence – Mabel glanced back at him and said: "You paddle like an expert."

"It's not so difficult," he smiled. He caught a whiff of the perfume on her person, and desire scooped a hollow in his stomach. He scowled in self-contempt, remembering Ellen's obscene gesture and seeing himself on a par with her. With an excruciating desperation he wished he could burn all physical urge out of his body. Christ! Why must he want not to feel desire for a woman and still have to!

She glanced round and surprised the scowl on his face.

"What's the matter, Gregory? You don't look cheerful, and I've been hearing you're full of high spirits this week."

"Who told you that?"

"Who else but Olivia?" She stopped paddling. "Let's drift along for a bit."

They were passing the mouth of the Ibi Creek, and he had a glimpse of cattle grazing in a small clearing. She stretched back and touched his knee. "If you knew how much I love you," she said.

He rubbed his hand along the wet paddle and kept looking toward the bank at the indifferently glittering profusion of trees but all the time aware of her face with its look of tenderness. Compassion was warm in him, but it had for company a stale bitterness that was the sum of other faces with tender expressions directed at him… "If you knew how much I love you." The number of times he had heard that said to him – and with exactly the same breathless murmured sincerity…

He smiled and touched her arm.

"I wish I could write poetry," she said.

Two *aeta* palm seeds went bobbing past, shiny and purple, and with the solid look of precious stones.

"I have so much I want to tell you, and I can't. It's too – too mixed up and deep." Her voice grew husky. She blinked and turned away her face. He told her not to mind.

"Let's make for the other side," she said. "It's shady there."

"Yes, the sun is getting a bit uncomfortable."

"You've got very brown."

They paddled across to the other bank. She had to direct him once to avoid a *tacooba* that was completely submerged. "It's just there," she said. "If you look carefully you'll see the water swirling a bit. When the tide is at dead ebb it shows itself an inch or two."

The jungle reached out at them with a cool lushness. It was very pleasant in the shade, after the blistering sunshine. They could hear the cluck and murmur of the water in the brown-dark grotto spaces that tunnelled to unknown depths under the over-hanging foliage. Every few seconds came the plep or chirp of some berry dropping invisibly and sinking – sinking for good, or sinking and floating up, though still invisibly because of the dusk cast by the dense branches.

"You like the jungle, don't you?"

"Yes," he answered.

"I can see it on your face – and from the way you're listening to the water and looking at the trees. I'd like you to look at me like that."

"Why? Do you identify yourself with trees?"

"No, I don't say that." She coloured. "Why pretend you don't understand what I mean."

"It's difficult to know when to take you at face value and when not to."

"Is it? Have I ever been evasive with you?"

He said nothing.

"That's not a fair thing to say. You can always take me at face value. I never say abstruse things,"

He smiled.

"What are you smiling at?"

"Nothing."

She caught hold of a branch and checked the drifting of the craft. The tide was falling. The leaves swished softly as the branch did its work as a brake. A swift musky smell of pollen swirled in the air, and a black ant alighted as though by magic on Gregory's knee. He brushed it off. "I wish I could get you to talk," she said. "You're still remote. As remote almost as when you first came."

He said nothing.

"It's so confined in this thing. We should have come in the skiff instead. If you sit very still I'll lean back and rest my head on your knees. Would you mind?"

"I... No, I wouldn't mind."

The *corial* rocked dangerously, but she managed it.

"This is much nicer than twisting myself round every time I want to say something to you. Are you moved?"

"Moved?"

"You are. I can feel you trembling. You're in love with me?"

Ants, or some other insects, kept up a subtle itching tick amid the foliage.

"Why don't you answer? I can feel you're moved. I am, myself. I wish it was night now. I'm going to come in to you tonight."

He started to speak, then stopped.

"Don't you want me to?"

The craft swayed.

"You'll overturn us. Careful, It's so hard to know what you're thinking," she said, after they were steady again. "You're so locked up. Why don't you tell me something?"

"There's nothing to say."

"Don't you want to make love to me tonight?"

"It's not always advisable to do what one wants to."

"That's true. But we have nothing to stop us from making love if we want to."

"Except the trifling circumstance that we're not married."

"Married? But – but we can get married whenever we like – if you'd want to marry. I…" She broke off, frowning puzzledly.

They had drifted round the bend. The settlement was out of sight.

She put up her hand and touched his cheek. "Look at me. Don't look at the bush. I want to call you darling, but I'm shy. You're so…"

After a silence, she said: "I'm sorry if I've made you uncomfortable. I should have remembered you see life differently. You think it wrong to make love without being married?"

"I don't say I'm as conventional as that, but… Look here, it's no use. Don't let's… I can't discuss this with you. And what you suggest is impossible. I can't make love to you. I…"

"But you want to. You wanted to a few seconds ago." He moved his head in assent.

"And why wouldn't you want to tonight if I came into your room?"

"You're making it very difficult for me, Mabel."

"Why? Does it embarrass you so much even to talk about it?"

"I'm afraid it does. More than that, too."

"What else? I know I'm being selfish, but… well, it might help you if you could tell me what's on your mind. Try to – please."

He smiled. "I've been made love to before, you know. I've had a lot to do with love. I want to get away from it."

"Get away from it? But you're only thirty-one."

"I know. It isn't possible, but one still wishes for what is impossible. I want to make love to you, but I despise myself for wanting to. The memory of the past inundates my imagination, and I get a feeling of satiety. I want to go beyond the flesh – to be safe and at peace away from the passions that plague the body."

She was thoughtful a moment, then said quietly: "I remember what you asked me that Saturday afternoon – about the magician: what superhuman power I'd ask for if a magician offered to bestow on me—"

"Yes, we were sitting by the landing-place."

After a silence that threatened to become awkward, he stroked her hair and said: "You haven't got to stop talking altogether, you know."

"But if I talk I'll have to talk about you and how I feel."

"Do I obsess you as much as that?"

"Please don't say it in that flippant tone." She kept looking at his face. "I wish you'd let yourself go." She took his hand and rubbed it over her breasts, and when he withdrew it, said: "Why should you want to get away from the flesh – and passions? Passions don't plague the body. They give pleasure. You seem as if you purposely don't like doing things that give you pleasure. You almost make me sorry for you."

He remained very still, looking out on the water.

"Fondle me. Forget about wanting to get away and be at peace. I can give you peace. Fondle me. Please."

He grunted. "Perhaps it's just as well you're not very sympathetic."

"I'm purposely trying not to be. I can feel too much sympathy wouldn't be good for you. Rub your hands over me."

He tapped her cheek playfully with a finger and said: "I've done a lot of fondling."

"But not to me. And you want to – I can tell from your voice and the way you're trembling now."

"Quite right. But – Christ!"

She held his wrist.

"Ultimately," he said, "you might see I was wise not to touch you."

"Ultimately? Ultimately we'll die. Darling, please!"

"Shall we be going back?"

"I'm in torture, I love you so much." She shut her eyes.

"Let's go back."

"Not yet. No. I'm… it's still a little comfort resting my head on you like this." She opened her eyes. "Fondle me. Please."

"Were you as passionate as this with Robert and Waldo – and the others?"

"Yes. But I didn't feel the same about them as I feel about you. With you it's more than my body wanting you. My body wants you badly, but I feel soft and sorry inside and – and weak. I could cry when I think of you. Oh, I can't explain it. It's too mixed up. With you – no matter how you rebuff me I can stand it. I don't care. I can take anything from you – any insult…" She shut her eyes. Bit her lip.

He fondled her tentatively, then desisted and held the sides of the frail craft to dispel an anguished giddiness that attacked him. It passed in a second, and the drumming in his head gradually became an indeterminate murmur like the water under the silently impending verdure. An insect started to cheep. A noise like a bedewed strand of cobweb glistening in moonlight. Then it stopped. A dank fragrance of rotted blossoms, not unpleasant, drifted out of the varying depths of twilight behind the bush.

"I've just thought of it," she said, looking at him. "Who told you about Waldo? I only remember telling you about Robert."

"Did you tell me about Robert?"

"Of course I did. We were sitting at the landing-place. That same Saturday afternoon you asked me about the magician and what not."

"You told me you'd been friendly with Robert. You didn't say you had been his mistress."

Her eyes opened wide in wonder. "But I… But surely you must have understood that that was what I meant. If I say I was friendly with a man in a sentimental way I mean we've made love sexually."

"You're enlightening me. I didn't know that. It was your mother who mentioned it this morning. She said you've been having affairs since you were sixteen."

A look of comprehension began to come over her face. She smiled and said: "I think I'm beginning to see what's wrong. You think me immoral because I've made love with Robert and the others."

"Will you please let us not talk about it?"

"It's really silly of me! Of course I should have known how you would feel. Especially you being English. Oh, Gregory, please don't think me a bad girl or anything like that. I'm not. Are you jealous of Robert and the other chaps?"

He sat looking distressed.

"I've been too impulsive," she said, humility in her voice. "I shouldn't have let you know how I felt about you until I'd got to know you better. Now I've spoilt everything. Oh, this is terrible!" She tried to sit up, and he made an attempt to help her but suddenly changed his mind and pressed her down again, told her not to move and patted her cheeks gently, kept his hands pressed on her cheeks.

They heard parrots.

"I didn't mean to say anything to hurt you," he said.

The parrots passed low overhead and chattered gradually away into the distance.

"It's generally upsetting to discover that someone you thought green is not. When your mother told me what she did this morning I felt like an utter fool. After imagining you were so inexperienced... My conceit got the sort of jolt it's not accustomed to."

"I can't imagine you as conceited. You don't behave as if you were."

"I am – very much. I've been horribly spoilt. I think I've told you."

"Yes."

A swift frantic rustle came from the bush – and stopped.

"What's that?"

"It could be anything. A wild pig – or a snake. Go on talking to me. I feel weak from loving you." She touched his cheek.

"Have you dangerous snakes here?"

"Yes, but you don't come upon them often. The bushmaster is the worst. It's six or seven feet long sometimes, and it's deadly. The venom paralyses you in less than fifteen minutes, and a few minutes more and you're dead."

"Doesn't sound very pleasant."

"It attacks you, too. The other snakes won't trouble you unless you happen to tread on them or frighten them in some way – but not so with the bushmaster. It goes for you on sight and without provocation."

"If I'm not mistaken, the cobra is like that in temperament, too," he nodded. "What are you laughing at?"

"You and snakes. Oh, darling, darling. Rub my cheeks again. I like it. Do all kinds of things to me. Please. My head is swimming."

"You'll have us over in a second."

After a moment, when the craft was steady again, she said: "You look so incredulous."

He nodded.

"You *feel* incredulous?"

"Yes."

"Why?"

He shook his head.

"Tonight?"

"Perhaps. I don't... no."

"I feel as if fire is crawling in my stomach."

A bubbling noise made him turn his head alertly, but he saw nothing.

"Is it of me you're incredulous?"

He nodded.

"You didn't think I was like this?"

"Not so persistent, no."

"Have I fallen in your respect? Is that what you mean?"

He shook his head.

"You needn't be afraid to tell me. I like the truth."

"I do myself."

She watched his face.

"I'm touched – by your behaviour," he murmured. "And upset – that's all."

After a silence she said: "I think I know what."

"Yes?"

"I won't ask you again. I'll wait until you ask me."

"Ask me about... oh. About going to bed, you mean?"

"Yes."

He gave a grunt.

"I've begun to understand you better now," she said.

"I hope so," he smiled.

She took his hand and pressed it to her cheek. "Help me sit up, and let's go back."

"I'm not in a hurry."

"I'm not, either," she said. "I feel happy with you."

"I am, too, with you."

"You're sure? Or is it because of the jungle and the water?"

"That combined with you," he told her.

"I feel so happy I feel like mist."

The wind sounded far away in the jungle. Like sea on a beach.

"Don't stop," she asked him.

"I'll rumple it up if I go on."

"Rumple it."

"It looks too perfect. The way the plaits are arranged…"

"I'd like you to. Take it down – as Olivia does for me at night in bed."

He said nothing. He sat very still.

"I always forget, and when I get into bed she reminds me – and does it for me in the darkness."

It was like thunder in the south, the trembling that awoke in him. He seemed to hear it in the distances of his being.

Her lips parted as though to utter an enquiry, then the enquiry flashed out of her face in a lightning of comprehension. He saw it happen, and saw her, how she breathed quickly, and how her legs stirred against each other.

The *corial* rocked slightly. He held its sides, and the rumbling in his head rippled into quietude… Small lilac blossoms drifted past. And a palm seed that was strange to him; not an *aeta:* it was of a dirty yellow, and kept rolling over and over like a lost eye. Lost and diseased. He thought of the yellow eyes of the people in his nightmares… There must be no return… He seemed to hear it echoed in a gurgle that came out of the alcoved silence behind the fringe of green limbs… There must be no return… "As Olivia does for me at night in bed… in the darkness…" Long, awkward legs in bed, and freckled breasts. Where did ecstasy begin? In the knees, say, and then shivered up in quaking explosions to the throat… Oh, God!… Lilac blossoms… They knew no heat. Nor did black water… Could that be an insect making that steaming noise? Like the spittle of a caterpillar slyly spinning its cocoon… It stopped.

"Gregory."

"Yes, I… what's it?"

"No, you say what you want to say first."

"It's nothing. What's it?"

"You felt as I felt. You… just tell me yes, you did – if you did."

"Yes, I did." He said it in a whisper.

"Help me sit up. We can paddle a bit further downstream, and then go back."

He agreed with her that it was a good idea and helped her to sit up.

Just before she dipped the paddle she turned her head and smiled at him. He gave a grunt and smiled, too.

IV

"Death!"

Gregory heard the whisper at his door, and looking round, saw Olivia.

It was shortly after three, the following day, Tuesday, and since after lunch he had been engaged in putting the final touches to his picture. He was satisfied with what he had done, and his mood was buoyant.

"Come in and stop being silly," he said, with a smile.

Only her face was visible, and she was regarding him with an expression of drama. "Death," she whispered again.

"So you said before. Come in and tell me what you think of my picture."

She came in. Her chest bore long scratches, fresh and bleeding, as though she had been walking among wild pines or razor grass.

"What have you been doing with yourself to get scratched like this?"

She stood and eyed him, a brightness in her stare that, somehow, discomfited him. "I was exploring," she said quietly.

"Exploring?"

She nodded. "With Berton on the other side of the Ibi."

"What were you and Berton exploring there for?"

She did not answer. After a pause, she said: "Did you hear my message? Death."

"Death?" He laughed. "That doesn't sound so funny. Try again."

"We were on the track of the Green Bottle," she murmured, "but Death intravened."

He would have laughed again, but her manner checked him. She seemed on the point of sobbing.

"Look here, I'm feeling in too good a mood to be put out by your tommyrot. Stop putting on your act and tell me about the picture. Do you like it? Think it comes off?"

She looked at the picture, and after a long interval, nodded and murmured: "Yes, it's good. I like it. Very modern and abstrapt."

He waited, but she said nothing more.

"Is that all you have to say?"

She began to look about the room. Her hands were clenched tight.

"Go on. Tell me. No more comments?"

"That eye on the bell," she said, after a pause, "has a mysterious look. Like the eye of a jumbie."

"I intended it to represent something of the sort. It's regarding this house from the quiet and detached dimensions of another world."

"You're talking like one of us now." She stood, rigid, a half-smile on her face.

He frowned at her.

"Death," she whispered.

"Olivia, what's the matter with you? What are you up to now?"

"I keep telling you, but you won't heed me. Death is the matter."

He wagged his head. "I do wish you could be serious, for a change. I'll admit that a little fantasy mightn't be bad sometimes – but not all the time. Even your father doesn't advocate that."

"Let's stop talking and listen. Please humour me."

"Very well. Let's stop talking and listen."

A sound of hammering came on the still, hot afternoon air. A bird in the jungle gave out long, sweet notes like melting stained-glass windows… Tweep-reet!… Tweep-reet!… The hammering sounded again, insistent – and of a sudden stamped with the mark of vague portents.

"He's in the workshed."

"Who? Your father? And what about it?"

"He's making a coffin."

"A coffin?"

"Yes. *Hier leyt begraven*…"

"Is that what you came in to tell me?"

"Mother sent me. I didn't come on my own." She blinked and turned her face aside, gulped and went on in a barely audible voice: "While you sat in here painting, a dreadful thing happened."

"What sort of dreadful thing?"

"Death."

"Is someone dead?"

"Yes."

He felt the laughter draining out of him. It left a hollowed space in his stomach. He looked at her, and experienced a spinning unrealness, and knew that it was fear climbing up his spine.

"Who is dead?"

He saw her head tremble. "Your dearly beloved," she said.

"Now, stop being childish and tell me what you came in to tell me." He spoke harshly and with a false severity. He saw himself; an insect-size figure spotlighted in a cave, and he was shouting to dispel the gathering crepuscle. "Come on! Who is dead? Cut out this foolery, Olivia, and be serious for once in your life!"

She turned off, sobbing.

He dropped his palette and brush on the floor and caught her arm. "Don't be a little goat, you foolish... Stop it, I say! Tell me what's the matter. *What* are you crying for?"

"Haven't I told you? Haven't I told you?" She tore herself away from his grasp and threw herself down on the bed, shaking and whimpering.

He stood and watched her. A nerve in his chin twitched. After a moment, he said: "This – this wailing doesn't fool me. Get up from there!"

She seemed not even to have heard him.

He seated himself beside her and tried to calm her. "You haven't explained anything, you silly creature. Has there been an accident?"

She moved her head in assent. "Yes. She – she was on duty."

"On duty?"

"She was on duty when it happened. A snake bit her." She sat up and began to gnaw at her thumb and shake her head in a distracted manner. Her tears had left a damp patch on the bed. "She was so good. So good and sweet and..." Her brows twitched in her effort to control herself.

He began to speak, but had to stop and clear his throat. After a moment, he managed to say: "Let's hear what's happened. A snake bit whom? Mabel? When? Where did it happen?"

"She was walking along the track that goes to the Ibi depot. She was on official duty, and she had to go and see after the *corials*. They were loaded with produce – and they had to be sent off to Mr. Buckmaster's place."

"Yes, go on."

"I can't… It was a bushmaster."

"A bushmaster?"

"Yes. It sprang out on her from the ferns and bit her. Robert of Art Squad heard her scream and went to help her. He killed the snake. It attacked him, but it didn't get him. He killed it with a cutlass. He tried to suck the poison out of Maby's ankle, but it wasn't any use. It was too late. He took her to Benab Eleven, and a few minutes later she died."

"She died?"

She nodded. "I can't believe it. I spoke to her just a few minutes before Berton and I went across the Ibi. We met her at Benab Sixteen talking to Gunther and his wife. Oh, no, I can't believe it. I won't!"

"But… look here, where are the others? Aunt Joan and Uncle Gerald and – and Garvey? I don't…"

She had begun to sob again. He shook her and said: "Tell me. Where are the rest of them!" He uttered it like a statement rather than a question.

"Don't ask me! Don't ask me! I… They're in Benab Eleven – with Maby. I left them there. Mother asked me to come and tell you."

"Where's your father?"

"Daddy is in the workshed making the coffin."

"Making the coff – look here, I hope this isn't one of your silly pranks. Be serious."

She said nothing. Only sat gulping, her gaze in a corner. Her chest was wet with tears that had dripped from her glistening cheeks.

Gregory watched her, then paced off and came back and watched her. "I can't… no. Only yesterday morning she was telling me about bushmasters, how they attack…" He caught her shoulder and shook her. "I don't believe you! This is simply another ridiculous joke. And one in very bad taste!"

"But she's dead! She's dead! You think I'm joking? Maby's dead. You never take anything I say seriously. But she's dead! Dead! If you don't believe me go and see!"

She ran out of the room wailing hysterically. He heard her go into the next room and throw herself down on the bed.

He gave his head a shake, felt as if he would stagger, so made a grab at the bunched-up mosquito-net, missed, but did not stagger. The toppling was only an illusion. Other things could be illusory, then. His being in this room even. He shut his eyes, then opened them and looked through the window. From out the glare of the day wisps like phantom curtains seemed to take shape and enter the room... He heard the hammering in the workshed and the song of the bird in the jungle. All could be illusion – like bushmasters. And Benab Eleven.

He left the room, hesitated in the corridor, then went into the next room and watched Olivia on the bed. She whimpered softly, her face pressed against the pillows. His lips parted to say something but nothing came. He went out into the corridor again.

He moved toward the stairs, and when he began to descend heard Berton calling. He was somewhere outside the house.

"Ollie! Where are you?"

Gregory encountered him in the sitting-room. "Have you seen Ollie?" He was very pale, and his manner subdued.

"She's upstairs. What's happened? Tell me and no fooling."

"Didn't Ollie tell you? A bushmaster... it bit Maby. She's dead." He blinked rapidly, gave a cut-short whimper and hurried upstairs.

Gregory looked about the sparsely furnished room. At the portable gramophone on its bamboo table that stood near the fragile paperscreen that hid from view the camp-cots where the two boys slept at night. At the old-fashioned centre table with its carved legs. At the one leather-lined easy chair. At the two upright chairs arranged at the small unpolished table on which rested the chessboard and the box with the chessmen. There was no more furniture to look at. He looked at the pictures on the wall – three of them, one on each wall. One was a black and white sketch of a building with a tower – afterwards he asked and learnt that it was the town-hall in New Amsterdam. Another of *corials* on the river; this one – above the table with the portable gramophone – was an oil: Mabel's work, Olivia had told him one day last week. The third, on the wall in the screened-off section, was just visible above the screen; it was a black and white sketch of a bandstand set amidst large trees with spreading limbs: the bandstand on the esplanade in New Amsterdam, he found out afterwards.

Individual shivers moved up his legs and tickled their way up to his head. Silken tassels containing icy laughter, and the laughter rosetted within the ever-widening sphere where his brain lived.

The back of his throat felt dry. He went into the dining-room, trying to swallow. Moved into the pantry to the table where the water-goblet stood. Poured himself a tumbler of water and tried to gulp it so quickly that he could feel it congeal into a lump and travel painfully down.

He heard Berton's voice and footsteps upstairs. Olivia was sobbing still. Berton gave a sob, too. One dry, coughing splutter – and then nothing more. He might have had his throat cut.

Gregory went out of the house by the kitchen steps. He moved round the kitchen and stopped near the poultry-house. A dim memory rose. He tried to bring it into focus, but it resisted. Only a scarlet blob... He regarded the chickens pecking about the compound... A hen scratching. A Dominic cock, sturdy and important, stood with its head poised as though alert for some inimical move on his part... The memory took shape, was about to be clear, then, at the eleventh second, retreated, hazed. Evaded him... He looked at his hands, wondering at the flesh. He tapped his knuckles and heard the soft, sharp bony rattle they made. Real. No illusion here... He looked up at the weathered wood of the house. The sky dazzled him...

He gave his head a baffled shake, moistened his lips and passed a hand down his cheek. It was hot with sunshine. He turned and went back round to the kitchen steps. Stood and regarded the steps for a long time. He shut his eyes... A scarlet blob danced. Danced and slipped away into a haze of ultramarine shrinking rapidly and turning into green... Illusion, that... He opened his eyes. He rubbed his hands along the rippled hardness of his chest.

The feel of his ribs was reassuring; he could believe in his ribs...
He tapped his collarbone...

The dryness came back to his throat, but he felt it would be impossible for him to climb the steps back into the house to get to the water-goblet in the pantry... It might not even be there now; it might have vanished... He sank down on to the lowest of the treaders. Immediately wanted to get up, such a sense of insecurity swamped him. The sun slanted fiercely full on his face. Maddening at first, pushing him over to the side of the mist. He pulled himself back and faced it. It was only sun. His eyes watered, and he had to bow his head and knit his brows. An emerald splash danced on the ground.

The hammering in the workshed began to tunnel its way into his ken. He had stopped hearing it since he had left his room, and was not certain whether it had been going on all the while without his hearing it or whether it had stopped and had now started again.

A footstep thudded softly, and he saw Ellen. She had just appeared from around the kitchen. Perhaps she had gone to Benab Eleven. She was returning now, filled with the black juices of a gruesome sight. He wanted to get up and run. Run and shriek. See the voice going before him like a sandstorm of sawdust... He wanted to laugh... He held himself in and sat still, kept his gaze lowered. He heard Ellen stop near him, and knew that she was staring at him; waiting for the pyrotechnics... sand and sawdust sparks... But her voice sounded quite ordinary as she spoke. She said: "You hear de news?"

He made no reply – did not respond at all.

"She in Benab Eleven. They put 'er in dere."

He began to bite his thumbnail... A memory flashed in him... Olivia gnawing at her thumb and shaking her head... He stopped biting. Rubbed his thumb dry.

Ellen moved past him and went up into the kitchen. After a moment, he heard her crying quietly. Like a cat wailing. Not a cat in sunlight. A cat bricked away in a wall... the wall had a chink, and out of the evil darkness came the wailing... Poe wrote something... The hammering. A coffin being made... He got up and moved toward the landing-place. The sun licked his back, and the nape of his neck; it had saliva like acid... H_2SO_4... "You shouldn't sit in the sun bareheaded like this..." He listened to the water, and watched the plants that grew near the logs. Stems and leaves without motion. Each leaf glimmered with sunlight. One leaf of dragon's blood lacked the smallest trace of green; it sprouted among its fellows, a tapering streak of crimson. Could he be wrong? He bent closer to be certain. He was wrong. The central vein held a barely discernible tint of green... He laughed, feeling hope. Other things could be what they were not. Life could be death. Death could be life... As he watched, the leaf moved. It vibrated. The finger of a presence unseen had touched it...

He watched it. It was still again. He must keep his gaze on it. Never let it escape his vigilance; not for a decimal part of a second. The heat on the back of his head grew. The sun's saliva eating into his brain... He saw the leaf tremble again. No mistake... The tinkle of a bubble in the water pulled a gasp out of him. He stumbled back a pace, and was certain he had been pushed – an unseen hand had slapped him on the chest... He watched the leaf of dragon's blood. He wanted to blink but must not... From the underpart of the leaf a small grey beetle crawled, opened its wings and flew off, causing the leaf to tremble for the last time.

He straightened up and laughed again, but this time the laughter did not want to stop. He had to clench his hands and press them hard to his face before the spasms would subside.

He felt perspiration on his forehead.

A footstep made him turn. It was Logan. He was coming toward him. He walked without a limp now; his heel was better. His face had a blank, detached look; stupidity without the ribaldry that generally redeemed it.

"You hear wha' happen, Mr. Gregory sah?"

Gregory nodded.

Logan groaned. "What is man?" he muttered, his eyes downcast, his hands clasped in front of him. He wagged his black curly head. "You walking quiet-quiet on de ground, and before you know what de hand of Jehovah smote you. Ow! De iniquity of man!"

The wind swashed distantly in the jungle, with an anxious, rummaging noise. It seemed about to die away, but the swashing increased unexpectedly and rose in majestic awesomeness until a warm gust fanned past their cheeks. It came from across the river, and the bath-calm water sprang a pullulation of filmy wavelets. The trees around the clearing began to rustle, then the rustle suddenly ceased, and, on the river, the thousands of wavelets vanished as if they had been newborn spiders snatched away and slain by cannibal parents.

"In de hour dat we t'ink not, de Son of Man comet'."

The spasms of hysteria wanted to return, but sight of the ill-formed creature slouching before him checked them. Pity flooded the raw voids…

"We know not when de hand of de Almighty will smote us."

Gregory grunted.

"Yes, sah. We know not. Young or old, we know not," said Logan, as though encouraged by Gregory's grunt. "De wicked shall flourish like a green bay tree, saith de Prophet."

"Yes," said Gregory in a toneless voice – and started, for he had not intended to speak.

"She was forty-seven, sah," said Logan, further encouraged.

Gregory nodded. The water lapped against the logs. A secretive sucking… A wire tingled remotely…

"What's that? Forty-seven? Who was forty-seven?"

"Matilda, sah," said Logan, surprised.

"Who is Matilda?"

"Matilda who dead, sah. Ellen' mudder. You na hear she dead? She fall down wid a stroke."

"Ellen's mother?"

"Yes, sah. She fall down wid a stroke and dead. She was planting yams, and she fall down sudden and dead. Jehovah smote 'er."

"Where is she? Where is the corpse?"

"In Benab Eleven, sah."

"Are you telling me the truth?"

"Yes, Mr. Gregory sah. De parson meking de coffin now."

"Where – have you seen Miss Mabel?"

"Miss Mabel? Yes, sah. She in Benab Eleven wid de mistress and Master Garvey. It was Miss Mabel who help lift up Matilda and tek she to Benab Eleven."

"I see. I… thanks, Logan."

He set out for the house at a trot. He went round by the kitchen and made for the track that led to the Reservation. He tried to slow down to a walk when he was on the track but to no avail; he had to keep running. He heard voices ahead, and felt that he must slacken his pace. A question of dignity. But he still ran on.

When he rounded the next bend the voices took on bodies and dissolved into mild exclamations. The bodies were real. He shivered to a halt. Then he ran on a few paces, ignored Garvey's presence and held her to him and said: "My God! Oh, my God!"

She asked him what was the matter. He held her off from him and looked at her and said: "My God!"

Garvey uttered an ostentatious cough and moved on along the track.

"Gregory, what is it? Whatever is wrong, darling?"

He released her, stumbled back a little and leaned against the trunk of a huge mora tree. He looked up and saw the smooth bole rushing upward without finality; it got lost amidst the fronds of some tall palms. He let his gaze rest on her again, stared. Then he turned and began to walk unsteadily back toward the house. She caught up with him and insisted that he should tell her what was wrong, but he made no reply, said nothing at all. When they were emerging from the track, however, he glanced at her and smiled. "Let me be alone for a while," he said, "and then I'll come and find you and talk to you."

She smiled back and said that she would wait.

The first thing he saw when he arrived in his room was the cut-throat razor and the sheet of exercise book paper on his pillow.

"This," he read, when he took up the paper, "is the Grand Finalde to the real-life drama I started since you first came here. I wanted to bring it off as a gay Finalde tomorrow night at the chumming-up party, but I didn't foresee this marvellous countretempers today, meaning Matilda's sudden death, she had a stroke, poor thing. It was a cruel trick to play on you but I couldn't resist doing it, it isn't everyday you get a chance for Grand Drama like this, it might never happen again for years. Wasn't my acting good? And Berton wasn't bad either, was he? I won't ever plague you again after this. I wasn't really jealous of

Maby but I had to force myself to believe I was to make the Drama a convincing piece of histeronics. Your cut-throat razor returned herewith with my best love and fellowcitations and if you don't marry Maby and live happily ever after it will be your own fault. 'Ah, take the Cash in hand and waive the Rest; Oh, the brave Music of a *distant* Drum!' Yours lovingly, Olivia."

V

About an hour later, Gregory entered the workshed – the door stood ajar – and said to his uncle: "Could I have a chat with you, Uncle Gerald, as soon as it is convenient?"

The reverend gentleman, his face and chest wet with perspiration, stopped sawing and looked up with a smile that registered no surprise whatever; he might have been awaiting Gregory's advent. "With pleasure," he said. He put down the saw and fumbled out his Westclox watch from the fob-pocket of his shorts. "I'll be out of here in less than ten minutes. Would that do you?"

"Splendidly. Haven't you finished the coffin yet?"

"Yes, that's done. Stanley of Labour Squad took it off to the Reservation a few minutes ago. What I'm doing now is my normal day's work which had to be put aside because of the emergency. Making a new table – for Rufus of Book Squad."

"Do you make all the furniture here?"

"Practically all. I started cabinet-making as a self-penance. Found that in my spare time I wanted to stalk too many of the women on the Reservation. I detested it at first, but I soon got to like it immensely. Now I just can't do without it."

"I see."

"Of course," said the parson, after a brief silence, "when I say self-penance don't misunderstand me. I don't mean I felt guilty about stalking the women. I mean that it was necessary to discipline myself."

"Of course."

"How's the picture? Finished it yet?"

"Yes," said Gregory, leaning against the workbench. He pulled out his cigarette-case, then put it back. It might not be safe to smoke in here with so much wood-shaving about... He heard the bird in the jungle... Tweep-reet... Tweep-reet... He remembered when he had listened to it about an hour ago... He squeezed his wrist and took a deep breath. He liked the smell of newly-planed wood and linseed oil... Two small windows let in daylight, and he could see the coralita trailing along the sills. One or two tendrils hung down inside the shed.

"Satisfied with the picture?" Mr. Harmston asked, after a pause.

"Yes. As much as I can be," Gregory answered.

"Um. Naturally. It's a bad artist who feels entirely satisfied with what he's done."

Gregory grinned. "Why do you say 'naturally'? Do you take it for granted that I'm a good artist?"

His uncle brushed off an eye-fly. "Expressionist, aren't you?"

"Oh, I don't call myself anything, personally, but I admit I have been influenced by the Expressionists."

"Joan mentioned she saw the canvas you were working on. She seemed impressed by what you expressed."

Gregory smiled slightly. After a silence he asked: "When is the funeral?"

"Funeral? Oh, Matilda. We don't have funerals here, my boy," smiled Mr. Harmston. "Don't believe in making death more ugly than it is."

"Oh."

"Within three hours of death the corpse is underground – as quickly and as unobtrusively, even as stealthily, as possible."

"I see."

"No bell-tolling or grave-side mumbling," said his uncle, after a pause. "No crepe or cortège. In fact, if we could manage to keep a stock of ready-made coffins we'd probably have the corpse underground within less than an hour."

Gregory made no comment, and his uncle looked at him and smiled: "We're much keener on life than on death." He produced his watch again. "Minute and a half more, then we'll be out of here. By the bye, I'm glad to see you're adopting our mode of undress."

"Yes, I'm afraid I've been using up shirts at too rapid a rate. Don't see why I should give the laundry section of Labour Squad unnecessary work."

"Our laundry folk can never have too much work. Never come upon a keener lot. Yesterday I was having a word with Mary

310

and Sylvia, two of our best pressers. I asked them if they weren't tired of the job, if they didn't want a change of occupation. But they said no, they wouldn't give up their present job for anything."

"Yes, I know Sylvia. Isn't she the one with the light-brown eyes? She works in Benab Nineteen."

"Quite correct. I've often remarked those light-brown eyes. Unusual for an Indian. I'm glad to see you're taking notice of our people, my boy. Um. I must say, on the whole, you seem distinctly happier than when you first arrived."

"I am happier. In fact, the subject I want to discuss with you chiefly concerns happiness – the happiness of us all on this settlement."

"Ssh! Not a word about it until I've done here. I'm bubbling inwardly with anticipation. Don't spoil it for me."

A moment later, the reverend gentleman, with a glance at his watch, murmured that it was time to stop work. He put aside his tools, dusted his hands and said: "I think we can go now and look for some shady spot to sit in and have our talk."

"Perhaps," he added, when they were outside and he was clicking the padlock shut on the door, "the place of penal shadows will be best."

"The place of where?" asked Gregory.

"Behind this shed," said his uncle. "The terminology is merely my shockingly poor attempt at a joke."

"Oh."

"We'll be safe from the eyes and ears of the world behind this shed, my boy – and the atmosphere is restful. No glare – and the minimum of eye-flies."

"Yes, I notice eye-flies seem to bother one more in the sun."

Behind the shed, Gregory had to admit to himself, was certainly ideal for a private conversation. It was cool, and possessed an air of complete seclusion: an almost eerie seclusion, as though the many anguished wailings of Logan might have been hovering in astral clouds about the spot, ready to reveal themselves at any instant in ectoplasmic form... He smiled to himself at the fancy.

Mr. Harmston gave a long sigh as he lowered himself to the ground and made himself comfortable against the corrugated iron wall. In his manner Gregory detected what seemed a genuinely pleasurable anticipation; his eyes held a glitter of excitement, and there was a faint fixed smile around his lips like that of a schoolboy looking forward to a feast.

"Now, my dear fellow, let's hear all about it," he said, clasping his hands and resting them on his drawn-up knees. Even though he was perspiring he still had about him, Gregory noticed, an air of personal cleanliness. Cleanliness and good health surrounded him almost like a visible haze.

"It's nothing very startling," Gregory said. "It's just the question of my staying here – and one or two suggestions I wanted to make about general improvements." He paused and fidgeted.

Mr. Harmston pulled from a hip-pocket a large handkerchief and wiped his face and neck. It was a clean handkerchief and smelt slightly of carbolic. A black, shiny lizard darted swiftly past on the ground, and vanished with a dry rustle amidst some dead leaves.

"I understand you've been saving for some time towards acquiring a Delco lighting plant – and various other useful appurtenances."

"Very good word, that. Appurtenances. I've always liked it. Concatenation, too. Reverberant. Albuminoid. Lovely, lovely. But you were saying, my boy. Yes, that's perfectly true about the Delco plant. I take it Olivia has been supplying you with much information of a domestic nature?"

"Yes, it was she who told me. I've been considering it a bit, and I wanted to offer to finance these projects. I can afford it easily, and – well, I'd better mention that – that just before I came to the shed here I asked Mabel to marry me."

"Tch, tch, tch! Oh, no, my boy! Now, now! That's very bad technique."

Gregory coloured. "What do you mean?"

"Well, surely – I mean, you ought to have sprung that on me at the very end of our interview. You're a playwright. You should know by now that the dénouement comes at the end of the play – not in the middle of the first act."

He spoke with such earnestness that Gregory had to regard him seriously. Gregory discerned that he was genuinely put out; he was not being sarcastic. Suddenly, however, the look of irritation passed and he smiled and said: "Let's forget it, anyway. Go on with what you were saying."

Gregory laughed. "I'm sorry I didn't observe theatrical rules, sir," he said. "I'm not in the habit of –"

"I understand, I understand! Let's forget it, I said."

After an awkward pause, Gregory said: "You heard what I said – about the lighting plant and the other things? Do you – would you let me see about getting them? Let's say the piano, too, and the motorboat."

The reverend gentleman patted Gregory's knee lightly. "First, I must congratulate you, my boy, on your forthcoming marriage. I'm very glad to hear of it. I'm sure it will make you happy. Mabel is a fine young woman. I'm very fond of her. We're all fond of her. She's far and away too good for a spiritually diseased reprobate like yourself from barbarous England. She would have done much better if she'd married one of our Indian lads here, but if she's made you her choice I suppose it's no use making a fuss. Mustn't quarrel with Destiny. All I can do as her father is to wish you both enduring bliss in bed and out of bed. But about your offer to help us acquire a lighting plant and a piano and a motorboat, I'm afraid I must tell you that your offer is graciously refused. I appreciate the spirit in which you make it, my boy, but principles are principles. We have been perfectly happy – and are still perfectly happy – without electric light, a piano and a motorboat, and prefer to continue to be so until, in due course, we can see our way to make ourselves happier by procuring these necessit— these appurtenances."

"I see," Gregory murmured, his face white.

Mr. Harmston dabbed at his neck with his handkerchief. "Warm behind here despite the shade, isn't it?"

"Yes – somewhat."

"When do you and Mabel plan to get married? Fixed a day?"

"She suggested tomorrow, but I thought it a little early. I thought it best to wait until next week. Say, tomorrow week."

"Um. Excellent. Have you been to bed with her yet?"

"I… no. No, I haven't."

"In that case, your decision is definitely the better. Much more in conformity with the local myth."

"What do you mean?"

"I mean simply that putting it off for a week gives you both that long to live, in your fancies, the delights of the marriage bed. That is, of course, I take it, if you intend to be continent until the big day."

Gregory said nothing.

"Do you intend to be?"

"Yes," frowned Gregory.

A silence. Another lizard darted past, black and shiny and tailless. Gregory shifted his position slightly, and his hand touched the ring in the wall… The trees frowned upon them. He glanced up into the gloom of palm fronds and spider-webs, and creepers with thin hanging tendrils like dripping venom congealed in mid-air… A swish-swish of water came to their hearing. From the river, Gregory told himself. A man in a canoe paddling leisurely – even wearily.

Mr. Harmston tilted his head and murmured: "Odd."

"Did you say something?" asked Gregory.

"Yes, I said it's odd."

"What is?"

"That *corial* entering the Ibi now. Don't you hear it?"

"I thought it was on the river."

"No, the Ibi. When your ear becomes more practised you'll be able to tell the difference."

"What's odd in a *corial* entering the Ibi?"

"At this particular moment there shouldn't be one *entering*. Six of them left laden with produce about half an hour ago. Tomorrow is steamer-day, and the produce must be loaded from Buckmaster's wharf. Two or three more should be leaving in a few minutes. But I can't see why one should be entering the Ibi at this minute. Very odd."

"What do you presume has happened, then, to account for the fact that a *corial* is entering the Ibi now?"

"Can't guess, but it must be some untoward event."

"Like what?"

"Haven't the faintest idea. Just as ignorant as you. An accident most likely. Something. Anything at all."

"Why not let's go and investigate?"

"I've noticed that you suffer from a mania to 'investigate'. You simply must be present at out-of-the-ordinary events – even if it's only Logan being chained up. Why such an importunacy, my boy? Why such curiosity? Let us sit here and wait and enjoy ourselves in a fever of quiet suspense. Don't you like mysteries? A mystery can only be entertaining while it remains unsolved. Why the hurry to solve it, then?"

Gregory laughed.

"Go on talking to me. No more suggestions to make for general improvements about the place? Suggestions are always welcome, you know."

"I'm afraid – no, there's nothing else I can put forward." Gregory tried to introduce a note of coldness into his voice but knew that he only succeeded in sounding absurd. He fidgeted.

Mr. Harmston chuckled. "Come on. Don't be discouraged. Isn't there anything more you wish to discuss with me?"

Gregory hesitated, then said: "As a matter of fact, I – there was, but I can't see there would be much point in broaching it – after the way you've reacted to my first offer."

"Never mind. Let's hear what you have to say."

"I wanted to ask you if you would object to my having the clearing enlarged – say, on the southern side – so that I could have a small cottage built in which Mabel and I could live."

"There! Good thing you did bother to ask me, because I have no objections whatever. The land is ours to do with as we please, and a new cottage won't contravene any of our Codes of Living."

Gregory smiled. "Yes, but there's another little point. Suppose I want it electrically lit. Couldn't I install a lighting plant in the vicinity to supply my needs?"

Mr. Harmston laughed – not boisterously; with heartiness but with restraint – and clapped him gently on the back. "Very clever, my boy. Very, very clever. As despicably clever a move as any that your politicians in Europe or America might have conceived. Next you'll ask me with disarming sweetness: 'And would you mind me possessing a piano and a motorboat?' Ho, ho! No, Gregory my boy, up here we don't believe in wrecking our system of thought and conduct by such glib quibbles and prevarications. We don't believe in sentimental hypocrisy, either. The answer is no. I couldn't permit you to have a lighting plant of your own, because that would mean you would offer to extend lighting to my home – and then to the Reservation – and it would make the acquisition of another lighting plant superfluous and ridiculous. The same would be the case if I permitted you to have a piano and a motorboat. You would want to share these possessions with the rest of us here. No. You will have to do without these comforts and live in Spartan discomfort for the time being. Build your cottage by all means, my boy – and have it painted, too; and furnished as luxuriously as you wish – and I shall cooperate with you in every way possible, but you will have to makeshift with lamplight until our mission can afford to get a lighting plant."

Gregory was silent, his fingers lightly intertwined. "I hope," he said eventually, "you don't seriously imagine it was my intention to circumvent your authority by a 'despicably clever' move?"

"Um. To be honest, I do imagine so."

"You're wrong."

There was a silence between them. The reverend gentleman looked reflective. Abruptly he said quietly: "I believe you."

"Thanks."

During another silence, Gregory glanced surreptitiously at his uncle and saw his face twitch. His throat moved as though he were swallowing. He was staring at the humped root of a tree nearby, and Gregory saw his eyes blink rapidly.

"Have I…" Gregory began, but his uncle shook his head and pursed his lips as though to warn him not to speak. After an instant he tapped Gregory's knee and said in a low voice: "Never mind. Nothing to worry about. I was a little touched, that's all."

Gregory looked up at the slim trunks of the trees that pushed crookedly upward into the mysterious density of the foliage that kept off the glare of the sun from this spot. For no reason, he had the feeling that he was being watched – watched by vegetable eyes; the uncomfortable thought stirred in him that trees had intelligence: perhaps they could divine his mood and watch thoughts rising from him in vapour…

"If I may add to what I've said, my boy, just let me tell you this. Our mission never accepts anything in the nature of charity. Not through any foolish pride but because we have made it a rule that whatever we achieve we must achieve through hard work. We don't like plums to fall into our laps. Our idea is that nothing corrupts more than easy gains, the easy winning of amenities and pleasures." He spoke quietly, his brows vaguely troubled, his eyes reflective, even a trifle sad.

"I understand," said Gregory. After a pause, he asked: "Are you recognized by the authorities – as a marriage officer?"

"I am – yes, certainly. You need have no fear. Your marriage would be legal if I performed it."

"What form does the ceremony take – in your church here?"

"We have no regular form of ceremony." Mr. Harmston's eyes twinkled. "We just hold a party in the church, with or without hymn-singing, and in the course of things I just say to you: 'Gregory Hawke, do you want to become the husband of Mabel Harmston?' You say 'Yes', and I turn to Mabel and say: 'How about you, Mabel Harmston? Want to become the wife of Gregory Hawke?' She says 'Yes', and I say: 'You're now husband and wife. Best of luck. Come into the vestry and sign the register.' No fuss. No stiff insincere questions and answers. No vows that neither of you can be sure you could keep. In short, no pointless sentimentality, and the minimum of formality and hypocrisy. No female relatives shed tears at our weddings."

Gregory smiled. "Why are you so much against ceremonies?"

"Because we feel that ceremonial conduct, or formalized ritual of any kind, eventually leads to superstition."

"But I should have thought you would want to encourage superstition."

"You've misunderstood our aims, then. We encourage fantasy, but fantasy doesn't necessarily call for superstitious belief. Superstition results from ignorance – and ritualistic forms. That is why religion, as practised by your churches, is such an impotent factor in the affairs of your world. The honest, down-to-earth myth-scheme with which Christianity started out was obfuscated by ritual – a ritual which became more and more elaborate until now it is merely symbolical and, to the majority of people, meaning-less. It is as much an example of mumbo-jumbo as the practices of the African witch-doctors. Baptism, marriage, mass, funerals, matins, evensong... 'Whom God hath joined together let no man put asunder'... 'This is the body of our Lord Jesus Christ'... 'I baptise thee in the name of the Father and of the Son and of the Holy Ghost, Amen.' What could be more superstitious than that? And what could be more corrodingly monotonous to the sensibilities of a normally intelligent and imaginative human being? Good Friday every year Christ is crucified. Easter Day he's resurrected. Christmas Day he's born. Year after year, year after year. As a youth, my dear fellow, I was avidly pious. I went to church and I said my prayers before going to bed. But the church cured me of my piety before I was nineteen. Long before that age I could have said every church service by heart, from beginning to end. To this day the very sound of an organ depresses me. I mean it. Because of the church I can't enjoy organ music. Two months ago I was in New Amsterdam for a day or two. Passing a church about six in the evening, I heard the voices of choir boys – practising. I stopped to listen, for it was an anthem I knew and rather liked. But suddenly the organ started up, and I moved on. Instantly all the old boredom associated with the chanting of psalms and the intoning of litanies and the monotony of prayers and sermons on a Sunday in church attacked me, and instead of being enchanted I was annoyed and disgusted."

Gregory was smiling.

"You know," said the parson, "another little thing I've observed about you. You don't talk back very much."

"No," said Gregory.

"I think I can guess why."

"Can you?"

"Um. You're one of these people suffering from philosophy-fatigue. In a way, I can sympathize with you. You have sampled so frequently and variedly of the vintages of intellectual argument that the sediment of futility has clogged the machinery of your will to quest. You are resigned, in short, to the insolubility of the problem of living and see no point in philosophic discussion."

Gregory was still smiling. He murmured: "You're very perspicacious – and very fond of words."

"Words are my weakness, my boy. I like spinning them out. Hadn't I more pressing occupations, I should spend all my days spinning out words: words of meaning and words without meaning. Did you hear that?"

"What?"

"A sound of voices. From the pathway."

Gregory cocked his head and listened. "Yes, you're right. I wonder what's the matter."

"I told you it was odd – that *corial* coming into the Ibi."

"But if there's anything wrong shouldn't you go and see?"

"No. Berton is on official duty, I believe. He'll find me and give me a full report before long. No hurry. The longer the delay, the more pleasure in the anticipation. I do hope it's something with a good dash of juicy drama."

"Or juicy tragedy, perhaps?"

"One never knows. But why spurn tragedy? Isn't it part of the stuff of life?"

"But not always a pleasant part, I'm sure you'll admit."

"Admitted. But we must take the pleasant with the unpleasant. Tell me about your plans for the future. Think you'll bud forth into a sort of Gauguin of the Guiana jungle?"

"Oh, I mean to do a lot of painting. The mood is on – but for my own pleasure solely, not for fame, I want to paint. I – you're right about the world. It's sick, beastly. I don't want to go back. I prefer to die here unknown. There's so much in me I could tell you of…" His voice broke.

They heard Berton calling. "Parson! Where are you?"

"They always call me parson when they're on official duty."

"I've noticed that."

"I must say this about you. You're decent at the core. The maggots of your world have only succeeded in getting at the rind of you."

"Suppose you hadn't deemed me decent what would you have done – I mean now that I've decided definitely to settle here and marry Mabel?"

Mr. Harmston laughed softly and patted Gregory's knee. "Probably given you something nasty to drink and got you safely underground so that you wouldn't be able to contaminate any of us."

"Parson! Where are you?" Berton appeared and gave them a

look of surprise. "Oh, you're here. Parson, there's trouble. Can you come right away?"

"Certainly, my boy," said his father, rising slowly. "Anything very serious?"

"I fear so, parson."

Gregory rose, too.

"What's the nature of it?"

"Sigmund has come back. He came in the *corial* he stole."

"He didn't steal it. We discovered it was his own."

"Oh. Well, he's come back. He seems half-starved, but our people say he must not be allowed to stay on the Reservation because he's a criminal and a menace. They want him put behind here and chained up until his trial."

"Ah. Is it their voices I hear?"

"Yes, parson. They've brought him. About a dozen of them, led by Cedric of Music Squad. They want to get your permission to chain him up. Cedric says he must be considered an outcast who, because of his fourth major criminal offence, has to be regarded as incurable and thus worthy of death. The others agree with him."

"Um. Very well, my boy. I'll attend to the matter immediately. Let's go."

VI

They were gathered near the belfry – about a dozen men and two women. They stood in a rough circle around Sigmund who was squatting on the ground, his head bent, sullen-looking but, on the whole, with an air of indifference and resignation. There was no disorderliness, but animated discussion was in progress, punctuated with laughter and exclamations.

No sudden silence came upon the group as the parson and Berton and Gregory approached, a circumstance that surprised Gregory. The laughter did subside, but in a way that seemed to indicate that the time to be serious had come. A rather taller than average Indian stepped forward in a casual manner, a smile on his face, and said: "You've heard the news, then, parson? He's back."

"So I see, Cedric," nodded Mr. Harmston. "Harry predicted he would turn up before long. Didn't you, Harry?"

Another of the group smiled: "Yes, parson. I knew he would."

"He has cheek to come back," said one of the women.

The reverend gentleman, his face abruptly solemn, brushed off an eye-fly. "Most annoying little devils, these eye-flies, Edith."

Edith's face registered what seemed to Gregory instantaneous understanding. She smiled and said: "Most annoying. I'm getting married, parson. Robert of Art Squad and I. We meant to tell you tomorrow at the party."

"Splendid, my girl. Splendid. Remind me to drink a special glass of ginger-ale to you and Robert."

The others stood by with smiles; they had a waiting air, Gregory noticed. There was no urgency in their manner.

Sigmund had not even glanced up.

"We've fixed the day for Wednesday fortnight," said Edith.

"H'm. Did you know we have a wedding coming off Wednesday week?"

"No. Whose?"

"Gregory's and Mabel's."

"Congratulations," she said, holding out her hand to Gregory. Her very black eyes had a friendly, humorous twinkle that Gregory liked.

"Thanks," he told her. "And best of luck to you and Robert, too."

Cedric touched Mr. Harmston lightly on the shoulder.

"Yes, Cedric?"

"Sigmund can't remain on the Reservation tonight. We want him put behind the shed, and if possible could we have the trial this evening?"

Mr. Harmston gazed past Cedric at one of the others. "How's that hand of yours, Tom?' Coming round nicely?"

"Pretty so-so, parson," smiled the man addressed. "It's formed a scab."

Cedric, in no way perturbed, stood waiting. He whistled softly. The Habañera from *Carmen*.

"See and be careful with that gimlet next time," said Mr. Harmston to Tom. "Hold it in the position I showed you and you'll be safe."

Harry said: "About Sigmund, parson. He didn't go upstream as we'd thought. He went downstream. We've questioned him."

"I see," said Mr. Harmston. "Downstream, eh? Not upstream."

"He said he was afraid of being seen by somebody at Mr. Buckmaster's depot. He said he managed to pick up an odd meal or two at various homesteads downstream, but he couldn't get any work."

"Cedric, when are you going to get married, my boy?" asked the parson.

Cedric smiled: "I haven't made up my mind. Robert has gone and cut me out, or I would have married Edith."

"Don't bother with him," laughed Edith. "He's never given me a look."

"About Sigmund, Cedric," said Mr. Harmston, his face abruptly solemn. "Has he been given anything to eat since his arrival?"

"No, parson. We brought him straight here. He said he wasn't hungry."

"Does his wife Gertrude know he is back?"

"Yes. She's in agreement with our present action – but we left her in tears. The human element. Mary of Art Squad is comforting her."

"*In the golden lightning of the sunken sun,*" said Harry.

"Yes, lovely line, that," nodded Mr. Harmston. "*The pale purple even melts around thy flight.*"

"*Like a glow-worm golden in a dell of dew,*" murmured Edith.

"That's a favourite line of mine, too," smiled the parson, nodding. He brushed off an eye-fly. "Has the voting been unanimous on this action, Cedric?" he asked suddenly.

"Unanimous, parson," Cedric nodded. He began to whistle. The allegretto from Beethoven's Seventh Symphony. The reverend gentleman joined in, humming the tune softly. Edith shuddered. "That thing always gives me the creeps," she said. Harry agreed with her.

"Cedric."

"Yes, parson?"

"I ratify the vote."

"Thanks, parson."

"I think you did well in leading this little expedition here. I endorse your action."

"*What leaf-fringed legend haunts about thy shape,*" said Cedric.

"*Forlorn! The very word is like a bell,*" murmured Harry.

"Shall we move toward the shed?" said Mr. Harmston, smiling.

VII

Gregory did not wait to see them move off. He hurried toward the house. In the gallery he encountered Mabel who was on the point of going out. "What's happening outside?" she asked. "Did you have the chat with Daddy? What did he say?"

"One thing at a time. Yes, I've had the chat with him."

She frowned. "What's the matter? You seem so tense."

He held her arm and said: "Sigmund is back."

"Sigmund? Is that... you mean, that's what you were all talking about near the belfry?"

"Yes. Sigmund was there, too. Didn't you see him? Or perhaps you didn't. There was too much of a crowd. They're going to chain him up behind the shed now."

She looked dismayed. Then she said quietly: "I didn't think we'd have seen him again. Poor fellow. This is the end of him now."

"It needn't be. That's what I've come to speak to you about."

She stared at him.

"You're white, darling. What's wrong?" she said, after a pause.

"It doesn't take much imagination to guess, does it?" he said. "Look here, Mabel, I came to tell you this. Whenever this farcical trial takes place – I don't know when it's to be, but – but you mustn't give evidence against that poor fellow. I think it a disgrace that he should be treated like this."

"A disgrace? But he's a criminal, Gregory."

He said nothing, his eyes looking past her, unblinking.

"It's his fourth offence. He's incurable. He has proved it by breaking into here as he did that night."

"Sometimes," he said, "I wonder if you people are real – or simply shadows in a dream I'll wake up from. I..."

She touched his cheek. "I understand. But I'm real enough, don't you think so?"

"This sort of thing is Fascistic. It's... this is what thousands of poor devils are fighting against in Spain."

"But... you mean Sigmund's case? I don't understand. Why should you consider it Fascistic to get rid of a man who has proved himself a hopeless crime-addict? Don't you think four times enough? And he *knew* what the penalty would be if he was caught a fourth time. That alone should convince you that he's a mental case. He's warped. If we let him go free, after just punishing him lightly, his next offence might be murder. Surely you don't expect us to wait until he commits a murder before taking steps to get rid of him!"

"I'm afraid I do! You're no fool, Mabel. You've not been out of this jungle very often, but you're intelligent and you're well read. You have enough knowledge of the world I come from to be aware that a man is only put to death when he has been found guilty of murder. We don't execute him for committing a robbery."

"I know you don't, darling. Please, don't let's quarrel. Look, you're trembling. Do you really feel so strongly about it?"

"I do."

She gave him a long, puzzled stare. "I really can't see..." she began, and stopped. She held his hand and said quietly: "I'll do anything you ask, but – but this is hard, Gregory."

"Why should it be hard? You're not cold-blooded. If I thought you were I wouldn't have asked you." He gripped her arm. "My dear."

They looked at each other.

"I know how you feel," she murmured, "but you've got to remember I have been trained differently from you. Please understand that or – or I can see you're going to misjudge me badly. The things you get worked up about don't move me in the slightest. You see that, don't you? Please don't look so fierce."

He said nothing.

"I don't think you're being fair," she said, "but I can put myself in your place. I know how you look at it now." She touched his cheek.

After an awkward silence, she said: "I've read about your Fascists and Nazis. They're beastly, I know – but I can't see how you can liken our methods to theirs. We don't practise dictatorship of any kind. We don't try to terrorize anyone, or try to force

325

any fanatical doctrines down people's throats. We live as peaceably as we can, and we try to keep our outlook on life as balanced as possible –"

"Don't let's go into the metaphysics of the question," he interrupted. He began to tremble again. "I simply want you to promise me you won't give evidence in any – in any so-called trial. If the trial is a fair one they couldn't convict him unless you or I testified against him. And if we both refuse they'll have to release him."

"I suppose they will, but – Gregory, think carefully and tell me if you really consider it would be sensible to release him. Please. Don't let yourself be carried away by the emotion of the moment. Think, dear. Don't you see he'll be worse off for being pardoned. He's already sullen and embittered through what he has had to go through during the past week or two. He'd almost for certain begin to show violence. Look what happens in America. Those gangsters. They begin in a small way and gradually go from bad to worse. If the American authorities were sensible they'd wipe them out before they get to the homicidal stage and turn gunmen. It seems so absurd to let criminals shoot up and hack people to death when they could have been stopped by being put out of the way before they got to the point where their frustrations and hatred of society compelled them to take to violence. It's bad enough that nothing can be done about such people who suffer from various forms of introversion and who suddenly reveal themselves to be homicidal – but the types that openly reveal their criminal tendencies ought to be dealt with effectively. I… oh, you can see what I mean, Gregory. You understand why this is so awkward for me? Tell me you do."

He moistened his lips and said: "You'll give evidence, then?"

"But… Yes, I must. It's my duty."

"I see."

She held his arm before he could turn away. "Don't look like that. It isn't like you, Gregory. You won't want to exploit my being in love with you to – to make me do – to make me not do what I feel I ought."

He shook his head with a dazed look, gazing past her.

She continued to hold his arm, her manner rigid and desperate. "You see what I mean, don't you?"

He nodded.

She gave a shaky laugh. "You look just as you did when you first came – vacant and lost. Oh, heavens! I love you so much. It isn't reasonable… I shouldn't…" She broke off gulping.

After a silence, he smiled and murmured: "I wasn't lost then – only half in another dimension." He spoke as though to himself.

She seemed in a spinney of thought herself.

One of the boards in the floor creaked under their weight.

"Will it make a difference, Gregory?"

"What?"

"My giving evidence against Sigmund. It'll change how you feel about me?"

He winced and turned away. "Let's not discuss it."

"But we have to. It's so important."

He put his hands to his temples, and slowly rubbed the tips of his fingers down his cheeks.

"Don't deliberately try to create a problem now, Gregory."

He pulled slowly at his chin. A plop sounded on the floor, and he started. It was a gecko fallen from the ceiling; it was the colour of the ceiling: grey-brown like the unpainted crabwood boards. It sped across the floor in wriggling flashes punctuated by pauses fractions of a second long. They watched it twist a lightning line up the wall and disappear behind the picture of the New Amsterdam town-hall.

"Gregory."

"Yes?"

"You should see your face. It's… you look as if you envied it."

"The gecko?"

"Yes. As if you would have liked to be it and not yourself."

He smiled slightly. Stretched out and touched her arm. "Yes, I was wishing that."

"But why, my dear? Why? Tell me. Aren't you glad to be as you are? Aren't you glad you have me? Aren't you glad to be human?"

His eyes became shot with fire. "No. No, I'm not glad to be human. I'm ashamed! Disgusted! I'm… let's go somewhere. I can't talk about anything – least of all myself." His manner was distracted. He walked over to the picture of the town-hall and peered behind it. His head trembled so much that it was difficult to focus his eyes. But he managed to make it out – the gecko. A black streak amid the grey shadow cast by the picture. He saw its flat head turn slightly. It must be looking at him…

Footsteps sounded and Olivia came in from the gallery.

She stopped and uttered a soft exclamation of surprise.

"The lovebirds in here, eh? I say, have you heard about Sigmund?"

"Yes, we have," said Mabel coldly.

"Oh," murmured Olivia. "So you're annoyed with me because of my dramatic Finalde."

An inundation of laughter began to spread through Gregory. He looked at her and grinned. "*I* am not." He approached her and put his arm about her. "I ought to be, though. You're a dirty little deceiver."

She blushed. "It was awful of me – really awful. But I couldn't help it. And Berton and I acted magnificently, didn't we?"

"You did. I compliment you and forgive you. Let's go for a walk somewhere. Take me exploring."

"You want to explore? I don't mind. I've just finished taking the illiterates in English, and I can do with some jungle air after talking so much in the church." She glanced at Mabel whose face was still cold. "What about Maby? Maby, are you coming with us?"

"Just you and I," said Gregory quickly, without looking at Mabel.

Mabel opened her mouth to speak, then shut it and pursed her lips.

Olivia hesitated, then giggled and said: "All right, let's go."

Going down the stairs, she said in a voice of conspiracy: "I fathom the situation. You've had a row with Maby, haven't you?"

"No. No row."

"You're lying, but never mind. Shall we go to the ruins?"

"Yes, the ruins," he said. "We'll see if we can get a glimpse of our friend Luise."

She giggled again. "You're in a very grasshopper-ish mood this afternoon. I can't make you out at all. Is it something you want to confide in me? Is that why you want me to go exploring with you?"

"Not exactly, no. I want to talk to you, that's all. You're so distinctly refreshing."

"It was raining heavily when I was born – that's why. A rain-jumbie leapt in at the window along with some refreshing drops and danced on my chest. No, but seriously. Mother said it was raining when I was born. The window was open and the bed was near the window, and a sudden shower came down just as I was about to pop out – and when I popped out a gust of wind and rain came in and sprinkled me. Daddy rushed and closed the window, but the black dispenser from Ida Sabina laughed and said it was all right, I wouldn't get a chill. He gave me a slapping and I cried and he said I was a fine baby. He's dead now. He was only a chemist but he knew a lot about obstreptics, too."

"He did, did he?"

"Yes. The new dispenser is good, too. We only fetch him when we think it might be a difficult case – breech presentation or anything like that. And that's only once in a very blue moon. The Indian women don't have much trouble giving birth. They shoot out their babies before you can say Genie, and then get up and wash the baby and move around as if nothing had happened. Only one of them so far we've known to die in childbirth, and that was Osbert's mother, and she fell from the roof of her *benab* and hurt herself. She was trying to get down an old pail she'd left up there. It had nails and pieces of string in it."

"And what was it doing up on the roof?"

"I don't know myself. That's all I know. Her sister Rachel told me. She's dead now. She died last year. She was forty-one. By the way, I suppose you know these Indians seldom live to more than forty-five. They get old-looking very early. At eleven some of them can have children. Look! Did you see it? An agouti! It ran into the ferns over there! I haven't seen one since February."

They were now on the track that led to the ruins.

He said no, he had not seen it, and the way he spoke made her look at him. She could tell that his spirit was crouching among grisly herbs. She felt an urge to say or do something to put him right, but knew intuitively that nothing ordinary would suffice. It would have to be words drenched in the dew-mist of purple wild flowers, or an act done darkly with hands and glaring eyes and topsy-turvy tails. She remembered how, when he was not right in his mind, she had to pelt stones at trees to take his attention away from spectral calamities. She had even had to show him her Scar of the Hissing *Kanaima* that Saturday morning on the way to the ruins... No, I can't do that now. It won't have any effect, because he's different now. His shadow has gone into hiding... She thought of a plan, and said: "We are being followed."

"Followed?"

"Yes. Shadowed."

"Oh, I see."

"You don't see. It's a jumbie – one of Luise's friends."

"Male or female?"

"Luise's friends can only be male."

The queer look leapt out of his face. He grinned and put his arm around her. "Will you protect me from him?" he said.

"Yes, but you'll have to promise me something first."

"What's that?"

"You must stop thinking grisly things among the moaning herbs. When you think grisly things you attract grisly shadows."

"I see. But what would you call 'grisly things'?"

"Grim, greasy things that make you frown secretly and tremble and squeeze your hands."

He grinned again.

"I think," she said, in a solemn voice, "I know why you've come with me on this exploration."

"You think so? Well, tell me."

"It's because the freckled flesh has annoyed you and you want to be with the spirit for a change."

He gave her a sharp glance.

She laughed and said: "Have I guessed right?"

He made no reply. They had come to the fallen palm.

"I know I have. I'm infruitive. No, no! If we go that way we'll be on the longer track. Come round this way and I'll show you the shorter one. You haven't been on it yet, have you?"

"No."

"If the freckled flesh was wise it would have taken you exploring in the jungle and shown you all our secret tricks and tracks. Can I ask you a very plain question?"

"Go ahead."

"Are you in love with Maby?"

"Yes."

"See that? I knew you'd frown and look flivvery-flitting around your eyes when you answered. That's what I mean by thinking grisly things among the herbs. Why have you got to be so funny? It's just as if even though you say yes and want to feel happy about it you get a tummy-ache."

He said nothing, though his eyes twinkled.

She glanced back. "He's still following us. A big, strong slave with a bow and arrow. Poison is dripping from the arrow. If his skin wasn't black I'd say he was a *kanaima*."

He gave her an affectionate squeeze. "Where's Luise all this time?"

"We left her at home in the sitting-room?"

"Did we?"

"Yes. She has invaded your dearly beloved, didn't you know?"

They came upon the clumps of wild pines. "See," said Olivia, "how quickly we've reached the wild pines! I could have taken you by another track so that we needn't have come to this spot at all, but I wanted you to remember the Saturday morning when I called out *Indeed, indeed*… You thought it was Brenda calling, remember?"

"Yes, I remember. But if you don't want me to get morbid and think grisly things let's not talk about Brenda."

"You're wrong. I think that's what you ought to do. I believe it's Brenda's shadow that's making you still so worried-looking even though you're in love with Maby. If you talked about Brenda and gave her a good hard thinking about you might kill her shadow once and for all, and then you'd be happy ever after and not have to frown and tremble."

He came to a stop and looked at her with a feeling of uncanny crabs' feet scampering up his back. He began to speak then stopped.

"Say what you want to say," she said.

"You must be a witch, child," he murmured. He laughed jerkily.

"Of course I'm a witch. A which and a what and a what not. That's one of Berton's and my passwords. I say: 'A which and a what' and he has to answer: 'And a what not'."

Such a rippling deluge of lightheartedness rushed through him that he felt weak-kneed. He laughed until his eyes watered.

"That's how I like to hear you laugh," she laughed. "Not just that Cheshire-cat grin as if your jaw was stiff with Surrey frost."

"I'm not in a laughing mood, all the same," he said, getting serious. "I'm still very, very muddled, Olivia."

"Muddled over what? Why don't you propose to Maby and get it over?"

"I've done that already. Barely two hours ago. We're to be married tomorrow week."

"What! And you kept it to yourself like that! Or did you purposely mean to create dramatic suspense?"

"No. I simply didn't feel like mentioning it before. I've told your father. You'd have heard about it before the day is out, I daresay."

She reached up and kissed his cheek. "My congratulations, sweet young man! My best congratulations!" Her eyes were filled with tears. "Oh, I'm so happy. But why aren't you? Why aren't you hopping about and chirping instead of behaving like a volcano sickening for diarrhoea? Oh, you're too silly!"

"I am. I agree. But, unfortunately, I'm not as straightforward a case as you might imagine. I'm so…"

"Go on. Don't stop. I know what you want to say. You're so complex and ultra-sofriskticated that you can't make up your mind what is pink and what is yellow. That's stupid. You can be simple if you want to be."

"You mean if I could be. There's the rub."

"What rub? You think you're Hamlet? Look, let's sit down here and watch the pines and talk. Tell me about your complex complexities and let's see if we can't drive them away."

She scraped together some dead leaves, and they sat on them and hugged their knees.

"Now, tell me. Isn't it really Brenda that you've still got on your mind? You feel she swam out purposely and drowned herself because she was unhappy, don't you?"

He turned his head quickly. "Did that occur to you?"

"Of course it did. I never mentioned it, but it did."

"Yes, it occurred to me, too," he nodded. "In fact, I'm almost certain it was suicide. I never wanted to admit it to myself, but I've thought of it."

"And that's haunting you, eh?"

"Not at all, no. No, it isn't that, Olivia. The trouble is… I wish I could discuss it with you, but I doubt whether you'd grasp it."

"Perhaps you don't know yourself what's worrying you."

He laughed and gave her pigtail a pull. "Yes, I do know."

"Well, tell me."

"In a way, you mentioned it indirectly yourself a minute or two ago. It's the flesh, Olivia. The flesh against the spirit."

"The flesh against the spirit?"

"Yes. I'm tired of the flesh."

"But why? You're not an old man – and even old men don't all get tired of the flesh. Look at Mr. Buckmaster. Almost every Indian woman who works on his timber grant has had a child by him. But you mustn't mention that. The Government would fine him ninety-six dollars for each illegitimate child. It's against the law to have a child by an Indian woman."

"Is it?"

"Yes. Have you ever heard of a more silly law? That's partly how the Government shows it wants to 'protect' the aboriginals. But you were telling me about the flesh. Why are you tired of it?"

"That would be a long story – and not a story for the ears of a nice pleasant girl like you. Just take my word for it that I'm tired."

"All right, I will. But what can you do if you're tired of the flesh? You can't just go to bed with Mabel's spirit and nothing else. *She* won't be satisfied with that, I can tell you."

He laughed, flushing. "I'm sure she won't. I can agree with you on that." He looked at her. "I tell you what I want. I want somebody like you – living spirit, volatile and light, and with no murky passions to beguile me and remind me of the instinct-part of myself."

"Oh." Her face abruptly clouded over. "I think I'm beginning to see," she murmured.

"I wonder. Yes, perhaps. You have infruition."

She seemed not to have heard him now. She looked reflective. Mature. As though the child-spirit part of her had glided into the wild pines and been replaced by a shadow, blue-black and hirsute, from the gloomed tunnels of the spider-webs.

"But the trouble is that the very passions in Mabel that I want to escape from are in me – and very strong and active. And impure into the bargain." He laughed softly. Ironic and mirthless laughter.

"One day, in a few years," she said, after a pause. "I myself will be flesh – flesh wanting to be passionate."

"I realize that."

Tick… Tick…

A black, shiny lizard wriggled a multiple question-mark path across the ground – without noise. And vanished. They could hear the breath of the silence overhead amid the tangle of fronds and crooked branches, and the lattice of vines. And amid the saw-edged wild-pine clusters from where the tick, tick came. At longish intervals… Each black spider in its tunnel must have its fangs raised, waiting for the insect to make a false move and get entangled in its web.

It must be half-past five, thought Olivia. She looked slowly around. Night will soon be here, and the dead Dutch people and their slaves will begin to walk. I wonder if they feel lost because they're jumbies…

I wonder, thought Gregory, how this moment will appear in my fancy in retrospect. Will it seem imbued with the stain of absurdity, or haloed with a silver beauty?

Suppose, Olivia thought, a bushmaster were to show its head among the pines… I don't see anything like a good stout stick lying about…

Tick… tick…

…Sigmund chained up behind the shed… My hand touched the ring in the wall…

…we'd simply have to run for it, then…

A yellow leaf fell. It settled beside her on the sand. A minute black creature, like an exclamation mark in a book, was crawling on it…

… a few weeks ago – on the day I arrived – this leaf was green and glittering. Vigorous with sap…

…I wonder if it has a brain and can think. Has it got passions? And a spirit like a grain of powder that would live on if I put my finger on it and killed it? Is this jungle haunted by tiny powder-ghosts?… *Lo, some we loved, the loveliest and best…*

…now yellow and effete in death. About to join the other dead leaves piled up on this ever-thickening carpet…

…have trees spirits? I'd like to see a tree-ghost. It must look like a fan made of frozen firefly light…

"Have we both gone to sleep?" said Gregory.

She smiled. "No. We were in the grotto of the Green Genie."

"It was pleasant being there. What were you thinking about?"

"A bushmaster, that dead leaf that fell and the dot of a black creature crawling on it. And the spirit of a tree. And you were thinking about what? Tell me."

"This moment, Sigmund chained up – and the leaf. I didn't notice the dot of a black creature crawling on it."

"Poor Sigmund. A pity about him, but to do other than get rid of him would be false sentiment, and sentimentality is bad for people."

"More and more I see that your father is a good teacher."

She glanced at him quickly, then said: "Yes, he is. And his teachings are good, too. He's a truly civilized man. More civilized even than Clive Bell. Do you know Clive Bell? He's a truly civilized man."

"He didn't advocate Nudism in any of his books, though, so far as I recall."

"I know. That's why we're just a cut above him. He's civilized but cynical. We're civilized and natural."

He smiled and stroked her hair. "You're a lovely creature."

"Quaint, too."

"Yes, quaint, too."

They heard the church bell ringing.

"What's that for?"

"I don't know myself," she said, tensed. "Some unusual event. A countretempers. It's an alarm."

"We'd better be going back."

"Yes… I wonder… I know what. It's the trial."

"Trial?"

"Yes. The people must have insisted on an immediate trial for Sigmund. The bell is to call them to the church."

"Let's go."

VIII

Her guess proved correct. People were coming into the clearing. It was the trial. They met Berton, and he told them; yes, he said, it was the trial. There were long shadows in the clearing; in less than ten minutes the sun would be gone and all the shadows with it, leaving a young gloom.

"The people insisted that we should try him this evening," said Berton. He spoke in a subdued voice and with an air of nervous awe. He appeared to be in one of his faraway moods; he stood on a lonely rock… Gregory and Olivia watched him.

"Did Mabel," asked Gregory, after a pause, "say she would give evidence?"

"Yes," whispered Berton. "Yes, she said so. Daddy told her."

"Told her what?"

"He told her to be in the church by six o'clock to give evidence, and she said very well, she would be there."

A silence. They watched him.

"Why do you ask?" asked Berton.

"Nothing," said Gregory. "I just wanted to know." He began to move off in the direction of the house.

"Aren't you coming into the church to hear the trial?" Olivia said.

"You won't be able to get a seat," whispered Berton, "if you don't hurry." His manner was vaguely anxious and fluttery.

"I don't want to hear the trial," said Gregory.

Olivia moved after him and told him: "Don't be silly. Not because you don't agree with our ways. Come and hear the trial. It'll be good drama."

"Tragic drama," quavered Berton. He seemed on the point of tears.

Gregory made no reply. Continued toward the house.

They accompanied him into the gallery, Olivia still trying to persuade him, and Berton making soft sensitive sounds. But he would not change his mind. His manner got colder and his face looked pale.

"You have my love and sympathy," said Olivia finally. "You're a stupid young man, but I still pity you and adore you." As she moved toward the door she said: "I'll keep a seat for you until the eleventh second, in case you change your mind. I won't be surprised if you did, too."

She and Berton went out, and Berton began to talk to her in sudden quick bursts, as though the words had been wrapped tightly within his throat and the parcel had just cracked open. Gregory smiled slightly and paced aimlessly along the gallery for a few minutes. On the walls were two oil-paintings – Mabel's, he had been told – and two black and white sketches not quite as good as those in the sitting-room.

He went into the sitting-room. The sun was gone, and the young gloom grew old as though injected with a serum of senility… One, he thought, can almost hear it growing into night. He could not make out the pictures clearly. Not the details. He went into the dining-room. Mabel was not there. He knew now that it was she he was looking for. He went into the pantry and then into the kitchen. She was not there.

Ellen smiled at him and made a quick circular motion with her finger. She had just been in the act of lighting the lamp on the dresser, and the box of matches rattled as she made the motion with her finger.

He turned off to return into the dining-room, but she took a step toward him and caught his elbow. "They all gone to de church for de trial. You want lil' sweetness?" Her finger… The matches rattled…

Gregory smiled and said: "No, thank you. No."

She gave a low gurgle, sensual and excited. Exciting him for a tremulous second. He paused, rigid, then went on. He knew she had noted the pause.

He went upstairs and looked in all the rooms. Mabel was not there. He went into his room and stood at the window and watched the sky over the jungle. Thunder-clouds crouched, humped, in the south, and he saw a reddish flicker of lightning. He listened for the thunder, and after nineteen seconds heard a faint mutter that died away in the very moment that it began. Like the grunt of a baboon shot abruptly dead. A punt laden with timber was going past on the river, heading downstream as always. Under the palm-leaf shelter something was cooking in a saucepan. He could see the red glow of the fire in the coal-pot under the saucepan. A squatting brown man watched it while two others manned the oars. The craft moved very slowly. Irritatingly so. He pulled his gaze away from it and looked at Logan who was ringing the church bell. He rang it unevenly. Tolled it, then made it clang out, then stopped ringing it, then began, after a pause, to make jerky tinkle-tinkle sounds. It sounded mad and idiotic and grave in turn; joyous and whispering and bizarre. He squirmed himself into all sorts of contortions as he manipulated the rope. Broke into a jig as the whim took him. Suddenly he uttered a loud croaking wail, released the rope and began to gallop round and round the belfry. Some of the people on their way into the church laughed, and their laughter seemed to encourage him. He turned somersaults and let out hoarse quarks. He halted and threw up his arms and bawled: "Oh, Almighty! Look iniquity dis good evenin'! Ow, Gawd! Punish de sinners! Let de wicked burn in de flames of Satan!"… Garvey came out of the west door and told him to stop making noise. "Shut up and ring the bell, or go back to the kitchen!" Logan, unheeding, cried to the sky: "Jehovah! Cast down dine eyes and watch nancy-story tale dis good evenin'! De sins of man shalt find him out! Oh, iniquity! Oh, salvation!" Garvey moved threateningly upon him, and Logan set off at a hopping run toward the track that went to the ruins. Just before he disappeared into the opening in the bushes he trailed out a squeaky laugh that merged into the squeak of a swift silent bat that swept round the belfry-roof and vanished.

Gregory paced the room. Other footfalls began to accompany his. He halted. It must be Mabel coming up the stairs. He looked expectantly at the door. It was wide open. He never bothered to shut it nowadays.

It was Ellen. She came in and gurgled and made the motion with her finger. "We alone in de house," she said. "Tek lil' sweetness wid me quick."

He stood where he was and watched her, not even a faint smile on his face. She pointed at the bed. "Mabel won't know. Me won't talk." She came closer to him. Perhaps she had noted how his hands shook. Her voice became husky with conspiracy. "Wha' you waiting for? You na like sweetness? Why you always behave so funny when me offer you sweetness? Come on. Come." She made a quick plucking motion at his belt.

"Get outside," he murmured, putting his hands behind his back and squeezing them together hard.

"You na like sweetness? You funny man. Hurry up come, na? Lie down on de bed and me come in wid you." She made another tentative move with her hand toward his belt. She was shaking, and her eyes looked shiny-wild.

"Get outside," he said.

She gave him an unsteady look and then moved toward the door, paused and glanced at him again and gurgled. "Why you so funny?"

She continued to stand near the door watching him, as though sensing that there was still hope. She rubbed her hands slowly down her thighs.

"Get out!" he shouted.

She scurried out. He heard her footsteps in the corridor and then on the stairs. He began to pace again. He kept swallowing. His fingertips were cold. He tried to get them warm again by rubbing them together briskly.

He heard an odd noise and stopped pacing and looked round. A sort of itchy swishing. Like little straw scarecrows come to life and marching in the shadow of a farmhouse… Weird. Telling of a thirsty death… Cactus in the bed of a dried-up river… He saw what caused it. A centipede on the bed. Crawling leisurely. Six or seven inches long and brownish-black. If the dusk had not been so deep he might have detected a touch of green, too. A monster. A grandmother centipede. It was moving diagonally across the sheet toward the foot of the bed.

This was his second encounter with a centipede. The last one had been over a week ago. He had come upon it on the floor of the dining-room one evening before dinner. He had tried stamping upon it, but his rubber-soled shoes had proved ineffectual against its tough, shiny body-armour. Ellen had come in with a cutlass and chopped it into three.

He took up a book from the dressing-table – the *Oxford Book of Victorian Verse* – and used it to sweep the creature off the bed on to the floor. It hit the floor with a dryish plop, falling near the washstand. It twisted itself quickly into position and set off at a hurried squiggle, making for the wall. He jumped forward and stepped on it, felt it squirm, slippery and elongated, hard, under his weight. He looked about – then knew what he wanted. It was near at hand, too. On the washstand. The cut-throat razor which Olivia had returned a few hours ago. He let the creature half-wriggle from under his shoe, then sliced off its horny head and fangs in two precise gashes. He felt a remote satisfaction at the easy effectiveness of the razor. With a sense of security – a soothing safety – he raised his foot off the rest of the thing. The headless body moved round and round in wide, futile circles. He chuckled, glimpsing a phantom version of himself demon-grinning, heartless. He bent down again and chopped it into four… It was a menace. He nodded and grunted. "Couldn't let it live," he muttered. "It might have bitten me. It was a threat to my safety."

The four pieces moved round on their own. He watched them, smiling. But with gooseflesh on his arms. In the deep dusk he could just make them out. After a minute or so they grew still. One had reached the wall, but it could not climb. One stopped at the foot of the washstand…

One piece was crawling through his mind. Swimming in an amber twilight. He began to gaze round the room. Near the chest of drawers stood the expanding suitcase; it was the only one he had not unpacked. Because of the whisky. Somehow, he could not decide what to do with it. Alcohol was forbidden on this settlement, and no one here would want it. He could not empty it into the river; that would be wasteful.

…struggling to the top. But it would find no escape at the top. A human mind was hermetically sealed. He listened with half his attention to the voices in the clearing and in the church; the other half tried to listen to the voices in the room. In this dimness the furniture seemed ripe with intangible messages. Furniture in the jungle. Not London or Middenshot furniture. This washstand had no sophisticated eye to burn cynical holes into his soul… A

340

marble top... Well, you never knew. It might be second-hand. It might have come from outside this jungle...

Anyone would think I'd gone mad again...

...struggling impotently along the zenith. No attic window. No matter how it fumbled its dying legs. No matter if it had tears to shed. The sky had no windows. No gable-exists. Oh, Christ!... Only an imprecation, Christ. I'm not calling on you for help. Christ! Christ!

He held his head. He shut his eyes and saw Middenshot. The cedars on the fell. The tall holly hedges. Beyond the cedars, beyond the fell, parkland – and the towers and red brick splendour of Middenshot Manor... Rumble of an electric train... the Southern Railway. The green signs and the green coaches... A W.H. Smith bookstall... Grey-blue mist veiled the distant woods beyond which lay Bisley... Gorse in bloom...

He opened his eyes and watched the jungle. The over-luscious, everlasting cascade of summer greens. No winter here. No spring. No apple or plum blossoms. No hoar frost on the grass. No cuckoos to weave solitude in the still of early morning...

Whistling softly, he moved over to the chest of drawers. Pulled open a drawer and regarded its contents. Shirts, underdrawers, ties... He put in his hands and lifted as many out as he could, and took them over to the bed, put them down in a pile. Went back and lifted out the rest and took them to the bed, too. He went on whistling. No particular tune...

... struggling feebly and bruising its mechanical legs against the nebulae of infinity... A red brick cottage showing amid the woods; smoke rose from its chimneys... Virginia Water... Sunningdale... Ascot...

He had to light the lamp on the washstand... Dusk never deepened as rapidly as this in Surrey... He never stopped whistling... He had emptied three drawers now... the Thames at Richmond... at Staines... a pair of silk socks dropped. He retrieved it and flung it on to the bed.

About to move back toward the chest of drawers, he changed his mind. Whistling louder, he bent and pulled the trunk from under the bed. He threw back the cover and looked inside. Saw the few oddments... An old fountain pen, a writing-case, an orange-covered Penguin, white stockings soiled at Martin's Bay in Barbados, two ties...

...struggling outside the influence of its spirit. Numb with the frost of rigor mortis. But rigor mortis of the spirit, for it was the spirit that groped infections at the surrendering body...

He thought he saw something grey move. Yes – on the writing-case... He went to the washstand and brought the lamp... Yes – a scorpion two or three inches long.. It was going over the Penguin now... It died very easily when he pressed the fountain pen upon it. Though it curled up its hooked and venomous tail, seeking the enemy. He laughed as he left it a doodled smear on the Penguin...

He put down the lamp and went on emptying drawers... From the bottom drawer he took his dinner suit... There was no wardrobe or cupboard in which to hang suits. This was not Middenshot. Not London... The white tie slipped from within the jacket where he had tucked it when he had put away the suit, and fell to the floor. He nearly trod on it. After he had placed the suit on the bed he stooped to pick up the tie. But he did not pick it up. He straightened up again and stared at it... The lamplight on it turned gradually harsher, whiter. A white tie in electric light... A shaded wall lamp, frosted so that it was not hard on the eyes... The telephone rang... "Do pop round after the show, old boy," said Eugene... Hypocrite! Wearing a white tie. Hypocrites wearing white ties. Hypocrites in black evening gowns... "There's a frightfully good place I know in a mews off Curzon Street..." Red...amber...green... "Oh, darling, I'd weep the night long if you don't show up. Oh, I will – really I will..."

He kicked it. Noiselessly it slid along the floor and lay coiled languidly against a leg of the dressing-table... A white tie.

He moved his head from side to side slowly. Blood and lamplight blended; the lymph and the photons could merge if you let them, if you thrust your thought like thread through the needle-eye that gave entrance and exit to the binding forces. Sift the dream through the reality and distil the reality into essence of new dusk – the dusk of crowded trees. But let the dregs of the old reality sink into the silt of the past, and nevermore probe in the silt... Nevermore, oh Christ!... You bloody pests! You stinking gobs of rottenness!...

He stumbled, but righted himself. He whimpered softly and shook. His lips moved soundlessly. He moved a step toward the trunk, looked into it and shook his head. He sat down on the edge of the bed and was still for a long time. Then he got up and began to take the clothes back to the drawers. When he had done, he shut the trunk and pushed it back under the bed. He gave short, husky laughs. He glanced toward the window and had a glimpse of a firefly. A fuzzy bead of light arcing past in the dark.

He went to the window, smiling.

The sky, he saw, had not yet lost its light. In the east and south-east it was split up into fans of pink and crimson: a trick of refraction. One would have thought the sun were setting in the east. The thunderclouds had drifted further to the west; they had turned a deep purple, rimmed with pink or bright yellow, and stood out against a haze of orange that melted upward into the mauve and lapis-lazuli of the zenith: it might have been that a rain of cosmic pollen were falling behind them and throwing up its spray back toward the source of the shower.

Every detail of the sky lay reflected in the cool river. The river, untrembling in the windless air, gave to the inverted version a glazed and staring reality that even the jungle, which with its own reflection scored a silhouette boundary between the actuality in the sky and the illusion in the water, could not nullify or lessen in fascination. So much so that, after a moment, he heard a drone of doubt within him. It swelled into an overwhelming conviction that it was in the water the actual existed and in the sky the make-believe.

Some lines of a poem came back to him... Edward Thomas... He tried to recall the title, but it evaded him...

> ...shall I now this day
> Begin to seek as far as heaven, as hell,
> Wisdom or strength to match this beauty, start
> And tread the pale dust pitted with small dark drops,
> In hope to find whatever it is I seek,
> Hearkening to short-lived happy-seeming things...

He remembered the title now. *The Glory...* He tried to think how it went on after that. He moved from the window and sat on the edge of the bed. Became aware that people were leaving the church. He heard their voices. He could not see the church from where he sat, and had no desire to get up…

> … or must I be content with discontent
> As larks and swallows are perhaps with wings?
> And shall I ask at the day's end once more
> What beauty is, and what I can have meant
> By happiness? And shall I let all go,
> Glad, weary, or both? Or shall I perhaps know
> That I was happy oft, and oft before,
> Awhile forgetting how I am fast pent,
> How dreary-swift, with naught to travel to
> Is Time? I cannot bite the day to the core.

The crimson, he saw was fading from the sky, and the fans were not so clearly delineated; they were merging into each other. The thunderclouds were out of his range of vision from the bed here. He shifted his head aside, and saw that they looked more indigo than purple now.

"The human element…"

The phrase drifted up from among the ragged fragments of conversation outside. The man who uttered it had an excellent enunciation… Another phrase of his came in… "Not tonight, I assume…"

He rose and took a cigarette from his case on the dressing-table. Lit it and sat on the bed again. Watched the sky and listened to the voices trailing past, getting remote, going toward the Reservation pathway.

He began to hear footsteps and voices in the house, down-stairs. In the gallery. In the sitting-room. On the stairs. Someone was coming up. It sounded like Mabel. You couldn't mistake the uncertain, awkward tripping way she stepped. He smiled – with tenderness.

She came in. Stopped just within the threshold.

"You weren't at the trial, I heard," she said.

"No," he said. Love moved in him.

She approached and sat beside him on the bed. After a silence, she said: "You killed a centipede."

"Yes." He spoke curtly. But love moved in him.

"A big one, it looks like."

"Yes. It was on the bed here. A menace."

"What?"

"A menace," he said. "I had to get rid of it. A scorpion, too – in my trunk. Two menaces in quick succession."

"Oh."

After a silence, she grunted with what seemed amusement.

Only a dull ochre remained in the sky. Incredible that only a few minutes ago there had been such a rich display of hues. The mauve higher up had deepened to violet and indigo, and in the part where it was indigo stars were twinkling. He moved his head to and fro and up and down to take it all in, and she asked: "What's happening outside?"

"The sky – I'm looking at it. Did you see the pinks and crimson, and the yellows on the thunderclouds?"

"Yes, I saw the pinks – through the church windows. What's that near the dressing-table leg? Is it a tie you've dropped?"

"Yes. A white tie."

"How did it get there? What were you doing with a tie?"

"It fell from my dinner jacket. I was unpacking my things from the chest of drawers."

"Why were you doing that?"

"I intended putting them into my trunk. I was getting ready to leave by Thursday morning's steamer."

"I… oh. And you changed your mind?"

"Yes. I have a weak character."

The smoke from his cigarette crawled lazily toward the lamp on the washstand, enveloped it and branched away into the gloom under the dressing-table. They heard Olivia laugh downstairs.

"So the trial is over," he said.

"Yes."

"When is the execution to be? Tonight?"

"He's been released."

"Why?"

"Because I wouldn't give evidence."

IX

Up in the twilight of the rafters the bats were black blobs, silent and without movement, for it was morning – the morning after the trial – and the new day's mist of sleep clung dense around them. Not even the harmonium would disturb them, Olivia knew.

The only sounds came from under the church. Bumps and scraping whispers. Her father and Logan were under the church looking for wood-ants' nests. Now and then she heard her father murmur and Logan answer with a grunt or a raw drawling. She stopped playing often to listen to them, and though she could not make out any words she would smile, feeling comforted and safe.

Morning light came in through the green-painted windows, which were all shut, and turned the church into a hive where unseen genii swirled their ribbon selves about her, weaving a honeycomb of magic drama. Dots of sunlight filtered through the flaked spots in the green paint on the window panes, and lay haphazard on the pews and on the floor like honey dropped by the genii as they worked.

She thought about the party tonight, and the magic fluff suspended in the air danced and rippled so much around her that she had to play a special passage on the harmonium, made up on the instant, as an accompaniment. She cocked her head, and was sure she could hear thin water-clear flute music coming from the Reservation. It must be Edith and Harry of Music Squad practising. Tonight they would bring their flutes, and George would bring his violin, and with Garvey they would form a small orchestra and play what pieces they knew. Mabel would play her flute, too… If… If she were in the mood… It was likely that she would not be. She would want to go walking in the darkness with Gregory. Or she and Gregory might want to make love in a quiet spot – in the school-*benab*, perhaps… About an hour ago, after breakfast, the two of them had left in the skiff to take an outing on the river, and they had not yet returned. They must be drifting on the tide, near the bush on the other bank, trying to hear the songs of the morning-jumbies in the dank night-caves among the trees. They must be very happy. Unless… Yes, unless… It might be that every other minute his soul wreathed out of the boat and went off into the moaning herbs. Mabel would be lonely then, and would call to him and ask why he had deserted her; didn't he love her anymore that he could let himself be lured away?… "Come back to my dotted flesh, dear! Come back! Or I shall die from the fumes of rank berries!" And she might cry a bit and tell him how she had behaved at the trial last night, how she had, at the very last minute, shaken her head and said: "I won't give evidence." How she had defied the Secret Code before all the people: she who should have been an example to them… "For your sake, dear. All for love of you, my darling! Oh, come back from the death-bell herbs and fondle my speckled breasts!" And of how the people had groaned and looked disappointed, and how they had smiled and forgiven her… "The human element! It cannot be helped. These things must happen. The human element, my friends…"

She looked round her, and knew that the air was brewing psychic tremors. Thin-legged spiders of electric fire crawled over her bare back and chest, and she wanted to breathe quickly. She thought she heard a cluck-click noise in the vestry, the spitting of a horned demon from the tomb of a dead wild flower. She glanced at the open vestry door, but saw nothing. She looked up at the bats, but they were still black blobs of silence in the twilight of the rafters.

Then she knew what it was. Out of the corner of her eye she saw him. Dicky. In the last pew, near the font. She had not seen him since that evening of Gregory's arrival.

She made to get up, but changed her mind. She would stay. It might be unwise to sit here instead of going into the vestry, but she would risk it. Dicky would not harm her. It might even be that he wanted to tell her a secret; he might know the howling hole where the Green Bottle lay hidden. It might be that he was trying to push through the fog-walls of the farther dells to touch her in friendship. She felt herself tingling into powder. She played her favourite tune – the Peer Gynt suite morning tune – and she could see the notes hopping over her head and going to him in soft friendliness. He must be smiling and thanking her for being so kind. She was not uneasy at all now. She took a quick glance back, and saw that he had gone. But she knew that it was only from the back of the church that he had gone. He stood near the pulpit now – invisible but more there than ever before. The body was nothing; it was the spirit that was something. He was struggling, struggling hard with the last strands in the star-mist barrier... Oh he was right behind her now. If he touched her she would be spirit like him, and the Genie would laugh and reach out friendly smoke-lassoes. And all the unknown wild flowers would pour perfume on her to welcome her to the Lair of the Lovely Lonely Lost Ones.

He was not free yet. He was a breeze standing still at her shoulder. More real than the moving breezes that swashed through the jungle. They were made of atoms only; he was of moonlight and ether.

She waited, playing a few more notes of the Peer Gynt tune. Then the feeling came on her that all was changed. The change was not outside her, though, but in her. She disbelieved, and in this instant of disbelief she knew that only nothingness stood behind her. The minutes had overtaken her. She was getting old. She had just heard the tolling of the bell in the wild-pine catacombs. She would never see Dicky again. This was the first big death of loveliness... But she did not mind. She knew it had to come. One had to grow old and be less fanciful. One could not always walk in the maroon mists of childhood.

She changed the tune to the Liebestod from *Tristan*. She was smiling.

Her father and Logan still tapped and murmured under the floor. She heard Garvey's voice calling: "Parson!" He was on official duty. He was coming to make his routine report. Though it did seem a bit early in the morning for him to report. Not ten yet, she was sure.

She felt very happy. Veils had fallen away. Pretty-pretty veils; and she had loved them. But one must never regret. One must look into the distance for more phantoms. There were always phantoms.

She let her mind return to Mabel and Gregory in the skiff

drifting on the river and whispering to each other. Deaf to other voices. Safe from circling ghouls. There were always ghouls, but you had to see that they only circled and not settled. Love was a good antidote against ghouls.

Yes, Love was good. She was glad for Mabel and Gregory. All between them was tranquil now. Mabel had not given evidence, and Sigmund had been released; Gregory had had his way, and he must be pleased. The barbarian. Tonight was the party, and next Wednesday the wedding would come off. Work on the new cottage would begin within a fortnight. Gregory would paint many pictures, and he and Mabel would live happily ever after...

"Parson!"

"Yes, my boy! Here I am!"

"I have a report to make."

"Um. Usual mid-morning report?"

"No, parson. It's not ten o'clock yet. This is a special report."

"Special, eh?"

"Yes, parson."

Silence. Olivia listened, waiting. Her father and Garvey, too, must be waiting. In dramatic suspense. Logan must be waiting, too. Open-mouthed.

"Something serious, my boy?"

"I'm afraid so, parson."

"Phew! Hot work looking for these wood-ants' nests."

"Have you found any so far?"

"None yet. We dealt with them pretty drastically last time. Painted all the beams with creosote. This is more or less a routine check-up."

"Quite right. Can't let them undermine the building."

"Exactly. Anything that is an undermining factor must be watched. Looking forward to the party this evening, my boy?"

"Very much, parson."

"So am I. We've ordered an extra amount of ice and soft drinks. Hope the steamer comes in early. What's this report, by the way?"

"Sigmund, parson. He's dead."

"Dead!" cried Logan. "Oh, heavenly Almighty! Oh, iniquity of Satan!"

"Um," said the reverend gentleman.

"He was found on the track that goes to the coconut grove."

"Um. Sad."

"Egbert of Labour Squad found him."

"H'm. Very sad."

"Yes, very sad."

"Snakebite, I presume?"

"Yes, parson. Snakebite."

ABOUT THE AUTHOR

Edgar Mittelholzer was born in New Amsterdam in what was still British Guiana in 1909. He began writing in 1929 and despite constant rejection letters persisted with his writing. In 1937 he self-published a collection of skits, *Creole Chips*, and sold it from door to door. By 1938 he had completed *Corentyne Thunder*, though it was not published until 1941 because of the intervention of the war. In 1941 he left Guyana for Trinidad where he served in the Trinidad Royal Volunteer Naval Reserve. In 1948 he left for England with the manuscript of *A Morning at the Office*, set in Trinidad, which was published in 1950. Between 1951 and 1965 he published a further twenty-one novels and two works of non-fiction, including his autobiographical *A Swarthy Boy*. Apart from three years in Barbados, he lived for the rest of his life in England. His first marriage ended in 1959 and he remarried in 1960. He died by his own hand in 1965, a suicide by fire predicted in several of his novels.

Edgar Mittelholzer was the first Caribbean author to establish himself as a professional writer.

CARIBBEAN MODERN CLASSICS

2009/10 titles

Jan R. Carew
Black Midas
Introduction: Kwame Dawes
ISBN: 9781845230951; pp. 272; 23 May 2009; £8.99

This is the bawdy, Eldoradean epic of the legendary 'Ocean Shark' who makes and loses fortunes as a pork-knocker in the gold and diamond fields of Guyana, discovering that there are sharks with far sharper teeth in the city. *Black Midas* was first published in 1958.

Jan R. Carew
The Wild Coast
Introduction: Jeremy Poynting
ISBN: 9781845231101; pp. 240; 23 May 2009; £8.99

First published in 1958, this is the coming-of-age story of a sickly city child, sent away to the remote Berbice village of Tarlogie. Here he must find himself, make sense of Guyana's diverse cultural inheritances and come to terms with a wild nature disturbingly red in tooth and claw.

Neville Dawes
The Last Enchantment
Introduction: Kwame Dawes
ISBN: 9781845231170; pp. 332; 27 April 2009; £9.99

This penetrating and often satirical exploration of the search for self in a world divided by colour and class is set in the context of the radical hopes of Jamaican nationalist politics in the early 1950s. First published in 1960, the novel asks many pertinent questions about the Jamaica of today.

Wilson Harris
Heartland
Introduction: Michael Mitchell
ISBN: 9781845230968; pp. 104; 23 May 2009; £7.99

First published in 1964, this visionary narrative tracks one man's psychic disintegration in the aloneness of the forests of the Guyanese interior, making a powerful ecological statement about man's place in the 'invisible chain of being', in which nature is a no less active presence.

Edgar Mittelholzer
Corentyne Thunder
Introduction: Juanita Cox
ISBN: 9781845231118; pp. 242; 27 April 2009; £8.99

This pioneering work of West Indian fiction, first published in 1941, is not merely an acute portrayal of the rural Indo-Guyanese world, but a work of literary ambition that creates a symphonic relationship between its characters and the vast openness of the Corentyne coast.

Andrew Salkey
Escape to an Autumn Pavement
Introduction: Thomas Glave
ISBN: 9781845230982; pp. 220; 23 May 2009; £8.99

This brave and remarkable novel, set in London at the end of the 1950s, and published in 1960, catches its 'brown' Jamaican narrator on the cusp between black and white, between exiled Jamaican and an incipient black Londoner, and between heterosexual and homosexual desires.

Denis Williams
Other Leopards
Introduction: Victor Ramraj
ISBN: 9781845230678; pp. 216; 23 May 2009; £8.99

Lionel Froad is a Guyanese working on an archeological survey in the mythical Jokhara in the horn of Africa. There he hopes to rediscover the self he calls 'Lobo', his alter ego from 'ancestral times', which he thinks slumbers behind his cultivated mask. First published in 1963, this is one of the most important Caribbean novels of the past fifty years.

Denis Williams
The Third Temptation
Introduction: Victor Ramraj
ISBN: 9781845231163; pp. 108; May 2010; £8.99

A young man is killed in a traffic accident at a Welsh seaside resort. Around this incident, Williams, drawing inspiration from the *Nouveau Roman*, creates a reality that is both rich and problematic. Whilst he brings to the novel a Caribbean eye, Williams makes an important statement about refusing any restrictive boundaries for Caribbean fiction. The novel was first published in 1968.

Roger Mais

Roger Mais
The Hills Were Joyful Together
Introduction: Norval Edwards
ISBN: 9781845231002; pp. 272; August 2010; £10.99

Unflinchingly realistic in its portrayal of the wretched lives of Kingston's urban poor, this is a novel of prophetic rage. First published in 1953, it is both a work of tragic vision and a major contribution to the evolution of an autonomous Caribbean literary aesthetic.

Edgar Mittelholzer
A Morning at the Office
Introduction: Raymond Ramcharitar
ISBN: 978184523; pp. 215; May 2010; £9.99

First published in 1950, this is one of the Caribbean's foundational novels in its bold attempt to portray a whole society in miniature. A genial satire on human follies and the pretensions of colour and class, this novel brings several ingenious touches to its mode of narration.

Edgar Mittelholzer
Shadows Move Among Them
Introduction: Rupert Roopnaraine
ISBN: 9781845230913; pp. 352; May 2010; £12.99

In part a satire on the Eldoradean dream, in part an exploration of the possibilities of escape from the discontents of civilisation, Mittelholzer's 1951 novel of the Reverend Harmston's attempt to set up a utopian commune dedicated to 'Hard work, frank love and wholesome play' has some eerie 'pre-echoes' of the fate of Jonestown in 1979.

Edgar Mittelholzer
The Life and Death of Sylvia
Introduction: Juanita Cox
ISBN: 9781845231200; pp. 366; May 2010, £12.99

In 1930s' Georgetown, a young woman on her own is vulnerable prey, and when Sylvia Russell finds she cannot square her struggle for economic survival and her integrity, she hurtles towards a wilfully early death. Mittelholzer's novel of 1953 is a richly inward portrayal of a woman who finds inner salvation through the act of writing.

Elma Napier
A Flying Fish Whispered
Introduction: Evelyn O'Callaghan
ISBN: 9781845231026; pp. 248; July 2010; £9.99

With one of the most delightfully feisty women characters in Caribbean fiction and prose that sings, Elma Napier's 1938 Dominican novel is a major rediscovery, not least for its imaginative exploration of different kinds of Caribbeans, in particular the polarity between plot and plantation that Napier sees in a distinctly gendered way.

Orlando Patterson
The Children of Sisyphus
Introduction: Kwame Dawes
ISBN: 9781845230944; pp. 288; August 2010; £9.99

This is a brutally poetic book that brings to the characters who live on Kingston's 'dungle' an intensity that invests them with tragic depth. In Patterson's existentialist novel, first published in 1964, dignity comes with a stoic awareness of the absurdity of life and the shedding of false illusions, whether of salvation or of a mythical African return.

V.S. Reid
New Day
Introduction: Norval Edwards
ISBN: 9781845230906, pp. 360; August 2010, £12.99

First published in 1949, this historical novel focuses on defining moments of Jamaica's nationhood, from the Morant Bay rebellion of 1865, to the dawn of self-government in 1944. *New Day* pioneers the creation of a distinctively Jamaican literary language of narration.

Garth St. Omer
A Room on the Hill
Introduction: John Robert Lee
ISBN: 9781845230937; pp. 210; September 2010; £9.99

A friend's suicide and his profound alienation in a St Lucia still slumbering in colonial mimicry and the straitjacket of a reactionary Catholic church drive John Lestrade into a state of internal exile. First published in 1968, St. Omer's meticulously crafted novel is a pioneering exploration of the inner Caribbean man.

Titles thereafter include...

Wayne Brown, *On the Coast*
George Campbell, *First Poems*
Austin C. Clarke, *The Survivors of the Crossing*
Austin C. Clarke, *Amongst Thistles and Thorns*
O.R. Dathorne, *The Scholar Man*
O.R. Dathorne, *Dumplings in the Soup*
Neville Dawes, *Interim*
Wilson Harris, *The Eye of the Scarecrow*
Wilson Harris, *The Sleepers of Roraima*
Wilson Harris, *Tumatumari*
Wilson Harris, *Ascent to Omai*
Wilson Harris, *The Age of the Rainmakers*
Marion Patrick Jones, *Panbeat*
Marion Patrick Jones, *Jouvert Morning*
Earl Lovelace, *Whilst Gods Are Falling*
Roger Mais, *Black Lightning*
Una Marson, *Selected Poems*
Edgar Mittelholzer, *Children of Kaywana*
Edgar Mittelholzer, *The Harrowing of Hubertus*
Edgar Mittelholzer, *Kaywana Blood*
Edgar Mittelholzer, *My Bones and My Flute*
Edgar Mittelholzer, *A Swarthy Boy*
Orlando Patterson, *An Absence of Ruins*
V.S. Reid, *The Leopard* (North America only)
Garth St. Omer, *Shades of Grey*
Andrew Salkey, *The Late Emancipation of Jerry Stover*
and more…